Let's Scare Cancer To Death

A Charitable Anthology

with all proceeds going to the V Foundation

http://www.jimmyv.org/

Let's Scare Cancer to Death
©2014 May December Publications LLC

Printed in the U.S.A.

ISBN— 978-1-940734-11-8

Introduction

Write what you know. Write what haunts you. Scribe those phantoms and nightmares that intrude through the mouth, that seep under the skin, that drive sharp icicles into your heart. For years, I have obsessed after my battle with cancer—the halcyon ignorant time before, the rage of the fight during treatment, and the years of uncertainty after, dancing on the edge of a cliff with broken toes. I have sliced open my arteries and poured the crimson ink onto page after page, dressing the lymphatic tumors in various guises, the masks of dark doctors of compassion, or wild dragons and in many cases, piloting the mindless bodies of zombies. This has been my catharsis.

In my late adolescence, the cancer came quick. I had suffered an intense antibiotic treatment for Lyme disease, which I had contracted while fishing for carp along the canals. It went undiagnosed for two years and did its damage. The disease and treatment weakened my immune system. One night after shaving, I found that someone had lodged a golf ball under my skin below my ear. It took all of twenty minutes to blossom. Two days later, a surgeon cut it out along with most of the inside of my face. Have no worries. The man was also a brilliant plastic surgeon, and I'm still just as beautiful. It took them time to diagnose the rare kind of cancer: a combination of both Hodgkin's disease and large cell lymphoma. Large cell kills in months. This rare combination, only seen before nine times, had never been successfully cured. I began an experimental treatment, enduring heavy doses of chemo and six months of daily radiation at extreme doses. And by divine mathematical miracle, I survived. And as I've often said, the hardest time in any cancer patient's life begins on the day he's told he is in remission.

And I live with it every day, every moment. Each time a cell divides, the die is cast. I understand that this is a reprieve, and I fight to get the most of my time, even against the debilitating side effects from the treatment. When I draw from the well for inspiration to write, I come back and back again to my experience, my journey, my fight against the intractable storms. I have published many stories about cancer patients and their battle, often horror, the cancer symbolized by myriad monsters. For May December Publications I wrote *New World*, a novella in their *Realms of Undead* novella anthology. In the novella, zombies are the device that compel my protagonist, a cancer patient in remission, to confront the stagnation of his life, to fight for his love so far away in Florida. Two forces do battle for his soul: that the universe is one of meaning, of life, of purpose or that life is a mistake, an aberration, a disease of the cosmos. This nihilistic point of view is that of the Rainbow Cult, a self-pronounced cult of lunatics and con artists who preach the futility of life. The zombies represent the cancer that is destroying the world, and the living, all the living now understand what we cancer patients have always known: the compulsory truth of the finite nature of life. Everyone understands it, but they don't believe it. For those with cancer, we have suffered our own personal apocalypse, as everyone will eventually.

All profits of this book will go to support research for a cure by The V Foundation. Formed by athlete, basketball coach and sports announcer Jimmy Valvano, a tremendous human being that was struck down with cancer at age forty-six, the organization promotes cancer research. The group seeks to bring new minds and fresh perspectives to cancer research by investing in the careers of young doctors and scientists. Their goal is to help facilitate new research into applications to help cancer patients, shortening the distance from the laboratory to the hospital bed. The V Foundation has awarded more than $100 million to more than one hundred facilities nationwide and proudly awards a hundred percent of direct donations and net event proceeds to cancer research.

Jimmy did not survive, but we do, and we carry on the fight in his indomitable spirit and name.

So please enjoy these wild tales of the living dead and who knows what else that lurks within. In just reading, you support the battle against this disease and ease the suffering of its victims, those patients suffering cancer and those who love them. As a modern bard, my work in art and writing heals. This is my faith. In reading *The Sick and the Dead*, you join me in my journey. For that I thank you.

T. Fox Dunham

A note from the editor, TW Brown

Every single year, one of the things we try to do at May December Publications is to offer an all-for-charity anthology. (Last year it was the Red Cross.) This year's decision was actually very simple.

As you will see in the coming pages if you take a moment to read the dedications, just about all of us have been affected by cancer in some way. Whether it was a friend or family member—or even more directly in some cases—we have felt the sting.

I lost my best friend in the world to cancer. Not a day goes by where I don't think of Steve Hobart. Cancer is a nasty thing that needs to go away. And while I sure as heck don't have the brains to make any progress towards the cure, I hope that I can send a few bucks in the direction of those who can.

If you are reading this, then you are helping as well. Thank you. It is only two words, but I mean them to the depths of my soul. And I can't speak for everybody else involved, but I am betting you have their thanks as well.

One last note, I originally set out to make EVERY story be about somebody with cancer. I chose to allow some leeway in order to include some very talented writers who really wanted to be a part of this but did not have "exactly" what I had been calling for. Please accept them into your hearts as well and share your appreciation for every contribution.

Again, thank you for doing your part in supporting this endeavor by making your purchase. And if you would be kind enough to submit a review, you will actually be helping more than you know. Believe it or not, those things matter to the "Amazon Gods" and will actually put us in front of more people.

TW Brown

Contents

1

Z Children
By Eli Constant

This story is dedicated to two men, two men that I love and cherish deeply.

To my grandpa, Jeffrey Blaisdell. You were a fighter, strong and uncompromising; you were a great man, full of kindness and love. You never would have submitted to cancer or any other illness. You would have fought until the end. I know this to be fact. God had other plans though, taking you home in a car accident, sparing you anymore pain. I'm glad you're okay now—no second round of chemotherapy, no oxygen tank to haul around, no more days of weakness and weariness.

I know you're in a better place. I hope the air is fresh there and you can take long, deep, painless breaths. I love you more than words.

To my supportive and wonderful father-in-law, Alexander Constantopoulos. You won the fight against prostate cancer. I didn't doubt that you would, not for a second. You are also strong, uncompromising and full of kindness. I'm grateful to have you in my life. I love you.

Tuesday morning.

A good morning, because I didn't have to go to work. A bad morning, because I did have to take Sophia and Marcel to the doctor. They'd just turned six years old. I had them on the recommended tract for vaccines and they were due four shots: the DTaP, the Inactivated Poliovirus, MMR and Varicella. Doctor Lynn had wanted to finish the vaccine series at age four, but I'd wanted to wait. I'd never been totally comfortable injecting my children with things I couldn't pronounce, let alone understand, but that was the way of the world, the way we kept our children healthy and alive. Age six was the latest the kids could get the next set of vaccines, according to Dr. Lynn and the CDC. So, I was going to bite the bullet today and endure the bright yellow smiley-face bandages and inevitable tears, doing what was 'best' for my children.

I don't know why I was having such a mental issue with this set of injections, but my feelings went far beyond the mild apprehension I'd felt during past vaccine visits to Dr. Lynn's cheery, child-friendly office. When Sophia and Marcel were younger, the shots would make me super uncomfortable, but that was the extent of it. Now though…on this morning…thinking about vaccines made me want to vomit.

***

Gregory, my ex-husband, had always wanted to have children. Specifically, Gregory wanted to have *our* children, but I wasn't able to carry to term. My womb was incapable of retaining a suitable environment for fetal growth. The fertility doctor had said something a little more scientific, not that his precise words mattered. I'd endured three miscarriages before I'd finally called it quits and realized that a biological child wasn't in the cards. Gregory wasn't happy with my decision.

In all honesty, I welcomed the infertility news. I knew in my heart that I'd never wanted to have Gregory's children. He was callous. I'd learned after only a few months of marriage that the kindness he'd shown me pre-engagement could not outlast his own desire for personal gain. I like to think that he really loved me at one point... but who knows?

I remember the adoption argument vividly. He'd not wanted a 'foreign' child, so worried that darker skin or slanted, wide-set eyes would reflect badly on us. He was always worried about things like that; I guess as Town Mayor you have to be concerned about your image. I didn't care though. Not really. Boy or girl. Black or white. As long as the child was mine completely, to have and to hold forever. That's what marriage is supposed to be like- the having and holding and forever. Enough of that though. Sometimes things just don't work out.

From the beginning of the adoption journey, Gregory had been one foot on board and one foot solidly on the dock of disagreement. When I'd shown him the pictures of Sophia and Marcel, he'd winced. I'd known why. They weren't white or black. They were Hispanic, a nationality frowned upon in our moderately-sized Tex-Mex border community.

The 'Americans' didn't want the Mexicans in our country; they didn't want to lose factory jobs to harder workers who'd take less pay. It was a solid concern. Our town relied on the textile mill; it was our bread and butter, but slow production and repeated union strikes had made the mill owners shift toward inexpensive labor across the border. The decision hadn't been made yet, but the rumors said it was imminent. And rumor mills always run the same, efficiency sacrificed for accuracy, half-truths traded for full pleasure.

For my part, I had been ecstatic, beaming at the photo of my soon-to-be children. They were gorgeous, tiny little newborns who needed immediate placement. Their mother was headed back to her hometown across the border, but she'd given birth in our small hospital and immediately put the twins up for U.S. adoption. The interpreter had been very clear on one point- the children stayed together. And that's why we were able to get them. No one in our town wanted a Hispanic child, let alone two.

3

They could have gone into the system, maybe even been tossed across the border to an ill-funded orphanage like so much trash, but I wanted them both, with all my heart, and I'd started the adoption paperwork, telling my husband the good news. Of course, he hadn't thought it was good news at all.

Gregory made it very clear the evening I'd shown him the twins' picture that he did not support my decision, that my actions on the matter would *'concrete the future of our marriage.'* I chose to hear his words, but not understand them. My mind was set on being a mother and not just anyone's mother. I wanted to be *their mother*, Sophia and Marcel's landing ground of love.

Gregory had come to every adoption meeting, interview, scheduled playtime with the children. He'd acted the charming, kind man the town knew him to be. No one had questioned whether he'd make a wonderful father. I should have questioned it, but I'd ignored all the signs, all the thinly-veiled threats and hints. I was blind in my desire for motherhood. I was even momentarily blind to the utter lack of love between myself and the man I called husband. During those meetings, all I saw were two lovely babes and a handsome husband making small talk with the social workers.

So stupid... I'd been so *utterly stupid* for months. After every visit with Sophia and Marcel, we'd leave the hospital and Gregory's demeanor would change, become coarse and cruel. He'd revert to the man I knew him to be, not the town's glowing idea of him. It was smoke and mirrors, a supportive façade masking deep-seeded hate. Yet I continued to ignore his behavior, pretend that everything was perfect.

He hadn't come with me the day I'd brought the babies home. I'd had to purchase and install the two car seats myself. I even spent an entire Saturday at the small boutique on main street, Baby Bliss. Sherry, the owner, was a dear friend. Although she thought my decision was oddball, she helped me pick out darling clothing, cotton diapers, baby rattles and other sundries. I'd spent most of a month's wages that day and I hadn't even blinked- which was strange for me, since I was usually so frugal.

I'd held Sophia and Marcel in my arms before, but nothing could prepare me for the feeling of holding them and placing them in the car seats I'd purchased. Strapping them in, buckle by buckle, the adoption became reality. I was a mother. And Gregory was a reluctant father.

When I'd finally arrived home with the children, all smiles and ecstasy, I'd found my house key didn't work. I remember trying every key on my chain in the door lock, all the time knowing that the first key with the pink rubber cover was the house key and that something was wrong. Confused, I'd knocked and waited patiently, knowing Gregory was home since his car was in the driveway.

His shiny black BMW was parked next to my twenty-year-old Volvo. He'd offered to buy me a new car, saying he didn't want the Mayor's wife riding around in a POS, but I'd refused. Bessie had seen me through a lot; she was a good, solid car. Gregory had tried to sell her out from under me one time, but only my name was on the title, so he couldn't. That had really burned him up. Gregory hadn't wanted me to work either, but I loved teaching. So, at least I'd stood up for myself twice in our marriage.

Sophia and Marcel were asleep in their carriers, sitting on the brick stoop beside my feet. It wasn't cool outside, but I'd still have rather been inside, settling the children into their room, introducing them to blue elephant and yellow giraffe, the two stuffed toys I'd purchased at Baby Bliss and left in their cribs as 'welcome home' gifts.

After a few minutes of waiting, I'd knocked again, harder that time. Almost instantly, the door had opened, revealing Gregory in the foyer, along with his suitcases and several large boxes. My eyes wide, I'd stared at the scene, not wanting to comprehend. Although, I knew... I knew what it all meant.

"What's going on, Greg? Why are all your suitcases packed?"

"You know what's going on, Susan. I made it clear how I felt about those children. I left the decision up to you." The expression on his face was remorseless, almost void of emotion.

"No... no. Greg, you never said it would be like this. You came to every meeting, every interview." I'd pleaded. "You never said you'd just leave. I thought you wanted children. You always said you did. Here they are." My finger had pointed at the beautiful newborns, barely a few months old, knowing what he would see and how it would contrast to the shining angels I saw. "They're beautiful and they're ours. We can have a family, even if it's not the way you'd hoped."

"I can't have a family with *them*. I wanted my children. *My children*. And you couldn't give that to me. That's all I wanted and you couldn't do it. I was willing to keep trying, but you gave up."

"*Three miscarriages,* Greg. I lost *three babies*. I couldn't do it anymore. Do you even realize how difficult that was, how... how... heartbreaking?"

"My mother said I shouldn't have married you. She knew this marriage would turn out badly. I should have listened to her. You've always been a little too ethnic-looking."

I was five seven, with hazel eyes and nearly black, curly hair. Living near the border as a child, I'd often been teased that I looked Hispanic. I wasn't, but that didn't matter to anyone; people only believe what is visible on the surface, not the truth underneath.

"So that's it. You're just leaving me." I'd looked down at my feet again, where Sophia and Marcel slept cozily under blue and pink blankets. Tears were threatening. Keeping my head down, I'd raised my hands, palms up, pleading again. "You can't leave me, Greg. You just can't. I can't do this alone; I can't raise them by myself."

"You chose, Susan. You chose these children over me. You knew how I felt. I supported you, but only to give you the opportunity to choose the right path, but you didn't. They're not even *American* for God's sake, Susan. What do you want me to do?

6

Be Mayor of a town that hates illegal immigrants, but have a brood of Mexicans raiding my pantry."

"Is that all you care about, Greg? Your image? What about me? Don't you love me?"

"A woman I love wouldn't do this."

"This," I'd glared, anger finally burning through the heartache building in my chest, "is the best decision I ever made."

"Fine. Live with it then. And enjoy the house. I'll have the lawyer put it in your name. I'll even throw in a little child support. I'll get reelected for being a selfless martyr, supporting my conniving wife and her illegals. At least some good will come out of being married to you." Gregory had moved forward then, raising his hand and a set of freshly-cut keys. I'd flinched reflexively. He had never struck me. He'd always had to get his way and I was always wrong; he had hit me with words many times, but he'd never physically hurt me. Tonight though, I was worried he might.

"I'm not going to hit you, moron." He'd shoved the keys at me and I'd taken them, my fingers curling around the cool metal. They'd weighted me down, like a giant anvil. "I changed the locks, thinking I'd kick you out, you ungrateful bitch, but that was before my lawyer said it would hurt my image and reelection chances, not to mention how much dough I'd have to fork over to divorce you if the judge sympathized. Not that I think that's likely." He'd stopped talking, watching me stare down at the keys, my brow furrowed in disbelief. "Don't worry, I didn't keep a key. Last thing I want to do is visit this house. It'll smell like beans and rice by morning."

"That's not why I was looking at them... What about all your things?" I'd asked softly, the quick anger already burnt out in a hot flash.

"Most of my things are already moved. This is the last of it. I'll stay in the apartment above the barber shop until I can find a suitable home. Maybe I'll build again. That's the only thorn in my side, losing this house."

When he'd loaded his suitcases and boxes into his car and driven away, I'd quietly lifted Sophia and Marcel and taken them into the nursery I'd painstakingly prepared over the past two weeks. It was beautiful—all soft grays and pale greens. Unstrapping and lifting the babes one by one, I'd placed them in their cribs.

They'd looked so tiny and defenseless; only a few months old and already fatherless. That thought had demolished the flimsy dam holding back total breakdown. I'd fallen to my knees, both hands gripping Marcel's crib, and I'd sobbed. The pity-fest hadn't lasted long though. Sophia's small whine had broken into my pain. That sound, more than anything in the world, had the power to make me strong.

***

I still lived in the same town with my children, which might seem insane, given my history with my ex-husband and the rampant prejudice in the town, but it was home; it always had been home. And I had support. My father was always over, playing with his grandchildren. He was a wonderful man, didn't have a racist bone in his body. If my mom, Nancy Grace, was alive, I knew she'd love Sophia and Marcel as much as my dad.

Mom succumbed to breast cancer when I was in my teens; there weren't as many treatment options twenty years ago and she was in the advanced stages when her condition was discovered. Whenever I had a little extra money, which wasn't often, I'd donate to a research foundation, hoping that someday no one would have to die of cancer or endure months of grueling, exhausting treatments.

My boutique-owner friend Sherry had been a huge help after Gregory left me. She'd expanded her store into toddler and youth clothing over the years. Each time I went into Baby Bliss, my wonderful friend would talk about some insane sale she was having and, as fate would have it, the sale was always on the items I needed- shoes for Marcel, leggings for Sophia. I teased her about it, but was beyond thankful. I worked at the middle school and a teacher's salary wasn't much to support two children on. It had been a struggle to keep my job; many of the parents saw me as a pariah. It didn't help that Gregory's word was gold in the town and, according to him, I was an uncompromising, irrational woman. I'd overcome though, after more than two years of social awkwardness and a few really great parents backing me up.

I hadn't been able to keep the house. Gregory had kept his promise, having his lawyer put it in my name, but the yearly taxes were insane and the property was too much for me to manage. As soon as I'd put it on the market, he'd approached me about buying it for half of its value. I'd refused, but he had power in the town. Not a single soul came for any of the open houses. I had one viewing the second month it was listed; the family was from out-of-town, looking to make a fresh start in a small community. I'd been honest with them, saying that our town wasn't made for new beginnings.

Six months was how long it took me to realize that Gregory would never let anyone else buy the house; so I'd sold it to him, walking away with barely enough money to buy the next home- a lot less than his original offer of half the value. He lived there now, with his new wife Bethany. He'd met her months after our separation and they'd married the day after our divorce was finalized. They had a blue-eyed, blonde son named Gregory Junior. He'd turn four soon. Gregory had gotten everything he'd wanted—a fertile, obedient wife and biological child.

I loved our house now though, and Sophia and Marcel loved it, which was all that mattered. It was just outside of town and we had three neighbors, all elderly without young children. The house was small, roughly twelve hundred square feet, with three bedrooms and a single bath, which would get complicated as Sophia got older. She already loved drying her hair and playing with my makeup. The kitchen was long and thin, but my dad had helped me knock down the wall between the kitchen and living room. The long island we'd built could seat four people on barstools- perfect for me, my dad and the kids. Sunday mornings were Sophia and Marcel's favorite day, because Grandpa Carl would come over and make pancakes- 'S' shaped for Sophia and 'M' shaped for Marcel. He always added chocolate chips. I never complained about the morning candy.

***

This morning, my dad had come over special, knowing the kids had a doctor's visit. He said chocolate pancakes were the right way to start off a day that involved needles. I couldn't argue with him there.

My three favorite people were sitting happily at the island, mouths full of pancakes, butter and syrup. Sophia was swinging her legs back and forth. Marcel was leaning against his grandpa, his little butt half on the barstool and half off. I was so blessed.

The time to leave for the doctors came quickly and both kids groaned when my dad told them to put on their shoes.

"Grandpa, do we have to go get shots?"

"Yep. How else are you going to stay strong and healthy, Sophia?"

"Well," Sophia paused, her little mind working quickly, "then you need to come with us. You're old, Grandpa, you need more shots than me to be strong."

"Oh, I've had my shots for the year," my dad smiled, "but if you want me to go with you, I can."

"Really!" Sophia looked at me, a wide smile brightening her face. "Can Grandpa come, mom?"

"Of course, but only if you go put your shoes on. Marcel's already got his on like a good boy." I watched my little angel with the deeply tanned skin and long brown-black braid swinging against her back, hop off her barstool and run to the hallway, where nearly a dozen pairs of shoes were lined up against the wall. That's one habit I'd never been able to instill in the kids— putting their shoes up in their closets after taking them off. I didn't set a good example though, since I just tossed off my own shoes and left them wherever they fell. I'd wake up in the morning and line all the shoes up against the wall and by the evening, they'd be all over the place again.

After neurotically checking the oven to make sure my dad had turned it off, we headed out the door. The drive to Dr. Lynn's office took ten minutes; we passed the kid's school, Liberty Elementary, on the way. Once inside the small office, Sophia and Marcel made a beeline for the books and puzzles with Grandpa trailing behind them. I signed us in. The wait was never long, only a few minutes or so, but the receptionist said to expect a longer-than-average wait time this morning.

I was surprised at the number of patients in the office. The majority were sitting in the 'sick child' area. There was one infant in the 'well-child' area with Sophia and Marcel; the mother was reading and paying little attention to the cooing child in the car carrier. I recognized one mom sitting in the sick patient section—Jennifer Payne from church. She'd always been nicer to me than the other mothers. Her four-year-old daughter Mary was very pale, her forehead glistening with sweat.

I walked over to Jennifer and her daughter, concern wrinkling my face. "Hi, Jennifer." I looked at the blonde toddler, now shivering uncontrollably. "Is Mary okay?"

Jennifer's face mirrored my own, "I don't know. She's been like this ever since our visit last week when she got her four-year vaccinations. I called here the next day, but Dr. Lynn said side effects were natural and to give it some time to settle in her system."

"Did she get all the vaccines on the normal tract?"

"Yeah. She got everything except her flu shot for the season. They were out of the nasal application and the injected version is totally synthetic this year so my husband didn't want Mary to get it."

"I can understand that. I've always been more than a little leery of vaccinations." I looked at Mary again; her condition seemed to be deteriorating rapidly. "I really hope she starts to feel better soon."

"She's just getting worse, Susan. I don't know what's going on."

I nodded, my most sympathetic expression splashed across my face as my mind focused on my own children. The apprehension was building to boiling point in my body. I walked back to the check-in window. The sliding glass shifted open as I approached. The receptionist that had checked me in was gone; Nurse Kayla sat in the rolling burgundy chair now, her hip fat folding over the sides of the seat. I really didn't like her; she was always a little too rough with the children.

"Hi, Nurse Kayla. I was just talking to one of the other mothers and she seems to think that her daughter started getting sick after her four-year vaccinations. Has there been a vaccine recall or anything? There seems to be a lot more sick patients than normal."

Nurse Kayla glanced around the office apathetically. "I guess." She looked up at me, clearly bored. "It's also autumn and the beginning of flu season."

"Oh, okay. I guess that makes sense." But as I walked away from the window and looked around the room again, my gut told me otherwise. All the children were roughly the same size, possibly around the same ages. Something was wrong. I began to walk again, but froze in my tracks almost immediately, movement catching my attention. One young boy sitting in the sick area stood up. His skin was pale and the folds around his eyes were nearly grayish, but he wasn't shivering like Mary. I blinked rapidly, thinking the boy's glassed-over expression was a trick of the overhead fluorescent lights.

The small figure, he couldn't be much older than Mary, walked slowly toward the well-patient area. His movements were a bit uncoordinated at first, as if he were new to walking, but as he gained confidence, his pace quickened slightly. His shoulders were slightly slumped, his mouth barely parted to reveal a sliver of off-white teeth.

The boy walked nearer and nearer to Sophia and Marcel. I began to move, unsure why apprehension had suddenly mutated to panic. I was feeling the pain-in-my-chest type of fear that I'd felt so rarely in my lifetime, but on a good note, the need to vomit from uneasiness had waned in the face of debilitating fear.

I was only a few feet away from my beautiful babes, when the slow-moving boy with the vacant expression changed course, a small cry carrying to his ears and drawing his attention. The infant in the car carrier…the tiny defenseless creature warm beneath a soft blanket had woken up.

The mother still wasn't paying attention, reading a magazine and rocking the carrier with her foot. The boy approached, knelt on the ground and buried his face against the blankets. The baby's mother heard the scream though, the high-pitched yelp of pain from her daughter. Her eyes shifted from the glossy pages of *Heavenly Hearth* to the floor. Instinct took over and the woman kicked out, knocking the boy away from the car carrier.

When I saw the blood painting the boy's face, I knew it was too late. The baby wasn't crying; the mother was screaming. I closed the distance between my children and myself and their position gave me a perfect line of sight. The boy had bitten through the infant's neck. And, as I grabbed Sophia and Marcel's hands, I saw the boy lunge forward and wrap his mouth around the mother's forearm, exposed by her short-sleeved shirt. Her cotton zip-up hoodie lay useless, draped across the arm of her chair. Not that it would have provided much protection on. It would have been something though…something between sharp toddler teeth and flesh.

My father looked as confused as I felt, his eyes wide and staring fixedly at the deranged boy munching on the woman. "Come on, Dad!" I screamed.

Sophia and Marcel's faces were warped with terror, but they allowed me to pull them along, toward the exit and toward Bessie, the now ancient Volvo. "Grandpa!" Sophia said loudly and tugged on my sleeve when she realized that my dad wasn't following us.

"Dad!" I screamed again; my second yell pulled him out of his motionless state. He began to move as quickly as he could with one bad knee and a year-old hip replacement. I yanked open the glass door and pushed Sophia and Marcel through. "Hurry, Dad!" Behind him, the other children in the sick-area were turning rabid, biting ferociously at anything nearby. The parents were confused, not knowing what to do or how to respond.

Like the situation was just a simple case of bad behavior, they tried to hold their children back, telling them to stop in raised, anxious voices.

Then the screams began, as the mothers and fathers realized that something was terribly, terribly wrong with their children. One woman was cradling her face, a large chunk of flesh hanging from her cheek by a single, elastic ribbon of skin. One father was still trying to save his child, holding her against the hard, tiled floor with strong hands as the girl thrashed wildly, growling and spitting. That father's voice, above all the other disturbing sounds, pierced my consciousness. *"Tessa, Tessa, stop! It's okay; daddy's here. You have to calm down!"* The other guttural sounds emanating from the doctor's office were better suited to a zoo exhibit.

My dad nearly fell through the door and I closed it quickly, slamming it against a brunette boy's face. A trail of blood from the kid's nose wetted the glass. He pulled back and body-slammed against the door, his hands clawing at the see-through surface futilely, his mouth opening and closing like a dying fish out of water.

"Sophia and Marcel, get to Bessie!" I ran closely behind them, their six-year-old legs pumping quickly back and forth. Marcel's sneakers lit up with every ground-fall, sparkling with red lights. They were his favorite sneakers. When I'd realized how attached he'd become to the shoes, I'd run to the store and purchased two more pairs in larger sizes so I could replace them as his feet grew without upsetting him. You plan to do a lot of things in the future, before the today turns to shit and the tomorrow loses importance.

I fumbled with the car keys in my hand, the automatic door opener had long-since died. I'd poured money into Bessie over the years and I'd always meant to replace the watch-sized battery, but I never had. I could kick my own ass for never replacing that stupid battery. To think such a small oversight could become so life-saving important at the turn of a killer kid.

The driver's side door was open now and I hit the automatic door lock on the armrest to open the other three. The kids were standing behind me, their bodies plastered to the car. My dad was near the rear of the vehicle, nursing his knee. "Get in!" I yelled, but their eyes were glued to the building we'd just run from.

"Mom." Marcel's voice was low and full of unmasked fear.

My head swiveled, turning to look at what held my children's attention. The mostly glass door and the large, adjacent windows making up the front of Dr. Lynn's building seemed little barrier between us and the blood-covered children and brutalized adults. They were pushing against each other, pushing against the glass, small hands made red, smeared prints. The parents had succumbed; even that father, so determined to save his Tessa, stood in the crowd filled with void eyes.

I saw Nurse Kayla in the center of the undulating, sickly huddle. She was the largest; her stomach, now bulging out of the button-up scrubs, pushed a red-haired child's face against the window. The child was trying to futilely shift his head sideways, his mouth ferociously snapping open and closed, trying to bite at the fat body pinning him down.

"Get in the car," I said again, trying to keep my voice calm. "Dad, get them in the car."

My dad opened the rear door and literally picked Marcel and Sophia up and tossed them onto the backseat. I watched them scramble inside, each getting seated in their booster and buckling- Marcel on my side of the car, Sophia on the opposite. My dad started limping around the car. Just as I was turning the key in the ignition and he was closing his door, I heard the shattering of glass and a distinct tinkling that said: barrier broken, glass falling on concrete, seriously demented, flesh-eating children and adults escaping.

I backed out of the parking space, my eyes flitting between the car mirrors and the doctor's office. Were they people? What the hell was going on? The children seemed to move a little faster than the shambling adults, their younger bodies apparently more agile and resilient to whatever was affecting them. Many of them were small enough to squeeze around the slow-moving adults and exit the building first, avoiding some of the sharpest shards of window glass.

I watched Nurse Kayla fall as others pushed to escape the building. The great mass of her body fell against the angled stalagmites of window glass. An especially tall shard exited the center of her back; her blood wasn't normal looking. It was nearly brown on the glass and then it oxidized quickly and turned into wet, shiny obsidian. Nurse Kayla thrashed about like a large, beached whale. The red-haired boy she'd been pinning against the glass stayed behind as the rest of the 'people' pushed to freedom. He crouched down on top of her body, making small jumps on her back to shove her down against the spiked glass. Nurse Kayla did not scream, as if she felt no pain, but it must hurt...*surely it must hurt?*

The boy seemed to lose interest quickly, crawling off the still-flailing body of the nurse and joining the crowd pursuing Bessie. His face tilted slightly upward as his nose tried to catch the lingering scent that was our uninfected flesh. I was pulling out of the lot now, watching the shambling bodies in the rearview. Some were close enough to bang the trunk with curled, stained hands. We all screamed as Sophia's door was wrenched open. The boy—the boy that had attacked the newborn babe—launched himself into the car; his body landed on the floorboards between Sophia and Marcel's feet. In my panic, I jerked the steering wheel, jolting my passengers, but the sharp movement kept the murderous boy on the rough carpeting a few moments longer.

My dad, not the most limber man on the planet, shoved himself over the center armrest between our seats. His arms strained for the boy who was now trying to crawl toward Marcel, his mouth already wide open and reaching for skin. The kid had on striped pants and bright yellow suspenders against a white polo shirt. He was dressed for success and I got the feeling his parents banked on the best for their kid—all name brands and private schools—hoping he would grow up successful and spread the wealth, maybe even choose one of the nicer nursing homes to dump mom and dad in when that time came.

Two strong hands gripped those brightly colored suspenders and lifted the boy off the carpet. "Kids, pick your feet up. Get them out of the way!" Sophia and Marcel both yanked up their legs, perching their shoes on the edge of the booster seats, obeying their grandpa without question. All the while, the boy growled and moved erratically.

The car was still moving; I didn't want anyone...*anything* else to try and get into the car. Sophia and Marcel's eyes were wider than I'd ever seen them, bulging out of their sockets. Without being asked, Sophia pushed her already ajar door wide and my dad simultaneously pendulum-swung the boy out. His body flew in a low arc, his head slamming against the metal doorsill as he exited the vehicle by force.

The impact caused the boy's head to bust open like a piñata, brown-quickly-oxidizing-to-black wetness oozing out. Several droplets flew into the air, catching Sophia in the face. I hit the gas, going from ten miles an hour to fifty, leaving the unmoving carcass of the yellow-suspendered boy and the rest of the rabid, slow-moving bunch behind us.

I slowed down as we entered the elementary school zone, the yellow lights weren't flashing, but slowing was habit. At first glance, the school, offset from the road by a wide partition of grass and the student drop-off lane, looked normal. After closer study, my heart did a free-fall into my stomach and the need to vomit came back with a vengeance. The windows were plastered with children, beating themselves against the glass, trying to exit

17

the building. The main entrance was propped open, the school office likely taking advantage of the fall breeze, but those double doors, let things in *and out.*

I pushed my foot down, compressing the gas and speeding up rapidly. Children were flooding out onto the lawn. A few kids seemed healthy, normal, running as quickly as they could from the voracious appetites of their demonic counterparts. The looks on their faces made my stomach roil with acidic anxiety; the 'I need to vomit' feeling intensified. I was suddenly yanked in two directions; my mother's instinct wanting to get my own children to safety as soon as possible, but also wanting to rescue those few kids running from the Reaper.

But I knew that I couldn't get to them in time; even if I turned the steering wheel to the right and barreled over the grass partition at full speed, it would be too late. Or maybe that's just what I was telling myself, relieving my mind of the guilt I felt from not trying to help them, those kids that obviously needed saving. My priorities were in the car; I had to protect Sophia, Marcel and my dad at all costs. No one in the world could rank above the three people sitting inside Bessie with me. If that made me a terrible person, oh well.

I was driving fast now and had there been a cop nearby, I knew I'd see flashing blue lights, but I didn't, so I kept driving fast and furiously through the streets. I headed for our house outside town limits. The neighbors didn't have children; we should be safe there for a while. I hoped.

When I pulled into the driveway of our little house, I saw no activity in the three other homes nearby. That should have struck me as odd. About this hour every day, Mr. Roseburn should be outside raking leaves. He was neurotic about that, hating each individual leaf that fell onto his pristine lawn. This past summer, he'd even had four perfectly healthy trees removed, just to minimize the falling leaves that would plague him in autumn. He'd wanted to cut down a large tree on my property and hadn't been pleased when I'd told him no.

I idled for a moment, waiting for the automatic door to rise and reveal the small single-car space, then I pulled Bessie into the garage. I hurried my children and father out of the car and up the concrete stairs and into the house; all I wanted in that moment was to have the garage door down and our house door bolted, a tactile barrier between ourselves and whatever the hell was going on in the outside world. As I was threading the chain lock, Sophia and Marcel started untying their shoes.

"No, leave them on," I barked, quickly realizing my tone was not soothing, "I don't know how long we're going to stay in the house, so leave your shoes on. Okay?" Their little heads nodded in unison. "How about going into the kitchen and getting a snack. I just re-stocked the treat drawer." We had a small drawer that was only opened as a reward for good behavior. It had sugary, chocolate-coated granola bars, puddings and single-serve packs of cookies. Sophia loved the peanut butter filled cookies; Marcel was more a butterscotch pudding guy.

They raced off toward the promise of a sweet treat and I turned to my dad. I didn't need to say anything for him to understand the questions warring inside my head. "Maybe there's something on the news?" he said, his voice sounding like he actually was calm instead of just trying to put up a good façade like me.

"Yeah," I took a deep, centering breath, "that's a good idea."

We only had one small television; I'd never let the kids watch much TV—just Saturday morning cartoons and a kid's channel movie now and then. For the most part, we'd go to our town library after school every Wednesday, listen to story time and rent a film from the small collection. Sophia and Marcel had gotten in the habit of picking the same movies over and over again. It got a bit tedious, but at least I could be sure the movies were clean; so if I were cleaning or concentrating on something else, I didn't have to worry about language or distasteful content.

The television came to life with a crackle; I really should replace the thing, but money was tight and until it broke completely...

"...reports are coming in from all over the country..."

My dad flipped the channel, heading toward what he considered the most reliable news source.

"A beloved Pediatrician, Dr. Bush, was found dead this morning by local police inside his ransacked office outside..."

Click.

"...CDC is scrambling to figure out what is affecting the U.S. population and why the epidemic has not touched other countries, but..."

Click.

"...bitten, please immediately report to the nearest hospital or..."

Click. The hand holding the remote lowered to my dad's side and rested against his thigh.

"People have described the attackers as rabid, animalistic...the 'living dead.' Authorities have no answers as we enter into the fifth hour past the first reports of the rapidly spreading infection. The CDC has offered one preliminary finding—that there is no patient zero. There are patients, thousands of young children ranging in age from four to six, originating the sickness. It seems to spread through bodily fluid exchange. If you are bitten or come into contact with blood, saliva or any other fluid from one of the 'infected,' report to an emergency care center immediately.

"We do not know what has caused the children to fall ill, but we are being assured that Washington is doing everything in its power to halt the epidemic. There seems to be no prejudice in victims of the infection. The CDC has asked us to help our viewers recognize the warning signs of, what the government has coined, a 'Z child' or an infected adult. Be on the lookout for vague expressions with eyes that might be coated in an opaque blue-white film, a graying of the skin with some signs of post-mortem decay, primal behavior, such as an increased use of ol-

factory senses and heightened saliva production, causing the appearance of excessive drooling.

"The infected will not respond to social settings, recognize their names or react to negotiation. Their only drive seems to be the most basic need: to satisfy hunger. They are ferocious, unrelenting and dogged in their pursuits. Do not be fooled by the childlike appearance of the Z children or the friends' faces that may mask the Z infected adults. They are not your children or your friends. They are, in the words of two eye witnesses, zombies.

"Get to a safe location, secure food and water. Our team at Channel Nine is dedicated to bringing our viewers the most up-to-date information on this unfolding national crisis."

"What's a...*Z child?*" a high voice said quietly behind me. My dad quickly turned off the television.

"Nothing, sweetheart." I walked toward Sophia and knelt down. "It's nothing you need to worry about."

Then I saw the dried blood on her face and my heart plummeted into my stomach. I picked her up and rushed toward our only bathroom. The door was closed. "Mom, Marcel's going potty." She grunted as I turned quickly, ran into the kitchen and plopped her butt on the counter next to the sink. "Mom...what's wrong?" Her voice was anxious.

"I just want to clean your face off. It has some dirt on it." My dad was beside me now, already wetting a paper towel and handing it to me.

"It's not near her mouth, Suz." He placed a hand on my shoulder as I wiped the dried black blood from Sophia's face. I didn't realize I was shaking until his grip steadied me.

"Yeah." I sighed in relief. "You're right. It just freaked me out."

Sophia didn't say anything; she just gave me a quick kiss and hopped off the counter. Amazing how resilient children are.

Marcel came out of the bathroom then. "Mom, my stomach hurts."

"Oh, I'm sorry." I filled a glass with cool tap water and handed it to him. "Drink some water and if it still hurts later, I'll give you some of the pink stuff." I brushed his hair off his forehead.

Marcel made a face; he hated the taste of the brightly colored medicine, but Dr. Lynn told me to keep it around for him since he seemed to have a really sensitive stomach. Thinking of the doctor, I realized I hadn't seen what happened to her. She hadn't been in the hoard of the infected coming out of her building. Was she okay? I doubted it.

I turned to the kids. "Let's go put on a movie."

"Can we watch the one from the library?"

"We watched that yesterday!" Sophia complained; Marcel had picked the movie this week.

"Why don't we watch *Polar Buddies* instead? You both love that movie." Both kids agreed that was a good pick; I knew they would. Even I had to admit that the yellow lab puppies in it were beyond cute. When the movie was playing and both kids had drinks and a second snack, my dad and I went into the kitchen.

"Dad, what should we do? The news said hole up, stay indoors, but…" My voice trailed off, weakening as I realized that we didn't have anywhere else to head. My dad lived in a one bedroom apartment in town. His building housed dozens of families with *children.*

"If the news is right, only the U.S. is being affected. We need to get out of the country."

"A million other people are going to have the same idea."

"A million people don't own a boat in Corpus Christi."

"You're not seriously suggesting we load up on your sailboat and drift off to paradise? You go down once a year, do a little work and never even untie it from the dock. Is it even seaworthy?"

"She's in good shape, Suz. The engine's reliable. I replaced the sails this summer and she's stocked with food."

The *Nancy-Grace* was my dad's tribute to my mom, a 1988 Hallberg-Rassy with five berths, a manual toilet, shower and a decent kitchenette. She'd always wanted to live on the water and sail to exotic locations. He'd purchased the sailboat when she'd started chemo, but she'd never gotten to step foot on it, dying before they could make the short trip to Corpus. The boat was in decent repair now, according to my dad, but he'd never tested it in the open ocean…which didn't give me much confidence.

"I know it's our best option, Suz."

I considered his words. The *Nancy-Grace* would get us off land, away from the population. Maybe the food on board would last us or maybe we could find a new home, in another country. Even if the diesel engine crapped out on us, we'd have the sails and wind to carry us to safety. Considering the other nonexistent options…

"Alright." I gave a resolute nod. "Time to pack."

My dad and I worked for over an hour, stuffing clothing for Sophia and Marcel in their school backpacks. I didn't take much for myself and luckily my dad kept a few changes of clothes and toiletries at our house for when he spent the night. The kids were always asking Grandpa Carl to sleep over and play board games. It was especially helpful on school nights when I had papers to grade.

Lastly, we went through the pantry, putting everything shelf-stable into a box. We took all the pastas, beans and rice, even though those had to be cooked. My dad had a few pots and pans and the boat's gas stove ran off a propane tank. The *Nancy-Grace* was outfitted with a rain reservoir and filtration system too. As long as it rained, we'd have water. We just had to get to Corpus, get to the boat.

When we were finished, my dad packed Bessie. His car was a lot newer, but it was also smaller, so we didn't even discuss taking it instead. While he loaded the vehicle, I spoke with my children, telling them where we were going, trying to make it sound like a vacation. My children were too smart for that though.

"Mom, is this because of those Z kids? Are they bad? Is that what happened at the doctor's office today?" Marcel stared hard at me, his eyes crinkled in thought. "Sophia said she heard about it when you and Grandpa were watching the news." His little hand moved down to his stomach and he rubbed reflexively. The movement made me think about medicine and how I hadn't packed any.

"Yes. You're right, sweetheart. And we have to leave to stay safe. Do you need some tummy medicine?"

"No, I'm okay, Mom." The hand that had been rubbing his stomach moved toward Sophia, who was standing stoically beside him. She took it; their fingers grasped each other tightly. "Mom?"

"Yeah, sweetie?"

"What about Aunt Sherry?"

My mouth dropped. I hadn't even thought about Sherry. My best friend for more years than I could count and she hadn't even crossed my mind. "I'll give her a call and make sure she's okay."

Marcel nodded and Sophia pulled him a little closer. My dad came in then. "Dad, get the kids in the car. I'm going to grab the medicine tote in the kitchen and I'll be right out." I didn't wait to see my dad hustle the kids to the garage, but went straight into the kitchen and grabbed the medicine. I had everything in the tote from aspirin to fiber supplements. My cellphone was on the counter. I checked it; there were three coverage bars. I'd call Sherry after we were on the road. Grabbing as many cold sodas as I could carry, I headed to the garage. Everyone was in the car; it was already started, thrumming loudly and quickly filling the closed space with carbon dioxide.

I hit the garage door button as I walked down the stairs, pulling the house door closed behind me. That was probably silly, considering I may never see the lovely little home again. I was just stepping off the stairs when I heard a distinct scratching. The garage door was a foot off the ground and rising slowly. A pair of small legs crouched next to the door outside, hands clawing at the thick vinyl of the automatic lift door.

Freezing, I kept staring at those legs, slowing lengthening into a torso, a neck, a deranged, blood-splattered face. Oh my God...my mind reeled. Mr. and Mrs. Roseburn's grandson, Jackson. I remembered Mrs. Roseburn telling me last week that he'd be visiting while his parents took a second honeymoon. How could I forget? *How could I forget?* The cold cans of soda fell from my grasp, clunking down the stairs.

Behind Jackson, standing in my yard, stood my elderly neighbors, each in various states of undress, their faces void of human emotion. They shuffled about the yard, focusing on nothing in particular. Mr. Mayhew was missing an ear, ebony blood streaming down his face, soaking the collar of his torn nightshirt. His right hand still gripped the morning paper he always retrieved at lunchtime—usually wearing nothing but that same striped button shirt and tatty boxers.

Mrs. Roseburn's body was the most disheveled. Her floral, long dress had a jagged rip in the middle of her chest, where a large chunk of flesh was missing. Her right leg seemed bent at a wrong angle, but she was walking...walking without purpose, dragging the damaged limb behind her like so much unwanted baggage.

Jackson, the Z child, lifted his nose into the air and sniffed deeply. His position and expression was better suited to a wild dog than a small human; a thick trail of saliva hung from his lower lip, lolling back and forth like a playground swing.

The screams from inside Bessie pulled me out of my motionless, come-bite-me-I'm-easy state. I lunged for the car door, trying not to trip on the soda cans and thanking God the space was so small. Jackson leapt toward me at the same time. His undisciplined jump landed him near me, but a large blue tub, filled with already-wrapped gifts I'd been stockpiling for Christmas in case money became tight, thwarted his attack. He knocked into the eighteen-gallon storage container and fell forward. As his body hit the concrete garage floor, I heard a resounding snap.

The sound of screaming and the falling storage bin caught the attention of the infected adults. They broke from their repetitive movements and began to travel in our direction; their gaits were slower than Jackson's, but I'd noticed that before…at the doctor's office when the Z children had been so much more determined and focused than the mauled parents.

I was in the car now, the driver's door closed. I didn't bother to buckle, throwing the gearshift into reverse and hitting the gas. My infected neighbors were directly behind Bessie now and the old girl did me proud, slamming into their bodies and tossing them left and right.

Jackson was up again, his left arm hanging limply. Black-stained, white bone protruded from his forearm. Again, I was struck by the absence of pain. Like Nurse Kayla, her body being shoved into sharp glass, he uttered no agony-soaked cry. He was making his way out of the garage, moving slowly, but gaining momentum. I hit the automatic door closer and the gears shifted into motion, rolling the vinyl access downward. It was too slow though; Jackson got outside well before vinyl touched down on concrete. He was motivated and our flesh his goal. I was beginning to think that fictional zombie 'norms' didn't apply to Z children.

I screeched out of the driveway and shifted gears. I tried to accelerate too fast, making Bessie's rear end fishtail violently. Lifting my foot just a fraction off the gas pedal, I controlled the vehicle, easing her forward at a less break-neck speed. When my infected neighbors were out of sight, I fished my mobile out of my pocket and called Sherry's number. The line rang six times before Sherry's voicemail message picked up. I waited until the beep.

"Sherry, it's Susan. Call me as soon as you get this. Hopefully, you're okay. I've got my dad and the kids. We're going to Corpus. We have some place safe there. Call me, please." When I hung up, I dropped the phone into my lap.

"Want to go by her store? See if she's okay." I looked at my dad, his face concerned. Sherry meant a lot to him too, almost like a second daughter.

"I don't want any detours, Dad. I just want to get out of here."

He nodded, understanding, but I could see that his pain matched mine—his pain and his hope that Sherry was somehow safe and unharmed.

The way out of town toward Interstate-10 went right by Gregory's house, the large 'nearly a mansion' that I'd once called home.

Call it poetic justice, call it whatever you like, but passing that house and seeing my ex-husband, his wife and their all-American son trolling the yard, drooling and growling at each other like depraved lunatics, was a medicinal balm to my frayed nerves and uncertain future.

***

Bessie was down to a quarter of a tank and we'd only been driving two hours; she'd had half a tank when we'd fled the house, so I'd known we couldn't drive forever, but Corpus was still nearly four hours away. I didn't want to stop, but what choice did we have? Dad said he'd take over driving after filling up. That was fine by me. I wanted to close my eyes, feel the car vibrations beneath my butt and float to la-la land. Sophia and Marcel were already asleep. The events of the day had exhausted them, their apparent resilience only surface-deep. Still, children were amazing creatures.

My children were amazing anyway, considering the other children I'd encountered recently were crazed ankle-biters.

Several miles down the road was a city, only slightly larger than the border town we'd recently fled from. The welcome sign was brightly painted, as if some municipal worker had been given the singular job of keeping it fresh and happy, a wonderful 'hello' for all the strangers passing through. Not far past the sign was a gas station, the kind with older pumps so you could fillup your tank before paying. I quickly scanned the adjacent buildings and streets; they seemed deserted, which made me uneasy, but we needed fuel. No way to avoid that truth.

Wishing I could idle the engine while filling the tank, I turned Bessie's key. The quiet that engulfed us after the sound of the motor died was unsettling; the stomach juices already wrestling in my belly became more excited, jumping and scorching my esophagus with their acidity. I sat still for a second, trying to forcefully calm my nerves and belly, but sitting motionless didn't help; it made me feel worse. I threw the driver's door open, leaning over quickly and finally vomiting. Yellow foam and bits of breakfast granola splashed on the ground grossly. As soon as I'd finished, I sat up, feeling instantly relieved, both emotionally and physically.

My dad patted my back. Sophia and Marcel still slept. I was glad they hadn't witnessed that. I got out of the car, avoiding the barf, and peered at the convenience store. I turned, hearing the passenger door open and close. My dad was leaning against Bessie, testing his bad leg before walking. Sometimes, long periods of sitting made his hip sore and his bad knee too stiff to move immediately.

"I'll see if there's an attendant."

"I can go."

"You can hardly walk right now, Dad."

"Hey, I got one good leg."

I rolled my eyes at him. He wasn't taking getting old very well. He'd always been so active. "Well, use that one good leg to pump the gas and I'll be right back." I walked toward the small building; large window stickers advertised slushies, candy and lottery tickets. Tiny decals on the door showed the accepted forms of payment. They took credit cards, which was good, since I only had ten dollars and some change in cash, not enough money to fill up the Volvo.

My hand gripped the long steel handle and pushed hard, expecting the door to open. I frowned, pushing harder…until I saw the word 'pull' written in large red letters. Great. I'm sure I looked like an idiot to whoever was in the store. Wearing an expression of chagrin, I pulled the door open and walked in.

At first glance, there didn't seem to be anyone in the store. A melted, ten-pound bag of ice was leaking out onto the floor to my left. "Hello?" No one responded, but I heard a rustling over near the soda machine. I headed in that direction, first glancing out the window. My dad was standing by the car, the nozzle already in Bessie, filling the old girl up. Behind that scene, across the street, were a few buildings. I hadn't scanned those before pulling into the station.

The name of the central building was *Sunny Valley Daycare*. I stiffened, realizing I'd put my family yards away from a potential Z child hive. "Hello?" I said in earnest. I was turning the corner around a potato chip display. I found the store worker, but even if he had wanted to respond to my 'hellos,' he couldn't have.

He was splayed out on the ground, his nametag askew on the gray lapel of his shirt. The lower half of his face—chin, lip and jaw—were missing. An assortment of candy wrappers littered the floor around his body, their shiny wrappings looking odd against his still-red blood. Perched on his thighs, was a girl. Her right hand clutched an open, half-eaten, peanut-covered caramel bar coated in blood. Her left hand was wrist-deep in the man's stomach, rooting around like a hog's snout searching for truffles in the ground.

Her hair was dark brown with sun-yellowed highlights. I thought I saw bright blue eyes, but it was hard to tell beneath the milky film that marked the infected. She must have heard my voice; she must know I was here, but she was too focused on her task. I tried to back away quietly. Her nostrils flared and she made small sniffing sounds, but still she did not look at me.

The Z child's void face suddenly gave a small jerk, her lips almost pulling up in satisfaction as her hand extracted a large wet chunk. It looked like the liver, but I wasn't sure. I didn't want to be sure. I backed away a little quicker, trying to round the corner toward the exit without taking my eyes off the girl. My angle was wrong.

My body hit the chip display and it toppled over. I fell with it, landing awkwardly against the metal stand. The girl's head jerked up, the loud sound enough to pull her attention in my direction. Like a wild animal, she crawled up the dead attendant's body, her gaze fixed on me with determination. A thin drop of drool left the corner of her mouth and traveled down her face to hang from her chin. After a moment, it released its hold on her skin and fell toward the tile floor. The mucous glistened grossly on the dirty tan surface.

I scrambled, working my way quickly to a standing position. The Z girl was so close to me, still moving on all fours. I lifted the display, which was surprisingly light, and threw it at her. It hit her right shoulder, but she continued moving as if nothing had happened. *They don't feel pain, idiot. Just run!*

And I did. I made for the door like an Olympic sprinter, glad that this time I could just push through and shove the door closed behind me. There was no way to lock it though and nothing nearby to use as a barricade. I firmly pushed my back against the door, planting my feet in front of me and leaning backwards. My knees locked solidly, giving me the maximum force to keep the door shut against danger.

"What's wrong?" My dad's voice carried toward me, slightly alarmed. "Were you able to pay?" He'd just finished pumping and was screwing the gas cap back on.

My eyes frantically met his; I screamed as the door pushed partially open. The infected girl was trying to get to me, to the fresh meat. I reacted quickly, slamming my body harder into the door to re-close it.

"Suz! What's wrong?" my dad called again, his voice more frantic. His eyes widened and I knew he'd seen the monster kid I was keeping at bay. "Oh my God...Suz!"

"Get the car started!" I yelled. "I have to make a run for it."

In seconds, my dad was in Bessie with the engine running. I was about to relinquish my post and make a dash when my eyes were drawn upward, past the car and across the street. The day-care door was now open and children were spilling out, falling over one another in their zeal to exit. At first, I thought they were normal, uninfected. Then I saw the grown adult emerging into the sun, her auburn hair bright against the black blood oozing from a gaping head wound. Her green dress was ripped in a dozen places, her body seemingly covered in small teeth marks.

My dad's head turned to look at what held my gaze; my expression must have betrayed my fear. The door moved under my hold again; that pulled me out of the trance caused by a dozen Z children coming in our direction. The rabid girl trapped in the convenience store was actually moving away, back toward the soda machines. Her right hand opened, letting the empty caramel bar wrapper fall to the floor. The door's glass was smeared with black blood and bits of candy. Such a strange combination.

The daycare children were halfway across the street and Bessie was moving, my dad swinging the vehicle around the pumps and toward my position. It wasn't a far distance. I closed my eyes for a second, took a deep breath and ran. When I got to the car, I yanked on the passenger door, but it wouldn't open. The doors had automatically locked when the car had started moving.

I slammed my palm against the window. "Unlock the door!" I screamed.

When the lock shot upward, I wrenched the door open. The children from across the street were mere feet away. I sat down quickly, kicking out at a boy that was reaching for my door. I missed and his hand gripped the frame, his fingers wrapping inward. I grabbed the door handle and pulled; the boy was yanked forward and as the door slammed shut, his fingers severed, falling one by one and rolling across the carpet to settle next to my feet. My heart was racing wildly. Sophia and Marcel were awake, their mouths hanging open, tears streaming down their faces.

I don't know why, but my dad drove slowly down the street and through the mass of Z children. Maybe it was their appearance; they were still so small. Maybe he just couldn't fathom running over any 'person.' At this point, I thought I could. The infected adult was still in the daycare parking lot, walking in circles, her shoulders slumped, her lips moving as if she were try-trying to say something.

We made it to Corpus on that tank of gas. It was a larger city and the streets were littered with the infected. We stayed on the outskirts, on our way to Padre Island where the *Nancy-Grace* was docked. I could only imagine what the inner city looked like.

How had it come to this? Just this morning…just yesterday, the world had been normal. Now, the Z children were taking over, attacking and infecting with every nibble.

Sea Ranch Marina was deserted. We took everything in Bessie to the *Nancy-Grace* in one trip and my dad made short work of getting us out of port. The boat's living area was decorated with dozens of pictures of my mom. I loved seeing her face; after the day we'd just had, I needed that image in my mind. In one of the pictures, my mom was smiling softly, her hairless head covered in a pale pink bandana.

***

We were standing on deck now and everything seemed like a fleeting dream as the boat cleaved through the water and away from land.

I looked at my children. Marcel was smiling and standing next to my dad. Sophia was staring at the water, her mouth a straight line. I walked toward her, ready to offer comfort.

As I saw the slightly opaque glaze coating her eyes, I thought back to cleaning the black blood off her face and my dad saying not to worry, that it wasn't near her mouth.

But it had gotten in her mouth…hadn't it.

ABOUT THE AUTHOR

Eli Constant lives in Virginia with her husband, two daughters and rescue dog. She spends her days mothering, puttering about the house doing this and that and, of course, writing.

Her debut novel, *"Dead Trees,"* was published in the winter of 2012. It is a dystopian thriller focusing on the trials of a mother across a post-apocalyptic, hostile landscape. Eli is obsessed with human nature and the choices people make when faced with insurmountable odds. She hopes to approach this obsession with every piece of writing, examining the nuances of humanity's many faces.

Her published works, available on Amazon and at various retailers, are *"Dead Trees," "DRAG.N," & "Mastic."*

Learn more about Eli at www.eliconstant.com. Follow her on Twitter @Author_EliC.

Let's Scare Cancer To Death

2

Of The Dead
By Alyn Day

For John, my Hero.

There were four of us left that night, after Gray's Brigade split off from Deland's Dynamos out on recon. Four living, breathing humans fighting for our lives. Just another day, I guess.

It was just before sunset when we knew we'd never make it back to base before full dark came on. We'd gotten held up trying to sweep a house with plywood over the windows and a swarm of ghouls inside. We weren't expecting them. It had been months since we'd seen them out in full force; that many clustered together, anyway. I think most of us had started to hope they were beginning to die off all by themselves. No such luck, though, not if this house was any indication.

Grady went first. Sergeant Grady Gray always went first. He was tall and imposing, built like a linebacker with these flat black eyes like chips of flint set into his skull. Tonner went next, his pale skin making him look like a ghost as he slipped into the shadows. Next was Ambrose, ducking his head to fit his lanky

35

frame under the doorway. I followed them all, bringing up the rear like always. Tyce. That's me.

Deland's group swung around back. There were six of them, but I don't know their names. Learning people's names nowadays is dangerous business. Sometimes the less you know about someone, the less you care, the better off you are when they bite the big one.

Like I said, I didn't know Deland's group from a hole in the wall…but one thing I did know about them, they were cocky. Gray may have been a hard ass, but he kept us all in line, kept us sharp. Even before that first scream as some poor bastard on Deland's team lost his life, we were ready to rock and roll. We couldn't save them, though. Best we could do was to put down the pus bags, contain the area, and end the misery of the two unlucky chumps that got bitten but not taken out by Zed. Grady saw to that job personally. I admired him for that; for not making his team do the dirty work. I hoped when my time came, I'd get as good an end as those two pukes got. Better than stumbling around, covered in shit and blood, groaning and making a meal of some poor fool who forgets his safety procedures.

At the sound of that first scream, we all knew what to do. We all had our orders. Maybe not right then, out loud, but we all knew what we were doing just the same. Gray had drilled us on this situation so many times it was like singing a damned nursery rhyme it came so easy.

I dropped to one knee, bringing my backup weapon around to bear. It was a long barreled AR-15, a custom job with a pistol grip and a black matte finish. Fully automatic. Extended magazine. Flashlight rigged up to the end, just like the rifles Ambrose and Tonner packed, though theirs were black market Russian jobs. Tonner swept around to my left like a damned ninja. I felt the air move as he passed by me, a slight breeze and the rustle of his gun strap, then he was gone. Ambrose went right, not as stealthy as Tonner, but quiet. His breathing was heavy and sort of raspy, his footfalls punctuating the silence after the screams had died, much like the screamers. Gray stood behind me facing the opposite direction, his back inches from mine. I touched my ammo store silently, reassuring myself that I had enough. It had been some time since we'd seen any real action. Mostly just swoop and sweeps, marking off block after block as "clear", sealing off buildings with a single stripe of protective yellow tape before moving on to the next one.

That scream came again, weaker this time. It ended in a gurgle, like someone trying to breathe water. I heard a rifle shot. Suppressed. Close. Followed by another. It came from the west. Tonner.

I moved forward, still in a squat, as Grady checked either side of the door before we swung out to join the fray. It was quiet at first, shadows already darkening the lawn, growing out from the house as the sun sank behind it. After a few seconds, as Gray and I made our way around the western side of the house, there came another handful of rifle shots. We turned the corner and found Tonner and Ambrose standing over what remained of half a dozen ghouls. The older ones were pale and desiccated, the flesh peeling back from their swollen joints. Just beyond them were two of Deland's boys, their goddamned pieces still holstered. What kind of half-assed operation had Deland been running? Not much of one, considering he was one of the bodies Tonner was toeing over onto its back. Gray frowned as he took the other leader's weapons and ammunition from his mostly headless corpse. He gestured with his chin towards the house. Ambrose and I looked at each other and nodded once, covering each other's backs as we went in for the kills, the sources of the groaning and the wet sucking sounds we heard just inside the doorway.

Just inside the glass double doors, which had been thrown wide (another rookie mistake) two more Zed chewed on the guts of an unfortunate greenie. That's what they called us all back at base—Greenies. On account of the green uniforms I guess. The scientists and doctors were White Coats. All the others were just civvies. At first, I thought the guy on the ground was dead, but when my flashlight beam swept over his face, he looked towards me with pleading eyes. His torso rose up a couple inches off the floor, face tied up in a taught grimace, and stretched a bloodied hand out to me, shaking with effort. One of his fingers was missing, strings of tattered flesh hanging from the wound. I was too stunned to do anything but gape at the guy. I hadn't even heard Grady come up behind me, not until the gunshot. The chewed up greenie fell back to the linoleum with a wet thwack, a fresh bullet hole right between his eyes. Two more shots and the ghouls fell on top of him in a bloody heap, one of their heads completely gone from the nose up. I glanced back at Gray over my shoulder. He'd seen me freeze, that was for sure, but he didn't reprimand me or even look upset. Instead, he nodded again towards the interior of the house, and Ambrose's back as he disappeared into the gloom. I followed.

By the time we cleared the house, putting down another three ghouls, and bitten greenies in equal number, there was more shadow than daylight and what was left was fading fast. Somebody, living or dead but probably the latter, was sure to have heard that commotion and probably get curious. We had no choice, we had to move out.

Gray and Tonner piled up the bodies, Zed and former colleagues all tossed in a dripping pile together in a corner of the fenced in yard. They doused them with kerosene and set the whole mess on fire while Ambrose and I finished the sweep. We taped over the glass door with our signature strip of yellow, so that if anyone entered, anyone dead anyway, they'd rip the tape and we'd know about it. Looters, they were smart. The people dumb enough to reject our offer of sanctuary out of some military prejudice or outdated fear of tyrannical dictatorship and go it alone had only survived this long by playing it safe. They knew our habits, what to look out for, how to hide their tracks so we didn't find them. Only once or twice had we caught them, shadows moving inside a house with a yellow stripe over the door. But we knew they were around. Sometimes we heard gunshots or shouting. Zed don't shoot, and he don't shout either. Pretty much the only thing Zed does is eat. Anything and everything in his path. Human or otherwise, it don't matter. As long as there's warm blood and a heartbeat. I've seen the chewed up remains of every animal you can think of—dogs, cats, horses, even rats. You name it, Zed has stuffed it down his rotten gullet. What a way to go, huh?

After the bodies were burning bright enough that we knew they'd keep on for a while, Gray pulled everyone into a circle on the opposite side of the yard. That's where he broke the news. "We can't go back," he said, looking each of us in the eye, "Not tonight. One, we'd never make it. Two, you know as well as I do that the perimeter guys'd shoot us dead before we got close enough to shout."

Tonner and I nodded, but Ambrose looked shaken. "So, uh, what do we do?" he asked, looking at the burning bodies.

He was breathing through his mouth, trying to block out the smell—we all were—but I think he had it the worst. Ambrose isn't much of a soldier, honestly. He'd be better off doing tech support in a nice safe office somewhere. Too bad no place is safe anymore, too bad there haven't been any tech support jobs since the lights went out eight months ago.

Gray looked off into the distance, east, towards home base. "Well..." he sighed, "...we can't stay here. We move out, find a secure building, check the perimeter, and fort up for the night. Two men on guard duty, two men sleep. We'll keep up a rotation, switch off every two hours 'til sunup, then we go home and take a goddamned shower."

There was a chorus of "Yes, sir!" and we all moved out, exiting the back gate in a single file, Ambrose bringing up the rear. I glanced backward and saw him close the gate after us before crossing himself and muttering something towards the still burning bodies.

Unfortunately, this wasn't a regular area for us. We were pretty far from our usual stomping grounds, so there weren't a lot of yellow stripes around. We ended up stalking silently through the darkness for far too long looking for one, and when we finally found it, I don't think any of us were thrilled at the prospect of spending the night.

It was an old apartment complex, one that had probably looked rundown long before Zed ever took residence. Three stories, lots of boarded up or broken windows. Peeling paint and cracked stucco. We all sort of looked at each other, almost daring one another to go in first.

As usual, Gray barged ahead, not even bothering to peel back the tape before he opened the door, he just pushed his way through it. It snapped with a sound like a dry old bone breaking. "I don't like it either, guys," he said, "But we can't stay out here."

Tonner and I followed him in, sweeping our beams over broken stair railings, ripped up carpet, and walls stained with— we didn't want to know what the walls were stained with. Ambrose followed us, bringing up the rear. He was shaking. I could see his beam trembling as he came up the stairs. Poor guy.

We did a cursory sweep of the second floor, up and down the hall with our beams. Pushing on doors. Most of them were locked. We didn't want to risk making more noise by busting them down and Zed had never been good with locks anyway, so we left them alone after listening for a few seconds at each one. The last one we tried was open. It pushed inward easily, creaking a little. Kind of unsettling in the dark stillness of the abandoned building.

We followed our usual procedure. Always better safe than sorry. Always. Gray went first, sweeping his beam around like a light saber. Tonner and Ambrose went next, side by side like little green army men trudging into the unknown, their flashlight beams like spears in the darkness. I followed them all, turning my back to them so I could keep a watch on the exit behind us. I swept my own beam through the dusty air, and that's when I saw them.

Three ghouls, crouched on the opposite landing, eating something wet and red. Somehow, we'd missed them on our initial sweep and they'd been too occupied with dinner to notice us.

I swallowed. Hard. It felt like choking down a rock. How many more of them were in here? I forced myself to remember my training, not to panic. I whistled a quick one-two note, our designated signal for Zed, then tapped a .556 on the butt of my riffle three times. Three ghouls.

Tonner turned smoothly on his heels, dropping into barrier position. Ambrose locked up for a moment before turning and dropping to one knee, ready to provide cover to Gray and me if needed. Gray stepped between them, weapon raised. I aimed at the ghouls, throwing a shaft of light over them all, lighting up what remained of whatever bloody thing they were eating.

Discharging our weapons in here was a risk, sure. Even a suppressed shot would make noise in a big old empty building like this, so we hesitated to pull the trigger. Using our guns could be dangerous; however, not using them and letting Zed roam free in a place where we intended on sleeping, that was almost certain death. Gray took the first shot, placing a bullet right through the top of the biggest one's head. It toppled over onto the unfortunate thing that had been its last meal, stained mechanic's coveralls glistening with blood and bits of sinew. Zed never even looked up.

I took the next shot. Zed had long, matted hair and a pink housecoat. I missed the mark a little low and ended up blowing a whole through its lower jaw and out the back. It still got the job done. Gray and I both swept our weapons to the final target, a much smaller Zed still munching away on what I started to think might've been a housecat. Our beams overlapped, lighting up the ghoul as it tore bits of meat free. The little ones were always hard for me. They made me think of Angie, my own little girl. At least she had been, before Zed came to town and took her away from me...and her mother, too. Was this what was left of her now? Some brainless eating thing? My little flower?

I caught myself and prepared to take the shot, but Gray beat me to it, as usual. I heard the hammer release, then Ambrose stood up, knocking the gun away. Gray's shot went way wide, a little puff of dust kicking up on a wall across the way. Gray looked at Ambrose like he was mental, which maybe he was, but the look on his face stopped us all cold.

"Sarge!" he said, voice quivering, pointing at Zed with a shaking hand. "She ain't dead! Look at her eyes!"

And we did. My beam was still locked on it. I hadn't moved a muscle since I took aim. Sure enough, Zed Junior was blinking and squinting into my flashlight's high intensity beam. Yeah, Zed does a lot of things—moaning, eating, infecting, mostly— but one thing Zed sure as hell don't do is react to light.

We all just sort of looked at each other, then back at the Zed Thing. The wheels in our heads were turning. I sure as hell couldn't shoot it now, not after I'd seen that reaction. What if it were alive somehow? Living with the ghouls like some sick parody of a kid being raised by wolves? What then?

Doc would want to see it/her, that's for damned sure. Like most science nerd types, our doc was obsessed with researching Zed and any and all irregularities from the norm. Unlike most science nerd types, our doc was tall, blonde, and leggy. We'd all noticed, of course, but especially Gray. I'd seen him making eyes at her during the routine inspections following decontamination protocol, trying to sound strong and brave and coming off like an awkward schoolboy with his first crush. It was kinda sad, really, and we all gave him crap over it. But it hadn't done a thing to change his behavior towards her. I knew Gray well enough to see the gears grinding in his head, imagining her reaction when he delivered this prize on our return, how she'd swoon and call him a hero, maybe even throw her arms around him in gratitude, maybe more...

I think Ambrose was looking for some kind of salvation from this whole gigantic mess. Maybe we all were, but him especially. I think the thought of a cure, of people still being alive somewhere out there, of humanity making any kind of a real comeback, was like a beacon of hope for him, and this maybe-Zed/Maybe-not had instantly become a symbol of that hope.

Tonner, like me, had lost a kid in the early days of The Collapse. I didn't think he could've shot it/her any more than I could've. So we all stood there, frozen, gaping at each other while the Zed Girl Thing continued eating what was left of the maybe former cat. As usual, it was Grady that made the first move. Our fearless leader swept up behind it/her and knocked it on the head with the butt of his rifle. This served two purposes: One, it proved she was still living. Any true Zed would've shrugged a blow like that off like nothing instead of collapsing like a sack of potatoes like Zed Girl Thing did; and two, it incapacitated her, bought us some time to figure out what to do next. Something was wrong with it/her, that's for damned sure, but how dangerous was she? I had no idea, but just to be on the safe side, I didn't plan on snuggling up with her and reading her any bedtime stories.

Tonner grabbed it/her by both wrists and started hauling her around the head of the stairs, towards the open apartment we'd been sweeping when all of this began. Ambrose, Gray, and I took the opportunity to heave both bodies along with the heap of blood, fur, and bones over the railing. The sound they made when they hit the foyer below is something I don't like to think about.

When everyone was inside and the door was barricaded as well as it could be, we conducted a more thorough sweep of the place. Maybe our operations were a bit out of order, but given all we had to worry about, getting inside somewhere relatively safe seemed like the best option. Securing the Zed Girl Thing was number two on our list.

Ambrose had cleared a bedroom that once belonged to a little kid. There was a twin sized bed, still made up with cartoon birds on the sheets. We pried off the headboard and strapped the unconscious Zed Girl Thing to it with duct tape from Grady's kit. Duct tape: Never leave home without it. Then we brought her/it out into the main living area and propped the headboard upright against a wall. We closed all the inner doors and forted up as best we could for the night. Tonner and Gray took first watch, though none of us could sleep right off anyway.

I leaned against a shabby, faded couch. Still in full gear of course, my rifle cradled in my arms like a teddy bear. I kept glancing over at the Zed Girl Thing. Her eyes were closed like she was sleeping. Maybe she was. In the dim bit of moonlight filtering in through the partially boarded over windows, she might've been my Angie, a few years younger and maybe a little blonder, but her coloring didn't matter much in the darkened living room. I wondered what color her/its eyes were.

After a few hours of staring into the darkness, listening for sounds of trouble, and wishing I could be anywhere else, it was my and Ambrose's turn to take watch. Tonner and Gray retreated to the couch; Grey stretching out the length of it, Tonner leaned against one arm, propping his legs up on an ottoman.

Ambrose and I stationed ourselves near the entryway, just off the kitchen. I stood against the wall where the hall split, one arm coming from the front door towards the living room, the other branching off towards the bedrooms. Ambrose put his back against the wall opposite me and slid down it until he sat, clearly exhausted. I wondered if he'd been able to grab any shut eye. I'd been too focused on the Zed Girl to notice. I looked over to check on her again. She was still tied to that painted headboard, still had her eyes closed. As I watched, I could see the slow, steady rise and fall of her chest. So peaceful. Like my Angie when she used to fall asleep in my lap when we read *Good Night Moon* or *The Cat in the Hat*. She looked cold. I glanced over at Ambrose, who appeared to be snoring, then decided to get a blanket from the kid's room, just to cover her up so she didn't get sick.

Ambrose didn't notice as I crept down the hall, rifle at the ready just in case. No one heard me as I slowly creaked open the bedroom door and stepped inside, into brighter shafts of moonlight. I guess they hadn't had enough boards to cover the windows in here. I avoided looking outside, afraid of what I might see, but even more afraid of what might see me. Instead, I bent down and picked up a *Hello Kitty* coverlet. Underneath it was a much loved teddy bear. I took that, too.

She was still sleeping. I was starting to worry that maybe something was really wrong with her. Well, besides the bits of dead cat still matted in her hair and smeared on her face and front of her shirt. Maybe Gray had done some damage when he hit her. But what did I know? It wasn't like I could help her, anyway. None of us could until we got back to base and had the doc look her over. I tucked the teddy up against her chest and wrapped her and the headboard with the coverlet. Then I went back to my post to watch Ambrose snore until Tonner and Gray relieved us. It felt like weeks instead of just hours.

Tonner stood and stretched, yawning. He stopped, frozen in mid pose, when he saw the girl. "What the hell?" he asked, snatching the teddy bear from the sleeping Zed Girl. He tossed it to the floor in disgust.

I said nothing. He glanced over at the sleeping form of Ambrose, scowling contemptuously. It was clear he had already pinned the teddy bear on him. I decided not to argue. Tonner kicked the teddy bear down the hall as he came over to wake Ambrose up. I nudged him none too softly with my boot. Then the girl woke up, groaning and gnashing like Zed. That shut everyone up real quick.

Like lightning, Gray was up, ripping the blanket to pieces. He shoved a wad of the pink material into her mouth and then wrapped her head with a long strip of it. He wrapped more strips around her and the headboard, binding her tightly. She struggled, her eyes wide and flashing, but she was held fast. I wondered if maybe she had just been reacting to waking up in a strange place like this, tied to a piece of plastic after everything she'd already been through, but I knew better than to question Gray. I kept my mouth shut. We all did.

After a few minutes of relative quiet, Gray pointed at the window. "Gear up, boys," he said. "Dawn approaches."

We'd strayed from our designated area after the incident at the last house we scrubbed. I wasn't great with directions, but I thought we'd headed vaguely east. Tonner had the map and was trying to figure out where we were and how to get back to base.

He and Gray had the big piece of colored paper unfolded on a table in front of them and were discussing movements like a coach and a quarterback discussing plays. Ambrose and I sat on the couch. Ambrose looked despondent. I stared at the girl. Maybe I was imagining things, but she seemed to be begging me with those eyes, pleading with me to just let her loose and give her something to eat and a clean change of clothes. She looked like she needed both.

"Alright!" Gray exclaimed, clapping his hands together to draw our attention. Ambrose and I went over. "We believe we're in this general vicinity." He circled a ring about an inch across with his index finger. "That means we'll need to cut across here," he gestured at a wide expanse of empty green, "and go overland for about two miles before we're in the clear." We nodded in unison. "Tonner, I want you to carry Zed. We'll strap her to your back over your pack. She weighs nothing, you won't even feel her."

Tonner looked like he was going to protest, but in the end he said nothing. We all packed up and got ready to jump ship. Just as the first glints of orange filtered through the boarded over windows, we began making our way outside.

It was still dark and shadowy outside the apartment building, even with the big orange globe of a sun peeking over the horizon. We kept in a tight cross formation, Gray in the lead, Tonner and Ambrose flanking him, me bringing up the rear. I kept looking at the little girl tied to Tonner's back. She looked so lost, so afraid, so like my little Angie. I just wanted to reach out and stroke her cheek, to pull the makeshift gag free and tell her everything was going to be alright, that daddy was here and he'd keep the monsters away. But instead, I just kept moving.

We crossed a few streets before the buildings began petering out. As we went, there were fewer and fewer of them, until we were standing in front of a great big field full of chest high overgrowth. That was dangerous. Anything could be waiting in that grass. Zed, looters, rabid, half-crazed dogs, anything. Gray stopped us before we could enter, raising his arms out to his sides.

We halted behind him, still in formation. I looked at the girl. Was that a tear in her eye? Was she crying? Was the tape hurting her? Was it too tight? I tore my gaze away as Gray barked orders.

"Hold Position!" he commanded, "Backs to the center. We cross as one. NOW!"

Still in our cross pattern, only now each of us facing a different direction, we started across the open expanse of grass and overgrown weeds. It was slow but steady, and everything was going fine. I kept glancing over my shoulder at the girl. Twice I caught her looking back at me, like she wanted me to save her.

We were about halfway across the field, holding steady, when Ambrose went down. His finger was on the trigger when he fell so his weapon discharged right into Tonner's leg. Rookie move. He hit the ground, too. I turned to see what had happened and was shocked to find Gray on his back, surrounded by half a dozen Zed. Their upper halves, anyway. Gray was done for, I could see that right off. He was covered in blood from a dozen or so bites and some of his insides had become outsides. Zed was going after Ambrose next. It looked like he'd done some damage to his leg when he'd tripped over Gray—the downside of walking with your back to your squad, I guess. He was toast, too. My gaze swept to Tonner, who still had a chance, albeit a slim one—and then I saw the girl. Angie. My Angie.

Without a second thought, I ripped the duct tape off her and snatched out the gag, leaving a screaming, bleeding Tonner writhing on the ground. I swung her up into my arms and felt the warmth of her breath on my neck as I had so many times before—then I felt a new warmth: blood, as it ran down my neck over my chest. She bit me. She fucking bit me.

ABOUT THE AUTHOR

Alyn Day is a computer geek, a foodie, and a horror writer. She's also a 2 time cancer survivor. Her publications include So Long and Thanks for All the Brains, Daily Frights 2012, Women of the Living Dead, Zombie Tales, Here Be Clowns, Horror on the Installment Plan, Quick Bites of Flesh, Zombies for a Cure, and the upcoming Daily Frights 2013. Find her on twitter @Z0mbiegrl or at her website,
http://alyndayofthedead.blogspot.com

3

Memories
By Heath Stallcup

For Dad and Nana

We had been working together for nearly twelve years. The enzyme that Brenda developed showed such promise in laboratory tests that animal testing was the next logical step. Her husband, Roger was so excited when the research hospital approved the request and the animals arrived. He and I had been best friends since college and it was actually my fault that he and Brenda met. She and I had been lab partners for an anatomy class and since I didn't like blondes, I introduced her to him. How was I to know they'd fall in love and get married? How was I to know that the three of us would end up going into medical research? How was I to know that...well, let's just say that if I could have known then what I know now, I'd have never introduced Roger to Brenda, we'd have followed a far less dangerous field (like maybe podiatry) and I wouldn't be the last of us still struggling to make Brenda's miracle enzyme work in humans.

I'm sure that if you're listening to this, you're probably asking yourself how in the world medical research could ever be considered 'dangerous'. Well, normally it's not. *Normally.*

49

It's such a long story, but seeing how this is the night shift and I'm the one left wandering the halls, I might as well relay the story to you. You'll need to keep up though. I'm making my rounds and I have quite a few stops to make.

First stop is to check on some cultures. Yes, I'm still growing cultures in the lab. Research 101. You see, we're working on a cancer treatment and we still grow cells in Petri dishes for research. Oh, I still have a few animals down in the basement, but the first step is to test the variations on the cultures. I've only got about seventeen different variations that I try each new batch on, and if all goes well, then I'll sacrifice an animal in the name of science.

Since we're using rabbits before primates, it tends to get expensive, and Roger really was the brains of this outfit, even though it was Brenda that came up with the enzyme. Roger just...well, he tweaked it. He almost perfected it.

Hold on. I need to adjust the temperature here. I don't want these to get too warm...

Anyway, Roger was the brains and I just sort of was the idea man. He'd bounce ideas off of me and I'd tell him how they wouldn't work. Or I'd *try* to tell him how they wouldn't work and then he'd find the way to work around the walls I'd put up for him. It really worked well.

Well, it did. Until Brenda got sick, that is.

Here, this is a picture of them at their wedding. She really was beautiful. Too bad I didn't like blondes, huh? Anyway, she was so busy working that she...well, she missed it. It was breast cancer. And it had spread to stage four. It had gotten into her nodes, and by the time they discovered it, well...she didn't have long. It really hit Roger hard. So hard, in fact, that he...well...here. Let me show you.

Once we get up onto the fourth floor, that's where the patients are. And that's where Roger is. He's basically in a coma. He thought maybe that if the most promising version of the enzyme would pass human trials, that maybe it could help her, but we were so far away from human trials. It had barely made it through the first round of primate trials. Anyway, he got desperate and injected himself with it and...I found him. Slumped over his desk. I wouldn't have known what had happened, but he kept notes and had his recorder going. He's been up here ever since.

That's him on the bed there. It's been nearly two years. Don't mind the nurse there. She's just checking his vitals. You'd think we don't exist the way they work here. You'll see them come and go, and they're nice enough to speak to him when they're interacting with him. They'll talk to him when they're about to change his sheets or give him a sponge bath or clean up after him or...but damned if they'll ever speak to me. I think they blame me somehow. Like I could have stopped him.

Come on, let's leave them to do their thing. Yeah, I'm telling ya, they act like I'm not even here. They'll walk right past me and not even make eye contact. They all loved Roger. They knew how much he loved Brenda, and I think, deep down, they know why he did it, and they probably think it's all romantic and whatnot, but honestly, it was just plain stupid. We were *this close* to finding a cure. Not just a treatment, but a CURE. I honestly don't think I can do this myself. I just don't have his brilliant spark.

Anyway, I need to go down and check on some of the lab animals now. If you want to follow me, I can fill you in on the rest. Yeah, just hit the 'B' button, because that lab is in the basement. So where was I? Oh yeah. So, anyway, Roger was all distraught and used himself as a human lab rat. Didn't go well. You saw all the machines that he's hooked to. Minimal brain function, ventilator, catheter, IVs. The guy is kept alive by machines. He didn't think to sign off on a DNR before he did it.

But I've been keeping at it. I'm actually using some of his blood draws and running tests. The enzyme is staying active in his body. It's doing what it's supposed to do, but since he didn't have any cancerous cells, it attacked his immune system. That was where he messed up. Had he used Brenda instead, who knows what the results would have been. But since he used the last of that known enzyme, I've been going bonkers trying to replicate it. Brenda was too sick to make more, too distraught over Roger to assist and...well, let's just say I was left on my own. She passed not much longer after Roger pulled his stunt.

See this little guy here? He is specifically engineered to pick up any and every kind of cancer known. Can you imagine being bred and born *just* to have cancer? Unreal. Anyway, that's his purpose in life. And I injected him with the enzyme a little over two weeks ago. Guess what? His scans came back clean. His blood panels are all perfect. If you were a vet, you'd think he was the picture of health.

And this chimp here? He was purposely given leukemia and he's beaten it. Then the poor little guy was purposely given one of the most aggressive bone cancers I've ever seen. He's just been pronounced in regression. Nobody likes to use the 'C' word. Ha! I know that look, no, I mean *'cure'*. But he doesn't have a cancerous cell left in his body. Healthy as an ox.

Right now I have human tissues growing in Petri that will be ready to test tonight. If the enzyme is good, then...>sigh< I may have finally found it.

So, that's it. I need to go back up to the second floor now and check my dishes and see if the cultures are ready. If they are, I can give them a diluted enzyme bath and just wait and see.

It's just too bad that Roger couldn't have been here to help me with this. Or that he couldn't have waited just a few more days before he...I mean...I'm sure that between the two of us, we would have gotten where I am now back then and he wouldn't be where he is.

***

Don't mind me. I'm just reviewing Roger's chart again. No improvement. I wasn't expecting any, but I still like to check. I come in here and check on him while the nurses aren't around. Ya know, the last four or five time I was in here and they were messing with him, I'd ask them a simple question and they didn't just give me the cold shoulder, they'd flat out ignore me.

It's a shame they got his face all covered up with crap. It's been so long since I've even seen him...

Anyway, they'll be in here shortly so I'm going to make myself scarce. I've got plenty to do downstairs. If you want to come down there with me, I'll show you what's happened since yesterday. Some of the results are looking more than promising.

You know those animals I showed you? Well, I've also been running the same enzyme through some tissue samples. Cancerous tissue samples. Ha-ha-ha, I can see by the look on your face that you're not really following me. Well, think of it this way. Pumping an active enzyme into a living animal is one thing. The body can utilize it easier and pump it into the cancerous cells itself. But a sample of tissue? It's just a cluster of cells laying in a nutrient media. It's not connected to a heart or lungs or...well, a living organism to keep it alive. So washing it in the enzyme? It isn't the most promising of tests.

Press 'Two' for me, would ya? My hands are full. So anyway, I basically took a diluted wash of the enzyme, spritzed it over the tissue sample and let it sit overnight. Now you have to keep in mind, this tissue sample is basically eaten up with tumors. I'd say it is over forty-five percent cancerous cells. Well when I came in this morning, nearly all of the tumors had shrunk by more than half their size. In less than twenty-four hours! The surrounding healthy tissue is completely unaffected. I'm going to go in and spritz it again and let it sit until tomorrow and just see what happens. If this works like I hope it will, I'm kind of hoping that maybe purposely giving Roger cancer and then utilizing the enzyme might...well, I don't know. Maybe it will help reverse some of the damage. Maybe it will give the active enzyme something to work on besides his immune system. Hey, don't look at me like that. I know it's completely unorthodox, but considering he's been laying in that bed for how long now? He's not improving. His brain function is minimal. He's basically a vegetable.

Turn right. The lab is down the hall here.

Anyway, yeah, I could lose my license for something like

that, but I look at this way. Roger was my best friend. Brenda became like a best friend. When she passed it was…well, it just wasn't the same. Then when I lost Roger, I lost interest in everything else. I'm not able to actually practice medicine so if they pull my license, so be it. If it helps Roger, then it's worth the price. If I don't help him, what has he really lost? I mean there is such a thing as quality of life, right?

You know, the last time Roger and I spoke about something like this, he told me, "Jake, no matter what happens, don't let them hook me to a bunch of machines. That's not living." So you tell me. Do you really think he'd want this? I honestly think that he'd want me to try.

No, I'm not going to do anything until I'm convinced in my mind that it will work. I'm not going to pull a 'Roger' and do something that risks his life unless I am one hundred percent convinced that the enzyme is ready.

What? No, this enzyme that I'm working on is actually a derivative of the one that is in him now. They shouldn't interact. In fact, once I basically give him cancer, the two enzymes will work in tandem and have it under control before it can even create feeders. Oh, um, those are capillaries that feed the tumors. Cancerous clusters have a way of causing the body to grow capillaries straight to the tumor just to feed it. That's just one way how they grow so quickly. The enzyme that is in Roger now will not only prevent that, but it will shrivel those capillaries up like plant roots pulled from the ground. The body just reabsorbs it.

The enzyme that I'm working on now actually attacks the cancer cells themselves. So it's kind of a one-two punch in his case. If I could replicate the enzyme that is in him now, combine it with the one I'm working on in the lab, I have no doubt. But…I can't.

Hand me that little bottle there. The one marked two-seven-seven. Thanks. After I spray these tissue samples, I can come back tomorrow and see if they've continued shrinking. Wow, just in the time I was gone, they've visibly shrunk. This is looking so promising. I'm really hoping that this will pull him out of this and...what?

No, it doesn't work that way. Think of it differently. When Roger injected himself with the enzyme, it *needed* cancerous tissues to attack. Since cancer cells are great mimics, they are able to avoid detection by the body's immune system. They can go on unhindered and do what they do, growing and growing and getting out of control. The closest thing to cancerous cells is the immune system itself. That was why it attacked his and left him vegetative. If I give it something else to attack, it will quit shorting out his central nervous system and I'm hoping he'll wake up.

No, I don't *know* that it will work, but I'm hoping. To be honest, I tried the same test with a primate and it did work. The orang I used basically slipped into a coma because he was healthy. But once I infected him with cancerous cells and the secondary enzyme...he snapped out of it. And he came out with a clean bill of health. The only difference is, I dosed him with a different enzyme the first time. Why? Because I didn't have any more of what Roger used on himself. It was based off the same previous work, but I can't be certain it was identical.

Anyway, I'm going to check the tissue samples in the morning and if all looks right, I'm going to follow through. The only thing that would stop me now is if you say something to someone who might try to put an end to my work.

Good. The nurses are usually out of his room between two PM and four PM. If you want to, you can come with me and together we can see if my plan works.

***

Oh good, you're back. I was beginning to wonder if you were going to make it. I just finished checking the tissue samples. You're not going to believe this but...well, here. See for yourself. Do you see this pinkish white blob here? Yeah, that's the tissue that just yesterday was eat up with cancerous tumors. Take a look now. Completely clean. And all I did was spritz it with the enzyme. I can't believe how fast that this thing is reacting. It's unreal. I already took a section of it and viewed it under the microscope. I used a gram stain to make sure and it's clean as a whistle.

See there? Nothing. It's all normal cells now. You can't even see where the nodules were. Totally gone. I'm still not sure what's happening in the tissue samples since there aren't any support systems to assist in the reabsorption of the cells. It's almost like they're being converted back to normal, healthy cells.

Anyway, I was just about to prepare both the infectious vector and the new enzyme to infect Roger with. We still have time since the nurses are preparing for their shift change. I'm sure they're used to seeing me come and go enough that they won't think nothing of it when I go to 'visit' him. It will just be a few more minutes while the enzyme finishes production.

You know, I still remember when I walked in and found him sitting at his desk. He was facedown and his lab coat was pulled up over his head. Almost like he was ashamed of what he'd done. I keep asking myself if he somehow knew what was about to happen. And…you know, I never told anybody this next part, but, I was so panicked that instead of trying to help him, I ran out of the office and yelled for help. Can you imagine that? I'm a freakin' doctor for crying out loud, and I panicked. Yeah, don't look at me like that. It's not like I'm a practicing Emergency Room physician, okay? I mean, I admit it, I panicked. But, truth be told, there isn't a whole lot I could have done for him even if I had tried to help him as soon as I discovered him. The damage was done. The enzyme was in his system. The nurses did all they could and the on call physician tried everything. Chelation, blood transfusions, you name it. The enzyme was bound to his cells. I guess I've been harboring the guilt all this time. I guess that's why I felt like I had to risk everything to try to help him. I mean, besides him being my best friend.

Ah, it's almost ready. Hand me those syringes, would ya? Thanks. I just need to make sure this is properly mixed and we'll be ready to go. I have to tell ya, I'll be glad to see that damned respirator tube out of his mouth. Get all that tape off his face and maybe let the guy breathe on his own for a change. And to be completely honest, if this works the way I'm hoping it will, after a few months of hardcore physical therapy, he should be right as rain. It will be like it never happened.

What? No, even if this is finally approved as a treatment for cancer, I wouldn't dream of calling it my own. Brenda came up with the idea and really, it was Roger who perfected it. I'm just...*re*-perfecting it. I mean really, we were this close to having it. He just jumped the gun. If anything it will be dual credit, with the grand majority going to him.

Okay. Well, it looks like we're ready. I have the syringes and if you'll get the door, we can...what? Oh, well, the first one is more like a prep for the cancer itself. It will help lower his immune system a bit and give the cancer a fighting chance against the enzyme that is already in his system. The second one is the cancer itself. This third one is the secondary enzyme. I want to wait until the last second to give this one to him.

So, if you'll get the door, we can be on our way. Thanks. Yeah, I want to keep the syringes upright in my coat pocket. I don't want to risk anything bumping them, so if you'll mash the elevator button.

Okay, so look. When we get to the floor, just act normal, okay? I doubt seriously the nurses will say anything to us, but if they do, just smile and nod, act perfectly normal. We're just stopping by to check on Roger and make sure he's doing okay. Just like I do every day. We'll make small talk and keep our voices low and...see? They're busy with their shift change. Just get the door for me. Thanks.

And there he...wait. Who's that sitting next to him? Wait here a second while I pretend to check his chart. Whoever it is has his back to us and I can't see, so just hang back and I'll see if maybe I can get rid of him.

Whoever he is, he looks familiar under that beard, I just can't make out who he...oh, my God. Roger? It can't be. If that's you, then who's in the bed?

Why are you sobbing, Roger? Why are you crying? Jake? What about me? Roger…I'm right here. Roger?

Why are you ignoring me, too? You're as bad as these damned nurses…

Roger? This isn't funny.

Why do you keep saying you're sorry, Roger. You didn't mean to…what?

Wait…if that's you there, then who is in the bed?

Oh, my God…no. It can't be.

I can't be in the bed. I'm right here. That can't be me…how could it be me? I found the *cure!* Damn it, Roger, I found the CURE!

ROGER!

Will somebody please acknowledge me? Wait, how can *you* hear me? Who are you? Why did you…Brenda? Am I dead?

A coma? Brain dead?

No….that can't be. Roger injected *himself.* I saw him slumped across his desk and…what? That wasn't me. Roger didn't infect me…did he?

If Roger infected me, then what are in these syringes?!

What do you mean, *what syringes?* THESE syrin…they were right here in my pocket.

I found the cure. I have the lab results downstairs.

Roger, please don't cry. Somebody, please tell me this is a dream.

Why do I feel so funny…

ABOUT THE AUTHOR

Heath Stallcup was born in Salinas, California and relocated to Tupelo, Oklahoma in his tween years. He joined the US Navy and was stationed in Charleston, SC and Bangor, WA shortly after junior college. After his second tour he attended East Central University where he obtained BS degrees in Biology and Chemistry. He then served ten years with the State of Oklahoma as a Compliance and Enforcement Officer while moonlighting nights and weekends with his local Sheriff's Office. He still lives in the small township of Tupelo, Oklahoma with his wife and three of his seven children. He steals time to write between household duties, going to ballgames, being a grandfather to four and being the pet of numerous animals that have taken over his home. Visit him on Facebook.com for news of his upcoming releases.

4

Project Arizona
By Gregory Carrico

I would like to thank May December Publications for including this story in this special anthology. I offer Project Arizona *in honor of my Nana, Juanita Early, who succumbed to breast cancer when I was eight years old, and also in honor of her daughter, Nancy Cathey, who I call Mom. Mom is a breast cancer survivor, and has been cancer-free for almost two decades; living proof that projects like this can, and do make a difference.*

Henry wept. Naked, cold, and except for his eyes, unable to exert his will over any part of his body, he could do little else. For three days he had believed with ineffable certainty that his captors would realize their mistake and let him go, offering embarrassed grins and apologies for their error. After all, ordinary people didn't get arrested for crimes they didn't commit. Nor were they ever mistakenly moved from a local jail cell to a maximum security psychiatric hospital. And ordinary people were never-ever quietly whisked from their cells and subjected to unnecessary and barbaric medical treatments against their will.

No, things of this sort simply didn't happen to ordinary

men, and Henry was the most ordinary of all men.

He would be angry when they finally let him go, but he would forgive them. People made mistakes. It was human nature. God knew that Henry had made plenty of mistakes, too.

But if he couldn't speak, he couldn't explain this funny sequence of tragic mistakes, and he might very well come to a not so funny end.

Dr. Evans, typing on a muted keyboard a few feet away, competed with the soft hum of medical monitors and I.V. pumps for mastery over the thick silence that otherwise dominated the room.

Over the soft background noises and through the closed door to the hallway, the sound of heels tap-tap-tapping the tiles came closer. The sound sparked an inexplicable fear in Henry. His discomfort no longer mattered. Nor did his anger over the injections or his frequent, confused awakenings from drug induced blackouts. The gravity of his predicament forced him to accept that he would never leave this secret laboratory prison alive if he couldn't overcome his paralysis and speak. He knew beyond reason and logic that those approaching footfalls were tapping out the remaining moments of his life.

Dr. Evans' typing faltered, then picked up speed, then stopped for frantic backspacing and mouse-clicking before racing on again. He clearly felt the approaching heel-wearer's menace too.

Henry heard the sounds of the opening door and of Dr. Evans standing. A moment later, she stepped into his straining, tear-blurred field of vision. He felt her touch before he saw her. She lifted his arm by the wrist, looking him over from head to foot.

She was pretty. Petite. Nicely dressed. Maybe he had pegged her wrong.

"No," she said, dropping his arm to the cold table with a metallic thud. "Absolutely not."

The tall, balding Dr. Evans stepped up to her side.

"Well, Dr.--" he began.

"Please explain to me, Dr. Evans, how the presence of a three centimeter tattoo on the subject's right shoulder escaped your notice. You did, actually perform a clinical examination, didn't you?"

"Of course, I was—"

"Because even a drunken pre-med sorority pledge with the eyesight of a mole would have noticed it. Well? Are you going to explain yourself?" She tapped her foot in a quick, impatient tempo.

Henry thought that his sense of dread at her arrival may have been warranted, after all.

Dr. Evans, though a foot taller and about three times heavier, looked as if he had just been reprimanded by a teacher. He dropped his eyes and stuffed his hands into the pockets of his iconic white lab coat.

"W-well, Dr. Greene," he stammered, wiping sweat from his forehead. "I didn't miss the tattoo, it's just... Well, I didn't expect you for another hour. I haven't completed my report and recommendations." He took a deep breath, perhaps waiting for some sort of rebuke, but was met with a chilly silence. "Anyway, the new laser can remove even the most clinically unacceptable tattoos in only a week. Two, at the most." His sentence ended in a weak mumble.

"A week?" she asked with dangerous calm. "Did you say a week?"

"Or two," Dr. Evans offered with a resigned sigh.

"You know how much fucking time we have!"

Henry could only blink at her explosive show of anger. This couldn't be good. No matter how much he struggled, he still couldn't speak.

"Get another one. Fast. I'll be back after my meeting. Fuck this up again, and I'll have you on that table."

When Dr. Evans looked at Henry's face and stared into his eyes, Henry knew he was about to die. He stopped worrying and struggling, not that either had done him any good anyway. Now that there could be no doubt of his fate, he felt calm. He was pissed off. It wasn't fair. He didn't deserve this. But in the end, that didn't much matter, did it? This was bullshit.

"I'm sorry," Evans whispered to him, taking a syringe from a tray beside his metal bed.

Dr. Green shoved Evans out of the way. She looked at a piece of paper and met his gaze. "Thank you, Henry Duncan," she said. She took off her glasses and stormed out of the room, her long dark hair bouncing against her back. "Whoever you were," she added under her breath.

Click-click-click— the clear sound of her heels on the tile.

Dr. Evans removed the cap from a syringe and injected something into his IV Drip.

Tears leaked from Henry's eyes and a powerful weariness overcame him.

Click-click-click...

His chest felt thick, heavy. His breath escaped, and he couldn't draw another.

Click-click-click... softer, now. Distant.

His eyes were closed, but he still saw her face. Gray-blue eyes so clear, so cold.

Click-click-beeeeep.

***

The maître d' led her though the main dining room and up the narrow stairs by the bar. "It's just through here," he said.

Tara's pleasure at seeing the empty, private dining room was quickly dashed when he opened the door to a balcony with a single table. She hated dining *al fresco*. She sat, trying to smile across the table as the Arizona sun seared her fair skin.

"Tara," he said with a convincing expression of pleasure. "I'm so glad you could make it. I started to worry that your stress-factory research gig had won out again." He dropped his iPhone into a jacket pocket and sat down. "I thought what a glorious February afternoon; we should take advantage of it. You don't mind, do you? I took the liberty of ordering our drinks. It's your usual," he smiled, his eyes twinkling.

"No, not at all," she said, shading her eyes from the unrelenting sun. It was unnatural that he could be as comfortable as he appeared wearing a suit in this heat. After too much wine the night before, she had been rather looking forward to some iced tea and mint. The sun burned into her face, and she swore silently to herself for leaving her sunglasses in the car. She had agreed to a late lunch, not a fucking picnic. What kind of idiot insists on eating outside with the bugs, the wind, and the blinding sun?"

"How was work today?" James brought her out of her thoughts.

"Fine," she lied, trying not to look hung-over and or worried. She crinkled her nose playfully and batted her long, dark eyelashes. James' usually pleasant southern twang was grating on her. Did he have to say absolutely everything like he was reading for a part in a Louisiana adaptation of Shakespeare?

"Have y'all been seeing much of this new flu at the prison" he asked, "I hear half of Texas is closed up on account of it."

"No," she lied again, "not really." The sun finally taking a reprieve behind some patchy clouds, she was able to clearly see James. He was handsome, nicely filling out his dark, expensive suit beneath a crown of perfectly messy black hair; she could see why women of all ages stared at him wherever they went. None of her friends or family could believe it when she had turned down his proposal last spring.

He'd have been a great catch for any woman. A Southern gentleman of obscene wealth, from a well-known and respected family, and an up and coming politician, *they* said. But at twenty-nine, her career was top priority. She had been assigned to the armpit of Arizona almost two years ago from the excitement and prestige of the nation's capital, and was counting on this breakthrough to get her back in the limelight.

But that would require Dr. Evans to start using his brain. Well, if he didn't find a use for it pretty soon, she knew a thing or two she could do with it.

"Tara? Welcome back. Are you ready?" James again pulled

her out of her thoughts as the sun reappeared from behind the clouds.

"Yes, of course," she said, hastily opening the menu.

Lunch went on with the usual friendly banter over work, the weather, the latest flu strain, and James' new Mercedes.

She almost sighed with relief at 4:00 when he said he had to skip desert. There was no telling what she'd find if she didn't get back to the lab check on Evans soon.

James walked her to her car, stopping along the way to show off his new toy. To be fair, it was gorgeous car. She didn't know what the AMG or the SLS GT badges meant, but it was sleek and sporty and had pleasing growl.

"Perfect," she declared. A quick kiss on the cheek and she sped off to the highway and back to the prison. Looking in the rear view mirror, she waved as James turned off to head north, noticing a newly formed freckle on her forehead. "Fucking sun."

***

Tara found Dr. Evans in front of his computer pouring over cranial CT images.

"I've found one," he boasted with uncharacteristic confidence.

"You found one?" she almost sneered. After ten months at that 1970's era phase-one lab, and twelve more long months in this place, how could this be best she could hope for? She had put in her time, done the hard work, kissed the right asses, and sabotaged her competitors when they made lucky breakthroughs. She had earned this, and now it was about to fall apart because of an incompetent assistant.

The odds that he really had found a good candidate now, at the last possible moment, were a statistical impossibility. She looked at Evans, and pictured his flensed, mostly de-fleshed skull bobbing in a pot of simmering water and meat tenderizer. And who says you don't learn anything useful in college? She could still smell the last body she had cooked down to the bone.

Thanks to the lax security at the forensic anthropology lab and the extra door keys she made when she was a research assistant, she never had to worry about what to do with the bodies.

"Will you at least look?" Evans asked.

Yep, she thought. He's going in the pot.

She leaned back against his desk. "You know," she said, "Texas and their so called flu are already dominating the media. We've even seen half a dozen cases here in the last ten days. Shit, in a month it will be up and down the west coast. They've done their part. All eyes are on us, now. And what do we have to show besides a string of failed experiments, nonstarters, and mistakes?" And bodies.

"No, really. I think he's the one we've been looking for," said Evans.

"We are out of time Evans. Don't you get it?" she said, banging her fist next to his keyboard. "It doesn't matter if this candidate is perfect. What if he has drug reactions? What if he dies in surgery or his body rejects the transplants? What if he gets through everything we're going to do to him and then it just doesn't work? Perfect doesn't exist in the real world. There is success and there is failure. You know what happens to failures like us who work on top secret projects that could topple the government? Hmmm?" she asked, poking Evans in the shoulder.

Evans looked up at her and shivered visibly. "Tara... Dr. Green, will you please shut up and look at these scans? No birthmarks, no identifying features, no dental work, nothing abnormal in any of the CT or radiographic images. There's nothing to suggest he has ever had any hospital treatment."

She perked up. "Tattoos?"

"No tattoos, no healed fractures, nothing," he said, practically gasping with excitement.

"What else?" She leaned close over his shoulder to scrutinize the images on the monitor.

"Arrest and court documents identify him as Walter Clarks, aged twenty years. Arrested for possession of narcotics and resisting arrest."

"Well, well," she said, with her first real smile all day.

After thoroughly examining this perfectly ordinary twenty year old male, Tara signed the approval to push the project to stage three. She loaded a carpule of the F3-K drug from the Alaska project and handed the syringe to Evans.

Evans stepped up to the subject, but hesitated.

"Grow a pair, you little girl," said Tara with impatience. "Go make the call." She took the syringe and nudged Evans aside. Leaning close to the subject, she wiped the tears from his boyishly handsome, yet generic face.

"Thank you, Walter Clarks, whoever you were," she whispered in her softest, sweetest voice.

"This Ar P2, ready for the Phase Three team with subject A_e. En route to surgery now," Evans said. He read the security key code and hung up.

***

Project Journal of Dr. Tara Green

Arizona, Phase Three.
Day 2
Subject A_e is doing much more than holding together. Twenty four hours after surgery, he is completely recovered and stronger than ever. Kudos to the Beaufort Regeneration team. We can tell them the human trials are a success, so far. Lobotomy and cranial com implants have taken hold and are functional. Nano-cellular regen-bots have vastly exceeded post-surgical expectations, and continue to replace damaged tissue a full day after surgery.

Lesson learned from subject A_d. A_e fitted with sub-dermal composite armor skull cap. One on one personal combat trials pushed ahead of schedule were a triumph. A_e improvised and severed an inmate's nose with his teeth.

Day 3

68

A_e has not resumed speech, even when prompted by the Control group. His silence is raising questions and comparisons with *One Flew Over the Cuckoo's Nest*.

A_e was reintroduced to prison population at dinner. He has not eaten yet, but shows no signs of fatigue or lethargy. When an inmate and former acquaintance reached for A_e's fruit cup, Control triggered a rage response. There were no survivors. A_e looked so normal and graceful in his combat. Aside from his calm efficiency, he was indistinguishable from the other inmates by his movements and actions.

Dr. Evans was visibly disturbed by the violence and death. He will have to be managed soon.

Day 4
Subject A_e was re-assessed and found to have minimal, indeed, no sustained damage. Dr. Evans expected more physical distress from normal wear and tear.

The national director has been notified of our success and is reviewing the full case file before passing A_e on to phase four, which will be executed by another group. A_e has been retrieved by helicopter, and I will meet with my group administrator for final debriefing this evening.

***

Tara cleaned out her desk, removing her extra pair of black shoes, toothbrush, medicine kit and personal protective items, hoping tomorrow she would get word to head back to DC. Not having an extra bag, she jammed stuff into her already full purse and the pockets of her extra coat.

She said a hasty goodbye to Evans and set off for the long drive home. As much as she wanted to invite him over for that last pot of stew, she couldn't touch Evans now that their project had succeeded. If they had failed it wouldn't have mattered, since they would have met with tragic accidents anyway. He was lucky. Besides, he always came through for her when she needed help "cleaning up" one of her messes, even though he hated her for what she made him do.

Still driving down the desolate highway around midnight, she turned the radio on to combat her exhaustion. Unable to find a decent driving tune, she tuned in to the news channel and heard of an enraged drug addict who killed dozens of people at the Dallas Fort Worth airport. Despite being shot several times, he escaped and is still on the loose. Witnesses said he was like a mindless zombie, killing with his bare hands in silent rage. A CDC spokesman very calmly announced that while there was no reason to expect it, he could not say definitively that there was no connection between this incident and the mutant variation of the ongoing flu epidemic.

"Ha," Tara said. "That was quick."

She entered her passcode at the gated entrance to her neighborhood and was feeling a bit nostalgic pulling into her driveway. While she would be on the next plane back east in a heartbeat if she could, she wondered if she would miss this house and the vastness of the night sky. *Nah*, she thought, she was an East Coast girl, and the openness of everything here intensified a feeling of loneliness that she always carried with her.

She unlocked the front door and was surprised and a bit bemused to find James sleeping on her sofa, an empty Champaign flute and an open bag of chips on the end table. He sat up when she closed the door.

"Tara. You're home," he said groggily. He gestured at the snacks. "I guess you can see I've been waiting."

"What are you doing here? You aren't going to make me turn down another proposal, are you?" Despite the surprise of finding him here, she was glad to see him. It would be nice not to fall asleep alone when she should be celebrating her success.

"I'm very proud of you. Well done," he said clapping his hands. "I told them from the start you were the one. All of Dallas is on lockdown. The real number of fatalities at the airport is over a hundred, and he escaped! Well, you don't look the least bit pleased. Come have some champagne."

Tara let her purse fall to the floor and took a few steps into the room. "But..." she rubbed her head, acutely aware of a throbbing headache. "What are you talking about? What does that LSD crazed kid have to do with me?" Shit! How did he know? Now she'd have to kill him, too.

"Well," he said coyly, "I didn't want to say anything, but now that you've pulled it off I can tell you that I recommended you for your position here. We have been watching you since killed that girl in medical school, testing you along the way. I am so proud of you, so proud Tara."

"But..." was all Tara managed say.

"Remember the man who beat that little kid with a golf club? The son who begged you to end the suffering of his cancer ridden father? You weren't afraid to do the right thing. You came through every time."

"That...no, that's not possible," Tara said. "Do you have any idea how hard that was on me? I still remember every one of their faces. "Do you know what you've done to me? What you've turned me into?" The memories flooded back to her. Her head throbbed.

"Come on, Tara. We didn't do anything to you except put you in situations where you could show your true colors. You proved yourself every time. You were exactly what we needed."

"Is this a bad dream?" she asked. "Have I fallen asleep at the wheel?"

"I am sorry I couldn't tell you sooner, but with daddy being in office, I just couldn't risk it. His arms and security company, though, of which I am currently majority shareholder, should go through the roof on trading tomorrow, all thanks to you." He paused and raised his glass of champagne to her.

His eyes twinkling, he reached out to touch her hand. She pulled away, shoving her hand in her jacket pocket.

"Shit," she said. "I did all of this work so a couple of rich good ole boys could get richer? I can't believe I bought that crap about the greater good, saving mankind from itself, that a little bit of instability would bring the nation together, save lives, end our oversees occupation, blah, blah, blah. All bullshit." She picked up her purse and removed her keys.

James grabbed her and pulled her into a hug. "Knock it off. No one made you kill those people. You made those decisions, not us. We didn't even have to help you get away with it. There is more to this than money, too. How do you think the good guys get funding to keep fighting the bad guys?"

She dropped her keys again, but not the syringe she had pilfered from the lab. Flipping the lid off, she injected it into James' butt and guided his fall to the ivory sofa. "Like this," she answered.

She hadn't expected him to go down so easily, and was disappointed he hadn't put up a bit more of a fight.

Well, I guess I'll need someone to clean this up, she thought.

She reached over to the end table and picked up his Merc keys. Walking out the door, she hit the key's buttons and saw lights flash three houses down. Getting in the car, she was reluctantly impressed with the supple leather seats and the high tech dash. She turned it around and tore off out of her development.

"Evans, it's Green. I need a pick up and cleaning. Yep. No, at my house. No, just have the team bring him to the prison; I'm on my way. We've got our next subject. Nope, a new experiment. Uh-huh. What? Look, I'll brief you when I get there. You can tell me about it then."

She hung up the phone and was pleasantly surprised to find AC/DC in queue on the iPlayer. Evans had been going on about new attacks in and around Dallas. He had also mentioned a detective from Baltimore asking questions about the group's funding and relationships with certain members of the US Senate. That had potential to be troublesome, but it wasn't anything she couldn't handle.

Speeding off into the darkness, she happily sang along and drummed on the steering wheel to *Thunderstruck*.

ABOUT THE AUTHOR

Gregory Carrico is an Amazon.com Best Selling horror and science fiction writer and 2013 HFA Author of the Year Finalist. He enjoys crafting bad guys that readers will both care about and despise.

When not creating new worlds and plotting their destruction, he advocates for adopting rescue dogs, and politely urges slower drivers to get out of the passing lane.

Other titles include:

Apocalypstick

King of Rats

Children of the Plague

The Shadow of the World

Anthologies:

Tales from the Mist

Addictive Paranormal Reads Halloween Box Set

www.Gramico.com/blog

Let's Scare Cancer To Death

5

Just Life
By T Fox Dunham

"The rumors of these reanimated corpses are entirely unfounded," Doctor Hobbes said. "The Helsinki Protocol could not cause such a thing. No. Alive is alive. Dead is dead. And we have worked hard to make sure you remain with us."

Robert laid tense on the stretcher. He shivered, naked beneath the paper sheet. The cool surgical suite like a butcher's freezer chilled his fevered body. The staff moved about him in green surgical robes, faces concealed with masks like theater, like a dancing pantomime. He thought of old tribal priests wearing the masks of their gods preparing a sacrifice on a stone altar.

"I don't want to open my eyes as one of them," Robert said. Doctor Hobbes chuckled beneath his mask, the bristles of his beard poking at the fabric. "A few slices. A couple of cuts. The mass will be gone. Your head will feel lighter."

"You told me it was over. The protocol had worked."

"Yes," Doctor Hobbes said. "God does not always let us in on His plans."

A nurse stepped over to the table, adjusted a light. It burned Robert's eyes. She held a syringe in gloved hand and fondled the

I.V. hanging from his saline bag. "Close your eyes, sweet prince," she said. "Count back from ten."

In those thoughts before painless oblivion, the promise of the Rainbow Cult, Robert thought of his Andrea and the sum of his broken promises now growing in her stomach, devouring the vessel that devours. At the count of seven, he joined the Rainbow Cult heaven and felt nothing.

The nurses painted the wound brown. The surgeon labored at his trade and lifted his scalpel to the mass below Robert's ear. It poked out like a buried golf ball and tightened the skin. For moment, he thought it flexed, pulsed, twitched under the skin, a buried insect, a beetle burrowing into the flesh to nourish and lay eggs. He shook it off.

"Been working too hard," he said.

He pressed the scalpel to the skin, pressed the blade into the flesh, lightly slicing open the patient's body to excise the tumor. He had to take care not to damage the eardrum or canal and any major vessel carrying blood to the brain. Still, most of the malignant tumor grew on the exterior, a lymph node gone rebel signaling the return of the lymphoma, even after the miraculous salutary results of the Helsinki 221 trial. The mass felt like it moved beneath the scalpel, jiggled like orange JELL-O. He steadied the blade.

"Too much coffee."

The nurses smiled perfunctorily, as was expected.

"It's...it's moving. Bring up the scan." A technician summoned the C.T. scan on the monitor over the theater. Doctor Hobbes studied it, looking for abnormality or habitation.

"Doctor?" the surgical nurse asked.

"Might be fluid. Let's get it removed and find out." He sliced deeper, working the edges of the pink and white gelatinous mass like cutting up a chunk of raw chicken. They cauterized a bleeder, smoke wafting from the site. The mass pulsed.

"A muscle spasm in the jaw. Are you sure he's under? Remember what happened last year? The hospital can't afford to pay for anymore incompetence."

"I'll page the anesthesiologist," the nurse said.

"The fuck?"

The tumor constricted then expanded, almost like it breathed. It flexed, pulling away from the bone with the behavior of a muscle. It struggled, ripping free from tissue and vein, evacuating from a bleeding crater in the patient's face.

"Doctor? Doctor?"

Doctor Hobbes stepped back from the patient, holding the scalpel before him in a defensive stance. The tumor, propelled by its own locomotion, jumped from the patient's head and landed on the surgical tray. It paused there, pulsing and flexing, a black ichor suffusing through its cells.

"Nurse," he yelled. "Isolate it!"

The surgical nurse moved forward holding a metal basin, ready to trap the emancipated tumor. She crept over to the new child, preparing to strangle it at its impossible birth. The tumor stilled then turned, aiming at her, sensing her approach. She dropped the basin and turned to run, but the malignant mass compressed then released like a spring, launching from the tray. It bounced onto her neck, staining her scrubs with black ooze. An orifice ripped at its base, and stiletto teeth grew from the hole. It pierced the flesh on her shoulder and chewed, razors digging deeper. Blood spilled down her chest. She screamed. The rest of the staff backed into the walls, knocking over a respirator and heart monitor. Pans clattered to the floor. The nurse raked at her neck, pulling at the tumor, fighting it, but it clung on. It nursed on her flesh and swelled in size. The nurse paled and collapsed to the floor.

"Get the patient," Doctor Hobbes said to the remaining staff, those who hadn't run from the room. "Roll him out of here." They moved on the tips of their toes, unlocking the table, rolling it out of the theater. The mobile tumor made no threatening moves, still and content like a child suckling from its mother. "I don't think she's breathing." He leaned over to take her pulse, careful not to make any sudden moves. A bump rose on the back of the tumor, blowing up like a balloon. It pulsed and launched, landing on Doctor Hobbes' hand, his fine hand that paid for his new condo. He shook it like it burned with fire. He yelled, sounding through the Pre-op and Post-op ward.

***

"I'm so terribly sorry," said a voice through the darkness. "It seems you've survived."

Robert clawed through the darkness. He opened his eyes to the sunlight pouring through the windows in his hospital room. Several bandages strangled his head, clamping along his jaw. A plastic tub dangled from an incision below his ear, draining fluid into a tube hanging down over his shoulder. He tasted bitter chemicals in his dry mouth.

"The world feels lonelier," Robert muttered, half in a dream, speaking to the pooka standing over his bed in a pink bunny outfit. "Am I dead, or are you a fat old man wearing a pink bunny outfit? Or am I dead and you're God? A fat old omnipotent being wearing a pink bunny outfit."

"One of those I guess. All of the above. What the hell do I know?"

"Where's Doctor Hobbes?" Robert reached for the alert button to ring the nurse's station in the hall. What was next? What had to be done? Before they found the lymphoma, he'd always wondered how cancer patients survived a single day, facing death, facing harsh life, no longer safe in their delusions of immortality. Then, he joined the oncological army, his brothers and sisters at arms. He learned that anything could become routine, that a cancer patient just got from treatment to treatment, appointment to appointment, from one vomit bucket to the next, surviving each trial as it came. It was just life. Just life.

Bunny man shrugged.

"Are you here to cheer me up? I'm a bit old for that."

78

"I'm here so you can cheer me up," Bunny man said. "You've got the good words."

"Wait. I know you. You're the leader of that cult."

"The High Priest himself. I do hospital rounds sometimes, come in to make myself feel better. Once in a while, I start feeling hopeful, positive about life. What a burden that can be."

The nurses still hadn't come in to see him yet. He watched the door into the hall. The intercom spit out muttered requests for doctors to dial numbers. He heard carts rattling, nurses running, muffled moaning coming from down the ward.

"They ain't coming," Bunny man said. "Got their hands full. New disease making the rounds. I hear it's bad. I hear it's the deliverance."

"High Priest. Do me a favor, and I'll preach your litany until I die."

"Shoot."

"I need you to check on another patient for me. I don't know what room she's in. She came in the same time I did. We were both patients in the Helsinki 221 Protocol. The retrovirus that can cure cancer. Worked like a dream for about six months. That's how we met."

"Yeah. I've heard about that witchcraft shit. Our founder was in the trial. He knew it wasn't going to work. Just a delusion. A dream. He bribed his way into the trials to dance in the futility when it failed."

Robert checked the digital clock on the wall. It ticked just before noon. Still time. When the cancer came back, when the miracle failed, the cancer burned like wildfire in dry wood. Many from the trial had already been cut from this world. She couldn't breathe last time they spoke. He heard her gasping on the cell phone. He'd dialed 911.

He leaned up out of bed, untangling the tubing and the wiring, and looked out the window down into the parking lot, overlooking the ER parking. Two EMTS and a cop wrestled with a bloodied guy. The dude had most of his neck chewed off, yet he clawed and raged on the three. Robert swore he was biting at them. Must have been high on PCP.

Finally a rotund nurse came in, her black hair up in a bun. Blood stained her purple scrubs.

"Yo. Fat rabbit. Out."

"What?" asked the pink bunny. "No kiss?"

"You've been warned. Coming in here and messing with our patients. Telling them there's no hope, no light. That Jesus ain't waiting for 'em."

"You let in priests and wise men to tell them about the afterlife."

The nurse twisted the pink bunny's arm behind his back and pushed him out of the room. He grinned at Robert before he left. Robert waved.

"Our soldiers are marching," Bunny said. "Hungry they are. Join the legions."

The nurse returned several minutes later. "I apologize for that, Mister..." She checked the chart. "Robert? That okay?"

Robert nodded.

"Doctor Hobbes was hurt. I think."

"What happened?"

"Some kind of accident in surgery. From the way nurses tell it, it was something out of you. Some kind of bug living inside you, but that's BS. I think one of the nurses went a little crazy, maybe popping pills. Attacked him. They're both down in the unit, pretty sick. They had to restrain the nurse."

"Did they get it all out of me?"

She shrugged again. "You'd have to talk to your doctor."

For a moment, a frisson of time, he'd allowed himself the comfort of security, of knowing the firm ground beneath his feet again, to believe he existed firmly in the realm of the living and no longer dangling over the edge, caught between two worlds. Both faded from him. No answers. Limbo.

"A ginger ale?"

"Sure, honey," she said, smiling. "You've got a cute ass, you know that?"

Robert had no idea how she could tell, having not gotten off his ass since waking up. She slipped out of the room, and he picked up the phone and dialed zero for the hospital operator to ask about Andrea. No one picked up. He swung his legs over the side of the bed. The side of his head throbbed. The bandages itched against the hair bristles growing in after chemo.

This had to be the surgical floor. Andrea should be in the system, somewhere, maybe even in ICU. He'd just get his ass up and go look for her. Robert grabbed the IV pole and pump and unplugged it from the wall. It chirped three times, and he expected the karate nurse to come back in, discover what he plotted and put an end to it by throwing him back into bed. Something crashed down the hall, and a woman screamed high opera. Sometimes old people get scared on these floors.

Robert strolled into the hall, trying not to look guilty, like he belonged there and could be up out of bed after a major surgery. He spied the nurse's desk, ducking behind a stack of pink dinner trays sitting on a tall cart. The phones rang. Patient room lights flashed. The staff had deserted the desks. Something cracked from outside in the parking lot. It couldn't be gunfire. Who would be firing a gun at a hospital? Patients moaned, though he couldn't determine the direction. Not his problem. He had to find her.

He dragged the pump pole to the front desk and sat down at one of the computers. The doctor had gone off still logged in. Robert navigated the system and found patient billing records then typed in Andrea's name. February 2nd. Her birthday, same as his. Billing had her in room 203, one floor down. They'd listed her condition as critical. A pain pump had been ordered, but that was the only thing listed. Doctors used a specific phrase:

We're going to make sure you're comfortable.

And thus your life ends.

At least it used to. They changed the game.

Someone groaned behind, and he spun the chair around, expecting to get yelled at; however, what could they say to a cancer patient probably dead in a few days? He didn't give a damn. A patient came out of the nurse's office, wearing a blood-ied hospital gown. His wild gray hair knotted around his ears. He looked like a rather sick man from the ashen pallor of his skin.

"We're the lucky ones," Robert said. "We know the truth of it."

A saliva stream spilled down his chin. He must have been on Thorazine, perhaps escaped from somewhere. He turned and looked at Robert with eyes white as hardboiled eggs. He moaned again and lurched. Robert stood up from the chair, but his blood pressure dropped. His head throbbed, and he nearly toppled over. He caught himself on the desk. The patient tackled the chair, hitting his arm on the desk. It cracked. Then he got to his feet. He'd broken his arm below the shoulder, and it hung there limp. He didn't wince once in pain. He moved for Robert again, and he stumbled back into his IV pump pole, nearly falling over. Robert twisted around, and the tube ripped from the tape on his arm, pulling out the needle. Saline leaked from the free tube, spilling on the floor. He moved for Robert, stepping in the pud-dle and slipped, cracking his head. The patient might have broken his neck from the bone protruding through the skin. Still he crawled, chomping at the air. Free of the pole, Robert stag-gered back, fighting his low blood pressure and spinning head.

Robert got down the hall, ignoring the moans and hissing coming from some of the patient rooms. He looked in and saw some of them strapped down. In one of the rooms, karate nurse lay folded over herself in the corner, sitting in a viscous blood pool. She twitched.

Judgment day. He had lived with living death for the last year, always one step ahead, resenting the ignorant living. Now the disease had manifested, had taken arms and legs and piloted them. Robert didn't understand why, but some deep primal part of his brain understood what he had seen, what they had become. George Romero had really given the term meaning. But Robert refused to call the walkers that. Instead, he named them Retribu-tion.

Let the world burn down. He had one choice now, the only real choice of any consequence: How would his consciousness end? Find Andrea. Leave this world together, holding each other.

The power died in the hospital. Lights dimmed. Emergency lighting lit in the halls. Machines sung in high pitched chorus across the building. Emergency generators kicked on, but power conservation practices kept the halls dark. Robert crept in the shadows. He slipped out of the ward. He couldn't use the elevators with the power off. Ahead, a couple of doctors shambling up the hall. He hid in the shadows until they passed then scurried down the corridor, pausing in the corner behind fake potted plants to let his head calm. A nurse ran by screaming, a mob of Retribution stumbling after her, keeping up good pace. They smelled like sweet road kill, of death, of foul shit and urine. He gagged and focused, concentrating as he did when suffering chemo, swallowing back the vomit. One of them crawled behind the mob, its legs gnawed off through its jeans. It clawed itself forward, dragging its colon behind him like a pet snake.

Robert found the stairwell, checked it first. Looked clear. He listened and heard not one moan. Did it hurt, being one of them, being the dead? Life hurt. He lived on morphine and Duragesic patches to calm the pain in his throat. When Andrea kissed him, it left. Robert carefully took the stairs, climbing down a flight, reaching the next landing. He slipped open the door, spied down the corridor, the identical hall with the elevators and potted plants and living dead hospital staff. More gunfire popped outside. He looked out a window in the well and watched as a wing of A-10 Warthogs flew low to the ground, sailing like kites, heading to Philly. St. Mary's hospital rattled from the force of their engines.

Robert rested a moment. His heart sped, tapping in his ears. He paused in the darkness, considering the next few meters of his journey, the last few. He knew it would come to this. He would define himself by his last actions, as millions defined themselves today. The end of the world had come, but he had known it early in his own personal apocalypse.

Robert pushed open the door from the stairwell and stepped into the shadows. Her ward was down along the corridor, beyond the radiology department and sports medicine. The hospital was shaped like a square with a courtyard in the center and several intersecting wards. Two of the wards had been shut from budget cutbacks and would be empty. You could walk in a circle again and again.

He made it to the double doors of the ward and looked through the door windows: full of Retribution, staggering about aimlessly. The foul aroma of newly rotting flesh seeped through the cracks under the door. He lost his stomach and vomited on the floor. He could see her room, just a few doors down. The door was shut. Maybe, maybe she had barricaded herself inside, waiting for rescue, hoping for him. He could feel her close. She'd be thinking of him. She'd never stop as long as her higher brain functions sparked and buzzed.

At least a dozen Retribution stood between the door. They hadn't noticed him yet. Their attention span focused on whatever was in front of them. A few of them, a mix of nurses and patients pale in skin yet not rotting, pawed at one of the windows in the hall, reaching for house sparrows busy at work on their nests, oblivious to the change in ownership of the planet.

They didn't seem fast, more like drunken buggers, chasing after some skirt running from a bar after happy hour. If he kept fleet of foot and stayed ahead, he could get through them. Still, they could mass, block passage to Andrea's door. If he could get them away, provide distraction.

Robert threw the door open. It slowed to shut. He spread his arms out and said:

"Though lovers be lost, love shall not;
and death shall have no dominion."

The poem by Dylan Tomas was his mantra, his battle cry through treatment. It prophesized meeting Andrea in the radiation-oncology ward at the Hospital of the University of

Pennsylvania in Philly where he endured daily radiation therapy. Her dark hair had just started growing, giving her a tomboy look, detailing her raven eyes.

They turned their heads, raised their backs, reached. Some staggered forward, gaining momentum, crying out. Pain shown in their eyes, a hunger, a need made manifest from the soul into the physical. Their flesh required no nourishment, yet still they desired to satiate that which would never be satisfied. It drove them until their skin, bones, muscle melted to soup and the soup dried to dust. He pitied them as he pitied the living.

Robert jogged away, slow enough to allow them time to catch up. He led the herd up the hall and round the bend, watching for any lone dead ahead. Most of this floor had been shut, the lights off, covers on the equipment, empty desks and barren office doors. He dodged a janitor's cart, knocking out a broom and a bottle of cleanser.

Certain he had the majority in pursuit, Robert sped up. His heart thumped. Radiation had burned his lungs, and he struggled with forty percent capacity. Cold sweat soaked his robes. He carried on, fighting muscle cramps in his legs. The radiation had fried his brain stem, spine, and nerves misfired or declined to function. He existed midway between the living and the walking dead. He'd probably find the transition easier than most.

Did they do this? Was this the Helsinki protocol? Robert took some pleasure in that. It's like what the bunny man preached. They had been chosen, selected as prophets to bring the truth to the world, the real state of existence. They'd deliver to them oblivion. Robert no longer ran as fast. He wasn't escaping. He was a general leading troops, an army.

Robert turned the corner again, running the length of the hospital. He thought he had time to rest, to catch his wind, but soon as he stopped, Robert heard them close behind. The reek turned his stomach. A lost nurse with smeared mango lipstick led the pack. Slime stained her white stockings. She kissed the air between, sniffing for him.

Robert ran again, passing an empty nurse's station then slipping out of that ward. He pressed a wedge under the door then hared through a slim corridor. Light poured in through the skylights and many windows. Outside among the hedges, the world looked normal, still. He turned the corner again, on the home stretch. He hoped that the other doors to Andrea's ward would be unlocked, had to take a few things on faith. There was no other choice, as was often the case of faith. Cancer patients learned early that control was an illusion. Just life. Always and always just life.

He saw the ward doors ahead in shadow, by a nest of doctors' offices. Their doors hung open, but Robert sensed no movement. He jogged by, reaching for the door when something tackled him out of the darkness. Cold hands dug into his shoulders as it pulled him to the ground. He had little strength with which to wrestle and twisted, rolling into the light from a window. He recognized Doctor Hobbes, his oncologist. Even in living death, he still beheld the distance in his eye and aspect, the clinical miles between patient and physician, keeping himself clean, untouched, unspoiled by the death around him in his chosen field of profession. There had been days when Robert wanted to press his thumbs to the doctor's eyes and scream at him: see me, know me, to weep for my coming death and his own. People like that made him feel like he was the disease and not just suffering it.

He chomped for Robert's shoulder. Black slime dripped from his teeth, stained his lips. He locked on with obsessive purpose, and Robert fought the force of his muscles, still tense and without fatigue. The doctor would never stop. Never give up the hunt. Robert twisted away, knocking him into a medication cart, banging his head. It seemed to shock him, and the Retribution paused. Robert reached up and grabbed a syringe from an open tray. Popping the cap, he drove the needle into the doctor's right eye and pressed the plunger. The orb bulged with fluid then burst. The Retribution twisted his head in obvious discomfort, the needle still stuck. Robert reached for his other eye and

86

pressed down his thumb. It popped like a grape. The doctor recoiled. He'd exist in the dark now. Still, his compulsion
overtook him, and he dropped to his knees, crawling, searching
for Robert. The mass of Retribution caught up to them, and Robert crawled to the doors and slid one of them open. He pushed it
shut behind, got to his feet, and wedged a chair under the handle.
They banged against it, moaning, pressing gray flesh on the
glass.

A few of the new ones still lingered in the hall, and he
dodged them. They seemed without purpose, perfunctorily chasing Robert and giving up, lost in a post-animated melancholy.
One woman in a pink sweater pawed the floor for something.
Robert spotted her glasses on the table. Her eyes squinted. Robert knocked them off the desk to the floor for her to find. She
reached for him but gave up.

Robert stood before Andrea's door. The pressure of the distance uncoiled. Hands and arms shook. Body near collapsed
from weakness, gravity overwhelming. He struggled to stand,
heard a crash down the hall, and watched the Retribution push
the chair out of the way. They fell over each other.

It was not the thought of finding her dead that kept him
from entering. He knew one day soon she'd be taken from this
life. He worried she had gone, evacuated, that he'd walk in to
find an empty room. Still, he had to know and stepped into the
private room.

Her song like mockingbirds, like the gold finches in the
woods, hung low, a few chirps, a few notes that arranged into a
rhythm. They stopped and stuttered, yet she sung. It lifted him.
The pain vanished and legs strengthened.

She sat on the edge of her bed, straight up. He'd not seen
her sitting up in a month. Her back was turned to him. Robert
walked to her and ran his fingers through her short dark hair.

"One last moment for us, with us," he said. "Then we shall
join them, my love."

She turned her head to see him, gazed on her love with
hoary eyes where winter clouds snowed, where ice froze over

the world. Her skin glowed white in the sunlight from the windows. Her gown had torn away, revealing the soft curve of her shoulder, the turn of her breast. A Hickman catheter hung from her chest, half torn out. She sung softly, mindlessly, going through old motions, old songs, most her mind burned out, playing the melody like a music box. Robert wanted to join her, needed to be with her just for a while longer, to rot together.

"Kiss me, Andrea."

He pressed his lips to her mouth. She sunk her teeth into them, tearing the flesh away. The pain seared through his face, but he had known pain, knew how to distract, to disable. Blood poured down his face, and he worried he'd look unseemly to her. She bit his neck, chewing through artery. Robert's blood painted her skin, giving her color. In his last moments of this life, he moved his fingers down her flesh, finger-painting in his blood, washing her skin in warmth.

They wouldn't be together forever. Nothing ever could, not in a cruel cold universe. Still, he'd take every moment. And even in the numbness of death-life, he'd still feel a cinder at fire buried beneath the cold flesh and dirt. Death could never entirely extinguish it.

T. Fox Dunham resides outside of Philadelphia PA—author and historian. He's published in nearly 200 international journals and anthologies, and his first novella, New World, was published by May December Publisher. Martyr, his second, will be published later this year. He's a cancer survivor. His friends call him fox, being his totem animal, and his motto is: Wrecking civilization one story at a time.

Blog: http://tfoxdunham.blogspot.com/. http://www.facebook.com/tfoxdunham & Twitter: @TFoxDunham

6

Choices
By Claire C. Riley

This is the bit where I'm supposed to write something really profound and meaningful isn't it? But what can I say that hasn't been said before? I mean, what will touch you and make you admire all the brave fighters of this horrible disease any more than you already do?

I've been touched by cancer, both near and far, but it matters not by whom, only that they fought with everything they had. That they were afraid, yet showed great courage, and I am both proud and humbled by them. But they know this already.

So how about this...how about I dedicate this story to cancer? In that case, I only have one thing left to say. Cancer...we're coming to get YOU!

A cancer fighter once told me, 'if I can't laugh about it, then it's already killed me.'

One.

Adam Walker wondered if this might be his last blissfully ignorant day on earth. He'd endured nine months of chemotherapy, radiotherapy, and lots of other therapy, all because of some stupid fucking lump in the left side of his nutsack, and he wasn't getting it confused with his *actual* balls. This lump was a deadly kind, and one his girlfriend of six months, Maria, had both found and been disgusted by. Apparently she wasn't quite ready to be with a sick old man. She was young—barely in her twenties— and didn't want to spend the rest of her life looking after him. Christ, he was only twenty-nine himself, and little did she know that he only had a fifty-fifty chance of surviving it anyway.

Adam shook off the doom and gloom. Today was going to be a good day. Today he got to find out if the hell he'd gone through for the past nine months had been worth it—the sickness, the shits, the hair loss, and the humiliation. More importantly, today he got to find out if he would live or die.

With his hands deep in the pockets of his jeans, and his cap low over his eyes, he made his way across town to the hospital he'd been visiting since Maria had found that fateful lump. He didn't even need to look where he was going anymore; he'd been there so many times over the course of the nine months that he knew the way like he knew the way to the bathroom in the middle of the night and didn't need to turn the light on. Yes, it was a twenty minute walk from his apartment to the hospital. Across eight intersections, four right turns, and three left. Twenty sets of traffic lights. One video store. One gas station One florist. Three grocery stores and nine coffee shops. Nine, for Christ's sake! He'd been in each one of them and sampled each type of coffee they all held. *Betty's Heaven* was the worst, and he'd subsequently renamed it *Betty Gave Me the Shits*. Of course it could have been the treatment that did that, but he preferred to blame it on good old Betty.

Adam was halfway across the third intersection when a car whizzed past him so quickly it blew his baseball cap clear off, exposing his bald head to the world. He wanted to shout and drop a load of F-bombs at the driver, but instead he chased after his cap, which had now blown up onto the opposite sidewalk. He grabbed the cap and tugged it back down over his head with a grumble, pulling it low enough to shade most of his face. He looked sick these days, and he hated the looks he got. They were always looks of either sympathy or worry. Worry that he was either a crackhead junkie or had some sort of infectious disease, or sympathy because of course everyone and their uncle knew someone who had died of cancer. He could almost smell the sympathy rolling off them in waves, threatening to swallow him whole. The worst looks, though, were the ones he always got when he told people he was fine. When he told people that he would be okay, that he'd get through this, that he was being treated and the outlook was positive. His poor mother had broken down and cried until she passed out from exhaustion when he had first told her, and now he hated having to visit her. Every time he did, it was a constant flurry of questions and a fresh bout of worry. For her and for him. Yeah, people's pity was the worst.

Adam looked down the street as another car approached and sped on by, ignoring the red stop sign and narrowly missing a small pickup truck on the opposite side of the road.

"Jesus," Adam mumbled with a shake of his head.

The car kept on going down the road and through another set of lights as if seventy was the new speed limit and the driver didn't have a care in the world.

Adam shook his head again and kept on walking. He stopped in at *Marco's Grocery and Tobacco Store* and bought a pack of Camel Lights, mumbling a quick hello to Marco as he paid. He hated smoking. Before he got the news he had cancer, he hadn't smoked in ten years. The first thing he did when he left the doctor's office on that August thirteenth was go straight to the nearest liquor store and purchase two bottles of Jack Daniels and a pack of Camel Lights. He hadn't even bothered to wait until he got home to open either of them up, but had forgotten about the shop assistant trying to hand him his change, turned, and walked out while twisting the cap off one of the bottles. He'd downed half of it before he'd made it to Community Park, whereupon he sat under an old oak tree and smoked and drank until his throat burned and his eyes felt like they had razor blades in them.

Anyway, today was going to be a good day, and once he had the news that he had the all-clear, he was going to give up smoking again. He didn't even enjoy it, but it took the edge off his frayed nerves.

Adam lit up his cigarette as he left *Marco's*, taking a deep pull on it and exhaling the long plume of smoke. He checked his watch, noticing that he still had thirty minutes until his appointment with the good Dr. Kerr, and set off again, slipping his cigarettes into his jacket pocket.

He watched his feet as he walked, ignoring the sounds of cars passing him, honking horns, and people arguing. He had no time these days for petty disagreements. However, the sound of a gunshot had him look up and nearly walk straight into an attractive blonde woman and a little girl who was crying. She was so busy looking behind her at someone approaching that she didn't notice Adam until he was gripping her by the shoulders to stop her from stepping on his new sneakers.

She screamed, long and hard, and swung around, slapping him hard enough across the face to make him see stars, and then pushed him away with another scream. The little girl screamed too, and started crying harder than previously, tears pouring down her chubby little cheeks as she clung to the woman's leg like her life depended on it. The crazy woman swung her arm back, readying herself to hit him again. Adam tried to grab her, but she continued her onslaught until he backed away.

"What the hell's wrong with you, lady?" Adam stumbled back another step, his hands held up in front of him as a sign of peace—and as a defense, in case she continued to try and beat him.

A man behind the blonde reached forward and grabbed the young girl, and it was only now that he was close enough to them that Adam could not only see the guy in all his glory, but could smell him too. He smelled like a walking sewer pipe, but it was his face that was the true kicker—or what little was left of it: flesh seemed to be hanging from his left cheek and chin like wallpaper in an old person's home. Rotted and blackening skin with an almost green tinge to it was literally hanging from his face.

Adam stared, his mouth hanging open, as the man dug his nails into the little girl's shoulder, breaking the flesh, and sending an arc of blood out from the wound. The man—thing, whatever-the-fuck it was—groaned and snapped yellow teeth at the girl. The blonde was pushing and hitting him, screaming and crying, and yet still Adam watched on in horror, unable to break whatever spell he seemed to be under. The thing used its other hand to grab the girl by the hair and pull her closer to him, and when he reached down, his mouth open wide and his teeth snapping, the young girl let out a scream that could break even the toughest of hearts as he bit down into her shoulder blade with a loud crunch.

"Jesus!" Adam's eyes went wide, and he finally broke out of his frozen panic and ran forwards, shoulder barging the monster in front of him with every ounce of strength his body still had.

The thing toppled over, releasing the girl but ending up with Adam on top of it instead. It didn't seem to mind, and it went straight for the jugular to prove the point. They rolled across the sidewalk—Adam, monster, Adam, monster—until they were a blur of limbs, blood, gore, bald-headedness, and a cheesy joke about a nun and a penguin rolling down a hill. The thing was finally on top of him, and as its jaw dropped down and it let out a throaty groan, globules of blood and spittle dripped from its lips and landed on him.

Adam felt fear and panic rise up inside him. They were the same feelings he'd felt the day he'd found out about the cancer. He gritted his teeth and placed his hands on its chest, pushing and pushing until he felt a strange movement from within its ribcage and, mercifully, the thing fell sideways, loosening its grip long enough for Adam to scramble up to his feet. The thing had started to stand back up, its movements slow and sluggish, seeming like it had drunk way too much tequila.

Adam stumbled backwards, turning to look for the blonde woman and child. He spotted them running; they were halfway down the street—with the child screaming and blood pumping from the bite mark on her shoulder—when a truck rounded the corner too quickly. With screeching tires, the truck skidded and flipped onto its side and plowed on top of them both. The child's screams were extinguished immediately.

Two.

Bile rose to the back of his throat, his hand simultaneously clutching his mouth to stop the vomit coming out as he turned his attention back to the monster in front him. Its nostrils flared, and its lips peeled back as it growled at him.

"Adam!"

He heard the voice behind him but couldn't tear his eyes away from the walking abomination in front of him. For every step it took forwards, Adam took one back without even realizing he was doing so, until his back bumped into the liquor store wall behind him and he turned, ready to strike out. A sense of déjà vu washed over him.

"Kill it!" Marco was behind him, offering up the baseball bat as he came out of the storefront. "That's not a man anymore. I don't know what it is, but it needs to die." He glanced back at the shambling, rotting man before making eye contact with Adam. "It needs to die *again*."

Adam numbly took the bat, his fingers curling around the metal handle and flexing before he gritted his teeth, stepped forward, and swung at the thing. Its head bounced off the metal, making a strange sound that echoed around them. It continued to move forward despite the fresh trickle of black-and-brown ooze that was now seeping out of its left ear. Adam moved to the left and the thing followed, one eye swiveling awkwardly within its socket.

It didn't seem to care that it had just been hit over the head. It didn't seem to care that it was about to happen again, either.

96

Its eyes were glassy and unfocused, yet completely fixed on Adam. The bat flew through the air and hit the thing again on the side of its head. This time, the bat seemed to sink into the skull, making an indentation. The thing paused, its shoulders slouching as Adam pulled at the bat. It made a sucking sound as it finally pulled free. Adam didn't need asking twice. He swung furiously, over and over again, hitting it until it dropped to its knees; and then, even as it still scrambled for Adam, brown blood seeping from every orifice in its face, including the new ones, Adam struck it again. It fell face down on to the sidewalk, still growling, its hands twitching and reaching for him.

His arms felt suddenly weak, too weak to hold the bat, too weak to have killed this…man…thing…whatever it was. The bat fell limply from his hands as he stepped backwards and away from the destruction.

He continued to walk backwards until he saw Marco reach down and grab his bat, and the thing moved again. He turned away from the sight of Marco hitting it again, finally completely crushing its skull and destroying what little was left of its brain.

Adam walked fast, the streets a blur, the sounds of screaming, shouting, and gunfire growing rapidly as he got farther into the city. He didn't even know where he was going anymore; it just somehow seemed safer to keep moving until he thought up a realistic plan.

A car swung wildly from around the corner to his right, slamming into a lamppost, and the driver flew up from his seat and crashed right through the windshield, sending shattered glass in all directions. The body fell limply onto the hood of the car, arms and legs bent in uncomfortable directions as blood trickled from the side of the man's mouth. If there were ever a public service announcement for wearing a seatbelt, this was it.

Adam stood gaping for several seconds, unsure what to do. That was until he heard moaning. His eyes followed the sounds as more and more moaning joined the chorus. Several of the sick people were coming from all directions, attracted by the noise of the car crash. Adam backed up until he hit the wall behind him and he jumped involuntarily, afraid for a second that one of those things had come up behind him and would now…what? What would they actually do? The one before had looked like it wanted to take a chunk out of him, but would it really have done that?

His stomach churned. Yeah, they would bite him—eat him, even. He looked around him and dipped into a side alley, watching curiously as the things approached the man on the hood of the car. The man was finally waking up. Only one eye opened at first and looked around him, then the other opening slower. His face contorted in agony as he tried to move, and a cry of pain left his lips. It seemed to spur on the sick people, who shambled faster to him. The first reached him and grabbed on to his leg, tugging him closer. The hands of the man from the car crash pawed and clawed at the smooth surface of the hood, trying to find something to grip onto even as the first mouth bit down on his calf muscle and he screamed.

Adam stared in horror as more and more of the sick reached for him, tearing at his clothes and flesh and biting down on parts of his body, their mouths coming away with stringy sinew and bloody muscle. Adam swallowed down the venomous chunks that were threatening to cascade from his mouth in a waterfall of vomity gunk.

What the hell was happening? What was wrong with these people?

A loud bark behind Adam made him jump again, and he cursed at himself. He turned to look, seeing a sandy colored Labrador retriever baring its teeth at him, the hairs on its neck visibly bristling.

Adam held up his hands in defense. "Easy, boy, easy now." He swallowed hard, looking back between the dog and the group of—well, let's face it: they were zombies in every sense of the word, though he wasn't quite willing to say it out loud just yet. Especially since the barking from the retriever was attracting the things to his location.

"Hush, hush, boy." Adam put a finger to his lips like the dog would understand the gesture.

To be fair to the mutt, it seemed to acknowledge that he was different from the rest of the people, and with a wary glance at him it barked once more, turned on its heel, and ran back down the alleyway. Adam looked towards the lurching…people, and followed after the dog.

As he reached the end of the alley, he turned left, catching sight of the dog again as it turned another corner. Why it seemed important to follow the damn thing was beyond him, but since it was trying to get as far away from the sick as he was, it seemed like a good bet it would know where to hide.

Three.

Every alleyway looked the same—Dumpsters overflowing, rotten food, cardboard boxes being used as shelter; but now no one lived underneath these temporary homes. His lungs weren't what they used to be and Adam had to slow down to catch his breath on several occasions, hands to his knees as he bent over trying to draw the breath into his lungs. Sweat poured from him, mocking the shower he had taken this morning. Thank God he wasn't going to have his nuts fondled by the good Doctor Kerr today; he wouldn't wish that job on anyone, given the amount of sweat coming from him. A thought occurred to him as he looked up and saw the white hospital at the end of the alley.

Today he was supposed to find out if he had beaten the cancer. He was supposed to find out if he was going to live or die—though under the current circumstance of zombie hordes eating people alive, the results should have seemed pointless. But they weren't pointless, not to Adam.

He pulled off his cap and wiped his bald head with his sleeve. His results were in there—in that building. He glanced behind him. There was no one following, no sick people chasing after him, and he knew it wasn't chance that had brought him to this building. Sure, he'd been following the damn dog to safety, but he knew instinctually that he had to go inside; he had brought himself here, and he had to go get those results.

His gut was telling him he was an idiot. Hell, even the dog had come back and was watching from a safe distance as he weighed up his options, but the fear on the mutt's furry face told him it was stupid to go inside. A hospital had to be the worst place he could go.

The world seemed to have gone quiet; silence seemed to span several blocks. No more gunshots, no more screaming— just the wind, and his raging heartbeat. Adam looked up to see the Labrador coming closer and he gestured to it with his up-turned palm, offering up a sad smile. It came close enough to touch, and he let his hand run the length of its back as it brushed against his leg with its muzzle as it whined.

"What should I do, boy?" Adam crouched down, ruffling the dog's ears with his hands. "I've gotta know." He looked into its face. "You know?"

The dog sneezed at him in response.

"I know, I know, but it's right there!" He pointed to the hospital. "I could be in and out before anything happens. My brother lives with my mom out on a farm in the sticks. You and me could head back to my apartment, grab my truck, and make our way there. We'd be safe there, no one around for miles. And I'd know…" He swallowed. "You know?"

The dog whined again and nudged his leg.

Adam stood up. "I know." He pulled his cap back onto his head. "It's stupid—to go in there." He pointed at the building. The dog sat down in stubborn agreement. "But it's stupid to be talking to a dog, and I'm still doing that." He sighed. "I'll never find out if this thing is killing me or not if I don't go in there. Whether I just wasted the last year of my life fighting it when I should have been off traveling and seeing the world, saying my goodbyes and fucking living like every day was my last day on this earth." Adam swallowed, choking up on his own words.

The dog nudged his leg again.

"I know, Yeller." He smiled at the nickname that tumbled from his lips, despite his inner turmoil. "I know it's stupid, and none of it matters anymore, not with all this going on. But I have to know!"

Yeller stood and glanced behind him, giving a soft growl. Adam looked and couldn't see anything for himself—but that didn't mean that something wasn't on its way. It was time to choose.

He looked down at Yeller. He had no idea whose dog he had been, who had cared for him previously. "I'll understand if you need to go, but I've got to do this."

The dog backed away, his tail tucked between his hind legs, and Adam resigned himself to going in alone.

"Be brave, but not stupid. Stay hidden—stay safe, boy." He stroked Yeller fondly on the head again and started to jog towards the end of the alleyway. If he was right, then the main entrance was to this left, but there was a side entrance for deliveries around the back. That was bound to be quieter than the main entrance. Doctors Kerr's office was at the back of the building anyway, so it made much more sense to him. It was a thought he'd often had on the many occasions he'd come to this stupid building.

As he reached the end of the alleyway, he looked behind him. Yeller was gone. Sadness gripped him, and he hoped that the dog managed to find a safe spot to hide out while all this madness carried on. He still had a plan to stick to: get his results, get home, get his truck, and get gone.

He peeked around the wall. There were a couple of the sick crouched down on the floor by a car, chewing on what he could only presume to be a person. Jesus, he hoped whoever it was hadn't suffered. Adam realized that he needed a weapon. He looked around at the garbage and trashcans, hoping that they would provide him with something, but short of using a sack full of day-old rotten trash, there was nothing useful. Adam took his hat off and wiped his forehead again, his ears pricking at the sound of shuffling.

"Shit." Adam put his hat back on and peered around the corner. All the sick seemed to be preoccupied with the dead person, and he took the opportunity to make a run for it.

Every footstep seemed to echo around him, but he refused to look behind him until he got to a safe place. As the corner of the hospital came up on him, he rounded it and slammed hands-first into one of the sick. Thankfully for him, it seemed just as surprised as he was, and before it could grab him, he was pushing it in to the thorny rose bushes and running again. He saw the small delivery entrance and prayed that it was open. It normally was—he'd seen so many of the staff using the entrance as a quick slip-out for a sneaky cigarette on many occasions. Ridiculous really, considering where they worked, but no one knew more than he did the idealism of *'it'll never happen to me.'*

As his hands reached for the handle, he could practically hear the slobbering from the sick man behind him as it struggled to keep up. Adam's hand gripped the silver handle and turned it, and he almost screamed with happiness when the door opened. He dove inside and slammed it behind him as the sick man banged its hands against the glass with a furious growl. Adam checked behind him, noticing that the corridor was a mess—and quiet. There should have been all kinds of things going on, especially with something like this happening all around him—but there was nothing, barring the occasional flicker of a light and the banging of the sick man on the door. Adam took a moment to get a good look at the man outside. He checked him over, from his missing shoes and torn-open bloody shirt that revealed a gaping hole in his chest, all the way up to the large chunk of flesh missing from the side of his neck. The man's eyes were covered in a white film, moving and seeing—but surely they couldn't see properly. Adam took a step back, and then another. Pressing his back to the wall, he paused in his movements, holding still for as long as he could. The thing outside couldn't smell him, and from this distance with him unmoving, it couldn't see him. Several minutes passed before its frustration on the glass subsided and it grew bored and wandered off. At least the creepy foggy eyes these things sported were good for something other than just scaring people.

Adam took a deep breath and pushed off from the wall. Next to the exit was a fire extinguisher, and above that—an axe. Using his elbow, he smashed through the glass covering it and grabbed the axe, testing out the weight in his hand with a smile.

Feeling much better now that he had a weapon to defend himself with, Adam set off for Doctor Kerr's office.

Four.

The stairwell was dark, with only the red security lights to light his way. Each step sounded like a drumbeat, no matter how softly he tried to walk. Reaching the second floor, he peered through the small glass window on the stairwell door. There was no movement on this floor either, and he couldn't decide what was freaking him out more—the fact that there were none of those sick people here in the hospital and the movies had it wrong all this time, or the fact that he had basically just walked into a trap if those things had any form of consciousness left and were actually stalking him at this very moment.

He shook off the morbid thoughts. He was nearly there. He could see Doctor Kerr's office from his position; he just had to get down the corridor as quietly as possible, get in the office, find his results, and get out. How hard could it be?

With a roll of his shoulders, Adam pushed the door open. He half expected it to give out a long piercing squeal, like in all the horror movies he had ever watched, but it opened silently. He stepped into the corridor, looking in both directions. There had been trouble here; that much was clear from the destruction everywhere. Blood smeared the walls, lights were blinking on and off, chairs and papers were spilling out of rooms and into the hallway. He held his breath, listening intently for any sound that was out of place. An alarm outside had started up again, and an occasional buzzing was coming from the old PA system, but other than that—silence.

He stepped further into the corridor, and cautiously made his way to Doctor Kerr's office, stepping over some broken glass as he went. At each doorway, he stopped and peered around it, checking for the sick, but found nothing but empty—if not destroyed—rooms. The axe was growing heavy in his hands, and he wanted to put it down and rest for a minute. He wasn't as strong as he used to be, no thanks to all the treatments he had been having—not that he'd admit that to anyone. He was stubborn if nothing else.

Doctor Kerr's waiting room door was wide open, greeting him with the same carnage he'd seen in the other rooms, and also empty of any of the sick. He shrugged; maybe things would go okay after all.

"Famous last words," he muttered, flinching at the sound of his own voice. It made him painfully aware of how quiet it was in the building. The receptionist's desk was clear of all the usual crap she usually had on display—photos, files, and twelve bottles of varying shades of pink nail polish. Adam found the sign-in log crumpled beneath the desk and grabbed it, checking to see that the good doctor had in fact signed in that day.

Breathing a sigh of relief, he spotted Dr. Kerr's name and signature. A noise from outside the building had Adam running over to the window, though he wished he hadn't when he got there. About half a dozen of the sick people were crowding around a couple of young men who could only have been seventeen or eighteen years old. The men were jeering the sick people on, and Adam assumed that they either didn't know what the sick would do to them if they caught them, or they were just fucking stupid. He rolled his eyes; probably just fucking stupid. Teenagers these days seemed to think they were invincible. However, maybe they would feel differently if they knew that more of those things had just come around the corner and were now closing in on them from behind.

"Shit!" Adam scratched at his chin. They were backing right up on the sick without even realizing it, and if he didn't warn them they were gonna be human chow very soon. Adam grabbed the secretary's chair and dragged it to the window, unscrewing the small bolt that held the window closed as quickly as he could, and pushed the window open wide.

"Behind you!" he shouted loudly—not loud enough, he realized, since no one paid any attention to him. "Hey! They're behind you," he shouted again, drawing the attention of both the teenage boys and the sick people. He leaned out and pointed down to the sick people making their surprise attack. The boys finally glanced behind them before cursing and making a run for it down a side alley. Some of the sick followed and some of them looked up at him in wonderment, their arms reaching for him, even as high up as he was.

Adam climbed down and hoped to God no one else had heard him shouting—certainly none of those things that might be inside the hospital with him—before going over to the doctor's office to try to find his results. He pushed the handle down and stepped inside, finding Doctor Kerr looking up at him from his desk. His eyes were a milky white, his skin a bland gray, and half his hair was missing where it had been ripped out from his scalp. The doctor stood up from his desk abruptly, tripping over the body of a young girl on the floor, her insides spilling out beside her pink handbag. Doctor Kerr growled as he reached for Adam, and Adam backed away.

"Doctor, if you can hear me, I don't want any trouble." He knew it was pointless trying to talk the doctor down—this was a thing like the others now—but for the past year Doctor Kerr had been his friend, his enemy, and his confidant. The doctor was the only one to have seen him cry, the only one who knew how scared he actually was, and now Adam was going to have to kill him with a fucking axe. This could not be happening.

As the doctor drew close, Adam raised his axe, preparing to put him out of his misery, when the doctor's forehead blew open in a splatter of brown-and-black brains and thick sludge, and the doctor fell to the floor in a bloody heap.

Adam hadn't heard a gun, but his right ear was ringing like crazy, insisting that a bullet had come from that direction. He turned to see a policewoman coming towards him, her gun raised. He lifted his hands to the sky, signaling that he was harmless. "Easy, I'm not one of *them*."

"What are you doing in here?" She grabbed him by the scruff of his neck and slammed him hard against the wall, pinning him in place with her pistol to his head. Her cool gray eyes bored into his and took his breath away. Even under the circumstances, he could appreciate an attractive woman.

"Nothing—shit, I had an appointment!" He shrugged helplessly.

She cocked a dark eyebrow at him. "Right, and you didn't want to let the good doctor down, is that it?" she mocked.

Adam smirked. "Well, you know the cost of missed appointments these days."

A smile touched the corner of her mouth, but she kept her eyebrow raised and her gun aimed at his head without speaking while she waited for more of an explanation.

"I was coming to get my results." He shrugged again.

"Your results?" she repeated.

"Yeah, this is the cancer department. This is Doctor Death's office." He glanced behind her at the dead bodies littering the floor. Doctor Death was what he'd nicknamed Doctor Kerr, since he only ever seemed to have bad news these days. *'Yes, son, the cancer seems to be spreading,' 'sorry, but we are going to have to up the treatments if we're going to win this war against the cancer.'* The joke seemed in bad taste right now though, since Doctor Death was actually dead—twice now, in fact.

The policewoman loosened her grip on him, her eyes taking in his appearance. "I'm sorry, I didn't realize. I wasn't sure if you were one of them," she gestured to Doctor Kerr on the floor, "or a looter." She let go of him and put her gun away.

"What did you think I'd be stealing? X-rays and paperclips?" he snorted.

She ignored his question with a roll of her eyes. "Where are you headed? You know you need to get out of the city, right?

This infection, or whatever the hell it is, has been growing rampant across the city for the past twenty-four hours. It's not safe here anymore; it spread too quickly."

Adam pushed away from the wall. "I'm not going anywhere without my results." It was his turn to raise an eyebrow at her, daring her to try to stop him. The look would have held more strength, though, if he actually had eyebrows, but since the treatments had robbed him of those too, the cop just stared oddly at him.

"Fine, just don't take anything else."

He shook his head, dismissing her, and began rummaging through the doctor's desk. He came across several folders with patient information in them, but after a quick look, he knew they weren't his.

"Twenty percent chance...ninety percent...complete remission," he grumbled as he looked, annoyed that he wasn't the only one who didn't get their results today—though for the ninety percent, perhaps it was best they didn't know.

After checking all the files in the desk and not finding his own, he began to worry. The officer was in the other room, watching out the window, presumably watching more of the sick wandering about. Adam spun in a circle, trying not to panic. If they weren't there, he had no idea where they could be. He lifted his cap and wiped at the sweat building on his head.

"Did you find them?"

He looked up to see the officer watching him, her eyes glancing at his bald head. He shook it once and pulled his cap back down. "They're not there."

"No news is good news, right?" she offered.

"No, absolutely not," he scoffed. "No news means I have no fucking clue if I'm going to die or not."

Their eyes met. She stared intently at him—trying to work him out, no doubt—before he shrugged and looked away. Or maybe she thought he was a complete idiot, since it was highly more likely right now that he was going to be killed by one of the sick people than the cancer.

"I have to know." He swallowed the lump in his throat. "I know it seems ridiculous to you, what with everything else going on right now, but you have no fucking idea what I've gone through for the past nine months. I have to know."

She nodded, opening her mouth to say something, before he cut her off with a raised hand.

"Don't. Whatever you're going to say, just don't. I know you probably knew someone who had cancer, right?" He looked at her and she nodded. "Your brother's sister's, aunt's uncle's fucking goldfish or some shit like that? Well, that ain't the same, lady. This is my life. This is real for me. It's not happening to someone I vaguely know, it's happening to me. And before you start, I don't want your fucking sympathy either—"

"Will you shut up?" Her voice was soft.

"Excuse me?"

"I said, will you shut up?" She raised her eyebrow at him again.

"You know, people like you make me sick. You think you have all the answers, that you know everything just because—"

"I survived it," she stated blankly.

"What?"

"I had cancer, but I survived it. So I do know what you're going through—what you've been through—and all I was going to say was try the filing cabinet in the corner." She went back over to the window again, continuing to scout the area.

Adam felt like a real dick, and for once he didn't have a smart-ass remark to come back with. He made his way over to the cabinet, carefully stepping over the dead woman on the floor, but unfortunately mis-stepping and slipping on some of her guts that had been scattered around. He felt them squelch under his boot, further bodily fluids leaking onto the once plush carpet. He tried not to look; the feeling alone was enough to make him want to throw up—worse than *Betty's* nasty coffee ever had. And that was saying something.

Five.

Adam flipped through the file tabs until he reached *W*, quickly working his way through several files under the initial *A* until he found his own.

A. Walker

He sighed. This was it. This was what he had come for. He pulled out the file, readying himself to look inside.

"Hey, you got what you needed?"

He looked up at the officer, only now taking in the rest of her. Her blonde hair was pulled back into a tight bun, the start of dark roots coming through. Gray eyes, and long lashes, and a small, heart-shaped mouth.

"We need to go. There's movement." She looked at him quizzically as he continued to stare at her. "Dude, we need to go, put your fucking tongue away." Her voice was urgent but quiet, and snapped him back to attention.

He shook the folder at her with a grim smile. "Got it here. Just need to look inside."

"Well you're going to need to keep a hold of that. We need to get out of here now—we have company." She turned on her heel and left.

He folded the file in half and then in half again, shoving it into his back pocket. There obviously weren't many pages in there, but they held so much. The weight of his world was in it.

The officer was in the receptionist's office, stealing a look around the doorframe into the hallway. She stuck her head back in and turned to look at him, holding up two fingers and glancing at his axe on the floor. Adam felt himself flush with embarrassment. *It was a real smooth move, losing your weapon without even realizing it*, he thought. He picked it up without a word and went to her side. She held a finger up to her lips and pointed to the left, and he nodded to show his understanding.

Adam finally caught wind of the smell of the sick people, his face grimacing at the raw scent of rotting sewage they seemed to exude. The sound of them getting closer was enough to have both of them flat against the wall on either side of the door in the hopes that the sick would pass on by. The smell grew worse until the sound of feet dragging and a low moan was right outside. He closed his eyes and held his breath, willing himself not to make another sound. Willing himself not to spew out the meager contents of his stomach.

The sick were right outside—he could almost taste them on the tip of his tongue. Their smell made him feel dizzy, and when he opened his eyes and looked across at the woman, she seemed to be having the same problem. Her hands were in front of her chest, hugging her weapon to her and waiting to fire it. Saliva seemed to build in the back of his throat, and it was taking every ounce of willpower not to swallow it down in fear that the noise would draw the sick's attention. Adam closed his eyes again, feeling a trail of sweat move down the side of his head.

Woof, woof!

Adam's eyes flew open. There was a dog in the hallway. A fucking dog! The moaning started up again, louder now that the sick had something to focus on, louder now that they had a meal in front of them. He heard them moving away, and all the while the dog continued to bark. Adam looked over at the woman, who shrugged her shoulders in confusion; she peered out into the hallway and looked back in, gesturing for him to follow her as she left the room quickly.

He trailed her out, making it to the stairwell as quietly and as quickly as he could. She pushed on the door and Adam cringed as he waited again for the door to squeak. When it didn't, he finally let go of the breath he had been holding and they stepped through into the dark stairwell. As the door began to shut behind him, he took one last glance back at the sick people. They looked like they had once been a doctor and a nurse here at the hospital, but now they were covered in blood, their clothes ripped, and they certainly wouldn't be helping anyone anytime soon. As they continued to move towards the barking with shambling footsteps, a small gap opened up between the two of them, big enough for Adam to see the yellow dog from outside. It had backed itself into a corner and was now baring its teeth and growling, looking equally fierce and petrified as the sick approached it with outstretched arms. Well, as petrified as a dog can look.

"Shit," Adam cursed.

"What?" The officer peered through the small gap and looked back at him, confused.

"I have to help him."

"Him? You know that dog?"

"Sort of. Short version? I can't leave it," he said with a shake of his head.

"And the long version?"

"I can't leave him," he repeated with a sigh.

"Are you fucking serious?" She stared at him, incredulous. "It's a dog!"

"I know, but it just saved our asses." Adam let out a shaky breath and stepped back into the hallway. He cleared his throat to get the sick's attention, and when that didn't work he decided to make his intentions a little clearer. "Excuse me, but can you get the fuck away from *my* dog?" His voice traveled the length of the corridor, and slowly they both turned to look at him.

Vomit rose in his throat at the sight of their disfigured faces. The male doctor's nose had been ripped clean off, baring a bony hole in his face where it had once been; his lower jaw was hanging on by tendons alone, giving a full view of the inside of his mouth. The female's face was perhaps a little worse, with one eye completely gouged out, and the skin on the left side missing, exposing bone and muscle tissue.

The dog took the opportunity to dive between the two and came bounding towards Adam, its tongue lolling to one side. It skidded between him and the door—bumping into the officer, by the sounds of her shout.

Adam took one last look at the sick making their way toward him and shut the door. The dog bounded up at him and began lavishing wet kisses on his hands and face, tail still wagging as it dive-bombed him.

"Thought I told you to go find somewhere safe to hide, damn mutt." He ruffled behind its ears with a genuine smile. "How did you even get up here anyway, Yeller?"

"Yeller?"

Adam looked at the officer with a smirk. "I didn't know his name and he kinda reminded me of that movie, *Old Yeller*. Used to love that movie." He continued to smile as he stroked the dog down. "Speaking of names, I'm Adam." He held out a hand.

The officer looked amused. "I'm Officer Lisa McAndrew. Though I guess the officer part doesn't really make much difference right now."

"You'd be surprised. People find comfort in people of the law, and this could all turn around as quickly as it started."

Lisa looked away. "Not from what I've seen the past twenty-four hours. I'm pretty sure the world as we know it is over."

"That quickly? Don't be ridiculous."

"Yeah, that quickly." She swallowed and looked at her feet.

A banging made all three of them jump as the two sick people reached the door and started smashing their fists against the glass.

Adam flushed, embarrassed. "Better get going. My mother and brother live on a farm out in the sticks, if you want to come," Adam said as they made their way carefully down the stairs, checking for anything or anyone who shouldn't have been there. Yeller ran on ahead, no doubt scouting for them like the movie version of himself.

"I think I'm probably needed here." Even in the dim lighting, Adam could see the worry on her face. "I haven't seen my partner since our shift started last night. In all the confusion last night, we got separated." She swallowed, and the sound echoed to Adam. "To be honest, you're the first person that I've seen that was...healthy?"

"What's wrong with them? Is this it? Armageddon?"

They were passing the next stairwell door and Adam took a look through the window. There were several of the sick people on this floor, and he realized how lucky he had been to not bump into any of them on his way up.

"We don't know." Lisa shrugged. "We started getting calls yesterday morning about people attacking each other. The calls were so widespread, I couldn't even tell you where it all began. There were calls from houses, parks, restaurants," she gestured around them, "hospitals. How did you not notice anything out of the ordinary?" Her forehead scrunched up in confusion.

"I don't have a TV...not anymore, anyway. I live on my own—now, and I'm in a top floor penthouse apartment. That, and I sleep like the—" Adam chuckled.

"What?" Lisa looked at him, even more confused.

"I was going to say 'I sleep like the dead,' but it seemed inappropriate."

He looked at Lisa, her confusion breaking into a smile. She shook her head. "They said that there would be an evacuation of the city at some point, but I'll be damned if there are more than a handful of people left to evacuate."

"Was there a meeting point?" Adam had no idea if he wanted to go to wherever they were evacuating to. He had his family to think of, but watching this woman, he wanted to help her get to the checkpoint.

"By the harbor. I think they're going to load up everyone that's still healthy and take them to an offshore station."

Woof, woof!

Adam and Lisa's eyes locked again at the sound of the barking, and they descended the last set of stairs two at a time. Yeller was barking at the door Adam had come in by, his teeth bared, foam dripping from his lips. In the hallway Adam could see several tortured and destroyed faces of the sick.

"Now what?" Adam said under his breath.

"We either go up...or down. You choose." Lisa shrugged. "Neither seem like good options, but we have to get out of here somehow."

Adam looked at Yeller, who stopped growling, wagged his tail, and trotted off down the last set of steps toward the basement.

Adam and Lisa looked at each other. "Down, then," they both said as they started to follow Yeller.

Six.

The parking basement was darker than the stairwell had been, and Lisa pulled out her flashlight to lead the way. Every now and then Yeller would dart past their legs, making them both jump, but neither seemed to be able to stay mad at him. Scared shitless or not, they both agreed that he was trying to guide them in the right direction. How the hell he knew which way to go was a conundrum, but there it was. They say dogs have a sixth sense about things, and perhaps that's true. Or perhaps the furry little shit was just playing some sort of doggy joke and trying to scare them. Who the hell knew?

Neither of them spoke as they made their way across the parking lot. They had agreed to find a car close to the exit to try and make as little noise as possible—if things went to hell, at least they could make a run for it outside instead of running around in the dark.

Yeller bumped Adam's legs again, and Adam could just make out Yeller looking up at him with his tongue lolling out to the side. Adam couldn't help but smile. Lisa, on the other hand, scowled at the dog. She shone her flashlight around at their feet, trying to minimize the attention that they were bringing to themselves, but every now and then she would give a quick sweep of the flashlight around them. The sick were shambling around in there—somewhere.

The red EXIT sign was in ahead, beckoning them, and they quickened their pace. Lisa pointed to an old white truck and made her way over to it. She checked the doors but found them locked. Adam tugged on her elbow and when she looked around, he pointed to a sleek, silver Mercedes. Lisa rolled her eyes at him and shook her head, continuing to try the passenger door of the truck.

"Ahem," Adam cleared his throat.

He was standing by the Mercedes with a huge grin. He'd always wanted to own a car like that, and with the world gone to shit, it might be the only chance he'd ever have to drive something like this. He tried the handle, knowing it would be locked—but human nature made him check, regardless. What he hadn't banked on was the car's alarm, which began to blare at him, and the car's lights flashing on and off. It was loud, but in such a confined space it was even louder, the sound ricocheting around them.

"Adam!" Lisa looked over to him. "What the hell?" she shouted.

The lights of the Mercedes flashed, giving them both glimpses of the sick coming towards them, the moaning getting louder as they drew closer.

"I didn't think," he shouted back, running over to the truck.

Lisa used her gun to smash a window, the noise adding to the deafening alarm. Reaching in through the broken window, she pulled up the lock and opened the door. Adam ran around to the passenger side as she leaned over and unlocked it for him. He opened the door to climb in and Yeller pushed himself in first, diving onto the seat with a whine. Adam climbed in and shut the door behind him, keeping watch for how close the sick were getting. Lisa ripped the bottom of the dashboard down and grabbed the wires, twisting two together and then sparking them with another one. She hissed in pain as the spark touched her finger, but never once stopped trying. The engine finally roared to life after what seemed an eternity, and Adam breathed a sigh of relief even as the first bloody hand slapped the hood of the car, making him jump.

"Go, go, go!" he yelled.

Lisa began flipping through the compartments of the truck, throwing papers and knickknacks around until she found what she wanted. She grabbed a screwdriver and jammed it into the top of the steering column, hitting it with her other hand as hard as she could. More hands slammed onto the hood, another set quickly joining those. Yeller whined loudly again, his furry dog snout millimeters from Adam's face.

"Come on, Lisa," Adam shouted.

She hit it again, hearing a crunch and finally seeming satisfied. She revved the engine once more, pulling forward into the ever-growing crowd of sick people surrounding them. The Mercedes's lights flashed like a crazy fairground ride, illuminating each vile body for a split second and then enclosing them in total darkness again. Lisa grabbed her seatbelt and slid it over her as she drove forwards, increasing her speed as she pulled free of the mob.

Lisa hit the gas pedal, making the truck lurch forward and knock some of the sick ones down. They fell under the truck, getting crushed under the tires and making the truck rock from side to side. Adam tried to look away from their faces, his eyes landing on Lisa. Her face was a blank page, not a trace of shame or guilt at killing these things—these people. The truck moved free of the sick and Lisa floored it through the plastic barrier and into the sunshine outside. The daylight stung both their eyes, nearly making Lisa crash into the opposite wall before quickly rectifying the over-steer.

"That was too close," she said breathlessly.

"Yep," Adam agreed. He couldn't help worry that this was what life would be like from now on. It had only been that morning when he was in his own little bubble, and the only thing he had to worry about was the cancer. Now? There was *everything* to worry about. Entire families—mothers, wives, children, fathers, brothers, sisters. This sickness had to be stopped—or contained at the very least—before the whole population was wiped out. If this thing was spreading as quickly as Lisa had said, then there wasn't much time.

Adam reached into his back pocket, pulling out the file. With shaking fingers he held it, wondering what news it would contain and whether it would make a difference or not anymore.

Yeller whined into his ear again, licking the side of his face before nuzzling him. Adam reached a hand over and stroked the fur on his head. "I know, boy."

"So do you want to me to drop you off at the harbor with everyone else, or are you going to head to your mother and brother's place?" Lisa didn't look at him as she asked, her eyes watching the sick that they passed.

Adam shrugged. "I don't know. I mean, they should be safe out there, at least for now. It's remote, and David—my brother—he's a gun nut, so he can defend them both, no problem. What could I offer them anyway?" He stared at the brown file, daring himself to open it up. His life—hell, his *future* was in this file.

"You going to open that or what? Seems like an awful lot of trouble you went through, to end up just staring at it," Lisa mocked.

"Yeah, I uh, I'm just...I don't know, building up to it I guess." He glanced out the window. A group of the sick were surrounding something or someone on the ground. Blood covered the sidewalk, dripping down onto the road and trailing away like a river of red. He couldn't help whoever that was, that person was gone—dead. "What are these things?" he asked, watching one of the sick drop the leg it was chewing on and take two shambling steps forward as they passed it.

He looked at Lisa, who glanced sideways at him.

"We've been getting reports on and off for over a week from other districts that people were attacking each other, but it wasn't until last night that it hit us. Me and my partner answered a call at a property not far from the hospital. A husband had come home to find his little boy ripped apart. At first he thought they had been broken into by a gang or something, the Devil's Boys are a notorious gang around these parts, and are known for their viciousness, but this...this was something else. So anyway, the husband started to look for his wife, and he couldn't find her anywhere. The man, he's a wreck—" Lisa paused and took a breath, her voice sounding tight from holding back tears. "Can you imagine coming home to find your child like that? And then not knowing where your wife is?" She shook her head. "So we're taking the report down when we hear a crash from the house next door. Me and my partner, Malcolm, head over there, thinking that it's the fucking Devil's Boys again, but it wasn't…"

Adam stared, waiting for her to continue but already knowing what was coming next.

"It was his wife. But it wasn't her anymore. She was sick, attacking the elderly couple who lived there. Malcolm shot her and I tried to stem the blood flow from the old lady, but then we heard screaming outside. Malcolm ran out, and when the old couple stopped breathing I went outside too, but this was like something I'd never seen before. The world had gone insane; people were all over, running, screaming, fucking *biting* each other. I radioed through to the station to send backup immediately, but for most it was just too damn late." Lisa screeched the truck around a corner, pulling to a stop when she saw there were none of the things about. She wiped her eyes with her sleeve, and for the first time Adam saw the blood all over her hands and uniform.

"Before we knew it, the little old lady and her husband were behind us and ripping into Malcolm like he was a T-bone steak." Lisa sobbed loudly. She rubbed at her eyes with her sleeve again and swallowed before looking at Adam. "So to answer your question, I think they are the dead, zombies, whatever the fuck you want to call them. There is no cure for whatever they have. The only way out is a bullet to the brain—for the living and the dead. Whatever this is, we all have it. It's just a matter of time."

The truck was silent; even Yeller had curled up on the back seat and was watching them both with sad eyes. Adam stared down at the folder in his hand, his name staring back at him, begging him to look inside and seal his fate.

A walker.

He almost laughed at the irony. On the day he was supposed to find out if the cancer was killing him, he'd found out that something else was instead. Adam rolled down his window, tossed the file outside, and rolled the window back up.

"I thought you needed to know?" Lisa asked, confused.

He shrugged. "What's the point? If you're right, we're all dying anyway. May as well make the best use of what little time I have left—whichever is going to kill me." He smiled grimly when she looked confused. "If I look inside and see those results, *it's* won. The cancer fucking won. But I won't fucking let it win, I can't let it win this battle. If I see that I'm dying from cancer…shit, I know I'll just give up—when what I really want to do is go out taking as many of these things, these *zombies* with me."

"Isn't the saying 'the truth will set you free,' not 'hide and pretend it's not happening?'" Lisa asked with a raised eyebrow.

"I'm not hiding, and the truth is we're all dying now, and I'm going to go out fighting, *not* sick. The cancer can kiss my big white ass!" Adam grinned. "Now let's get going, we've got some zombies to kill and people to help."

Lisa barked out a laugh. "To serve and protect?"

"To serve and protect, yes ma'am," Adam laughed. For the first time in nine months, he felt free of the chains the cancer had wrapped around him. This was his life, and it would be his death—his way.

Yeller barked, panting closely to Lisa's face, until she pushed him away. He continued to cover them both with wet kisses, his tail wagging.

"I think we have a third partner," Lisa grinned.

"Looks like we're gonna need it." Adam pointed up ahead to a couple of stumbling sick people.

ABOUT THE AUTHOR

Claire C Riley's work is best described as the modernization of classic, old-school horror. She fuses multi-genre elements to develop storylines that pay homage to cult-classics while still feeling fresh and cutting-edge. She writes characters that are realistic and kills them without mercy.

Claire is the author of "Limerence," "Odium," "Odium Origins," and a proud contributor to 'Let's scare cancer to death.'

She lives in the United Kingdom with her husband, three little girls, and one scruffy dog.

She can be stalked at any of the following:
www.clairecriley.com
https://www.facebook.com/ClaireCRileyAuthor
https://twitter.com/ClaireCRiley

7

Dying Days: Mortality
By Armand Rosamilia

Stephen coughed blood into his dirty handkerchief and jammed it back into his jean pocket. If Laura saw he was still spitting up blood, she'd freak out. He needed to remain strong for her, especially in her time of need.

Laura was riddled with cancer. She'd been on chemo for weeks before the world took a wrong turn, and without a working hospital or electricity her health had taken a wrong turn itself. *It's not fair*, Stephen thought. *I'd trade places with her in a heartbeat if God would let me.* He coughed again and wondered if the Good Lord had taken him up on the offer.

They'd taken a chance a couple of weeks ago, Stephen borrowing their neighbor Shane's pickup truck and driving into Palm Coast, but the hospital was nothing more than a burnt husk; and they'd been attacked by them damn dead folks who still walked and bit at ya. Stephen wasn't proud of having to run a few of them over as he sped back down Route 100, but it was a dog eat dog world out here now. He'd kept his cool and went straight to the meat market, where he piled up the warm meat and all the canned goods he could pack into the pickup truck.

Laura had done better that night, enjoying some of the best grilled burgers, hot dogs, steaks, chicken and pork chops they'd ever had. The couple had spent an hour joking and playing around in the kitchen, taking advantage of the various expensive rubs and sauces they'd managed to take. After forty-three years of marriage, her black-eyed peas and rice were still his favorite, and she'd made an extra helping for both of them. But the meat was long gone, and what they hadn't immediately eaten had begun to turn. They were left with cans of vegetables and rain wa-water, and Stephen couldn't leave his wife long enough to forage farther than his block.

They lived down a dirt road you could only traverse by following another dirt row, their double-wide hidden in a copse of trees and bushes and behind a chain-link fence that wrapped around their two acres. Locals called this area the Mondex. Stephen just called it home. He'd lived here with his wife in this trailer since their wedding day, turning the land from a rocky uneven hill into rows of vegetables, a pen for the pigs and at one time they even had horses.

Stephen stepped outside onto the porch because he felt another coughing fit coming on. The vegetable patch had been overrun with weeds and torn apart by critters, the pigs and horses long gone. The barn was leaning precariously to the left and looked like a strong Florida wind would punch it over.

He was in the midst of a coughing fit, spitting gobs of blood into the bushes lining the porch, when he saw Shane's pickup truck coming down the road. Shane was the nearest neighbor at the end of the road a quarter mile away. He might be one of the only people still breathing right now as well.

"How's it going up here?" Shane asked when he'd parked and gotten out. He carried his shotgun even though I knew he'd been out of ammo for the last week when he went out to try his hand at deer hunting. Shane was a great guy, but not a great shot, and one small deer was brought home; not enough for his family.

His wife Madeline had been sick with the flu or something the last Stephen had heard, but Shane didn't talk about her much lately and Stephen didn't want to pry. If she'd been infected… Stephen wondered what he'd do if his Laura was bitten. Could he handle it? He didn't want to find out.

"Slow," Stephen said. "Just another day in paradise. Any word from the outside?"

"My cousin in Palatka said there was a fire at the paper mill and the Golden Corral was torched, too."

"Shame. I loved that place. They were cheap and they had decent fried chicken."

"Speaking of chicken…" Shane said and smiled. "I found a coop filled with them. I'm going over to try and move it back to my place without losing too many of them. I could use the help, although you don't look so hot."

"I'm fine," Stephen lied. "I just don't know if I can leave Laura for that long is all. I'd hate for something to happen when I was gone."

Shane waved a hand. "I understand. Not a problem. I'll still share my chickens with you when I return."

"That would be mighty neighborly of you. Maybe we'll get your family over here and have a good cookout. Laura might be able to sit up on the porch and at least watch the kids for a while."

"Sounds like a plan." Shane put his rifle on his shoulder and headed back to the truck. "If I can find dumplings I'll bring them along, too."

***

Stephen woke to another coughing fit and pitched off the bed, hitting the floor with both knees and crying out before he was fully awake. Laura was still asleep, chopping down a forest with her snoring. At least she'd fallen out.

He went to the porch and tapped his pocket unconsciously with a sigh. He'd given up his pipe and smoking years ago but still wished for the taste of it in his mouth and the smoke curling over his head while he listened to nature around him. Laura had been a big fan of healthy eating and clean living since they'd both had health scares in their forties. *Not that it helped any*, he thought and sighed again. *She was inside dying, and I'm outside doing the same.*

Shane hadn't returned and that couldn't be a good thing. No way would he go through the trouble of asking for help and then not coming back once the job was complete to brag about doing it by himself. Stephen didn't want to take a walk down the road, especially in the dark, to find out if he was home.

Something tapped against the chain-link fence to his right, but it was too dark to see anything. Stephen didn't move, looking with his bad eyes and wishing he had a weapon. One of Laura's big moves back in the day had been not having guns in the house. Of course, the hunting cabin west of Palatka was filled with the rifles he'd been able to hide from her. He knew she knew they were there, but it was an unspoken thing. After all, Stephen was a hunter. He'd been a hunter since he could walk, and he came from a long line of proud men who shot their own dinner. She knew it and she let him go off every now and then with the other men. As long as she didn't ask where the deer came from, he didn't tell; Win-win, as they say.

He hoped the perimeter was secure. Every morning at first light he'd spend an hour walking his property slowly, looking for problems. So far so good. He'd cut down some branches and even had Shane help him secure more chain-link fence from abandoned houses in the Mondex. You could never have enough fencing. If Stephen was a younger man he would be running a second line of fence around his property as well, so if there were gaps in the first line of defense he'd have time to repair it.

He knew he was running out of time.

Something hit the fence and shook it. How he wished he'd hidden one of his rifles in the tool shed. He didn't want to turn on a flashlight because out here, in the middle of nowhere, it would be a beacon for them.

Stephen felt another coughing fit coming on but he had no-where to go. Inside he might wake his wife but outside it would attract the dead. He went into the living room and buried his face in the couch cushion, coughing and staining it with his blood.

**

"Are you sure you'll be alright for a few minutes?"

Laura waved at him before closing her eyes again.

"I'm just going down to make sure Shane and Madeline are alright. I won't be but a minute. Can I get you anything before I go?"

"Go," she whispered. "I need sleep."

Stephen had spent the last hour sharpening one of the extra wooden fence slats, knowing it wasn't much but it would work in a pinch. He had two of his wife's steak knives on him but he didn't relish the thought of close combat with a monster. At least the five foot wood might keep them at bay long enough he could escape, although his creaking legs and weak ankles were telling him something completely different.

He hadn't spent the morning walking the fence line but there was nothing out of the ordinary to see. There weren't any dead people wandering outside his property. The road was emp-ty, birds singing in their perches and even the grunt of a wild boar in the distance caught his ear.

It took Stephen much longer to traverse the well-worn road, careful not to step into the rivulets years and years of pickup trucks had cut into it. In his younger days, he would've jogged down the road. But that was many years ago.

When he finally got to Shane's property, he leaned against the fencepost and gasped for air. Even a slow walk had winded him. Stephen was going to call out but he couldn't catch his breath.

Shane's pickup truck wasn't in the driveway.

Stephen looked around to see if anything was out of place but the day was beautiful, a slight breeze in the trees and the bright sun beating down on the clay. The actual double-wide was set back behind a shielding of trees. The only way you'd know someone lived out here was because of the fence and the dirt driveway that ran past the home. There was a set of garbage cans on a cement block just in sight and usually where Shane parked his truck. A rock walkway led to the door of the trailer.

Stephen went to the door and knocked. He kept his eyes peeled for movement, even though it looked like Shane's fence was intact. You never knew, and the back end of it was butting against the woods behind them. It would be easy for someone to climb over undetected and if there was a breach you'd never know until it was too late.

Shane kept saying he was going to clear it back so there would be better sight lines but Stephen knew he wasn't going to do it. He hoped the man was still alive to procrastinate.

He knocked again. Had Shane taken his wife with him to fetch the chickens? Stephen suddenly felt sick to his stomach. What if he'd talked her into going and something horrible had happened? Stephen would feel so guilty.

Another coughing fit came on suddenly and Stephen tried to be courteous and spit the phlegm and blood into the bushes and not get any on the trailer or the porch. When he saw how much blood he'd discharged he sighed. It was getting worse and worse.

A four-point deer ran through the yard, stopping every twenty feet or so and ears pricked. Stephen watched in awe as this thing of beauty, this gift from God, moved so powerful and graceful. He also wished he had his rifle because venison right about now would be a godsend as well.

Once the deer was out of sight he tried the knob on the trailer and found it unlocked. Knowing you didn't blindly walk into someone's home especially in these parts where everyone owned more than one weapon, he opened the door wide but didn't enter. "Hello? Shane? Madeline? It's Stephen. Anybody home?"

He reluctantly went in, not knowing if his worst fears would be realized: either they were both gone and he'd assume dead, or just Madeline was left with no sign of Shane. Either way he was sad.

The bedroom door was open and he went to it. "Madeline? Hello? Anyone home?"

He heard what sounded like a whimper. What if she was one of those things now? What if Shane had seen her turn into a monster but couldn't kill his wife? So he'd left?

Stephen held the sharpened stick in front of him and entered the bedroom slowly, the bed coming into view.

It was worse than Stephen thought.

Madeline looked gaunt, napkins and tissues covered in blood on the floor. She was asleep but breathing heavily, wheezing and whimpering.

When Stephen took a step closer Madeline's eyes popped open. "Stephen?" she whispered.

He nodded. "How are you?"

She smiled faintly and closed her eyes. "I'm dying of cancer."

***

Stephen didn't ask Madeline where Shane was. He figured he already knew the answer, and the selfish part of him wished the pickup truck was still here, because he wanted to flee. Take the two sick women and drive until he couldn't drive anymore. To where? He didn't know. He didn't know if anyone else was still alive.

"You got family in Palatka?" Stephen asked her an hour later when she opened her eyes. He'd been snooping around their trailer, inventorying their food and water in his mind and feeling guilty for doing it. But he couldn't leave her until he'd at least talked to her, even though his wife was in the same predicament down the road.

"Shane does. I'm not a big fan of some of them." She stared at Stephen. "Is that where my husband is?"

Stephen shrugged. "I don't know. I hope he's found us a safe haven. Maybe the military found him when he went to get the chickens."

"I told him not to go if you weren't going with him, but he said it was for the best because Laura is also so sick."

"I didn't know you had cancer."

She smiled faintly. "Shane didn't want to say anything, especially after we knew she was sick. You know my husband. He's so quiet to begin with. He didn't want to burden anyone else with our problems."

"I wish I'd known. Shane and I could've talked about it."

"Swapped war stories about your dying wives? He wouldn't want to do it," Madeline said. "He might even be upset you're here. It's just who he is."

"Can you get out of bed?"

"Only on my better days. Usually I stay right here."

"Same with Laura. She can't get out of bed most days, and lately even on her good ones. I'm really worried, especially without the hospital."

Madeline began to cry softly.

"What's the matter?"

"I'm going to die."

"No, not at all," Stephen said, knowing how stupid it was to say.

Madeline wiped eyes and smiled. "We're all going to die. I'm just going to go much sooner."

"I need to get you to my trailer or Laura here. I can't go back and forth."

Stephen's knees were hurting him and he didn't want to take the long walk back and forth and was hoping Madeline was in better shape than Laura and could walk. He needed to protect both women and needed them in one place.

He sighed. "I need to check on my wife. I'll be back."

***

There were two of them at the end of the road, stumbling through the spot where Stephen had dumped the topsoil last spring. They hadn't noticed him but he didn't dare move.

As slow as they were, he was even slower today. He'd woken this morning with his right ankle swollen from trudging back and forth to Madeline the last two days. Caring for his wife was a fulltime job, and now he had to double it and walk at his age.

Stephen didn't know how long he could do it. *Is it bad I wish one of them would pass?* he thought and looked to the heavens. *God, what should I do? And is it bad I just thought of my own wife dead?*

Shit. One of the zombies turned and looked directly at him with bloodshot eyes. And Stephen knew him. It was the Hutsell husband, and the other zombie was probably his wife. They owned a little farm about a mile away and directly through the woods from here. They'd wandered over and by the looks of them they'd been busy. Blood covered their mouths, hands and what was left of their clothing.

Stephen turned as gently as he could, trying to keep the pressure off his worse leg. He dragged his foot and shimmied sideways down the road. He used the board he carried as a cane.

He glanced back to see both of them were following at about the same pace he was moving. Stephen was reminded of an old episode of Seinfeld, where George Costanza is in a cart because his employer thinks he's handicapped, and he's being chased by a pack of older people in their own carts. Stephen thought he'd give anything for one of those carts right now.

The fence line for Shane's property was in sight but it looked like it was ten miles away. Under normal conditions Stephen had a rough time getting to the gate, and now, added pursuit was going to be the death of him. What would the women do? Slowly rot in their beds in agony or die of starvation since neither could help themselves?

A glance back told him the zombies were pacing but now another had joined from the woods. If one appeared closer he'd be in trouble, especially between him and the gate.

Stephen couldn't remember what his last words to his wife had been. She'd been sleeping soundly when he left. Last night he'd said goodnight, but had he told her he loved her or kissed her? He didn't know. Now he wished he'd kissed her even if she was snoring. Each moment needed to be precious, because it could be the last.

And it was looking like it was going to be his last, because a young girl appeared from the woods, blank look and missing an arm. She shuffled to cut Stephen off just as he reached the fence, but he had at least a hundred feet until he reached the gate, and he'd need time to open it with his arthritic fingers.

The little girl zombie was slightly faster than Stephen, and he had to chuckle at the irony of a dead person being faster than he was. At least he thought it was ironic. He never did understand the subtlety of the English language, and his ninth grade education sometimes tripped him up, but he more than made up for it with worldly experience. Stephen tried to will his body to move quicker.

He reached the gate the same moment the zombie was in reach and he poked her in the face with his board, but he was too weak to do more than keep her at bay. With his free hand he unlatched the gate. He could see the other two zombies in his peripheral vision.

The little zombie shifted to her right just as he thrust the board and it caught the side of her shoulder. Stephen tried to keep it balanced in his hand but he lost his grip and it fell. He popped open the gate and fell backwards onto the gravel road.

The other two zombies were against the fence and closing.

"God, please give me the strength," he yelled, more to psyche himself up before he completely panicked and covered his face.

He kicked out at the gate, managing to get it closed, but he couldn't lock the catch. He slid forward and kept his foot on the bottom of the gate.

All three zombies were pushing against it, but they couldn't get it open.

Stephen rolled onto his side, keeping his foot in place, and pushed up on one elbow. He shimmied closer to his feet and hooked his hand in the fence, careful not to get bitten. After several grueling moments he was able to pull himself up enough to reach the latch and click it into place.

He rolled over and stared at the long walk still needed to get to the trailer itself.

***

"What happened to you?" Madeline asked when Stephen stumbled into the bedroom. "You look like you got dragged around for a bit."

"I did. I'll live," he said and smiled. He was still out of breath and his ankle was one massive throbbing pain. "How are you today?"

"I want to die," Madeline said.

Stephen didn't know what to say. "Can I get you something to eat?"

Madeline smiled. "I want you to kill me."

"No…"

Madeline was staring at his ankle, swollen and stretching his jeans. "You can't keep doing this. They'll catch you one of these times and then Laura will be left alone."

"So will you."

Madeline looked away. "I'm already alone now that Shane is…gone. Maybe he found a younger, better model of me in this crazy new world. He's probably getting married to her right now, with zombies in the bridal party. We got married by Minister Boyette in Jacksonville. It was such a small wedding, but so nice. He looked so handsome."

"I'll make this work," Stephen said. "I just need to find a golf cart or a car."

"Where will you find one? If it's more than a mile away it will take you hours to walk to it with your busted knee. Stephen, please do us all a favor and kill me. I feel worse every day and I don't have the will to live. I don't want to survive another few days or weeks in pain. The cancer won't magically clear up. It will get far worse than this. I'm lucid right now. I want this to end before I slip further and further into the disease. You're my only hope. I'm too weak to even run a razor across my wrists and be done with it."

Stephen shook his head and felt awful because he was agreeing with her inside but couldn't say it out loud. There was no real point to any of this anymore. If it weren't for Laura, he would have ended it weeks ago himself.

"You have to," Laura said and began to cry. "I don't want to live."

"I can't...how would I do it, anyway?"

"There are knives in the drawer in the kitchen."

"No way."

"Take the pillow and smother me. I can't fight you."

"I don't have the strength to do it."

"Yes, you do. More than me. Plus, all you have to do is put it over my face and lean onto me. Your weight will help," Madeline said.

"No."

"Do it," she said and tried to pull the pillow from underneath her head.

"Let me help you," Stephen said, feeling awful again but knowing what he had to do.

***

Stephen wrapped his swollen ankle after slicing the legs off his jeans. He couldn't remember the last time he'd worn shorts.

He put all of the remaining food, water and supplies into a blanket and tied an end to his belt loop. He'd need to take everything worth anything with him so he and Laura would survive another few weeks.

Stephen stepped outside, the blanket dragging behind him, when he saw the pickup truck in the driveway. He was dumbfounded for a second until he saw a smiling Shane.

"Hey, buddy, I'm back. I found us a great place to stay, too. On the other side of Green Cover Springs. It's going to be a drive, but we can load up the truck and all four of us can get to safety. They have animals and crops and a clean water source." Shane seemed to notice the blanket for the first time.

Stephen looked away guiltily.

"Is that all my stuff? Where's Madeline?"

ABOUT THE AUTHOR

Armand Rosamilia is a New Jersey boy currently living in sunny Florida, where he writes when he's not watching the Boston Red Sox and listening to Heavy Metal music... and because of him they won the 2013 World Series, so he's pretty good at watching!

He's written over 100 stories that are currently available, including a few different series:

"Dying Days" extreme zombie series

"Keyport Cthulhu" horror series

"Flagler Beach Fiction Series" contemporary fiction

"Metal Queens" non-fiction music series

He also loves to talk in third person... because he's really that cool. He's a proud Active member of HWA as well.

You can find him at http://armandrosamilia.com for not only his latest releases but interviews and guest posts with other authors he likes!

And e-mail him to talk about zombies, baseball and Metal: armandrosamilia@gmail.com

8

Gift Wrapped Box
By Catie Rhodes

This story, especially its brave main character, is dedicated to my Gran who had the spirit and courage of a Viking warrior trapped in her sick, old body. The cancer may have taken her, but it never beat her.

The doctor recited Kaylee's death sentence in monotone, sounding like a kid called to the front of class to read embarrassing poetry. Kaylee understood his words just fine. Two months to live. Maybe more. Maybe less.

Her lips went numb as all the blood in her head roared in her ears. She felt this way once before—the night highway patrol came and said her parents died in a car crash. Same as then, she couldn't think. A white wall of shock blanketed her thoughts, protecting her for the time being. All she could think was, *I'm going to die.* Those words ran on endless loop until her lips formed them, tingling as feeling returned.

"Pardon?" The doctor interrupted his speech and stared at her across the desk at her, his liver-spotted hands resting on her file. "Did you say something?"

Had she? She didn't know. Maybe she'd spoken out loud. She shook her head, and he went back to his speech.

The son of a bitch didn't care if she lived or died. This was a script for him, a tragedy he played out again and again. She found her anger and clung to it, still unable to listen as the doctor talked about chemotherapy and hospice. She snorted and drummed her fingers on her thigh. It was her life they were talking about here, not a TV show. And here this jackass sat, talking like he was practicing for fucking toastmasters.

"Ms. Ferguson?" The doctor was obviously waiting for an answer. She didn't have a clue what he'd asked and said so.

"Your son. Do you have relatives who can care for him when you are unable?" He looked at his hands again, studying the manicured fingernails.

Terror surged through her, chasing away the shock and the anger. Landon. No, she didn't have relatives who could take him, not unless she counted Austin. And she didn't. Austin was twenty-two and full of dreams and schemes. With Austin, Landon would likely end up in foster care, where she lived after the night the highway patrolman came. But Landon was only five. He would grow up in the system, whereas she only spent three years. Her stomach writhed, the fear pitching and rolling inside her. A sneak preview of Landon growing to adulthood in the system flickered in the abyss of her imagination. Panic and fury choked her. She couldn't leave her baby to fend for himself.

She knew what she had to do. Not die. At least not until Landon was old enough to take care of himself.

"What about one of those clinical trials?" she shouted over the doctor's speech. He jerked as though slapped and leafed through her file.

"I'm sorry, Ms. Ferguson—Kaylee. There's nothing open right now. I'm afraid by the time you applied and were accepted, it would be too late." He arranged his face into a sympathetic expression. "Your time would be better spent getting your affairs in order."

She stood and grabbed her purse. She didn't need to hear more. This joker couldn't help her.

"Where are you going?"

Not bothering to answer, she bumbled to the door, tears blinding her. She found herself alone in the reception area and sat down in one of the uncomfortable chairs, put her face in her hands, and sobbed. Someone tapped her shoulder. She cut off her sobs, quick and clean, and wiped tears off her flaming cheeks. Struggling to regain her dignity, she focused on the stranger bent over her.

The most noticeable thing about this woman was the care she'd taken with her appearance. The eye shadow hid wrinkles rather than emphasizing them. Her lipstick was on her lips, rather than in the fine lines around them. Her teeth, obviously victims of a professional whitening, gleamed. She wore heels, but not too high. A royal blue dress with a wide black belt completed the look.

Kaylee was suddenly aware of her frayed blue jeans and t-shirt. These clothes worked fine at the tattoo parlor she co-owned with her brother.

"I'm sorry. I needed to…" Exactly what did she need to do? Erase the doctor's diagnosis?

"No need to apologize. If you're here, you're probably dealing with more than you can handle." The older woman plucked a tissue from the cardboard box on the end table and handed it to Kaylee. "Do you mind if I sit?"

"Of course not." Kaylee turned her head to wipe the tears and snot off her face. She wondered if this woman was some kind of social worker. The lady had that air about her, one of someone who worked in the system. Gathering herself, she waited for the woman to speak. The first rule Kaylee learned during her many years in the system was to never speak first.

"I'm Lily Geis." She held out a perfectly manicured hand. "And you are?"

"Kaylee Ferguson." She grasped Lily's Geis's hand and felt a moment of revulsion, which made no sense. Maybe it was the cancer. Already killing her judgment.

"I thought I overheard you ask Dr. Martin if he could get you into a clinical trial." Lily crossed her legs, her pantyhose whispering.

"He couldn't." Kaylee wondered how the woman heard anything through the doctor's door but figured it didn't matter at this point.

"I'm surprised he didn't mention Dr. Bubb's trial." Lily cocked her head to the side, frowning.

"Dr. Bubb?" Kaylee strained against the feeling of relief. This could turn into nothing. She might not qualify. It might not work. Even with those thoughts firmly in the forefront of her mind, Kaylee allowed herself a glimmer of hope.

Lily took a card from her purse, started to hand it to Kaylee, then hesitated. "Perhaps Dr. Martin had his reasons for not mentioning Dr. Bubb's trial. His methods are controversial."

"I don't care." Kaylee snatched the card. "I'll do anything not to leave my son an orphan."

Outside in the parking garage, Kaylee dialed Dr. Bubb's number with shaking fingers. The call connected and rang once, twice, three times.

"Please answer," she whispered through trembling lips.

"Dr. Bubb speaking."

Weeping with relief, Kaylee poured out her story and the reasons she needed this clinical trial.

"I can't believe Dr. Martin didn't mention me." Dr. Bubb sounded indignant. Kaylee hoped he gave Dr. Martin a piece of his mind. Uncaring sonovabitch. "Come right over to my office. You can fill out the paperwork. If it looks good, we'll start today. But I have to warn you. I'm unconventional. My methods require faith as much as anything else."

Kaylee didn't have much faith, but she tapped the address into the GPS and promised she'd be right over.

***

Driving to Dr. Bubb's office, Kaylee buzzed with hope. For the first time since old Dr. Parsons, her gynecologist, called her in to discuss his suspicion she might have ovarian cancer, the cold tendrils of dread were gone.

Her GPS led her to a rundown part of town where trash littered the gutters and buildings looked ready to collapse. A little fear returned. She did a double take and checked the slip of paper with Dr. Bubb's address. No. She hadn't made a mistake. Kaylee parked on the street and craned her neck to look at the building.

In the fifties, it had probably been nice. Now it was dirty, needed pressure washing, and looked mostly empty. At the door, she ran her finger over the names listed, almost hoping she'd made a mistake. She could call Dr. Bubb, ask him to repeat his directions. Then she found his name. Her finger shook as she pressed the buzzer.

The elevator didn't work. She climbed four flights of stairs to Dr. Bubb's office. In high school, she'd been able to run a five-minute mile. Now, she almost passed out climbing the stairs to the fourth floor. Black dots swam in her vision, and her stomach lurched. She sank to sit on the top step, cold sweat dripping from her chin. Any stray hope she wasn't really sick evaporated.

The stairwell door cracked open. A tall man with an expensive haircut stuck his head around the door and gasped.

"Ms. Ferguson. I'm Dr. Bubb." He stepped into the stairwell. His brown hair and eyes and high cheekbones hinted at exotic ancestry. His perfectly tailored suit hung on his lean frame like it belonged there. "When you never made it to my office, I became worried." He leaned over and offered his hand. Their fingers touched. Kaylee's insides shrank. Despite Dr. Bubb's handsomeness, his touch felt cold, impersonal, somehow wrong. She pulled away and used the handrail to pull herself to a standing position.

"I am so sorry." Dr. Bubb acted as though nothing had happened. "The elevator went kerplunk this morning, and I..."

Kaylee quit listening as he helped her into his office. She couldn't believe the ache of fatigue that had taken up residence in her bones. It begged her to take a break, and she knew there'd be no rest for her. Not when she needed to get well.

The astringent smell Kaylee had grown accustomed to over the last few weeks was absent from Dr. Bubb's offices. In its place was another odor, its spiciness reminding her of a Hare Krishna temple she visited when she first moved to Houston. She eased into a chair in front of his desk, and he walked around to the other side. Opening a wooden file cabinet, he took out a sheaf of papers, attached them to a clipboard and passed the set-up to her.

"You mentioned time is of the essence during our phone conversation." He steepled his fingers under his chin. "You fill out those forms, and I'll tell you a little about my trial."

Kaylee started writing. She could fill out medical forms in her sleep by now. This one asked all the usual questions, plus a few more. Mostly about family. Since she only had Austin and Landon, there wasn't much to write. As she wrote, she became aware of how still the air felt, how quiet the building. Compared to the bustling doctor's offices she'd been sitting in lately, it was a relief to her senses.

"My theory about cancer, and all other illnesses, is that the person's determination to get well has a lot to do with their survival."

Kaylee nodded and kept writing. A nasty tickling feeling settled over her skin. It felt like walking through spider's webs, leaving residue she needed to brush off. The sensation grew so intense, she stopped writing and swiped at her arms. She caught Dr. Bubb watching her.

"My other theory about these chronic illnesses is they're a poison in the system of the afflicted. One that must be purged. That's what I help you do. I help you purge your illness."

The last page of the paperwork consisted of an agreement full of long paragraphs and tiny words. Without reading it, she signed and handed it back to the doctor. "I'll do anything to get rid of this. My son, my Landon, would be parentless if I died." She leaned forward. "I can't die, Dr. Bubb."

The man nodded, a smile spreading over his face. "That's exactly what I like to hear, Kaylee Ferguson. Are you ready to get started?"

The question took her aback. "Really? There's no more hoops to jump through?"

"You've jumped through enough hoops to last a lifetime."

"Ain't that the truth?" The two shared a conspirator's laugh. Dr. Bubb stood and opened a narrow door behind his desk. He turned, holding a small square box. Its foil wrapping gleamed in the overheads, and bouncy curls of ribbon dangled from its sides. She frowned. How could this cure her cancer? Did Dr. Bubb gift each of his patients with some token? He took in her wonder and smiled even more broadly.

"This next part will seem odd." He set the box on her lap.

It seemed to weigh nothing. Coolness spread out from where it sat, seeping into her body. Her toes, fingers, and the tip of her nose grew numb with the cold.

"I want you to promise you'll bear with me." Dr. Bubb's brown eyes managed to convey vulnerability and charm at the same time. "Make no predictions on whether this method will work until you've seen it in action."

Kaylee pulled on one of the ribbons, watching as it bounced back. She glanced at Dr. Bubb and nodded. At this stage, nothing could hurt, and it just might help.

"I'm going to put the tips of my fingers on your forehead, right between your eyes. I want you to look inside yourself, locate your illness, and send it toward my fingers."

Unable to help herself, she giggled. This was the silliest thing she'd ever heard. *Think* her cancer at Dr. Bubb's fingers? Was he kidding? Some kind of joke? One look at his face told her it was not.

Sadness, so bone deep it seemed like an extra person, settled into Kaylee. This was bullshit. It wouldn't get rid of the cancer. In a few months, she'd be dead. Landon would be in Austin's custody or in foster care. She wondered if she could find adoptive parents for him before she went tits up. Probably not. At five, her baby was too old. Her throat tightened, tears welling up in her eyes. She wanted to fling the box into the charlatan's face. Beat him for wasting precious minutes of her life.

"Don't dismiss it until you try it," Dr. Bubb whispered and placed his fingers on her forehead.

At first, nothing happened. Then, Kaylee felt a hot spot inside her. The cancer started in her ovaries, but now she felt it through her body. How would she ever find the right place? Some part of her brain she'd never used before searched for it, found it inside her pelvis, and surrounded it, and pulled until it was freed. The mass of pain and sickness traveled through her faster, faster, faster, until it hit the bone of her skull right underneath Dr. Bubb's fingers. He took a deep breath, and she felt it leave her.

Dr. Bubb's face turned purple, his eyes bulging. He pressed his fingers onto the beautifully wrapped box. It grew warm on her legs and began to chitter, creating a sound like tall grass blowing in the wind. The box swelled, pulsing, as a glow came from inside. The glow matched the red of the sickness in Kaylee's mind. Just when she thought the box would burst, it shrank back to its original size. The heat from it faded.

"Still don't believe?" Dr. Bubb smiled.

Kaylee felt her face stretch into a grin. Wonder, the sort she hadn't felt in many years, danced inside. Something akin to fear hid behind it. She ignored it and met Dr. Bubb's gaze. They were conspirators again.

"Your illness is within that box," Dr. Bubb said. "But it'll need another host within the next twenty-four hours. It's your job to find one."

"What? I have to give someone else my cancer?"

"Choose well. The cancer is in its most aggressive form right now." He drew forth a gold watch and, after snapping it open to glance at the time, slipped it back into his pocket.

Kaylee's eyes followed the watch, mesmerized by the way the worn gold caught the light and the blue stone winked at the stem. The doctor seemed to notice her interest but only smiled.

"You might have had a couple of months left, dear Kaylee, but the box's recipient will only have days. Hours if they're already in bad health."

"But they'll die." Kaylee's heart pounded in her chest. She couldn't kill, could she? But what of her precious, innocent son growing up in foster care? She would do anything, including kill another, to save him from that.

Dr. Bubb watched her face as she thought. His eyes crinkled at the corners and sparkled.

"All the more reason to choose well."

***

Kaylee left Dr. Bubb's office, the box tucked safely into her bag, fairly sure she'd participated in an elaborate joke. But standing in the stairwell, looking at all those flights of stairs, a bolt of energy surged through her. She took the first few steps tentatively, waiting for that bone deep fatigue to set in. It never did. She reached the bottom barely winded.

It was easier because you were going down, not up. Her body said different. The insidious symptoms, subtly invading her life for no telling how long weren't there. She found herself believing Dr. Bubb's weird cure might have worked. If so, she had less than twenty-four hours to give her sickness to someone else.

The idea scared her. Who was she to play God? She couldn't give it to just anybody. It had to be someone at least a little evil. Kaylee got into her car, searching her mind for the right person. As she drove to the tattoo salon, she said the names of potential recipients of the box aloud.

By the time she arrived at Fevered Dreams in Ink, she knew exactly who deserved her cancer. She breezed into the tattoo salon, the familiar buzz of the tattoo gun and disinfectant soap bringing a smile to her face. She tucked her purse and the box in the drawer where she always kept it at the reception counter.

"How'd it go? Good news at the doctor?" Austin leaned over a nervous kid getting fashion statement ink he'd regret in ten years.

"The best news." They exchanged a smile.

"Told you so." Austin was still young and inexperienced enough to believe things turned out fine on their own. He earned enough money with his tattooing, which Kaylee had taught him herself, not to starve. That was all he cared about.

"I've got an appointment in half an hour. After that, I'm knocking off early, spending the evening with Landon. Can you handle this?" Kaylee knew Austin would put up the "Closed" sign as soon as things got slow, but tonight she didn't care. Tonight she had business. She barely heard Austin's mumbled agreement. She was too busy thinking about the gift.

She prepped and sanitized her work station. Her client, a guy working on a full back piece, arrived. They exchanged greetings. Kaylee turned on the stereo and got to work and got to thinking.

Ellie Grimes, her downstairs neighbor in the apartment complex where she lived. Ellie, a single, sour-faced, middle-aged woman, hated both Kaylee and Landon. When they made too much noise, she beat her ceiling to let them know. Never mind her loud TV at all hours. That alone didn't make Kaylee want to kill her. It was the situation with Smokey, a little gray abandoned kitten Landon discovered.

Kaylee let Landon feed the kitten on their doorstep because the animal was too wild to handle at first. She promised Landon he could keep Smokey for a pet if he could tame him. Landon patiently fed Smokey until the animal finally allowed itself to be petted. Ellie told him Smokey would break his heart. The old bat went as far as setting out a live trap with an open can of tuna inside. Kaylee disabled the trap, tearing it up in the process. The two women almost came to blows. Ellie finally backed off.

Landon made progress with Smokey. Kaylee called area vets and asked about bringing the cat in for shots and neutering. One day, Smokey showed up lethargic and hissed when Landon tried to pet him. The poor thing vomited blood before he wandered off. The next morning, they found Smokey dead with no wounds. Ellie Grimes never said a word, but Kaylee knew with a mother's intuition the horrid bitch poisoned Smokey.

Well, she had a surprise for Ellie Grimes.

Kaylee's client paid and left. Tired, she wandered into the break room and grabbed a juice from the refrigerator. Austin sat at the table.

"These chocolates ain't no good, sis." He spoke with his mouth full of something black and slimy.

Kaylee recoiled from the disgusting sight, her mind still on how she'd present the gift to Ellie, and sat down at the cheap card table. Then she saw the foil wrapping scattered around the box and the colorful curls of ribbon on the table. The inside had the same plastic shell as a candy box. All the rounded indentions stood empty, their contents already consumed, except for one. A black ball sat in it. It could have been chocolate, but it wasn't.

"Don't eat that." She knocked over her juice as she stood and slapped the box away from Austin.

"Shit," he yelled. "Don't get so excited. I'll replace them."

"But you...you can't eat those." Kaylee didn't know how to explain to her brother what he'd done. He'd signed his own death warrant. She looked into his eyes, those same eyes she'd looked into for twenty-two years. Grief buckled her knees. She'd killed her brother. She gripped the edge of the table, ignoring the sticky juice pooling around her feet. A nasty, bitter cat murderer wouldn't get the gift after all. Her sweet, devil-may-care brother would die for her selfishness.

"Don't get upset," Austin whined. "I'll replace them. You know how I can smell chocolate. And I've been here all day while you were at the doctor's. No lunch. I'm sorry, sis." He reached out and touched her arm.

"No." She took a trembling breath, willing herself not to screech at the horror of what she'd done. "You did nothing wrong. I was going to give those as a gift." She sat heavily in the metal chair.

Austin stood and went to the sink where he gathered cleaning products. He returned and began cleaning Kaylee's mess. She forced herself out of her chair and helped him. Kaylee's whole body stung with the impact of what she'd done. Austin took the last of the paper towels to the garbage can, and she knelt dazed on the floor.

"So what was the good news?" He bit into one last chocolate, grimacing, and finally tossing it back into the box.

"I don't have cancer." Kaylee gave him the response she'd prepared on the drive from Dr. Bubb's office. Her voice sounded hollow and monotone, like it came from a robot. Or a killer. "It was a false alarm." She tried to smile, but it felt like stretching uncooked dough.

"That's great." Austin gathered her into a hug and kissed the top of her head. "I didn't know what I was going to do, how I'd run this place, without you."

I didn't either.

Austin winced and broke the hug. He turned around, holding his stomach. He cried out, running in the direction of the bathroom. Alone, Kaylee put her face in her hands. She couldn't live with herself if Austin died. Even though she didn't always like the things he did, she loved him fiercely. They were all each other had.

The toilet flushed. Austin reentered the room pale-faced and sat heavily at the table.

"I think that chocolate made me sick."

"Go on home. I'll close up."

"But you were going to celebrate with Landon." He stood but immediately fell back into his seat.

"No...you go on. Pick him up from day care and tell him I'll be home as soon as I can."

It took a little more convincing, but not much. Austin was as sick as she'd ever seen him. Soon as he drove away, Kaylee turned the sign in the door to "Closed" and returned to the break room.

She had to undo this horrible thing she'd done.

***

This time, Kaylee noticed the numerous broken windows in Dr. Bubb's building. The front door hung ajar, the glass busted out and scattered over the vestibule. She stopped in her tracks, trying to figure out how this level of damage occurred in the last four hours. Crunching through the glass, she crept inside the dark building.

The smell, a combination of piss and puke, assaulted her. She clapped one hand over her lower face and stifled a gag. The elevator hung open, the car full of garbage. The brightly lit stairwell she used earlier was gray with fading daylight. Kaylee took a step toward it and stopped. Something bad happened in this place since her last visit. No telling what waited in that stairwell. As if on cue, a shuffling sound echoed through the old, obviously empty building. Kaylee jerked and tried to figure out where it came from.

Her instincts screamed at her to leave this place, to get far, far away before something awful happened. *What about Austin?* If Dr. Bubb told her the truth, Austin had days at best. He'd die of her cancer. It would be her fault. Every day she lived, it would be with the knowledge that she killed her brother. Kaylee picked up a tire iron from the debris on the floor.

This time, she didn't hesitate but went straight to the stairwell and started climbing. At the fourth floor, Dr. Bubb's floor, she eased the door open. The door hinges groaned. Gathering the last of her courage and tightening her grip on the tire iron, Kaylee marched down the hall to the office.

She stood at the door for a long time, unable to believe her eyes. The glass in the door twinkled on the office floor. It was old, dirty, indicating it had been there a while. Spray painted symbols covered the walls, which had been clean and freshly painted that morning. Confusion prickled at her skin, bunching her muscles into knots, mutating into stabbing needles of terror.

She stepped into the office and winced at the stench. This room, while free of the reek of human waste, smelled of roasting flesh. Her foot crunched into something, and she leapt backward, staggering into the wall. The corpse of a heavily decomposed cat lay on the floor. She moaned, dread coiling in her stomach and rattling its tail, waiting for a chance to strike. This was so wrong. She couldn't piece together what had happened. The shuffling sound came again, this time closer.

Kaylee stood by the door, her tire iron in a batter's grip. A young cop stepped into the room and shone his flashlight on Kaylee. A shriek tore out of her, very loud in the small room. The cop took one look at her and screamed back.

"Ma'am, put down the weapon," he yelled.

Kaylee complied, the clunk of the iron on the floor sounding ominous and final.

"What are you doing here?"

"I'm looking for Dr. Bubb," Kaylee said.

The cop cocked his head at her, studying her face. She stared back. He seemed comically young, square-jawed, and handsome in a way that would likely fade as the years took their toll. Right between his eyes, she saw a glowing, jagged-edged cross.

A wail built in her chest, and she took one step backward and stumbled on debris. The cop sprang forward to catch her.

"There's no Bubb in this building. It's been deserted since the seventies." The cross between his eyes flickered each time he spoke. A little fire flared out of it, bringing with it the odor of sulfur.

Kaylee moaned and tried to wiggle out of his grasp. He wouldn't let her go. She jerked her arm hard, wrenching it away, and took several steps backward, making a point to keep her eyes off the cop. It hit her she could be going mad. Terror sank its claws into her mind, ripping and tearing itself new digs. Maybe she'd hallucinated the whole 'Dr. Bubb' episode. Certainly she imagined the burning cross on the cop's forehead. She couldn't bring herself to look again.

"Let me help you out to your vehicle." Without waiting for an answer, the cop led her out of the building and to her car.

Late afternoon had deteriorated into evening. The cooling air hit her face, clearing her head. She glanced back at the building. She still wasn't sure what happened in there. There had to be a rational explanation. She unlocked her car and got in. The cop stood in the open door.

"Now what about this Dr. Bubb?"

"I have cancer. I came to him for a clinical trial." She didn't have to tell him details.

"Here?"

She turned on her GPS to show the cop the address. Out of habit, she glanced at herself in the rearview mirror. Between her eyes a glowing cross had torn open the skin, exactly like the one on the cop's forehead. She jerked and yelped.

"I knew you saw it." The cop squatted next to the car.

"Saw what?"

"The cross, Kaylee." His eyes narrowed. "We both know you don't have time to play games."

She reached up to touch the spot where she'd seen the cross.

"It's still there. Just like mine is."

"This is crazy." She shook her head.

"He gave you a box, didn't he? With candy in it. And he told you to wish your illness onto someone else. But the wrong person got it, and now they're dying."

Disbelief welled up, begging her to push him out of the way and slam her car door. Drive away from this place. Then she glanced at herself in the mirror again. The cross glowed. The truth set in, heavy and uncomfortable. "How do you know that?"

"There's no time to explain." He opened his ticket book, wrote something, and handed it to her. "Meet me at this address in one hour. It's an old library downtown. I'll be on the third floor."

"Wait a minute. I'm supposed to meet you, a stranger, in a strange place and you can't tell me your name?"

He smiled. "Jack Renner. Don't stand me up if you want to save whoever has your cancer."

He walked around the corner and disappeared.

Hands trembling, she started her car, breathing a sigh of relief as she left the old neighborhood. The whole scene took on the surreal life of an acid trip memory. Newer buildings flashing by, she convinced herself she imagined the whole ordeal. She'd go see Dr. Martin.

***

Kaylee arrived at Dr. Martin's office ten minutes before closing. She marched inside and rapped on the frosted glass separating the reception area from the waiting room. A young receptionist wearing aqua scrubs rolled it back, her face pinched in annoyance.

"I need to speak with Ms. Geis." Kaylee lifted a shaking hand to swipe her hair out of her face.

"Ms. Geis?" The young woman raised her eyebrows, crinkling her overly tanned skin. "I'm afraid you're mistaken. There's no Ms. Geis in this office."

Kaylee shook her head, a frustration and fear climbing up her chest. She flashed back over the scene at Dr. Bubb's building and felt her sanity slip a notch. "No. She has to be here. I spoke with her today." Kaylee heard her too loud voice but couldn't calm down. "She was dressed really well. Dark hair. Middle-aged. Very attractive."

The smaller woman shook her head and glanced behind her. "I'm sorry…"

An elderly woman stepped out from behind a partition drinking a cup of coffee.

"Who are you looking for, dear?"

"Lily Geis," Kaylee yelled. "We talked after my appointment with Dr. Martin. Get me the receptionist or somebody who knows what's going on here."

"Honey, I'm the receptionist." The woman's hand trembled as she set her coffee on the desk. "Have been since the doctor opened his practice thirty years ago."

"Then why weren't you here during my appointment?"

"My grandson had a recital. Not that it's your business. Now what is it you need?"

Another woman in scrubs walked into the reception area and approached Kaylee. She touched her arm but jerked back when she made contact. "I remember you. I weighed you. Do you remember me?"

Sympathy softened the woman's voice and eyes. She probably knew Kaylee's diagnosis. Now she likely thought the nutty patient was in the grips of some psychotic episode.

"I'm sorry," Kaylee said. "I don't remember. I was so scared, I couldn't focus."

"It's okay." The woman's eyes crinkled as she smiled. "Most people are scared when they come in here."

Kaylee didn't know what else to say. There was no Lily Geis in this office. They'd never heard of her. *Maybe you're crazy.* It almost sounded like someone had whispered the words in her ear. Kaylee whipped around in time to see Dr. Martin come out of his office.

"Another day's over, ladies." At the sight of Kaylee, his mouth fell open. She saw the mark between his eyes and began to wail. The world blurred as her knees melted, and she slumped to the floor.

It took some talking to convince Dr. Martin not to call the paramedics. Kaylee assured him and his staff it wouldn't happen again. They finally let her go. She stood on the sidewalk outside the doctor's office, tears streaming down her face, all hope of sanity lost. She slumped to her car, defeated. Jack Renner was her last chance.

***

Kaylee found herself in another part of Houston she'd never seen before. This area had passed rundown and was being converted into trendy shops and restaurants. The library sat at the end of a street, its red bricks arranged into arches over the windows and doors. The entryway looked like an actual keyhole. Kaylee parked on the street and paid the meter.

Inside the library was like stepping into another era. The high ceilings and the rays of sunset streaming through the windows caught every dust mote and sent it sparkling to the ground. People sat at tables, their heads bowed over newspapers and books. None had laptops, but some wrote on notepads. She crept through the stone quiet on her tiptoes and skirted the room, looking for the stairwell she knew must be tucked into a corner. Finding it, she opened the door, which groaned loud enough to wake the dead, and stepped inside before someone scolded her for breaking the silence.

Guiltily marveling at how good she felt, she jogged up the stairs to the top floor and eased open the door, hoping to avoid another noise like the one she made downstairs. The room she entered was set up like a parlor with couches and coffee tables. An unused fireplace dominated one wall. The stacks up here seemed to hold bound reports rather than books. Jack Renner sat at one of the long wooden tables, hands clasped in front of him, staring out one of the big windows. The red cross on his forehead glowed like it was on fire. Kaylee tiptoed to him, resisting the urge to reach up and touch her own burning red cross.

"Jack?" Kaylee whispered.

He twitched, the distance in his eyes clearing, and smiled.

"Sit down," he said. "I'll go get the papers you need to see."

Kaylee watched the clock while she waited. The second hand never stopped moving, a relentless reminder time was running out. Her nerves jumped with the need to do something to save Austin. As she decided to leave, Jack appeared holding a brown expandable file. He rummaged through it, muttering to himself.

Staring at the clock, Kaylee tried not to fidget. The constantly moving second hand marked the endless passage of time. What if this was another waste of time? She needed to be outside, fighting, working to save Austin.

"Here it is. Look at this."

Kaylee dragged her gaze off the clock to see what he had to show her. She sucked in her breath and leapt to her feet. "This is them. It's them." She snatched the photocopy and stared at Lily Geis and Dr. Bubb. Her spirits crashed. It wasn't them, after all. The couple in the photocopied picture wore Victorian era finery. The caption underneath the photo read: "Dr. Gideon and Rebekah Samuels circa 1875."

"I see you recognize them." Jack remained calm, still arranging the thin sheaf of papers he'd culled from the overgrown jumble in the expanding file. "I'll save you having to read all this. Dr. Gideon Samuels and his wife Rebekah were hanged by a lynch mob right here in Houston in the late eighteen hundreds."

"No, you don't understand. I saw both of them this morning." Dismay fluttered in Kaylee's chest. Suspecting she'd stepped into something beyond the realm of possibility and having it confirmed were two wildly different things. "These can't be the same people."

"I think it's you who don't understand. You keep looking at the clock, worrying you're running out of time. And you are. That's why you need to listen to me, and listen right now." Jack held Kaylee's gaze until she nodded.

"Dr. Samuels offered abortions to pregnant prostitutes. Once the prostitutes came to his office, he imprisoned them, forced them to carry the pregnancies to term. They sacrificed the infants as offerings to a deity they called Xouplae. One of the prostitutes escaped and went to the police. Word got out, and a mob formed. They stormed the Samuels's' home and hanged them in the front yard."

"This can't be right." Kaylee's mind churned the information, looking for the rational part. "I talked to them, the husband told me he could cure my cancer…and he did, sort of."

Jack simply handed another piece of paper to Kaylee. This one showed a pocket watch, opened to display the engraving on it. It read "Xouplae." Just the letters made Kaylee's muscles bunch. A slimy sweat broke out over her. Something about the watch wormed around in her mind, but exhaustion from the day's events wouldn't let her latch onto it.

"Gideon Samuels's pocket-watch."

"Who is Xou—" The name caught in her throat, so she tapped the watch.

"In all the years I've researched, I've only found one mention of that name." He pulled a piece of paper from the stack and passed it to Kaylee. "It's a German woodcut thought to date back to the fifteenth century."

Kaylee winced at the image. It showed a hideous beast made up of different animals holding a man over its gaping mouth. Another man lay on the ground at its feet, apparently dead.

"I interpret the man lying on the ground to be the deceased corporeal body, and the man being held over the beast's mouth to be the dead man's soul." Jack pulled a mini-magnifying glass out of his pocket. "Now, look carefully at the markings on the monster. They look like hieroglyphs. I've searched but have never been able match them to any civilization. They have both Egyptian and Native American properties. The bottom line, for me anyway, is this thing is old."

"It can't be real." Kaylee sat back on the couch, competing thoughts twisting in her mind.

"Can't it?" Jack's eyes bored into her. "Looters took souvenirs from the Samuels's' house, sold them as souvenirs. A traveling minister bought this watch and used it as a prop in his sermons. He was fond of saying the name aloud during his sermons."

"What happened to him?" A headache throbbed behind Kaylee's temples.

"He burned a tent full of people attending one of his sermons. Was incoherent when the Texas Rangers questioned him. All he'd say is 'They need the souls so they can hide from him.' One of the Rangers present at the preacher's execution claimed he saw a ghostly man and woman standing off to the side of the gallows. He identified them as the Samuelses after he came to Houston, researching the origins of the watch."

"What did he do with the watch?" An important piece of the puzzle flitted around Kaylee's mind, staying one step ahead, evading her at every turn.

"Sold it to a private collector. He owned it until he poisoned his wife and children in the early nineteen hundreds. While he was waiting to hang, he drew this." He handed Kaylee another sheet of paper.

Nausea brewed in her stomach. On the paper was a pencil drawing of Dr. Bubb and Lily Geis. Or Gideon and Rebekah Samuels. Tremors ran through Kaylee's hand. The piece of paper vibrated, making a chittering sound.

"I don't understand. What do the Samuelses get out of getting people to do these things?" The monster's name burned her tongue. She couldn't let herself say it. "Do they eat souls?"

"Maybe." Jack's gaze became unfocused, the way it had been when she first saw him sitting alone in the library. "I'm of the mind they eat the misery of their victims. Either way, they devour you until there's nothing left."

Kaylee stared at the floating dust motes. They flashed and twinkled, falling into obscurity, just like the truth. But they offered no solution, no way to get the sickness out of her brother and back into her.

"What happened to the watch?" She couldn't get the timepiece out of her mind.

"There's no record of it being recovered from the collector's residence. Someone could have stolen it, but I think the Samuelses took it. They'd finally gained enough power to use the people they tricked as an entry into our world."

A few pieces fell into place. Dr. Martin had one of those crosses on his forehead. Using Jack's theory, Lily Geis used Dr. Martin to get to her. She thought back to the deserted building where she and Dr. Bubb conducted their business. Had Jack been Dr. Bubb's portal? Was that why he insisted on helping her?

"So did the crosses take the place of the watch? Make a sort of door for Samuels and his wife to enter?"

"Maybe." Jack tapped the papers on the table again. She glanced at them and something clicked. The stubborn bit of information fluttering around her mind fell into place.

"That's it!" She slapped the table.

Jack glanced around the library, perhaps worried an angry librarian would come scold them.

"The watch," Kaylee hissed at him. "Bubb—I mean Samuels—has it. I saw it. He took it out and checked it while we were together."

Jack shook his head, brow wrinkling in confusion.

"What if I can get that watch from him? Destroy it? I'm no occult expert, but the watch obviously has power."

"Maybe," Jack said. "They believe it does anyway."

"Sometimes believing in something makes it real."

"Might be worth a try," Jack said. "What have you got to lose? You won't be able to live with the guilt if your brother dies of your cancer."

"Only problem is I don't know where to find them." Her mind latched onto something weird in Jack's words, but she was too focused on planning to go back over them.

"Gideon and Rebekah Samuels were buried in a potter's field not far from here." Jack pulled a slip of paper from his pocket. "A subdivision was built over the graveyard in the 1960s. The developer didn't bother to relocate the graves. Most weren't marked, and few people knew it had been a graveyard."

Kaylee took the address, wondering if she could beat the Samuelses. Jack's words came back to her. *You won't be able to live with the guilt if your brother dies of your cancer.* Jack had known her name without her telling him, too. She turned to him.

"How do you know—"

"It doesn't matter. Maybe I've got some wrongs to right." Jack put the papers back in the expanding file. "Good luck, Kaylee."

Kaylee impulsively hugged him and made her way back to her car.

The robotic voice on the GPS read directions to an older housing development, full of brick ranch houses on tiny lots. She parked at the curb of a house whose broken windows and kicked-in door suggested it was unoccupied. The house radiated malevolence, a wrongness she sensed but could not describe. At the same time, it invited her to come in, to see what secrets it held.

Alone on the street, she hesitated. Every bit of self-preservation begged her to run away. She reminded herself of Austin, how they'd grown up, gotten tough together. She took a deep breath and entered the monster's belly.

***

Trash littered the house's floors. Scraps of faded linoleum peeked through the debris. The walls, oddly free of graffiti, were stained with dark brown smears. Her raw and abused nerves tried to spur her into running away from this awful place. Whatever happened here hung in the air, greasy and heavy. A hot wind picked up and swirled the trash on the floors, making sweat ooze from her pores.

She slunk through the house, kicking piles of animal bones and filthy clothes out of her way. She wasn't sure where she was headed. It was as though she had a magnet inside her, drawing her to the right place. She opened the door to the hallway bathroom. A ripe, rotten stench rolled out to meet her. She

157

backpedaled, gagging. Wrangling her stomach under control, she pulled a bandana out of her coat pocket and tied it around her lower face and crept into the tiny room. The wall tiles lay in shards on the floor. The space where the tub once sat was filled with black, stinking muck.

A groaning noise broke the house's eerie quiet. The gore in the hole bubbled and roiled, thickening the stench. Kaylee, eyes watering, inched toward the open door. The thick soup heaved more violently and finally exploded. The gunk burned where it hit Kaylee's skin. She slapped at the painful spots, crying out.

"What do you think you're doing?"

Kaylee stopped her frantic motions and turned toward the sound of the voice. Dr. Bubb, or Gideon Samuels, stood before her dressed in Victorian finery. His wife stood next to him.

"You can't escape us," she said. "We made a deal. You wanted your cancer gone. You agreed to give it to another person. It's not our fault your brother ended up with it."

"Please." Kaylee shook all over, the bits of black ichor still stinging her skin. "I'll do anything."

"You have nothing left to offer us—"

"Unless you want to give us your son's soul in exchange for your brother's," Gideon Samuels interrupted his wife. "He is below the age of accountability. You could give us Landon."

"Don't ever speak his name." Kaylee bared her teeth at the specters. They laughed. With a sinking feeling, she realized they were right to laugh. She was nothing more than a squeaking animal, caught in a snare, panicked and desperate. Begging wouldn't work. Her only option was to surprise them. That morning Dr. Bubb took the watch out of his right pocket. Focusing on that pocket, she dropped to her knees and clasped her hands together.

"Can I have more time? Please? To say goodbye to my brother?"

The Samuelses came closer, pleasure brightening their faces. The cross between Kaylee's eyes burned and stung as they neared. She didn't have to fake her tears. The fiery cross hurt worse than anything she'd ever experienced.

"Please," she gasped.

Gideon Samuels, smiling broadly, took one step closer. Kaylee sprung at him, sticking her hand in his right pocket and closing it around the watch. He shoved her away, but it was too late. Kaylee opened the watch and read the horrible name. She closed her eyes and pictured the thing from the woodcut. She thought his name. *Xouplae.* She believed in him wholeheartedly because there was no other choice.

Rhythmic thumping came from somewhere near. Hoof beats. Had it worked? Had *Xouplae* answered her call? Oh, she hoped so. Her luck had sucked ass today. The hoof beats thundered louder than ever and stopped on the other side of the bathroom door.

"What have you done?" Rebekah Samuels's eyes grew until it seemed they'd consume her face. Her lips twisted, exposing her perfect teeth. "You don't know what he's capable of."

Kaylee hoped Xouplae was capable of whatever power she gave him.

The bathroom door swung open, hinges squealing. A hulking figure stood silhouetted in it, backlit by the glare from a streetlight.

Taller than any man she'd ever seen, the thing towered on two legs, but the legs were thick and rounded like an animal's hind legs and ended in black hoofs. They glowed with the symbols from the woodcut. Massive shoulders with arms that hung too long ended in three thin fingers, like a bird's foot, hooked like talons. The body was covered in whorls of gray fur.

"Gideon. Rebekaaaah." The voice, sounding like thunder, bubbling sewage, and razor-sharp gravel all rolled into one, emanated from a head with horns and a snout with fangs like a snake. "I've been looking for you for a long tiiiiimmme." Xouplae stepped into the room, his slitted eyes settling on the watch in Kaylee's hand.

Kaylee took a step backward and pressed herself into the wall, whispering a prayer she hadn't said in years. Hysteria swirled in her brain, begging her to let go of her sanity. She held fast to lucid thoughts and forced herself to meet the thing's gaze. The monster held out one talon-tipped hand for the watch. Hands shaking, her breath coming in wild pants, she looped the chain over one of its three fingers.

"What is your part in this?"

"I want my cancer back," she repeated. "And I want my brother to be well."

"Why would I do what you say?"

"Because I believe in you." Kaylee hoped this was right. "And because I've helped you find these two."

"Yes," it grated out. "I have wanted to eat their souls. They promised and then tricked me, hiding their souls in the watch. They existed on borrowed tiiiiime. But now we are all together again."

"You made a deal with me, and I'm not letting you out of it." Gideon sneered at Kaylee and then spoke to the monster. "And so did you. You said I could have your power if I sacrificed the infants to you. I never promised you my soul."

"But your soul is so much more tasty to me. Much more wicked." The creature took a step toward Gideon, who cowered. "You'll be so much more delicious."

Before Gideon could run, Xouplae reached down and grabbed him by his ankles. The beast's mouth elongated, the jaw stretching. The ghost bucked and howled but could not escape. Slowly, the monster lowered its prey into its mouth. At the shoulders, its mouth crunched down. The sound of bones breaking made bile sting Kaylee's throat.

The beast crunched and grunted through its snack. The whole time, Gideon never quit screaming. Finished, Xouplae wiped his mouth and turned to Rebekah. The woman tried to dive into the muck from where she'd come, but the beast caught her mid-leap. He ate her much more slowly, doing things Kaylee wished she could forget seeing. When he finished, he turned to Kaylee and flicked that snake's tongue at her.

"I want my cancer back," Kaylee told the horror in front of her.

"Are you certain?" He cocked his head to one side, studying her.

"Yes. It's what's right."

From out of nowhere, he produced an elaborately wrapped box and handed it to Kaylee.

"I think you know what to do with this. For your service, I grant you a boon—a little more time on earth to say goodbye to your people. Enjoy it." The beast flashed sharp, needle-pointed teeth at her. Kaylee shivered from a cold so deep she doubted she'd ever get warm again. The monster faded until he finally winked out of sight.

***

Kaylee opened the box and choked down the chocolates. They smelled rotten and tasted worse. She gagged several times but wouldn't let herself vomit. Clutching her stomach, which felt full of razors, she left the house. The morning sun confused her. Had she been in the house all night? She checked her cell phone. No. The date was still the same. Had she hallucinated the whole ordeal? Shock set in, throwing her off balance. She leaned against the cool bricks until the spell passed.

She stumbled to her car and drove away. After only a few blocks, she pulled over in front of a cemetery. She thought she was dying and hated to do it on the road. She leaned her head on the steering wheel, chills gripping her at uneven intervals. At the sound of a dog barking, she raised her head. A monument in the cemetery caught her eye.

It was a rendering of Jesus Christ, only it was made of some material that hadn't agreed with the humid Texas heat and blazing sun. The elements had turned the statue a dull, ugly black. Kaylee stumbled out of her car and toward the monument, wanting, *needing* to see who was buried there. She pushed herself, feet sliding in the dew-slick grass. Finally she reached the monument and sank onto a concrete bench in front of it. She read the name and froze.

Jack Renner
1950-1976

A cold chill crawled over Kaylee's skin, but she wasn't really surprised. Jack, too, had been a victim of the soul eater. Next to Jack was Tina Renner, 1960-1976. Phyllis Renner and Donald Jack Renner rested next to Tina. The family died within days of each other. What had happened to them?

"You okay?"

A hand appeared around Kaylee's arm and gently hauled her to her feet. She brushed herself off with shaking hands, very aware of how weak she felt. "Thank you for that. I'm fine."

She gasped when she saw who had helped her. Ellie Grimes, her horrid neighbor, stood before her holding a bunch of flowers.

"Here to see my brother, sister, and my folks." She set one bunch of flowers on Jack's grave and the other on her parents' grave.

"What happened to them?" Kaylee didn't want to know, but she had to.

"My brother was a cop. Got shot in the line of duty." Ellie swiped at her cheeks, though they were dry. "Some crazy idiot went into an office building and started shooting people. Jack responded. The guy shot him in the back and paralyzed him. Mom took us to see him in the hospital. She and my sister ate all his candy—nasty smelling stuff—while he was sleeping."

"You didn't eat any?"

"Oh no. I'm a diabetic. Have been all my life." Ellie knelt beside Jack's tombstone and brushed off the dirt.

"The candy made them sick, and Mom decided we'd go home. Crossing the street, a bus ran the light and hit her and my sister. Clipped me, knocked me a good ten feet. I slammed my head on a parked car." She held her hair away from her face to show Kaylee a deep scar. "Apparently, the EMS thought I was dead for a good long while. I woke up when they tried to zip me into a body bag." She walked over to Jack's tombstone and traced it. "By that time, Jack had already been told we were all dead. He took his razor apart and killed himself with it," she snorted. "Ten years old, and I had to pick what to bury him in. I chose his uniform." Her lips trembled. "He was such a handsome guy. Such a good brother."

Kaylee sent up a silent thanks to Jack Renner, who had done everything he could to help her beat Gideon and Rebekah Samuels. She hoped his soul could finally rest.

"I need to say something to you." Ellie Grimes stood a little straighter.

Kaylee's stomach turned a slow-flip flop, and the sick sweat oozing out of her pores turned clammy.

"The cat your son was feeding." She bit her lip, frowning. "I know you thought I was being mean, but there's a facility not far from the apartment complex conducting animal testing. Every once in a while, one of those poor animals escapes, sick and dying. I usually trap them and take them to be euthanized at the vet I used for my pets. It's the only humane thing to do."

"Why not call the SPCA or the Health Department?"

"Tried both. They'll come get the poor animal, supposedly file a report, but it got where it happened so regular that I started…"

"Doing the best you could?" Kaylee's cheeks flamed. Some of it was the cancer, but more of it was embarrassment she'd judged this woman so harshly.

"Something like that." Ellie Grimes blinked. "Maybe I shouldn't say this, but you look awful. Is there some way I can help you?"

Kaylee pushed down her pride and told Ellie Grimes about her cancer and that she needed someone to help her get home.

***

163

Kaylee lay in the bed Hospice had installed in her living room a month earlier. She'd insisted on being out here so she could see the tree during her final Christmas season. Landon and Austin played with the gaming system she'd given them as an early gift. She could certainly afford it. After she became too sick to work, Austin took over the shop, redecorated, and bought in an award-winning tattoo artist. Her irresponsible brother brought in more business than Kaylee ever dreamed of doing. She should have trusted him sooner.

He'd done okay with Landon as well, taking the boy to sporting events and whatever else he wanted to do. Kaylee worried her son wouldn't remember her in a few years. He'd only know his uncle as a father. The thought created an unbearable ache in Kaylee's chest. But she was grateful her son would have a parent to raise him to adulthood. That was the important thing.

The doorbell rang. Austin glanced at her, eyebrows raised. Was she expecting guests? She managed to shake her head, but even that small motion took a great deal of effort. Her brother rose and answered the door. Ellie Grimes poked her head around Austin.

"May I come in?"

Over the past months, Ellie had shown her true colors. After that day in the cemetery, she began cooking for the family, cleaning for them, and doing their laundry. During the long days, she sat with Kaylee. Today the older woman held up a fabric carrier as she entered the apartment. From inside came the unhappy yowl of a cat.

"He's not a kitten now," Ellie said in her brusque way. "But he was on death row at the humane society, and I couldn't leave him. I had him neutered, and I've got a litter box and food in my car."

The cat gave another mournful cry.

"Let him out." Kaylee barely recognized her own whisper of a voice.

Ellie opened the carrier door. The poor thing, an orange bobtailed tabby, stood stock still among all these unfamiliar humans. Landon got down on his knees and wiggled his fingers. The cat, tail undulating, went to investigate. Austin went outside to get the rest of the cat's things.

Ellie sat down in her chair next to the hospital bed and took out her crochet. Kaylee watched her son enjoy his new best friend, and the world around her grew dim. As her body cooled and her heart slowed, she struggled to focus on Landon, wanting her last moments to be filled with the joy he brought her.

Movement in the corner drew her attention away from her sweet little boy. As she watched, dark shadows swirled together. Ellie said something to Landon, but Kaylee couldn't hear it. Part of her had already left the living world. The shadows formed a head. Hoofs peeked out below the dark mist. The spot on her forehead, that awful cross, burned. Pain spread through her dying body.

Xouplae had come for her after all.

ABOUT THE AUTHOR

Catie Rhodes lives in the overcrowded and overly noisy Houston, Texas suburbs with her longsuffering husband and crazy little dog.

She misses the rural East Texas piney woods of her childhood so much used the setting for her Peri Jean Mace series. In addition to her Peri Jean Mace paranormal mysteries, Catie writes horror on those dark days and moonless nights when the shadows beckon.

When not writing, Catie loves to cook and is slowly teaching herself to crochet by watching videos online.

Connect with Catie at www.catierhodes.com or chat with her on Facebook and Twitter.

9

Tunnel
By J. Thorn

"Dedicated to Katy Sozaeva and her beautiful spirit."

Jeremy tried pulling the steel gate shut, but the pile of bodies in the corner kept it from closing.

His legs ached and the grime beneath made his feet slick on the tile as he fought the vertigo threatening to submerge him into unconsciousness. He cursed, pushing his hair from his sweaty forehead, wishing he were in jeans instead of a hospital gown. Another explosion shook the subway platform and Jeremy ducked as plaster and ceramic tile rained from the ceiling and past a poster of a long-legged model in a coat that would never see the new season.

"I'm heading into the tunnels. Ain't like that gate is gonna stop them, even if you could get it to latch."

The voice shook Jeremy from his thoughts. He turned to see a young man wearing blue overalls and a baseball cap with a growing paunch and a soul patch beneath his bottom lip. Jeremy noticed the man's filthy hands and the dirt nesting in the wrinkles at the corners of his eyes. The stranger spat and shoved his hands into the pockets of his overalls.

167

"Help me move them," Jeremy said.

"I ain't goin' nowhere near no bodies."

Gunfire punctuated the conversation, followed by shouts. Jeremy looked toward the light at the top of the dead escalator and back to the young man standing near the turnstile.

"What the hell's going on?" Jeremy asked.

The man shrugged and shook his head as if he could barely understand the question, let alone provide an answer. "All it takes is one to stumble down the escalator or for something to spark the dead ones over there and we're both in deep shit. Some take time to turn, and others hop right back up."

"But the gown...and I don't have shoes. I'm sick. Feeling better but still sick."

"You're gonna die, you stupid fuck. You keep standing there pulling on that gate and you're gonna die. I'm leaving right now. You coming?"

Jeremy took a last look at the top of the escalator, where he swore he saw movement through the shadows. He shook his head and looked back to the gate. The blood beneath the bodies had pooled at a depression in the floor where a tile was missing. The bitter stench of human waste hung in the air.

"I can't," he said to the young man. "I can't go into the tunnels. I've got a phobia, and my therapist said—"

"And your therapist would tell you to stay here and die, I guess. You comin' with me or not? I ain't about to get torn apart by guns or teeth."

Another explosion shook the tunnel, this one accompanied by the sharp retort of gunfire. The battle raging on the street was about to descend on them like an angry thunderstorm.

"You know where you're going?" Jeremy asked.

"I been repairing water mains down here for nine months. The Department of Environmental Protection got some lines they been using since the 1800s. So yeah, I know the tunnels."

Jeremy looked closer at the man's work overalls, a stitched patch displaying "NYC Department of Environmental Protection" on his left pocket. On his right was another that read "William."

"I'm Jeremy. Nice to meet you, William."

"It's Billy. Only my mom calls me William." Billy reached over and grabbed Jeremy's arm, yanking him toward the edge of the platform as the first of the zombies appeared at the top of the escalator, moaning and dripping dead flesh as they descended the stairs.

***

"So you didn't even have time to dress before running from the hospital?" Billy asked. His words were slathered with Bronx attitude. He looked past Jeremy toward the platform, knowing the dead would find their way into the tunnels.

"No. As I was trying to tell you back there, I don't have shoes or pants. Nothing but this hospital gown."

As the two moved deeper into the subway tunnel, following the rails, Billy flipped his headlamp on and spun to blind Jeremy with it.

"You were in the hospital?" he said.

"Cancer." Jeremy could hear the hesitation in Billy's sigh, so he filled the awkward silence. "Probably remission. Never got to hear from the doctor exactly. I was in for a biopsy, getting prepped but never made it to surgery."

"And then the shit started?" Billy asked.

"Yeah. I got out of the hospital as fast as I could. You?"

"Been working down here every day, twelve-hour shifts. First rumble made me think we got hit by another Muslim motherfucker. You know, like a plane or bomb exploding inside Penn Station. But we heard chatter on the radios, and dudes topside said it was something else."

"You alone?" Jeremy asked.

"Why you asking me that?" Billy clenched his fists and turned to face Jeremy, his feet spread apart and his chest heaving. "If you wanna make a play for my light or my shoes, let's do that shit right now. I ain't afraid of nobody."

Jeremy collapsed against the rail as he heard the squeal of a rat far closer than he liked. "I'm tired. Can we rest somewhere?"

"Gotta get deeper," Billy said, easing his defensive posture. "The stank might mask our smell once we do, and I doubt they can see this far in. Of course, you never know. Sack up, man. We gotta get deeper before I'm gonna rest."

"I don't have much left in the tank. I'll probably slow you down. Go ahead."

Billy stopped and turned again, putting both hands on his hips. "Goddamn you," he spat. He stomped a foot and continued to curse beneath the thin beam cast by the light strapped over his hat.

"I'll be fine. Go on," Jeremy said.

Billy hissed and reached down to grab Jeremy by the elbow. "Can't do that. Can't leave none behind."

"Thanks, man."

"Fuck you. If you turn, you ain't gonna be as slow as you are right now." Billy stumbled forward into the tunnel, dragging Jeremy along by the arm. The sound of gunfire and explosions faded as clicks and drips echoed from the unseen depths ahead.

***

The men walked for hours in silence until Jeremy broke it.

"Please stop. Just for five minutes, please."

"You got two." Billy let go of his arm and turned in a slow circle, his light illuminating rusted conduits, steel beams and ancient graffiti. "You got cancer?"

Jeremy raised his head and propped it up by putting his elbows on his knees. "Yes, but I think I'm in remission."

"Like you're cured?"

"Not exactly. The cancer, it's not getting worse."

Billy continued surveying the tunnel without another question.

"I've been stable for a few months, but the chemo treatments were a bitch. Still don't have all of my energy back."

Billy remained silent and Jeremy talked faster.

"I'll be fine, though. Just need to catch my breath."

"You wounded, Jeremy?"

Jeremy smiled at the first mention of his name in the conversation. "Like from the fighting, the outbreak?"

"Like wounded, motherfucker. Are? You? Wounded?" Billy spoke each word with increasing emphasis.

"I was just getting a biopsy. I'm fine."

"None of them got a scratch on you, dug their nails in or anything like that?"

"I got into the station on 34th before chaos broke out on the streets. I was hoping to catch the E Train across midtown."

Billy looked at Jeremy, turning the beam directly to his face. He waited several seconds as if searching for any sign of the sickness that caused the dead to turn. "Fine. Get up. We're done resting. There's an intersection several blocks down with an access door to a storage space on the northeast side. Me and some of the crew been stashing six packs and beef jerky in there for our overtime shifts."

He paused, expecting Jeremy to crack wise about the American workforce or union shops. When nothing came, Billy continued. "We stay there for a day or two and see if this shit blows over, whatever the fuck it is."

"But I got a wife and kid. I can't—"

"Then go back," Billy said, pointing toward the tunnel that reverberated the sounds of war from two stories above. "Get the fuck out. We're doin' this my way or we ain't doin' it at all. You hear what I'm saying?"

Jeremy nodded and pushed all thoughts of his family from his head. He wouldn't be able to protect them if he was dead. "That's cool. We do it your way. You know these tunnels."

"Damn straight, I do. What do you do, Jeremy?"

"IT. Tech support," Jeremy said. He could almost hear Billy's eyes rolling.

"You ever done construction, hole digging, plumbing, any kind of *real* work?"

Jeremy remained quiet, knowing nothing he could say now would satisfy Billy.

"Uh-huh. Thought so. If we get to the switchboard and it's still got juice, maybe you can check the grid. I'll get us there, keep us safe, and then you do your thing when I need it. That's the deal."

"Not like we have many options, do we?" Jeremy asked.

"You always got two, Mr. Help Desk. You can live or you can die."

***

The rumbles came in waves, each one coating the men with ancient dust as they walked north along the E Train line toward the 42nd Street Station. Billy could barely see Jeremy's hospital gown, now black as the grease on the rails. Water dripped in the distance, and Jeremy would shudder each time his bare foot brushed past the stiff, matted fur of the rats scurrying about at his feet. The explosions continued to shake the tunnels but without the sharp, bitter snap of gunfire.

The guide lights for the subway trains had been off since they climbed down from the platform, and now the track markers went dark as well. From the moment they hopped onto the rails, Jeremy had the feeling that getting electrocuted wasn't going to be a huge risk. From the looks of the hospital as he fled through the parking garage, the New York City power grid wouldn't be coming back any time soon, if ever. The billowing mushroom cloud above New Jersey crept over the Hudson River.

Billy kept the pace brisk, not slowing or accommodating for a barefoot and weak Jeremy. He felt his chest for the key to the padlock on the storage room door and sighed when his fingers touched the cool metal. As Billy looked at the markings on the tunnel walls, he realized he never thought he'd miss riding the hot, crowded 456 Train to the Bronx.

"We getting close?" Jeremy asked.

Billy ignored the question and kept walking, throwing the beam of light back and forth. With each turn of his head, he could estimate how far they were into the tunnel and knew approximately how much farther they had to go to reach the storage room near the 42nd Street Station.

"Got a phone?" Jeremy asked.

"No," said Billy. "Do you?" He leered, remembering what Jeremy was wearing when he first saw him at the gate on the subway platform.

"No," Jeremy said.

"We have to keep phones in our lockers. OSHA regs or some bullshit, I don't know. Either way, kinda doubt the grid is working. But I ain't the computer geek, so..."

"If I had one, I could try a few things, some codes."

An explosion shook the tunnel, raining down more debris. Billy shrugged as if that was all that needed to be said about phones and communication infrastructure.

"Nice gun," Jeremy said.

Billy stopped and laughed, placing his hand on the pistol grip in the side pocket of his overalls.

"No OSHA regs on firearms at work, I guess?" Jeremy asked.

"Not anymore, my man. The cop they was eating at Broadway and East 34th ain't gonna need this, now, is he?"

Jeremy stayed three paces behind Billy, focusing on the bobbing headlamp as they walked through the tunnel. Stopping ahead, Billy drew the pistol from his pocket and snapped it up in one motion until the barrel was pointed at Jeremy's head. It wasn't until after Jeremy heard the whimper that he realized Billy was aiming beyond him at the little boy slithering out from the gloom of the tunnel.

"Are you alone?" Billy shouted.

Jeremy took a step to the side and turned so he was no longer standing in front of the pistol. He squinted into the darkness and heard another stifled cry followed by a hitching sob.

"Take two steps towards us, son. Really slow steps," Billy said.

The child's eyes seemed to float in a river of onyx. His skin was covered in sweat, and his clothes were stained. Jeremy wondered if the child was hiding from the bedlam above or if he lived in the subways.

"Close enough," Billy said as the boy approached from an auxiliary tunnel. "What's yer name?"

"Seth."

"What're you doin' down here, Seth? This ain't no place for a kid."

"My apartment," Seth mumbled. "My parents. They…"

"It's okay," Jeremy said, stepping toward the boy.

"Stop," Billy yelled. "Don't get any closer to him."

"He's a boy," Jeremy said.

"We don't know shit. Keep back or I'll shoot you both, I swear to God."

Jeremy grinned at Billy and took another step toward Seth. He ruffled the boy's hair and looked at him from head to toe. "How long you been hiding?" Jeremy asked.

"I don't know," Seth said. Billy kept the gun pointed at Seth's head.

"Have you seen anyone else down here?"

Seth shook his head, and Jeremy looked back at Billy.

"Ain't enough for three," Billy said. "I can tell you that right now. I ain't gonna be responsible for a kid."

"We can't leave him here alone."

"The fuck we can't. Let's go, Jeremy. Don't make me shoot you."

"You wouldn't do that," Jeremy said, putting his arm around Seth, "because you don't know what would happen. Ain't that right?"

Billy shifted his weight from one foot to the other. His tongue curled out and licked his top lip. "I saved yer pansy ass, Jeremy. Don't go growing a pair now. I got the gun, and I got the safe room with food."

"Yes, you do. But you know we can't leave this kid. He's going to die."

"We're all going to die, you stupid motherfucker. Can't you see that?"

Seth stood behind Jeremy. Billy laughed.

"Cancer dude and a fucking kid. What a duo. I make the calls," Billy said while jabbing the air with the barrel of the gun.

"You're not going to use it, Billy," Jeremy said, straightening his back and taking a step forward. "In the time we've been walking through this tunnel, you've figured it out."

"Figured what out?"

Jeremy took another step closer, keeping his body between the boy and Billy. "That I might be weak right now, but if you kill me and I turn, you'll have a reanimated corpse that might be more than you can handle. You don't know how many bullets it would take, and I get the feeling you've already checked the clip. How many you got, Billy?"

Billy flicked the safety off the Glock and closed one eye. "Shut the fuck up."

"How many, Billy? I'm guessing less than three. That's why you didn't fire at me on the platform, or at the boy. In fact, you might be best saving those for your own suicide. Although I'd imagine one pull of the trigger with the barrel in your mouth oughtta do the trick." Jeremy stretched his arms out, and the hot air moving through the subway tunnel billowed his hospital gown behind him like a set of black wings.

"We ain't takin' the boy with us, and if I have to put you down twice, that's what I'm gonna do."

"Then it looks like we got ourselves an old-fashioned stand-off. I'm not leaving the boy, and I'm not backing down. So you're either going to shoot us both and deal with whatever happens next or you're going to put the gun down and keep walking towards the safe room so we can get out."

The blast from the gunshot illuminated the tunnel in a flash of white, a deafening sound reverberating off the walls.

***

Jeremy turned to see smoke curling from the barrel of the boy's pistol. Seth's arm was shaking, and he began whimpering in the same way he had when they discovered him. It took Jeremy a moment to realize Billy was lying in a pool of blood, his body motionless and arms spread across the rail like a grotesque crucifixion.

"Give me the gun," Jeremy said.

The boy dropped his arm and held the pistol grip out at Jeremy.

"Why did you do that?"

Seth stood still, mouth hanging open, staring at Billy's body on the ground.

"We have to get out of here. Right now." Jeremy coughed as the acrid gunpowder filled his nostrils. He exhaled the rank, hot air of the subway tunnel as he bent down. Mimicking what he saw on television, Jeremy put two fingers to the side of Billy's neck. The man's skin was still warm and covered with a layer of sweat. He moved his fingers around but could not feel a pulse anywhere. To be safe, Jeremy put a hand on Billy's chest and felt nothing. He pulled it away, his fingers covered in blood.

"Is he dead?" Seth asked between sobs.

"Yes," Jeremy said. He forced his hand back to Billy's chest until he felt the shape of the key. Jeremy yanked as hard as he could, but the chain didn't snap from Billy's neck. He slid it over the dead man's head before tossing it to Seth. "Put that on."

"What's going to happen to that man?"

"I don't know for sure, Seth, but we need to get out of here and find the safe room. We've got the key and the headlamp. I think if we continue until we come to the 42nd Street Station, we'll find it."

"I didn't want to hurt him, but he was going to kill us, wasn't he?" Seth asked.

Jeremy pushed a tear from the corner of his eye and looked at the boy. He thought of his own son, and a shiver ran up his spine. "Yes, Seth. He was," Jeremy said, trying to believe his own lie. "You did the right thing."

Jeremy strapped the headlamp on and held a gun in each hand. He considered stripping Billy's overalls until he remembered the faces of those who had turned in the hospital. If this was some kind of virus, the last thing he would want to do is put on clothes of the infected. He turned his back on Billy's corpse and bent down to look directly into Seth's face. He could smell the fear and desperation on the child. "Let's get moving, Seth."

Jeremy saw Seth's eyes widen at the same time that he heard a groan from the depths behind them.

***

Jeremy felt the hand on his shoulder before he had time to turn and fire one of the guns. The headlamp set Billy's face ablaze. Jeremy recoiled from the dead man's eyes showing white, rolled back into his head. Blood covered Billy's neck, and the dark stain had spread across his chest, obscuring the patches on his work uniform. Jeremy heard Seth cry out. He had to drop both guns to grab Billy's wrists, which were now wrapped around his throat, pulling him closer.

Billy's corpse snarled, and Jeremy could smell cigarettes, coffee and death. Billy moved his mouth toward Jeremy's face, his teeth snapping like a rabid dog.

"Run," Jeremy gasped. "Run towards 42nd Street."

It was all Jeremy could say before Billy's dead hands tightened around his neck. Seth ran around the two men locked in hand-to-hand combat and watched as the headlamp created erratic patterns on the wall of the tunnel. He could see Jeremy

177

kicking at Billy's legs as the man he shot dead moments earlier still stood, unfazed by the blows. Jeremy screamed and swore, but his words became breathy and shallow.

Seth waited and watched, despite Jeremy's warnings. Billy's head moved closer and closer to Jeremy's face until Seth heard a wet slap and a gurgling sound. The headlamp froze on one spot, bobbing up and down until it dropped to the ground and shone on the rail. A black shadow smothered the light, and Seth heard a noise that reminded him of feeding time in the tiger cages at the Bronx Zoo.

The boy shivered and took a step toward the intersection ahead. He ran deeper and deeper into the black hole beneath the city, trapped by the inevitable destruction behind and the unknown evils ahead.

ABOUT THE AUTHOR

Embrace the entire spectrum of human emotion – especially its dark realms – for a more meaningful story. Welcome to J. Thorn's world, where the ultimate escape from reality is the horror novel.

J. Thorn is a Top 100 Horror Author (Amazon Rank). He is a supporting member of the Horror Writers Association, a member of the Great Lakes Association of Horror Writers, and a writer for disinformation.com.

Let's Scare Cancer To Death

10

One Lonely Night
By Chantal Boudreau

To Barb McQueen

Quinn awoke to the sound of jagged fingernails scraping on his windowpane. The shrill squeal was enough to make him start and cringe. It took him a few groggy seconds to register what had roused him from his shallow sleep, one he had finally slipped into only minutes before, after more than an hour of trying. Then the wave of nausea and pain struck him, followed by a burst of frustration and anger.

Sitting up in his bed, he launched his pillow at the window.

"God dammit! There's nothing here you want! Why won't you give me a moment of peace?"

Considering how difficult it was for him to get to sleep in the first place and how tired he always was, there wasn't anything much more disheartening than having his rest disturbed—especially by one of "them".

The response to his outraged assault included a low rattling moan and more scraping at the window. The zombie outside his bedroom would not easily be deterred. With a groan of concession, Quinn got up and went into the kitchen to make himself a

181

cup of chamomile tea. He slouched in his chair, mug in hand and heaved a deep sigh.

Worse than the physical discomfort due to his failing health was the loneliness of being the only resident in his house, something that was even harder to bear at night than in the day. He had nobody to check on in the two smaller bedrooms, and only a cold empty space next to him in his queen-sized bed—nothing to comfort him when his condition made his life intolerable, and certainly nothing that would soothe him back to sleep.

"You were supposed to outlive me, not the other way around," he murmured.

Quinn had believed that his cancer diagnosis would be the most horrible event in his life, convinced he was doomed to die long before his time, but that fate hadn't been as bad as it would get. The cancer was still killing him, but it had actually spared him the quick death that had come to the rest of his family, and would prevent him from rising again, as they had done, once he had passed on.

What he had heard before he had lost contact with any other living human being was that his immunity to the virus was a result of the chemo. Nobody had been able to give him a scientific explanation as to why it kept the zombie virus from entering his system and why it repulsed the undead that had succumbed to the infection, but that was the assumption. In fact, the only people still alive seemed to be the survivalist types and those who had undergone cancer treatment at some point in their lives.

Another wave of nausea swept through him and he staggered to the bathroom to purge the tea from his stomach. He had bowel cancer that had spread to his stomach; sometimes things would stay down and sometimes they wouldn't, but he was gradually losing weight and growing weaker day by day. He had been in the middle of treatment when civilization as he had known it had come to an end. Without finishing his treatments, his cancer hadn't had the chance to go into remission. That left him plagued by the horrible symptoms of his condition, symptoms that spelled his end by means of a slow and painful death.

To add cruel fate to his agony, he would spend those torturous dying days alone.

Wracked by the shakes, Quinn forced himself to his feet. Perhaps he could try to sleep in Marley or Christopher's beds. They were much smaller than his queen-sized one, but at least there wasn't a zombie currently trying to claw its way through the window and into their room. He headed for what had once been Christopher's space, before the boy had died from the infection. Quinn thought he could ignore the memories that would come from seeing his son's belongings, but he was wrong.

Quinn couldn't help but glance around the room as he curled himself into a ball atop the child's *Star Wars* comforter. Posters of space ships, laser battles and costumed characters adorned the walls, and a mobile of the planets still hung overhead. His boy had been fascinated with anything involving space travel, and had dreamed of becoming an astronaut. The last time Quinn had seen Christopher, his son had not tried to make eye contact, half of his face missing, and his rotting internal organs draped over his groin. Even if Quinn had attempted to approach the zombie that had once been his son, he wouldn't have gotten very close. Those who had turned avoided Quinn like the plague, put off by his chemo-tainted smell.

Instead of sleep, all Quinn found was more pain, the heart-rending ache over the loss of his family far exceeding any discomfort caused by the cancer. The end hadn't seemed quite as bad when he had believed he would spend it surrounded by loved ones. Not like this, though. Never like this.

He couldn't understand why the zombie had chosen his window to assault that night. They were drawn to the house by the residual scent of the living, the earlier residents who had not ever been through chemo. The children's clothing and toys, along with his wife's things kept bringing them back, Quinn suspected, because the zombies certainly didn't want him.

Still angry, and now very upset, Quinn rose and began to tear down all of the posters and the mobile, which he piled onto Christopher's bed. Then he pulled the clothing, shoes and extras from his son's dresser and closet, adding them to the pile atop the comforter. Bundling everything together like a giant hobo pack, he dragged the comforter and its contents out onto his front lawn. Fatigued but not finished, he returned into the house and did the same thing in his daughter's room, piling all of her belongings onto her much smaller rainbow quilt.

By the time his wife's things had joined the heap on the lawn, Quinn was spent. He allowed himself to collapse onto his front steps and sat there limply, watching as a small crowd of zombies gathered and circled the mound of toys, ornaments and clothing. They still avoided Quinn, but shuffled and paused at a distance, sniffing at the untainted items that carried his family's scent, and moaning hungrily.

"Sorry to disappoint you, but I told you…I don't have anything you want."

Quinn had already decided he would burn it all, a giant bonfire that would eliminate the scent of his absent family and rid himself of the zombie annoyance for at least a while, giving him a chance to get some rest. The zombies shied away from fire even more than they did from people like Quinn. They would go away, likely for the remainder of the night, and maybe bother someone else for a change.

When he had gathered enough of his strength to get to his feet again, Quinn dragged himself into the garage where he still had an old container of gasoline for his lawn mower. He poured it onto the items gathered on his lawn, and then set them ablaze. Backpedalling, he dropped down onto his steps and watched the flames.

Just as he had predicted, the zombies fled once the fire was going strong, shying from the heat at first and then shuffling away as quickly as they could manage. Quinn hoped it would keep them at bay for hours. He knew he should stay outside and guard it until it burned down, in case it spread or even advanced on his house, but he didn't care anymore. He had nothing left to live for and no way to keep himself from dying even if he did. All he wanted to do was sleep, the longer the better.

The wind changed direction and the smoke made Quinn cough and stung his eyes, forcing him inside again. He headed back to bed, exhausted and ready to make another go at sleep. He had honestly thought that ridding the house of all mementos of his family would serve dual purpose: fend off the zombies and help him to forget that his family had been there in the first place. The zombies were gone, but shedding all reminders of his family did not allow him any peace of mind. If anything, having their belongings around had preserved something of them, almost making Quinn feel as though they were still there, even though he was aware that they would not be coming home. Now he had nothing, not even false hope.

As Quinn lay under his blankets, running his hand over his wife, Emily's, empty side of the bed, the loneliness overwhelmed him. He tried to remember her beautiful face the way it had been the day that they had first met, or during their first kiss. He dug deeper, trying to picture her on their wedding day, or holding Christopher and Marley just after his babies had been born. But try as he might, all he could come up with was the way he had found her when arriving home from chemo, the day she had died.

When he had walked into the house that day, the place had been in shambles. The children had already died and turned. They had attacked their mother, mauling her and tearing away the choicest pieces of flesh before leaving her bite riddled corpse bleeding and dying in the hallway. Quinn had no idea where his son and daughter had gone from there. He had caught a glimpse of zombie Christopher a couple of times, but not Marley. Maybe one of the survivors had gotten in a headshot and ended her undead existence. She would have been one of the easier zombies to overpower, having only been four years old when she had turned.

The shock of seeing Emily like that had shaken off all of the nausea and lethargy that usually plagued him after a chemo session. He had dropped to his knees and clutched her to him, demanding to know what had happened. She had told him as simply as she could, sparing him the gruesome details, and had begged him to find her purse. He couldn't understand why at the time, until he had returned with it and she had confessed that she had kept a small pistol in there once word of the viral outbreak had hit the media. Quinn had always hated anything dangerous. He had been severely phobic when it came to anything that was potentially fatal and had been obsessive about keeping guns, large knives and even prescription drugs out of the house. That hadn't stopped Emily, but the gun had proven worthless when confronted by her own undead children. She would have shot anyone but them, possibly even Quinn.

"Use it on me," she had begged him. "One shot in the head. I don't want to come back as one of them. I don't have much time—please, you'll do this if you love me."

It had been hard enough for Quinn just to grasp the gun and pull it from her purse. He had known she was practically dead already, infected even if her wounds hadn't been life threatening, but he just hadn't been able to bring himself to pull that trigger. He hadn't even been able to do it once she had died and risen again, because no matter what had happened to her, it was still Emily. After she had breathed her last breath, he had left her in the hallway, not wanting to watch her turn. She had left the house after that, no doubt hungry and repulsed by his very strong smell.

It seemed to Quinn like he remembered that moment when he really needed to avoid it most—when his spirits were at their lowest, like now. He had failed her, and that fact tormented him. He still had the gun, hoping he would find the strength to use it on himself when he could stand his own pain no longer, but he had already tried to twice and he hadn't had the heart to do it. He wanted to die, he needed to die, but now rather than lingering in his own filth for a couple of days once he grew too weak to take care of himself.

He couldn't manage to shoot himself, and he didn't exactly have any other options, none that he would ever follow through on. He didn't think he could overdose on aspirin or acetaminophen, the only drugs in the house. He supposed it was possible, but if he got it wrong, his death might be umpteenth times more painful, and he wanted to die to escape the pain, never having had much of a tolerance for it.

That was also why Quinn wouldn't be trying death-by-cleaner cocktail either. He had heard it was a horrible way to go, your innards on fire for however long it took you to die. Ironically, what should have been the easiest way for him to go, death-by-zombie, wasn't available to him. He would have actually picked that over going on alone, if he could have.

In truth, Quinn hadn't been alone the entire time since the loss of his family. He had managed to track down Amelia, one of the other cancer patients who had been receiving chemo treatment at the clinic where Quinn had gone for his, but she was no longer with him. Not that she had died from her illness or another cause. They had made do with each other's company for several weeks, scavenging for food and other supplies together until they had run into a group of the survivalists. The men hadn't been willing to take Quinn back to their enclave, only looking for able-bodied males, but they had been happy to take Amelia back with them. With a ratio of three men to every woman, they weren't about to be fussy with regards to the females they recruited. Amelia, apologizing to Quinn for abandoning him, but admitting she could not bear to live the way they did anymore, had agreed to go with them.

Quinn had tried to follow them back to their enclave, pleading with them to make an exception rather than take his only companion from him. They hadn't been totally unsympathetic to his plight, but they hadn't yielded to his demands either. Escorting Amelia away, they had soon outpaced Quinn, beating him to the enclave. The barred gate was well secured to keep out the undead, the lofty walls impossible to scale for someone in Quinn's condition and topped with razor wire even if he could make it up. They had refused to let him in. That had been the end to that.

Quinn drew in a deep breath, missing Emily and his children much more than Amelia, but sad for all of their losses. He wept, not worried if it would make him appear weak because there was no one there to observe or to care. He wished things had ended differently. In fact, he wished things had ended, period. If only he had had more courage, the deed would have already been done.

"Death-by-zombie...kind of like death-by-cop," he muttered, stirring in his bed. Quinn's obsessive nature still wouldn't let that idea go. That was how people sometimes did it before the world had been ravaged by the zombie virus, committing suicide by forcing someone else's hand when they saw no way out. But Quinn refused to see it as suicide. In his case, it would be euthanasia.

Death-by-survivalist could have been another option, but that group selectively destroyed zombies or any living people who posed a genuine threat. They hadn't viewed Quinn as any danger, and when he had lingered by their door after Amelia had gone with them, they had simply ignored him. Whether it was because they opposed killing any of the few remaining humans, or they hadn't wanted to waste ammo on him, Quinn wasn't sure. They may have even considered him somewhat beneficial while he was there, deterring the zombies from approaching their gate. Eventually, hunger, thirst and the need for shelter had driven Quinn away, and he had returned to his lonely house, devoid of Amelia's company.

A new pain started smoldering in Quinn's gut, one that suddenly shot piercing agony through his torso. He writhed on the bed, sweating profusely and moaning loudly until the pain gradually ebbed into something a little more tolerable. Those random attacks occurred more often now, paralyzing him for minutes and provoking behavior in him that was almost zombie-like, with the incoherent sounds and the flailing.

"Jesus, if the survivalists saw me like that, they wouldn't hesitate to shoot me," he gasped, clutching at his stomach.

The thought stayed with him, however, and as soon as his tension and panting eased, he lurched out of bed. He finally had a solution, but it might be burning up in the bonfire on his lawn. Rushing outside as fasts as his shaky legs would allow, he searching the pile of belongings for the specific thing he wanted. The light from the flames was enough to allow him to find what he sought, a small black case bearing pictures of a vampire, a ghoul and a Frankenstein monster on its topside. Quinn dove for it before the fire could reach it.

He dragged himself and the box back into the house again. The plastic had curled on the edges of the case from the heat of the blaze, but otherwise the container and its contents were unharmed. Quinn glanced through the tubes, bottles and sponges inside, contents that included liquid latex and fake blood. Christopher had begged for the make-up kit for his costume last Halloween. Ironically, the boy had chosen to go as a zombie.

And Quinn could use it to make himself look like a zombie too.

The undead wouldn't be fooled by the make-up; they would know him by his smell. The survivalists would be much less likely to recognize him, however, and they shot any zombies approaching their enclave, on sight. Quinn might not be able to kill himself by pulling the trigger, but he could still have his death-by-zombie—only *he* would be the zombie, sort of.

After examining everything to make sure it would still function as intended, not too dried up or crusty, he slid the case under his bed. It was too late to do what he intended to do now and it could easily wait until morning. With this knowledge, Quinn now had strong incentive to get a good night's rest. He would need it to make it to the enclave in his weakened state, even though he would be fueled by a motivating purpose.

The zombies were gone now, driven off by the fire, so nobody scraped at his window anymore. Quinn could even ignore the pain, comforted by what tomorrow promised. He would sleep better than he had in many nights.

And in the morning? Death-by-zombie. He would finally have an end to his loneliness and suffering.

ABOUT THE AUTHOR

Chantal Boudreau is an accountant/author/illustrator who lives in Nova Scotia, Canada with her husband and two children. A member of the Horror Writers Association, she writes and illustrates horror, dark fantasy and fantasy and has had several of her stories published in a variety of horror anthologies and magazines. Fervor, her debut dystopian novel, was released in March of 2011 by May December Publications, followed by Elevation, Transcendence and Providence. Magic University, the first in her fantasy series, Masters & Renegades, made its appearance in September 2011 followed by Casualties of War and Prisoners of Fate. Learn more at: http://chantellyb.wordpress.com

11

Sweet Release
By Mark Tufo

It took the doctor seven and a half minutes to tell Theodore Wright that the world as he knew it no longer existed. At least that's what it felt like. At thirty-two, he was on the fast track at the law firm he worked for. His wife was a model, they lived in an upscale apartment on the upper west side of Manhattan. He had box seat season tickets to the Yankees for chrissakes!

"Are you sure? I feel fine, I mean except for some occasional abdominal pain. How can this be possible?" Ted asked.

The doctor shuffled his papers around uncomfortably. He had just given the man sitting across from him a death sentence, and if his patient should break down and start crying, he would be sure to miss his 2:30 tee off time with his colleagues. "I'm forwarding you to the foremost doctor in this field. Dr. Simmons and I would like to start you on chemo and a drug regimen beginning Monday."

Ted looked shocked. "That soon?"

"Ted, if I could get you in today, I would. The cancer has metastasized. At least this way you can go home, you'll have the weekend to wrap your mind around this."

"I mean we caught it soon enough, right? I'll recover?" he asked with trepidation.

The doctor looked down. *Shit*, he thought as he watched the second hand of his Rolex click away more time. The doctor removed his glasses and pinched the bridge of his nose. "Ted, even with aggressive treatment, you're chances of survival aren't too good. It has spread."

"What's not too good? Fifty-fifty? I'll take that."

There was an imperceptible shake to the doctor's head.

"Forty-sixty? Friggin' thirty?"

"Three percent."

"You're fucking kidding me!" Ted said, sending his chair skittering backwards as he arose quickly.

"I wish that I were, Ted."

"Why bother with the chemo then?" Ted asked, circling the small office and then getting behind his chair subconsciously using it as a barrier between him and the doctor's cruel words.

"It's zero without it," the doctor responded evenly.

"Zero...three...big deal."

"I bet the bookies didn't give the Red Sox a three percent chance of beating the Yankees after the third game of the ALCS in '04." Ted allowed himself a small smile at the remembrance. "I had to wear my friend's Boston jersey for a week after that series. The only good part about losing that bet was I got so much food and drink tossed at me while I was wearing it, it was almost ruined by the time I sent it back."

The doc smiled with him. "Be back here Monday at eight and we'll go over everything you can expect," the doctor said as he rose.

"Eight, Jesus, what do I tell work?"

"The truth, I would imagine."

"You don't understand law firms, they smell weakness in me...I'm gone."

"There are laws in place to prevent this type of thing. Talk to your human resources department."

"I'm finished." Ted said as his head hung low. "Oh, at first they'll be all caring…but as soon as I need to take time off and I can't bill my clients, they'll find a way to let me go. A failed evaluation, or they'll find a client to lodge a complaint. I'll lose everything."

"Right, well…um…you need to concentrate on yourself first," the doctor said, doing his best to usher the distraught man out of his office. "I can still make it if I hurry," he said after he closed the door and looked at his watch.

***

"You're home early," Jennifer huffed from the living room. Her long, lithe body, stretched taut over her exercise ball. The woman demonstrating the technique on the large plasma screen could easily have been taking lessons from Jennifer.

Ted did not acknowledge his wife as he walked into the kitchen and grabbed a Lite beer. "Don't we have any real fucking beer!" he cursed. He heard the squeaks of the ball as Jen removed herself from it and padded softly into the kitchen.

"You alright?" she asked, wiping off her face with the towel she had draped over her slender shoulders. "Drinking at three? What's going on?"

His eyes were red rimmed as he looked over at her. He took three steps over as he touched her. "I have cancer," he practically wailed.

She stiffened and pushed back on him. "Is it catchy?" she asked as she escaped his embrace attempt.

Ted was too lost in the depths of his despair to notice the slight.

"When will you be better?" She took an involuntary step backward as he came forward.

"Maybe never," he said, something between a sob and a laugh escaping his lips.

195

"You mean you'll always have it?" A confused look on her face joined a rising dread in her chest that her fantasy world was beginning to fold in on itself.

"Yup, right up until the day I die," he told her flippantly.

A dawning recognition began to crease her features.

***

"I start chemo Monday, are you sure you can't postpone this?" Ted asked Jen. "I could really use your support."

"It's Milan, Ted, you know how important this is," she replied as she seemingly stuffed everything she had into her bags.

"Why haven't you said anything about it before?" he asked, tears threatening to fall from his eyes.

She nearly caved as she gazed upon his strong features. He was so handsome; she could not bear to remember him any other way than this. "I was going to tell you when you came home. It'll only be a week."

"You need all this stuff?" he asked her as the apartment doorman and porter placed all her bags on a luggage dolly.

"You never can tell what they'll want you to wear on these shoots," she said to him, her hand coming up to caress his face. She pulled it away just as it was about to make contact.

"I love you."

"Just get better," was her response.

After she had gone, Ted sat on their king-sized bed and took a good long look around the room. "She just left me," he realized when he saw that she had taken her jewelry, pictures, and any knick-knack she cared about.

He didn't know which was more treacherous—the cancer eating him away from the inside, or his wife.

The Mirror

He wasn't sure when he had become an alien. The last of his hair had swirled down the drain weeks ago. His once tight, tanned flesh hung pasty and sallow from his body. Sunken eyes and a moon face peered back at him where there had once been angular and determined features. He had lost over forty pounds of muscle mass, most he figured from the internal organs he must have heaved up through his go-around with chemo-therapy.

"Chemo-therapy," he mused as he reached out with a finger and stroked his reflection's cheek. "More scared of that then I ever was of the cancer. The cancer merely kills you, chemo makes you suffer."

He'd heard from Jen only once during the ordeal, and that was because she'd forgotten to take all of her shoes. She'd had the balls to ask him to ship them to her. He'd been tempted to throw up on the lot of them before he sent them, but thought better of it.

When Jennifer opened up the box a few days later, there was a small note on top of the carefully packaged shoes. She screamed loudly after reading it and checking out the package. 'Soleless shoes for a soulless bitch, Love Ted.' Every shoe had the sole neatly removed.

It was high summer in New York; inner-city kids had opened more than one fire hydrant. The Yankees sat perched atop the A.L. East. The Jets were in the middle of another off-field meltdown. The Dow had increased by two hundred points. A hit play called *Fallout Hill* had just opened up on Broadway. Ted cared for none of it. He dressed as if it were fall heading into winter; which, when he stopped to think about it, it was at least in *his* life. No matter how hard he tried, he had difficulty staying warm and the added clothes had the benefit of hiding the majority of himself from the rest of the world once he donned his wide-brimmed hat and over-sized sun-glasses.

The weight of the clothes pressed heavily on his nerve endings. Just the simple act of wearing them caused pain and discomfort. He contemplated going out nude, the worst that could happen was the cops would give him a free ride to the hospital and he could save the almost three bucks in bus fare.

"The psych ward's only one floor away from oncology," he said aloud.

Jennifer's first stop when she'd left her husband was the bank. She'd pulled out their entire savings. His firm, Stanley, Feinstein and Feeley had let him go two weeks after he'd informed them of his condition. It was a week and a half longer than he'd expected. He hadn't really been surprised when the charge of sexual harassment had been leveled against him by the Records Management assistant. That she was ten years his senior and at the time had outweighed him by a good fifty pounds was of little concern. He'd been given the option to quit quietly or have his name dragged through the mud openly and loudly.

He'd thought about opting for door number two. He had no one to embarrass; his parents had died ten years previously in a fiery car crash, his wife was busy carving out a special circle in hell for herself. The 'friends' he had at the firm who had been entrenched in his asshole when his shit didn't stink had bolted faster than rats off of a sinking ship.

"You too, Pete?" Ted had asked of his closest ally at the firm.

"You're a pariah, Ted. Listen, man, I loved you when I thought you could further my career, but now you'll just sink it. I have to look out for me and mine. Don't look at me that way. We're lawyers…you should know better," Pete had said as he shrugged off Ted's hand.

"Fuck, I've got an ex. You guys should hook up. Could probably make an anti-Christ," Ted said to Pete's back. Pete stiffened for a moment as he walked down the hallway, but his stride never broke.

Ted had sold nearly everything to hold onto his Manhattan apartment. He was surviving off his 401(k) and the meager buy-out his firm had offered him. On the plus side…his grocery bill had plunged to barely twenty bucks a week and most of that was Ramen noodles. It wasn't that he couldn't afford a little better, it was just that was the only thing he could stomach. And surprisingly on those occasions when it came back up for a visit it looked remarkably a lot like it did when it had gone down. Even the slightly off color yellow hue of the chicken stock flavor was the same.

He heard the sounds of summer all around him. Kids playing, couples fighting, ice cream trucks in the distance, horns, construction crews; he heard it all and paid none of it any attention. The pain muted life, it blotted everything else out but itself. His entire existence had been reduced to incessant pain and pill taking. By sheer volume of weight, pills were easily the largest intake to his diet. He took two breaks as he walked the city block to the bus stop. Whether consciously or sub-consciously New Yorkers as a whole shunned him, most times just merely ignoring him, other times actively moving away. The benefit to this was that he always secured a seat on the bus, even if sitting had lost some of its luster, he was too tired to stand that long.

His buttocks, which his wife used to playfully slap and call 'her buns of steel', had been as decimated as the rest of him. Unless there was six inches of padding on the seat, he could feel his pelvic bones rubbing raw against the remaining muscle. He was convinced that eventually they would poke through like mice that had chewed through a wall.

Ted's teeth gritted every time the bus ran over a pothole. He had a death grip on the seat ahead of him as he tried in desperation to minimize the shock to his system when the bus hit a bump.

"Look, mommy, that man is an alien!" a small girl of six said as she pointed at him. Her mother quickly grabbed the accusatory finger and pushed it down. The mother smiled wanly at Ted and quickly turned away.

"I was a man once," Ted said.

The mother and child got up to get off at the next stop.

"This isn't where we live, mommy," the girl had said.

The mother did not heed her daughter's words as she pushed through and off the bus.

"Must know my wife," Ted had croaked dryly.

***

Ted sat in the lobby of his doctor's office. His hands firmly entrenched in his pockets. He was shivering from the cold of the air conditioning; any thoughts of reading the outdated periodicals were quickly pushed from his mind. First, because that would mean he would have to take his clenched fists out of his pockets; and secondly, along with the degradation to his body, his mind had also been affected. The directions for preparing instant mac and cheese had taken him longer to figure out than the actual cooking of the food. He grimaced when he realized that it had also taken longer to cook than it had actually stayed in his stomach. That had not been a particularly easy clean-up job.

"Mr. Wright?" a young nurse asked, as she looked around the waiting room, her gaze passing him over more than once. He realized he'd almost wasted away to the point of not being seen. She looked somewhat surprised when he arose, as if from thin air he had materialized. "How are you doing today?" she asked plastically.

"Are you fucking kidding me?" he asked back.

She appeared taken aback from that. The common courtesy had never been thrown back at her like that. "I'm…I'm sorry," she answered when she couldn't figure out what to say. "Do you want to take your jacket off while I get your weight?" She directed him to the scale.

"This jacket is the only thing holding me to the floor," he told her.

"One forty-two," she said aloud as she wrote in his ever expanding file.

"Jesus Christ I was one ninety-six when this fuck-fest started."

"The doctor will be in to see you in a minute." She led him to the exam room.

"We both know that's a lie," he told her as she shut the door.

"Hello, Theodore," Doctor Simmons said as he entered the room. "Chemo went well," he added, never looking up from the file. "First rounds aren't usually so productive."

"First round?" Ted asked in a panic. "As in there are more? Is it worth it?"

"We've bought you more time, Ted," Dr. Simmons told him earnestly.

"At what cost, Doc? Time itself is only as good as what you do with it. I spend more time in the bathroom than my bedroom. I live pain pill to pain pill, my biggest happiness is when my constant constipation finally allows me to squirt one out. And you should see the thing, it's almost as pale and shriveled up as I am."

Doctor Simmons wanted to tell him it would get better, but the odds were greatly against that being the case. "I can give you something for the constipation."

Ted barked out a laugh. "I don't know when I'd be able to fit another pill into my schedule."

"This would be more of a suppository."

"I think I'll keep what little dignity I have remaining."

"I'd like to see you gain a little weight back before we start back up, but I don't think we can wait too long. Your T-levels have evened out, but they're still entirely too high."

"Doc...Doc, look up from the damn chart," Ted asked. When he finally did, Ted continued. "Is it worth it? I mean besides putting some medical professional's kids through college or into braces, is it worth it?"

"I don't have a definitive answer, Ted, you have a shitty form of cancer."

"Shitty? That the clinical term?" Ted smiled.

"Listen, you asked for honesty, here it is. I figure your odds of survival to be somewhere in the five percent range. Again...shitty, but it's still five percent. It's worth the attempt. If I truly didn't think it was possible to beat this I wouldn't bother. The alternative is death."

"No eternal life, Doc? You don't believe in life after death?"

"Do those words even make sense? Life after death? You live and then that's it, Ted, there is no Heaven…no Hell. There's here and now. Man was smart enough to create that fantasy world as a means to calm the suffering."

"Aren't I suffering, Doc? I could use some calming."

"I want you to fight, Ted. I don't want you giving up because you think there's something better on the other side, because there isn't. When your time is up, it's up. You have a chance. With the chemo, radiation and the right mix of drugs, we can get you years. Your hair will grow back, you'll regain the weight, you could have your old life back."

Ted's face pulled back in abject fear.

"What is it, Ted? Are you alright?"

"Jen won't be coming back, will she?" he asked.

"Scared the hell out of me."

"I'll try, Doc, if only for you. When do I start up again?"

"I've scheduled you for Monday."

Ted's eyes opened wide; this time not in mock horror. "Yet another reason to hate that damn day."

Ted had fogged his way home, taking double the dose of painkillers as he absorbed the information the doctor had given. "I guess I always knew you weren't there," Ted said, looking up. "I mean, what kind of fucking cosmic joke would this be?" Ted had one step on the stoop to his apartment building. "How about I have a joke for you?" he said as he walked a block to a local variety store.

"Will that be all?" the girl behind the counter asked.

"A new pancreas might work, you got one of those? Maybe a wig…and how about a wife that doesn't leave at the first hint of trouble."

"Fresh out of non-psycho bitches, they don't stay on the shelves long," the girl told him.

"Come on, mister, this ain't no soap opera…gets your ass out of the line so I can plays my numbers," a burly man dressed in a Department of Public Works uniform said.

"Sorry, I didn't mean to mess with your retirement plan," Ted told him as the clerk handed him his change.

"Youse a funny one," DPW man said as he elbowed past.

Ted leaned against the store front once he stepped out. He was exhausted and slightly concerned that he did not possess the energy to get home. "A good a place as any," he said as he unscrewed the cap and took a large swig of the caustic liquor.

"Yo, Powder," a young man in his twenties said.

Ted turned to look at the man; scabs laced his arms and his face. Teeth the color of dead canaries lined his mouth. His eyes were a rough-shod red.

"You got any money I can have?" the man asked, scratching frenetically at his arms.

"You know how I know there's no God," Ted told him as he took another swig.

"Yeah how's that?" The man asked looking around.

"I bet you're as healthy as a horse, yet you care nothing for the life you decide to flush down the toilet with every hit of meth you take."

"Yeah? Well fuck you, mister, you don't look so hot yourself. You and your bottle of Jack can kiss my ass." He ripped a leathery flap of dried blood from his right cheek, puss oozed from the new opening. "You go bury yourself in your bottle, and I'll do as I please."

The sun was making its journey downwards when the store clerk's shift was over. She exited the store and immediately lit a cigarette. She turned to her left where Ted was sitting, his legs splayed, the bottle in between them.

"This is the best place you could think to do that?" she asked him, exhaling a large plume of smoke.

Ted looked up into her face. "Jennifer?" he asked foggily.

"Yeah, sure…whoever you want me to be. You live around here?"

"A block over on 156th," he slurred.

"Didn't figure you to be rich. Do you need some help home?"

"Why?" Ted asked.

"My dad died from lung cancer, you remind me a lot of him."

"Is it the hair thing?" he asked as she reached down and helped pull him up.

"The smell, you reek of rot," she told him.

"So I've got a distinctive malignant odor to add to all the other things I have going on? That's perfect."

She shrugged her shoulders just as she took on a significant portion of his body weight.

"Want a hit?" he kept asking her as they walked. Constantly sloshing the bottle in front of her.

"Recovering alcoholic...but thank you for making my clothes smell like a distillery, I was looking for a reason to reflect on all my bad decisions in life tonight."

"I was a lawyer once."

"Oh, so you've had a lot of prior experience on being an asshole."

"We're here," he told her.

"Fancy digs."

"Thank you," Ted told her earnestly. "Can I get you a drink...I mean of water or soda or something?"

"I've got to go, I've already missed my bus, and now I'll owe my babysitter overtime. Sixteen years old and I swear she's training to be in the mafia. It's extortion the prices she charges. You take care okay?" she said to him as she left.

He climbed the stairs to his apartment, walked into the kitchen, and poured the remaining contents of the bottle into the sink. He then sat heavily down on his sofa. He placed his head in his hands and sobbed uncontrollably for hours. He had meant to pill and drink himself to death, the one small act of kindness from the clerk was the only message he needed to discount all his doctor had said earlier.

"I was going to kill myself God," he wailed. "If there was no retribution for sins, then how could I be expected to have to atone for suicide? I'd be out of pain." A fear gripped his chest as he thought of how close he had come. "To die without a legacy...that is the true crime," he said. "I have done nothing noteworthy my entire life. I have no kids, friends or kin who will mourn me. When I die, that will be it, I will be erased as neatly from this world as if I never existed. I have to live, I have to make a difference. I have to survive if only for that."

He dreaded the whole idea of the radiation and chemotherapy regiment starting all over. It was worse this time around because he knew what to expect, there was something to be said about being blindly ignorant to what was to come. He turned quickly to his right when he felt the ice cold brush of a finger on his neck. It was a fleeting sensation gone nearly as quickly as it come. "Guess that's what I get for mixing booze and pills."

Sunlight was streaming across his face when he awoke the next morning. "My head is killing me," he said as he sat up. "Well...actually it's the cancer if I'm being specific."

He stood, fighting off a serious bout of vertigo. He let go of the side of the couch when he finally regained his balance. He took a long hot shower to see if he could scrub off the smell the store clerk had told him he wore, but unless he could get a Brillo pad inside himself, it probably wasn't going anywhere.

He took his time as he walked; partly because it was making him exhausted, but more so because he wanted to take everything in. The sun upon his face. The birds as they sang to one another. The young lovers on the park bench kissing. An older couple fighting about who was going to drive. He thought that maybe only those that were so close to death could appreciate life so much. He was at the market before he knew it.

The clerk looked up at him. "Round two?" she asked with a sadness in her eyes.

"I just wanted to say thank you," he told her. "It's been a while since anybody has even looked at me, much less done something kind."

"You would have done the same," she said to him.

He wasn't so sure. He was confident that his old self would have been like the vast majority of humanity, entirely too busy and self-absorbed in their own lives to stop and help a stranger, much less one that was so close to the other side. People did not like constant reminders of their ultimate destination. "All the same…thank you." He gave her a small wave.

She cocked her head slightly to the side like she had more to say or thought maybe he did. "Goodbye," she finally told him. He nodded before he exited.

Ted was in the best spirits he'd been in since the doctor had told him about his condition. He wasn't happy about it, but he'd come to accept that this was his life now. It was with this disposition that he boarded the bus on Monday morning. Hopeful, expectant, accepting, and resigned; all of these emotions swirled around inside of him each vying for its moment in the spotlight. "I have a chance!" was his mantra as he walked into the hospital.

When he emerged a few hours later, the chant was still within him, it just took too much energy to vocalize it. For a while he had found himself traveling from his couch to the bathroom, and then, when it just became too difficult to make the trek, he grabbed some of the throw pillows and made himself as comfortable as possible on the hard tile floor.

"This is the life," he croaked out in between upheavals. He had not meant it as sarcasm, only as an affirmation that he was still alive.

His body ached when he awoke, there was not much on him to offer in the department of cushioning. "You ready for this?" he asked his reflection. The reflection shrugged. He opened up his bottle of Oxycontin and shook two of the pills into his hand. "Not today," he said as he put them back in the bottle. "I've got one thing I need to do today before I go to the hospital." He went through his file cabinet, and when he found what he was looking for, he headed out. Trepidation knotted in his stomach.

"What if she isn't there?"

The pain the Oxy's usually kept at bay was pushing its way around his body. Painful spikes radiating out from his chest and reverberating throughout his body to crash into his skull, threatening to drop him to his knees.

"You alright? You look like shit," the store clerk asked him as she grabbed his arm; he had been leaning up against a yet un-opened bakery store front.

"We need to stop meeting like this. I...I don't even know your name."

"Stacy Grangor, why?"

"Is that with an e-y?" he asked, fishing the paper out of his pocket.

"Just the y," she told him, clearly confused.

He placed the paper up against the store front window and quickly filled it out and signed it. He handed it to her with a key.

"What is this?" She asked.

"Car title, cherry '69 Mustang," he told her, his teeth chattering from the pain he was in. "The key goes to the parking bay I pay entirely too much for over on 152nd."

"But why?"

"One kindness deserves another. Have a good life, Stacy Grangor." He moved as quickly from the scene as he could. "Just another step!" he prodded himself. He did not want to have to stop and rest. "It will be a bad ending if I can't even walk away." He forced himself forward, each step sending a shock wave of pain throughout him. He thanked God for small favors as the bus pulled up just as he got to the stop. He was in agony, pain flared through his extremities, it was beginning to tunnel his vision and he had no such illusions that the heavens would be so kind as to send another guardian angel.

His breathing became labored. "I...I don't think I'm going to make it," he said silently. His hands curled into tight fists. The bus stopped, he knew it was too soon for the hospital, he didn't bother to look up. A few moments later, he felt someone sit in the seat next to him, their arm brushing up against him. Where they made contact, a soothing sensation flowed. A liver spotted hand reached across his field of vision and gently grabbed his right fist.

"Wha—" Ted began, the all-encompassing pain easing. He was finally able to drag his eyes up to a familiar looking face. It was someone he'd never met, but he'd seen enough pictures of to recognize. "Grandpa?" he asked.

The wizened old man smiled and nodded.

"How?"

"It's a Sweet Release."

12

Uncle
By Michael James McFarland

For Tillie...

Too late, far too late to bring back the dead, I've come to realize the truth hidden behind my uncle's bedroom door. The night-rustlings, the soft sound of his idiot laughter, the single-minded fascination he seems to have with his left hand...

I see faces shrinking into a terrible black vapor—languid, increasingly pale—slowly devoured by the spider in their midst; unaware of the true cause or, perhaps suspecting, unable to raise a hand against it.

The cold, creeping realization...the *horror* of its method.

The calendar tells me it's only three months since my life began to unravel, but can that be true? How distant those days seem, almost as if the time preceding my mother's death were part of another life—a calm and orderly existence I'd somehow mistaken for my own.

But I'm getting ahead of myself...

***

The snare closed around my leg on March 21st, when word of my mother's passing arrived by telegram. My invalid uncle, who lived under my mother's care, was being attended to by a neighbor, and I suddenly found myself obliged to take a leave of absense from the bank to travel to Spokane, where I would assume responsibility for him. My father, of whom I can recall very little, was long dead—at once more and less fortunate than my uncle in that the war obliterated him completely from the face of the earth, imbuing his memory with the aura of a soldier's death. My mother's older brother, on the other hand, left the greater part of his humanity in a bombed out churchyard in France, returning to my aunt a useless shell, a vegetable. After she died—still relatively young, at 36—there was only Mother to care for him, her small pension supplemented by taking in laundry and cleaning houses. For my own part, I sent her everything I could after necessity devoured the greater part of my salary.

Now, with Mother's death, it fell upon me to provide for him.

Let me be perfectly blunt about this. I had no great love of the man; indeed, I hardly knew him, the sum total of our acquaintance being three or four awkward visits around the holidays. What I do recall most vividly was the three of us shut inside that suffocating little house, the wind and snow flying at the windows; and the nights, they fell so painfully early...

Looking back, I now see the life and vitality draining out of her: the day-to-day drudgery, without respite...the scraping for money, *always* scraping...with *him* as her only companion.

Yet how we underestimated him. His *tenacity* to survive.

Being so much older than Mother, I'd always assumed my uncle would precede her to the grave. In addition to his war injuries, his health had never been particularly stable, so there was little reason to believe otherwise. My impression, at least from my mother's letters, was that he was forever tottering on that final line between life and death, and that a prolonged cold or infection would be enough to tip him over. As a result, nothing had been put aside to provide for his continued care—it simply never occurred to us that he would last so long. As a bachelor with less than a year's seniority at the bank, I had no nest egg to draw upon. I'd not even accrued the security and stability to permit the basic pleasures of wife and home, much less a bed-ridden relation.

Other, more providential souls receive monies, stocks, or even properties for their inheritance; I received a millstone. My uncle had been a burden to my mother, and now he would become a burden to me.

Packing a hasty suitcase, I boarded a train and began my trudge across the state, the clack and carriage of the steel rails dampening my senses, pushing me deeper into the contours of my seat. The fleeting shapes of spruce, pine, and cottonwood trees whispered past the windows, giving way at some point to the bald stalks of telegraph poles. Inevitably, in a dull stretch beyond Ellensburg, the rhythm of the train lulled me into an unguarded sleep.

***

Snow was falling outside the faded sheers, creating a padded sense of isolation, as if the tiny white house were receding into limbo. To the north and south, the neighboring houses trembled and blurred with each new gust. Beyond that, the rest of the city might not have existed at all.

A feeble light gleamed dully off the wallpaper, imparting a drowsy forgetfulness to the interior. A Christmas tree stood in one corner, captured and defeated, shedding little of its gaiety to the cramped arrangement of rooms; the decorations hanging from its boughs chipped and lusterless, as old as memory.

I stood in the midst of it all, a giant in my service uniform, suitcases tugging at the ends of my arms, looking down as if from a great distance, as detached as the gods of Olympus. From behind there came a familiar creak and the kitchen door swung open: my mother in a clean apron ushering in the aroma of bast-

ed turkey and oven-fresh rolls. Cranberry stuffing, mashed potatoes and sweet pumpkin pie.

"Mother, you've gone to too much trouble!" I protested, offering a half-felt smile; in truth I was happy to see her, content to
be home, but the damping, almost stillborn presence of my uncle
in the back bedroom cast a heavy shadow over my mood. "And
the wine...you shouldn't have! It's too expensive!"

"Oh, *that!*" she said, waving it aside, busying herself about
the table, laying out the good china (settings for two, I noticed
with a measure of relief). "A present from Mrs. Yates for some
last-minute alterations to her dress...a lovely velvet and lace.
With young John away in France this year, it's just her and
George for Christmas. I suppose I let on that you were coming
home to visit; still, it was awfully nice of her."

She straightened and looked at the table with a critical eye,
nodding. The wine, the candles, the linen tablecloth...it floated
before me like an island of quiet elegance in the gathering storm,
a welcome haven from the cold outside. I raised my eyes to meet
hers and caught a tear before she could wipe it away.

"It's good to have you home, Davy," she said quietly. "I
was afraid the snow might keep you from me."

I smiled. "It's good to be back."

The moment faded gracefully, then was broken by a low
moan from the rear of the house.

Uncle.

Her eyes dropped to the floor. "My word, listen to me prat-
tle on while you stand there, arms full and dripping wet!" She
hurried around the table, worrying the folds out of her apron, and
planted a tender kiss on my cheek. "Let me have your hat and
coat to dry and you can take those suitcases back to your room. I
put some clean sheets on the bed this morning and made space
for your clothes in the closet and bureau. Just push aside any of
your uncle's things if you need more room."

A sound like long fingernails scratching plaster replaced the
moan.

I looked down the hallway toward the dimly lit bedroom. A jaundiced wedge of light fanned across the hardwoods and up the facing wall. I saw the foot of his bed draped with a woolen blanket and, above that, part of a pastoral scene hanging in an antique frame.

"How is he these days?" I inquired, turning back to her.

She sighed and some of the day's pleasure bled out of her expression. "No better or worse. He still has the use of his left arm and leg, but there's no real strength to them, and he won't use them one whit to help himself." She shook her head and gazed distractedly down the hall, obviously troubled. "Mostly he sleeps his days away and lies restless throughout the night…making his complaints. I've gotten to where I can sleep a good piece, if I leave a light burning on his bedside table; that helps some."

"Mother, you're fifty years old! You can't keep doing all this yourself!" I argued. "Isn't there somewhere…some *place* that might take him in and look after him? A home for veterans like himself?"

She turned away, watching the snow as it pressed against the windowpane. There, framed against the gray of twilight, I could see a reflection of her in silhouette, her hands busy at her apron.

"I did look into one of those homes once, a few months after you enlisted," she admitted, a sharp edge of emotion tearing plainly at her voice. "Right close to town…but I couldn't do it, not while I still had two good hands and an extra bed under my roof." She turned back to face me; I saw the tears I had known were there, rimming her pale blue eyes. "You don't remember him from before the war, do you, Davy?"

I shook my head.

"That's why you'll never understand why I keep him here, with me…because *I do*. He was my sweet big brother," she said fiercely. "How can I turn my back on him now?"

***

213

I stood in the bedroom, looking down at his scarred body in the half-light. He seemed ancient—incredibly so, as timeless as a fallen tree in a mossy glen. He seemed to sense the weight of my shadow and arched his back, rolling slightly in his bed, his eyes peeled back to cast a baleful look in my direction, as if I were somehow to blame for his wretched condition.

Finding himself awake, he moaned and shifted, his gaze rising to regard the knotted flesh of his left hand. An unsettling smile cracked his lips, as though he'd found something there to amuse himself.

"Hello, Uncle," I said aloud, uttering words that felt wooden in my mouth. "It looks like we'll be sharing a room tonight."

All the while, he continued to stare into the lines and folds of his hand, to the exclusion of all else…holding it just so, fingers splayed to catch the light, turning the hand slowly, as if it were a precious object on display.

Somehow it all seemed covetous, sickening to my eyes.

His mouth opened to smile, the muscles tightening, and his sides began to shake with silent laughter, toothless and barely contained.

A frightening impulse eclipsed my compassion and quickly, before it could take shape, I turned and fled the room.

***

I awoke to a shuddering squeal of brakes, bringing the train to a halt.

The day had turned to drizzle and tattered gray, the station itself subdued, uninhabited; perfectly suited for a funeral. I stood and collected my suitcase, feeling dazed and disoriented, as if I were stepping through overlapping ripples of time. There was a damp spot on the shoulder of my jacket, a slim thread of saliva on my chin.

I wiped it away as I stepped onto the wet platform.

Uncle

***

The smell of disease and despair leapt upon me as soon as I entered the house. Mrs. Culp, my mother's next-door neighbor, came out of the shadows to greet me, expelling exclamations of greeting and assurances that she would be happy to sit with my uncle until after the service.

I set down my suitcase and took a cursory look about the place. It had changed very little since I'd last laid eyes on it: the same brown and dreary wallpaper, the same claustrophobic feel. The clock ticked steadily on the mantel. There was another year's wear on the rugs and upholstery, another year's misery bottled up inside the rooms, but it all looked clean and well kept. Mrs. Culp's doing, I'm sure. The woman seemed a whirlwind of activity. All surfaces scrubbed and polished, all furnishings clean and expectant, like lonely pets waiting for my mother's return. I made a mental note to leave the woman something for her trouble, some token more substantial than an empty hand-shake and a thank-you. Perhaps there was something of my mother's she might wish to keep...

A low chuckle insinuated its way from the back bedroom, pairing itself in the folds of memory with a clenched hand. A tightly-held secret. "Your poor mother," Mrs. Culp frowned, flinching slightly at the sound of my uncle's laughter. She touched my arm in sympathy. "It happened so *fast*. Bless her heart, she was all used up."

***

All used up...

I was surprised—*shocked,* really—at how frail my mother looked. How *wasted.*

My God, I thought, swaying wearily in a hushed alcove within the funeral parlor. It had been four months since I'd last seen her, but the changes in so short a time were startling! She had never been a particularly heavy woman, but now what flesh she'd had looked to have evaporated away, leaving a brittle wraith in her best blue dress.

She looked lost in her clothes: dry bones connected by sinew to a pale and skullish face, her eyes virtually straining within their hollowed sockets.

I reached out to take her hand and immediately dropped it. It was just twigs and paper; nothing left inside to mourn.

Tears falling down my gray suit, I took a chair beside her.

***

The service was brief and merciful, the cemetery less than a mile from her little house. I'm ashamed to say I wasn't able to concentrate on the service as was her due. My mind kept wandering from the sodden gravesite: down misty lanes to the room where my uncle lay in his awful bed and loose-fitting clothes…waiting for a new charge to wipe and feed him, while he spent endless hours considering the mysteries of his own sinister hand.

It's not a responsibility I take lightly; truly, it's not.

Still, I wish it weren't so.

***

Rain began to fall again as the service reached its conclusion.

I walked the (too brief) three-quarters of a mile from the cemetery to my mother's house, trying to put my thoughts in order and delay the inevitable a few minutes longer. The renewed downpour soaked my hat and overcoat, weighing me down further as I turned up the walkway.

Mrs. Culp burst through the door and came flapping down to meet me, umbrella in hand. "Good gracious, Mr. Laurie! You're soaked to the skin! Why didn't you take a taxi from the service?"

Actually, it *had* crossed my mind to arrange for a taxi, but to an altogether different destination.

"Here you are." She thrust the umbrella against the sky so that my last ten steps to the house might be dry ones. "Come inside where it's warm," she prodded, stepping to avoid both puddles and cracks. "I've got hot soup on the stove and the makings for sandwiches! I wasn't sure if you'd have eaten but, being a man, I guessed you hadn't given it a passing thought. There's so much food left in the icebox; why, it would be a *sin* to let it go to waste!"

I thanked her kindly, shedding water from my coat before I crossed the threshold.

"I'll hang that up for you, Mr. Laurie," she said, shaking the umbrella closed and holding out a plump hand for my overcoat. "Your hat too, if you don't mind." She bustled off through the kitchen toward the utility, where Mother used to keep such things as dripping coats and muddy galoshes. "Sit down and make yourself comfortable. I'll be just a minute. I'm sure you're anxious to hear about your uncle."

I bit my tongue to keep the bitterness from leaking out.

Unbuttoning my suit jacket, I cast an indifferent eye down the hall. The door was shut, but I could hear him laughing through the panel; amused, no doubt, about the rain. With a sigh, I sat down and looked once again at the furnishings, this time with a more critical gaze. I might find space for some of the smaller pieces in my apartment, I thought, appraising the two end tables like a ghoul, but there was a great deal for which I simply didn't have the room. It would have to be disposed of somewhere. Hauled off, sold, or given away.

"There now, that didn't take long. Have you been back to look in on Clark?"

I shook my head. It's strange...most of the time I never think of my uncle by name, much less that he has one. That's awful, I suppose, reducing him to that level. Even cats and dogs have names. You might suppose he was no more than an inconvenient lump to me. A thing.

"Just as well." She bent to straighten a cloth on the arm of the sofa—where she'd been sitting, I realized, waiting for me, the lawn and walkway clearly visible out the window. "He's been sleeping most of the day; has his days and nights switched around, if you ask me, but he seems in good spirits now. I don't know how Bethany put up with it, the way he fusses through the night. I tell you it wears a body out!"

"Yes," I answered, "it certainly could." My mother was testament to that.

"Well now, how was the service? A dismal day for it, I can imagine. I was sorry to have missed it, the two of us being neighbors and all, but then we couldn't very well leave your poor uncle alone, could we?"

"No, I suppose not." She was quite obviously fishing for a word of gratitude and I was slow to take the bait. Slow, but not completely insensitive. "I *do* appreciate the sacrifices you've made staying here with him, and getting the house in order. I don't know what I would have done without you, Mrs. Culp."

She blushed and waved it away with a contented smile. "Don't think twice about it. I was happy to help out." She paused, letting slip some twitch or tremor of emotion. "Your mother was very dear to me, young man. I expect she knows that I was with her in spirit." Tears were creeping into her soft brown eyes.

"I'm sure she does, Mrs. Culp," I assured her, rising and laying a comforting hand on her shoulder.

She turned away, digging for a handkerchief.

It was then I noticed a small, rust-colored petal pressed damply against the fabric of her blouse.

"Why, Mrs. Culp," I said, pointing to the spot on the sleeve, just above her left elbow. "You've cut yourself!"

"What?" she yelped, raising her arm and tugging at the drab material, turning toward the light. "*Where*? Oh my gracious! Where on earth did *that* come from?" She pinched the stain between her thumb and forefinger and the tips came away red.

"Look at that!" she cried, holding her bloody fingers at arm's length.

Frowning, she wiped her hand on the front of her apron, leaving two streaks that looked like the tracks of a dying animal. She seemed inordinately troubled by the discovery, more so by her inability to recall how she'd received such an injury than the wound itself.

"It should be properly dressed," I cautioned, moving toward the hall. "Mother always kept a bottle of hydrogen peroxide in the bathroom cabinet. You'd better roll up that sleeve so we can have a look."

True to her habits, I found the bottle alongside a box of cotton gauze. I took them down from the shelf and returned to the front room.

"Here we are." I frowned at the expression on her face. "Mrs. Culp?"

Her sleeve rolled to a pale and doughy bicep, she was staring down the hall—right past the bathroom to my uncle's room.

"Mrs. Culp?" I repeated, a bit more pointedly.

She started, as if I'd suddenly materialized out of nowhere.

"It's all right." I smiled disarmingly. "It's only me."

"Oh, Mr. Laurie!" she stammered, trembling. "I don't know where I was! You must think I'm a frightful old goose!"

"Not at all," I assured her, setting the two containers atop one of the end tables. "Why don't you come over here to the light," I suggested, removing the cap from the peroxide.

She stepped obediently into the pale daylight, offering me her arm hesitantly, as if I might be hiding a razor.

A wad of soaked cotton in hand, I turned her arm gently outward, rolling the small wound into view. It was a small, neat puncture, a thin line of blood still oozing from the prick. It looked as if she had poked herself with something sharp, the tip of an ice pick perhaps, though surely she would have remembered that. Strangely enough, the puncture itself did not look particularly fresh; rather, it was somewhat bruised and ragged about the edges, as if it were a day or two old and only recently reopened.

"This may sting a bit," I warned, the dampened gauze poised over the wound.

I pressed it down and she screamed.

***

After I had the cut cleaned and dressed, Mrs. Culp insisted I sit down so that she could serve me lunch. Chicken salad sandwiches alongside a steaming bowl of barley soup. As I greedily ate she took the time to educate me in the finer points of my uncle's care, elucidating the highlights on the blunt tips of her fingers:

First off, he had to be turned from side to side, without fail, every two hours to prevent bedsores.

Secondly, all his food (though he ate surprisingly little) had to be pulverized into a uniform mash, then strained through a cheesecloth to prevent choking.

Third, he needed incontinent care almost as often as he was turned, "And it's not unusual for there to be a touch of blood to his urine, so don't be alarmed if you throw back the covers and find a pink stain where you might be expecting a yellow one. It'll take care of itself in a day or two."

Fourth, bathe him with good strong soap and water every few days, depending on his habits and my own good sense. "More often," she advised, "if the two of you are living in close quarters."

Finally, I was to take care that his bed was not too close to any windows. "His skin is sensitive to sunlight and he burns very easily. Once that happens, he'll keep you up all night with his fussing and moaning," she explained, refilling my soup bowl. "It may seem like a terrible inconvenience, but once you've left him out too long and he swells up with that awful rash, you'll wish you hadn't. And it takes forever to peel away, so mind you don't forget!"

And those five pearls, in a shell, were all she could offer to help me along.

"He's a strange one in his habits," she ventured to say, lowering her voice as she cleared away the dishes. "That odd fascination he has with his hand... You've noticed? Likes to lie back and stare at it, all the time chuckling away like it's some great prize. Doesn't seem to give a hoot for the other, but then I guess there's not much movement there." She dried her hands on a dishtowel. "Well, you'll see."

I nodded absently, scenes of my new life already tumbling about inside my head. It did not make for pleasant rumination.

The event I'd been dreading came a short time later. With nothing more to say, Mrs. Culp rose from the table and dusted her hands, as if ridding herself of an unpleasant weight. Buttoning her coat, she wished me luck and safe travels then left me alone with him.

After she'd gone, I realized I'd forgotten to ask her if she wanted any of my mother's things.

And she forgot to leave a number where I might reach her from Seattle should the need or urgency arise.

Or perhaps, looking back on that gray and dreary afternoon, she didn't forget at all. She simply wanted to be done with us.

***

Late that night in my mother's room, I threw back the covers and stumbled into the hall, frustrated by my uncle's incessant noise. Even as I snapped on the light, his agitations ceased and a brief shadow flitted across the wall, erratic as a moth. He stared at me with a baleful eye, as if I'd been the one who was carrying on for the past hour.

Turning toward the wall, he slapped his hand against the stained plaster, grunting obscenely as he rubbed it back and forth in a demanding manner. His palm made a hard, scratching sound, puzzling until I noticed the yellow glint of his wedding ring.

He turned back to the door, his eye sharpening, searching for a response.

With a sigh, I crossed the room and checked his bedding, turning him away from the wall, though this only served to upset him. He reached up and clutched my arm, his grip painful, and I pried it away. I offered him a glass from the bedside pitcher, but the tepid water simply ran out between his teeth again, unwanted and unaccepted. He hissed and sputtered and tried to knock the glass from my hand.

I retreated to the door, lingering by the switch. "Go to sleep," I told him and turned off the light.

He cursed two or three times in anger: raw, black outbursts that bristled against the walls. I went back to my mother's room, certain that sleep would be a long time returning. When it finally came, I dreamt of my uncle. He crept out of his room and stalked through the house, clenching and unclenching his fist. He found me in my mother's bed and loomed over me, his swollen fist making a sound like a living heart. Blood began to squirt from between his straining fingers, splashing against the walls in arterial streaks.

As dawn blossomed against the east side of the house, the dream seemed to fade. I awoke feeling tired and drawn, as if I hadn't slept so much as a wink.

I went in the opposite room and stared at my uncle, trying to judge his condition. He seemed to be sleeping, his left hand splayed loosely against the pillow. Within the folds of his palm I saw a dark speck, no larger than a pebble.

His eyelids hung partially open, allowing dim crescents to peep from beneath the hoary lashes; he might have been gazing back at me, it was difficult to be certain. His sleep seemed deep enough to swallow us both.

My eyes went back to his hand and, in an instant, I made up my mind to see what lay inside; what it was he so jealously guarded.

I crouched beside the bed, hardly daring to breathe. The inscrutable hand lay before me, less than twelve inches away.

Within the soft shadows of the palm, the pebble had turned a rusty red, as if scabbed over. Delicately, as if coaxing venom from a tarantula, I prodded two of his fingers. The overlapping shadows lifted and I saw that it *was* a scab. A dot of dried blood no bigger than a nail-head.

A cut or puncture kept gleefully open, I thought, allowing the fingers to wilt back toward their previous positions. He rubbed them together in a covetous manner then retreated back into his dreams.

Shaking my head, I rose from the bed, wondering what in God's name I'd expected. A golden coin? A rare gem, perhaps? A genie and three magic wishes? The man was an imbecile, after all; an aging vegetable...

Let him keep his worthless secrets.

***

Seattle again.

In the last three months, my life has taken on a lurid, surreal quality. I look in the mirror and find a face I no longer recognize. I sleep in fits and starts (much the way I imagine infantrymen must sleep in the heart of battle) and my appetite shrinks with each passing day. In the dim light over the bathroom sink, my skin looks waxy and sallow, almost gray around the edges, and my eyes are sinking into haunted pits.

Unclean. I feel fouled by the stench and nearness of *him*; my hands are raw from constant scrubbing and, when I make a fist, the knuckles crack and bleed.

My supervisor has twice asked me if I'm having troubles at home. On the second occasion, I explained my situation and, though he is sympathetic, he cautioned me to take care that my work doesn't suffer. Eyes are watching me.

April has drifted into May and still I haven't found a home to place my uncle. The waiting lists are extensive and my case, I'm told, is not an unusual one. Necessity has forced me to hire a woman to watch over him while I'm at work, but all he does, she says, is sleep. He won't take food, drinks very little, and though she is grateful for the employ, she feels that she is stealing money from my pocket.

Then, each evening after she leaves, my uncle comes awake, keeping me up into the dead hours of the night.

Never have I felt so helpless. So wrung out and depressed.

I find myself entertaining ideas I dare not commit to paper.

Terrible, unthinkable notions…

***

Late this afternoon Mr. Edwards—my supervisor—informed me that a policeman was waiting in the lobby, requesting to speak to me.

"A policeman!" I blinked, surprised. "Why would a policeman want to see me?"

"I'm sure I don't know," Edwards replied; perfectly calm and composed, as if the rest of the world stood apart from him, behind iron bars or a protective sheet of glass. "I *did* gather a certain sense of urgency from his manner, so perhaps it would be best not to keep him waiting," he suggested, gesturing toward an uncertain future.

I nodded, eyes moving over the cluttered surface of my desk, my mind racing. I rose to my feet, steadied myself, and glanced at my reflection in the window. It seemed that a ghost was staring back at me, a thing no more substantial than a passing shadow. I could only guess what my colleagues were thinking as I moved toward the front of the building, their glances stinging, insinuating, as if there were blood on my sleeves or bank notes fluttering from my pockets.

Halfway across the lobby I thought of my uncle. Had he finally expired? Had this policeman been sent to inform me? I dared hope it was true; indeed, I had myself so convinced that I rushed forward, eagerly, to hear of it.

The officer was a balding, badger of a man, thick in the waist and far progressed into middle age. Out of breath (as if from a heroic run) he seemed ill at ease, remaining just inside the doors to wait, his uniform cap clutched in his large, restless hands; clearly out of his element.

I introduced myself and offered my hand. "I understand you wanted to see me?"

He nodded, glancing around the bank as if it were a mortuary or private library—a place where voices were unwelcome and liable to carry. "Officer Stacy Malone." He hesitated, once again glancing about the lobby. "I wonder if we could speak outside, Mr. Laurie?" he inquired in a low, apologetic tone.

I looked over my shoulder to where Mr. Edwards had positioned himself. To my surprise, he nodded his discreet consent.

"Yes. Perhaps we'd better."

Outside, amidst the bustle of afternoon traffic, Officer Malone fit his worried cap back atop his squarish head and took a breath of confidence from the warm, spring day. We were now in his office, I realized, though he spoke in the same kindly manner. His expression, however, was grave, well suited to the subject at hand. A death in my apartment, he was sorry to report.

Unfortunately, it was Miss Schuller—my uncle's attendant—and not he whom I most desired to be rid of.

"My God," I gasped, mouth open in shock, feeling the weight of it in the pit of my stomach. This was not at all what I'd expected, nothing like I'd hoped for. "*H-how*?" I stammered. "What happened?"

Malone grimaced. "We're not altogether sure. The girl appears to have cut herself, and there's blood about the rooms, but not so much as to have done her in." He consulted a notebook. "Your landlord, Mr. Wenkman, heard a scream and went upstairs to investigate, but by the time he let himself in the woman was already dead. He found her lying in the second bedroom."

I nodded, knowing exactly where she had been found; if I closed my eyes, I could picture her there.

"The elderly gentleman sharing the apartment with you," Malone prodded. "A relation, I understand?"

"Yes," I heard myself reply from far away. "My uncle."

"An invalid?"

I hesitated. "Yes."

He regarded me for a moment in studied silence.

"Mr. Laurie, one of our detectives would like to ask you some questions…back at your apartment. Can you come along with me?"

I looked up. "Yes, I think so. I, I'll just have to clear it with my supervisor."

"Fine, then. I'll just wait for you."

And he did, too, just inside the lobby door, where he could keep a tight watch over me.

***

The first aberration my eyes fell upon was an overturned table, one of the two end pieces that belonged to my mother. I'd adopted it as a stand for a large plant; now the clay pot lay in pieces on the floor, dirt spilled in a fan over the bare boards; the plant itself tangled in the sharp fragments. On the wall above was a dark smear of blood, no larger than a finger. It seemed to point downward, drawing the eye back to the mess on the floor.

"Mind your step." Malone pointed, indicating a path of spilled droplets (almost invisible against the floorboards) running from my uncle's room to the bath. There was a groping smudge of red on the medicine cabinet, some clotting drops of the same on the porcelain. A photograph had been knocked off the wall, the glass within the frame shattered. I bent to rescue it, but Malone blocked my arm; they would take care of it later, he said.

I turned and my uncle's bedroom opened before us. There were three men in the room, including Wenkman, my landlord; he was calmly smoking a cigarette, while Miss Schuller lay sprawled under a sheet at his feet.

The curtains had been opened, the room much brighter than I was accustomed to. I worried that it might upset my uncle, but his only window faced north and his bed was tight against the

226

opposite wall. From what I could see he looked perfectly at ease, one blue eye shifting, as if he were gazing at a tall cluster of buildings. Occasionally he smacked his toothless lips together and let out an indefinable moan.

Malone made cursory introductions, beginning with the detective. Burgess was his name, Lieutenant Burgess. We shook hands over the sheet.

"Mr. Laurie, if possible…we'd like you to identify this woman?" He was watching me quite closely now, his eyes as sharp as glass.

I took a settling breath and nodded stiffly.

The second uniformed officer, whose name I'd already forgotten, crouched and gathered back the sheet. It pulled away to reveal a woman's back, which I immediately recognized as Miss Schuller's. There were spots of blood pressed against the sleeve of her white blouse.

"Angela Schuller," I whispered hoarsely, the smell of blood rising in my face.

"Wait until the officer turns her over, please," the detective chided, raising a cautionary finger.

She went over awkwardly, arms flopping loosely, her dull brown eyes fixed on the ceiling. Her face was a pale imitation of its former self, the color and vitality drained away, even from her lips.

"Angela Schuller," I repeated in the same strained tone.

"You're certain?" Burgess said, searching my face.

"Yes, of course."

There were questions—questions regarding the work arrangements and specific tasks performed by Miss Schuller, questions concerning the health and history of my uncle, questions probing my own whereabouts over the past six hours—and when the questions ran dry, Lieutenant Burgess scratched his head (clearly unsatisfied) and had the body carted away.

***

I closed the door quietly after their echoing footsteps and walked slowly back to the bedroom. Blood was still pooled against the worn rug—an alarming amount really, but as Officer Malone observed, not enough to kill her.

I looked at my uncle.

From outside came shouts and screams, the sounds of children playing in a nearby park.

His left fist lay curled against the sheet, lazy and satiated.

I pulled up a chair to watch and to wait.

***

Night has fallen.

The laughter of children has faded into the hum of the evening's traffic moving up and down Olive Way and, to the east, a fat, yellow moon is rising.

My uncle is quiet now, his lip curled back in a sneer, studying me. Occasionally he shows a toothless grin and lets out a thick, satisfied chuckle, holding his curled fist toward the light. He has a secret clenched there…something I could pry loose, but I think it will come away in its own good time.

Miss Schuller saw it. Mrs. Culp did, too, though she tries to convince herself otherwise, and *Mother…*

"My God," I said for the second or third time, sickened and repulsed.

I shook his shoulder roughly, to provoke him, then poured out my accusations.

Are you the disease in our midst, Uncle? The lingering cancer? Why do those around you wither and die while you go on and on? Will Wenkman find me *dead in a week or two? You laugh and smile, Uncle, but I think that he will.*

You see, I recognized your mark when they turned poor Miss Schuller over; I spied it the moment her arm rolled against the carpet. A puncture wound—exactly like the one on Mrs. Culp—just above and to the inside of her elbow.

Uncle

There's an artery there... one that you could reach as they were leaning over your bed, changing your filthy bedsheets. And that odd scab in the palm of your hand...what would I find, I wonder, if I were to peel it away?

I moved my chair closer to his bed. "What happened to you during the war, Uncle? After the artillery shell left you paralyzed in that muddy French churchyard, what happened next? I think I can guess. I can pity you, Uncle, but I can't forgive what you did to Mother...to your own *sister.*"

At this, his hand clutched itself tighter, the first glint of real fear in his eye.

"It's a shame what happened there didn't give you a hypnotic stare or dark, cruel lips. Dear Christ, it couldn't even make you walk again! All it gave you was an appetite for blood."

His lip curled back in a silent snarl.

"No teeth and not much jaw control, but you do have the use of one good arm. Not a lot to work with, but necessity finds a way. Necessity *always* finds a way."

Leaning back in my chair, I crossed my legs.

"So now I know what you are...the problem is, what to do about you?

"Can you read my thoughts, Uncle? You're not smiling anymore.

"Perhaps we'll talk about that tomorrow, you and I." I rose to my feet. "You see, I've planned a trip outdoors... away from the noise of the city. I do my best thinking there. In fact, we'll make a day of it.

"I hear the weather is supposed to be fine...

"Clear and sunny."

ABOUT THE AUTHOR

Michael James McFarland lives in Washington state and has been writing dark fiction for over 25 years. His novels include "Wormwood", "Duplex" (novella), "Blood On The Tracks" and "Fallow Ground".

13

The Legacy
By Julianne Snow

For Nanny and Pat—we lost you too soon...
"Death leaves a heartache no one can heal, love leaves a
memory no one can steal." – Irish Proverb

"I'm sorry...I've got what?"

"Grant, I know this is hard for you to hear, but you have stage four colon cancer. It's inoperable. Had we found it sooner, you may have had a chance, but it's in the first stages of metastasis and fairly soon it will have spread throughout your body. We can try an aggressive round of chemotherapy, but all that's likely to do is make you sicker. You need to think long and hard about how you want to spend your last weeks."

The cool detachment of the oncologist chaffed Grant. He could feel the anger boiling from within at news of his diagnosis and the demeanour of the person delivering his fatal news. He lashed out verbally at the doctor—the only concrete thing in his path.

"Are you fucking kidding me? I have cancer? Me?"

The doctor could only stare at him, used to the gamut of emotions that came from those who'd been recently diagnosed. No one wanted to believe it could happen to them and, based on past experiences, he just sat there, waiting for the storm to pass.

"This isn't supposed to happen to me. I help people! It's my job to keep people healthy..." Grant trailed off as his mind exploded with the treachery of his body. He looked up at the doctor and saw a charlatan; a man who spent years in school just so he could watch people die. The air around him felt foreign. All he wanted to do was leave the claustrophobic atmosphere of the office and drown himself in a drink.

Grabbing his coat and hat, he stood while giving the doctor one last parting look of disdain, "There will be no aggressive rounds of chemotherapy for me. If God has decided I must die of this disease, then that is my lot in life. It's simply too bad the world will be robbed of all of my future discoveries in the process."

Turning on his heel, Grant stalked out the office and into the chill of the early autumn air. Soon it would be flu season and the paranoia surrounding the illness would hit the streets. What superbug was coming our way this year? An H1N1 variant? Perhaps a less virulent strain of SARS would make an appearance. There was no telling what strain of influenza would strike and what mutation it would undergo while replicating in its hosts.

Grant Mazra turned up his collar and hunkered into the warmth of his jacket, his mind still spinning with the news of his diagnosis. He wondered what it all meant as he walked the six blocks to his office at Hubertson Pharmaceuticals, the drink forgotten for the moment.

As the biochemist in charge of new drug development, Grant had the rewarding job of helping millions of people. With his hands and mind behind so many of the recent discoveries, he was lauded as one of the most brilliant biochemists in the field.

None of that seemed to matter to his own cells however, and he cursed how they had betrayed him. Sitting behind his oaken desk, he could almost feel how they mutated and multiplied. He could see them in his mind's eye, turned black with cancer, tiny pieces breaking off and entering his blood stream in search of healthy tissue to infect.

His head dropped to the blotter on his desk, tears causing darker blotches to blossom on the paper. Grant's shoulders shook as he allowed himself the moment of self-pity.

As quickly as it started, it was over; and the fist slamming down on the desk rattled the picture frames that covered the top left corner. Grant looked up to see his secretary eyeing him warily over the cubicle wall surrounding her desk. He shook his head and smiled haphazardly. Not wanting his colleagues to know just yet, Grant decided to do the best he could to hide his cancer from them.

Figuring it was the best way to drown his sorrows enough to forget them, he dove into his work. Pulling up the newest data from the preparation of this year's flu shots, he concentrated on the molecular formulas and recumbent DNA curled into them. His mind began to spin and within a few hours, he knew he was well on his way to creating his legacy. One last discovery to bring the collective world to its knees in awe of his brilliance...

***

"Damn! Why won't this work?" Grant spoke, thinking he had the lab to himself. He jumped when the voice answered him.

"What are you working on, Dr. Mazra?" It was Lucille, a very talented PhD candidate who interned at the lab while using their facilities to research her doctoral thesis.

Grant's head snapped up at the sound of her soft voice so close to him. Shuffling his papers and angling his body in front of his computer's screen, he turned to give her his full attention, nervous at what she might have seen before revealing her presence behind him. "Ahh, Lucille, hello! I didn't realize you'd be working today...thought maybe you'd be off doing what young women get up to these days." He smiled in an effort to reassure himself he hadn't let her see his lack of composure.

Lucille smiled back before answering, always a little stilted and nervous when speaking to the senior biochemist, "I had to check on the samples for the Bovine Spongiform Encephalopathy study. Results need to be documented each day or we might miss something important. You know how it is." Her shoulder rose in a tiny shrug before falling back down.

"I certainly do, Lucille. Do you need any assistance?"

"No, Dr. Mazra, I'm fine. Just a few Petri dishes under the microscope, some notes about growth, and I'm good to go. Thank you, though, I always appreciate anyone's help when I need it." She smiled before moving away to a different corner of the lab.

Grant watched her put on a white lab coat before collecting her specimens from their labelled shelves in the lock-up. Observing her walk carefully to her workstation, Grant was struck by how self-assured she was in the lab setting and knew she would make a brilliant biochemist. She might even be the one to cure cancer...

He snorted at the thought, drawing a strange look from Lucille. "Sorry, was thinking about something I'm working on. I think the answer just hit me while watching you. Isn't it odd where we get our inspiration from?"

"Yes, I think that sometimes myself, Dr. Mazra. I can be driving to the lab and something in the traffic patterns can spark an idea. Or even the song on the radio can make me think of a process in a new way. I love how the mind can always be working on those little things even while it's concentrating on a different task."

"So true, Lucille. And on that note, I must get back to what I was working on. Please let me know when you leave."

Grant turned back to his workstation, and while keeping a wary eye on Lucille, he got back to work. He witnessed the cancer cells he'd harvested attacking the healthy cells through the lens of his microscope and frowned. Had he made them *too* aggressive? His legacy rested delicately on the aggressiveness of the cancer cells he was working with; if they were too aggressive, they may end up killing themselves. And that certainly wasn't in Grant's plans.

Having come from his own body, he now knew more than he ever wanted to know about them, but in experimenting with them, he was struck by their aberrant perfection. They had one simple job—the infection of other cells—and they carried out that job in absolute simplicity. Mutate, replicate and infect. Over and over and over again.

Could he revolutionize the way the world saw the cancer cell before he died? Grant believed he could, and on that cool October day, he made his breakthrough.

A cancer cell that behaved like a cancer for other cancer cells.

He was confident his research would be the cure for cancer everyone was looking for, but his motives were not completely altruistic. No one would ever see his work for what it was: his cancer would kill him, but it would kill the rest of the world as well. For, while he'd created a lethal cancer for cancer, he'd also devised a way to make his cancer virulent. Grant thought of it as a necessary side effect, but in truth, it was his way of evening the odds. It was too late for him thought; his body too far ravaged to be repaired.

Gathering his data, he shut down the computer at his workstation, erasing the files from it, and left for the day. Grant's mind was consumed with that he planned to do and he wondered if his resolve would withstand his conscience. In his heart he knew his plan was immoral and depraved, but his head didn't seem to care either way.

Grant gave himself the night to sleep on his decision, deciding he would know what to do when he awoke. For the first night in a long, long time, he drifted peacefully into sleep.

Waking with his alarm on Sunday morning, he showered and dressed, grabbing a quick cup of coffee on his way back to the lab. He had work to do and a new virus to synthesize; luckily he had no shortage of replicated cancer cells to work with.

The lab was empty, just as he knew it would be, and he set to work immediately, knowing it would take him days to synthesize enough of his new virus for what he was planning to do with it. Just as he was setting the DNA synthesis machine to begin, Lucille walked into the lab to check her samples.

"Hello, Dr. Mazra, I wasn't expecting to see you here today."

"Hello, Lucille, just working on a little something I think I've figured out. Sometimes the brain doesn't let you rest until you've started your next big project." With a smile, he turned back to what he was doing, unaware that Lucille was crossing the room toward him.

"What are you working on?"

Grant jumped at the sound of her voice in such close proximity. Whirling around, he closed his notebook and said, "Nothing for you to concern yourself with."

Said in such an authoritative tone, Lucille immediately backed away. "Sorry, Dr. Mazra, I didn't mean to pry."

"Not to worry, Lucille, I just don't want to share what I think I've discovered until the time is right. Check and double check—you know the drill..."

"Understandable, Dr. Mazra," she replied as she retrieved her samples and brought them to her workstation.

The two worked in silence at opposite ends of the lab until Lucille left for the day. Once Grant was alone, he relaxed and worked through the night. For the next week, he barely left the lab, stopping only for a few hours to sleep in his office in the middle of the night. He couldn't risk leaving his work unattended and open to prying eyes while the other scientists were working in the lab during the day. Plus, he needed to be there when each step of the preparation was complete. He only had a short window of time.

It was 3:47AM when it was finally complete. In total, Grant had synthesized over three litres of a highly virulent and continually self-replicating strain of his cancer. It was his crowning achievement and would affect the medical community in a profound way. He just needed to do one more thing with it.

Hefting the container into his arms, Grant walked the distance to the manufacturing area of the compound. He had only a small window of time to add his discovery to the newest run of flu shots that would be packaged over the next few days. While the three litres did not seem like a lot in terms of the volume of vaccination vials they would package in the coming days, he knew his addition would use the dead strains of influenza virus to continue its replication, infecting the entire batch. In fact, the virus he had created would likely withstand the sterilization procedures that were performed between batches. There was no way of knowing just how far this could spread.

Pouring the contents into the vaccine reservoir, Grant felt no remorse. He was simply completing his life's work. If he must die of cancer, so shall the rest of the world; Grant was just a little disheartened to realize he would not be around to witness the fruits of his labour.

Closing the lid on the reservoir, he made his way back to the lab and gathered up all of his notes. He erased the hard drives in both the lab and his office, then used a program he'd purchased from the internet to fry the mainframes completely. It wouldn't keep them out of his computer, but it would buy him some time. After that he'd be dead and unlikely to care which fingers they pointed at him.

As an extra level of security, he uploaded the program onto the server and let it run rampant through the databases. All of data from countless experiments scrambled and disappeared. It would take someone quite some time to reveal even the smallest of fragments. Careful not to disrupt the production side of things, Grant brought the development side of Hubertson Pharmaceuticals to its proverbial knees.

Taking one last look around the lab, he gathered his notes, donned his jacket and left for the night. Looking back at the structure of iron and glass, he let a small smile curl his lips. He would burn his notes at home and call in sick the next day. His co-workers would understand when he revealed the news of the cancer consuming his body.

***

Three weeks later, Grant Mazra was dead, the cancer having eaten more healthy tissue than his body could sustain. He was laid to rest in a simple ceremony attended by many of his colleagues and close friends. His eulogy outlined a legacy that started with his first synthesized drug for diabetes control and ended with his work to create a more comprehensive flu shot. None of them knew of his last discovery; his parting contribution to the world.

How could they have? Hubertson Pharmaceuticals was still trying to dig their way out from under a catastrophic computer failure in their development department. Production of flu shots continued uninterrupted and the demand this year exceeded their initial supply. More people were getting their preventative shot than in previous years, and more pharmacies were holding clinics to help inoculate the public.

Shipments of the flu vaccine were dispatched across the country, even around the globe as the demand rose along with stock prices in Hubertson Pharmaceuticals. All of those shipments were tainted with Grant's legacy as he had correctly predicted his new virus would be resistant to sterilization.

It didn't take long for the world to see the effects of that legacy either. The rates of aggressive cancer rose exponentially, but no one could figure out why and no one connected it to the influenza vaccine. There was no reason to suspect anything.

Anyone who received the tainted inoculation died within a few short months of its introduction into their bodies. With many of the doctors and nurses knocked out of commission in the early stages, the world's remaining medical community could barely cope with the steep rise in cases. No one knew what was going on; they just knew it was an event unlike anything they had ever seen. Like an apocalyptic culling of the population.

And the engineered virus didn't stop there. It continued to do what it was made to do. Mutate, replicate and infect…

ABOUT THE AUTHOR

Julianne Snow is the author of the *Days with the Undead* series. She writes within the realms of speculative fiction, has roots that go deep into horror and is a member of the Horror Writers Association. Julianne has pieces of short fiction in publications from Sirens Call Publications, Open Casket Press, 7DS Books, James Ward Kirk Publishing, Coffin Hop Press and Hazardous Press as well as the forthcoming shorts in anthologies from Phrenic Press and others. *The Carnival 13*, a collaborative round-robin novella for charity which she contributed to and helped to spearhead was released in October 2013. Be on the lookout for her contributions to a number of collaborative projects to be announced shortly.

Twitter: @CdnZmbiRytr
Facebook: Julianne Snow
FB Fan Page: Julianne Snow, Author
Amazon Author Page: Julianne Snow
Blogs: Days with the Undead & The FlipSide of Julianne

14

The Judas Contingent
By Blaze McRob

Cancer is no stranger to me. After being with Princess Little Trout for only nine months, she was snatched from my hands by the ravages of breast cancer. She was a loving lady and I miss her so much.

But it did not stop there. Angela died in my arms, again after we had been together for only nine months, and once more, the Reaper used breast cancer to take her away from me. She was a wonderful lady and fought with all she had, but she just wasn't able to beat the disease. She was a wealthy woman and gave me her estate, but she knew I would only turn the money over to St Jude. We both loved the children. She is buried where she wanted to be, watching the children on the ranch, hoping maybe, just maybe, that these children will be cured.

I first got cancer in 1986, was given six months to live but fought it off. Twenty years later it stopped for another visit. Once more, I sent it on its way. However, it has sneaked in once more, and as I write this, it ravages my body yet again. Pesky bastard. But I have too much work to do before I kick off, so I have to fight it with all I have yet again. Will I do it? Stage 4 says no. I say yes.

241

So, do I have a stake in the cause? You bet I do. I might be old, but I'm not ready to roll over yet.
Time to scare cancer to death...

Lights flicker in the room as the energy wanes and waxes depending on the needs of the machines. An impassive, almost plastic-faced, nurse stares down at me, looking into my pupils, hands on my wrist, checking my pulse. Blood pours from my mouth, diverted by thick gauze pads, and channeled in to catch basins along my sides.

Pain shoots through my mouth, virtually no part of it un-scathed by its ferocity. I cannot move: the straps! I'm fastened to the table by straps on my wrists, ankles, and some contortion-like machine attached to my head. There is no release! I must endure what is happening to me.

"Settle down, Mr. Heinz," the cruel voice attached to the emotionless woman says. "You don't want to tear out your IV or your transfusion tubes, do you? We have plans for you, you know. Big plans."

Plans! Yes, ever since the bone eating bacteria invaded my mouth, this medical center has had plans, but they haven't been concerned about me. It's not who I am that matters, it's what I might become. I'm a pawn in the battle of the big corporation versus the common man. Is there such a thing anymore in this day and age as a person who is valued for being a person, an in-dividual deserving of being respected? No more. Big corporations control everything

"Fuck you!" I shout, pissed off at this incessant amoeba in the Petrie dish, add this, add that, and let's see what happens treatment I'm receiving. Something big is ready to happen. There's no doubt about that.

Without saying a word, she flicks some sort of a lever which forces something into my IV. It's not glucose, that's for sure. My eyes spring back into my head, and I see fast little groadies, many different colors, chasing each other around, gobbling the smaller ones up, and being eaten by the larger ones in return. The bacteria…the bacteria are being consumed by something, but by what? The new entities forced into my body are taking over. Sure, the bacteria are vanishing, but something more ominous is occupying that space and advancing to the surrounding tissues.

"Congratulations, Mr. Heinz," the hideous one says, "the bacteria are leaving, but on the flip side, the cure comes at a price. We have injected cancer cells into your body. The good news is we might possibly have a cure for the cancer. Notice I said *might*. There are no absolutes."

Whatever type of cancer has been injected into me is fast moving, invasive to the point of instantaneous agony. My body screams for relief, my mouth, my throat, wailing for something, anything, to ease what is coursing through me. But it does not stop. The blood flows, the pain continues, and as much as I want it all to end, regardless of the circumstance, it is not up to me. I am merely a tethered experiment in the process of invasive modification of the human body: as much human as I am allowed to remain.

"Change the blood bag now! The one with the synthetics added. That's the one I want," a voice echoes, a lower voice, a man's voice, perhaps a doctor. I don't know; I don't care. Relief! I want some fucking relief. Damn pushing me to the limits of my physical tolerance!

Sweat pours off me, joining the blood running out of my mouth. I shake, not able to control the jerking and twisting, the sounds of my moans adding to the cacophony of the painful opera within me. But the fat lady does not sing, and there is no end to what I endure.

Invasive bastards eat away at the inner tissues of my mouth, gobbling through the flesh, and cause my cheeks to fall inwards because there is only an empty space, a hollow where nothing exists. My human tissue is being removed, first by the cancer and then by the new cancer-eating substance, that which has a huge appetite and is not happy with merely attacking the cancer cells.

My mind shifts to a graveyard scene where worms attack my flesh, eating their fill, rejoicing in the bounty that is me, but I am not in a graveyard. I am not in the ground, and worms are not my enemy. The mega corporations have decided my fate.

The doctor checks the machines, the gauges, and the bags attached to me. He peers over me and smiles. "You are doing so well, Mr. Heinz. Just a few more modifications and we will have you exactly where we want you. Yes, Bauckham Enterprises will be famous. You, sir, will be the first artificially cured cancer patient. There will be no rejections. From the seemingly insignificant bone eating bacteria we were able to destroy within your body with cancer cells, we immediately attacked the cancer with the bio-genetic material at our disposal, and soon...and soon, there will be no disease or pathogens of any kind able to take your life. You, sir, will be immortal. Just a little more pain and it will all be over for you."

He changes the blood bags once more. Another something, God knows what, enters my body, eating through the last batch of introduced modifications and becoming the dominant bio-artificial entity residing within me. This pain is far worse than what I have been subjected to up to this point, almost causing me to pass out from its severity, but I refuse to buckle under to the manifestation of agony. I *need* to know what's happening; I refuse to lapse into a subconscious stupor.

Over and over again, the edge of the abyss that decides between sanity and insanity comes up to me, taunting me with the realization that this is not a done deal. One cruel roll of the dice, and I could become fodder for shock treatment to bring me back. The irony there is this whole procedure has been nothing but one long extension of that very treatment. Physical perhaps, but where exactly is the line between the mental and the physical attributes of humanity?

With each procedure performed on me, I become less human and more...and more of what Bauckham is striving to turn me into.

The lights finally return to a steady state. Does this mean they are finished with me? Is the pain finished? Has the time for healing arrived?

Chuckling to himself, the doctor must be pleased with what he sees on the computer screen set up close to the bed. "Oh, Mr. Heinz, my good fellow, we have exceeded beyond our wildest expectations. You are so much more powerful now than you have ever been, than *any* man has ever been. We will, of course, be running many tests on you, sort of a fine tuning if you may. And, I dare say, Bauckham will pretty much be your home. You can't run around the countryside mingling with the common rabble. Besides, what is it to you? You have no one. Everyone has abandoned you."

He and nurse plastic-face leave the room and turn off the lights. Darkness. Finally I get to embrace its soothing calm. But sleep does not come with the dark. Something is wrong. That part of my makeup has vanished. I no longer feel the need to refresh my mind or my body. My brain is functioning as never before, reaching out, absorbing every sensory perception imaginable. I feel like a...shit, I feel like a computer: all knowing, able to sort out micro and macro functions at will, only I need no mouse, no voice over-ride, no nothing. My brain controls it all!

Damn it! I am a computer! The last batch of goodies injected into me were tiny computer chips. My flesh is real enough, and all my body organs seem to be working as before, but if something happens to threaten me, these mini-computers will find a way around the attack. I look at the computer next to the bed and sense it is there as a sort of watch dog, analyzing my thoughts, ready to report on me if I go too far with any ideas or physical actions which might threaten the authority within these walls.

Fuck the authority!

Using my newfound power, I easily neutralize the computer, hacking into it in a benign way, allowing the computer to function as before but only absorbing feedback I wish it to have.

Yes, it is last year's model. I am the new super computer.

While the computer plods along in one mode, I analyze all its programs, discovering their plans for me and others like me. The data shows that while I am the only successful product of their bio-engineering, many have died in this quest for human mastery.

The whole history of the past thirty years whirs through my brain, telling me exactly when and how the huge corporations such as Bauckham have taken over the country, the elected officials being merely pawns in a power grab of unprecedented proportions. Money rules; technology rules. The common man is no better than last week's garbage, as expendable as spit on black top.

I think of this and more. Yes, the reason I wound up here to begin with, and the fact the doctor was right. No one cares about me. I am truly alone. For whatever money given to them, people who I thought loved me deposited my carcass in the waiting hands of the staff here, glad to be rid of me and certainly not caring about their Judas approach to affection.

Cancer…cancer in copious amounts in seemingly every part of my body had me in such a state that I was barely able to care for myself, but somehow I avoided being remaindered to an assisted living facility, or worse. I knew full well that being in one of those horrendous hostels of physical limbo would only get me to a place such as Bauckham much sooner.

Enter my "trusted" lawyer and a supposedly grieving ex-wife who was so concerned for my welfare that she insisted on my being transported to the hospital. My children were too young to have a legal say in the matter, except one, and the dangling of the forty pieces of silver before her eyes must have been a huge enticement. Special care facilities like Bauckham pay well to use people such as myself for guinea pigs.

In the current day of "Big Brother" control, the average citizen is supposed to buckle under and do what he must for the common good. But that common good does not have anything at all to do with individual freedoms.

My anger builds, festering to the point of exploding like the Caldera lurking beneath the ground in Yellowstone, waiting to destroy the planet. But, the new me has more than one facet. I can control these feelings of vehement hatred and channel them to the side for now, somewhat like a coil under pressure, waiting to spring forward when needed.

It is 3:00 A.M. when they come to check on me, expecting to find a worn out man, exhausted from his ordeal and sleeping peacefully. That is the image my vital signs show them, but the passive energy becomes static, and all the hatred explodes, causing the visions of all the injustices done to me over the course of my life to flash before my eyes, blinding me to anything but revenge, and the only ones around now to be on the receiving end are plastic face and the doctor.

The leather straps snap like twigs, and Mr. Cancer and Mr. Bone Eating Bacteria tear the two of them apart, not caring when they shout out in pain. Who will notice down here? This is a house of pain and agony. Hee, hee. These are customary sounds. They come with the turf.

As their limbs are shredded from their bodies, the massive blood flows shoot everywhere, drowning everything in what was once a life giving fluid, now having become just one more color on the pallet of paints to create a masterpiece of revenge. Ah, the sweet visual presented with the adornment of the dominant color against the background of pristine white walls makes for a startling contrast, a paradox of retribution and virtue.

They handle more pain than I thought them capable of, and my calm veneer returns as I watch their struggles diminish as the end comes closer. It is so much better this way. They have been given time to think about their moral transgressions.

I turn the lights off once more, preferring to think in the dark, wishing to formulate my plans for what is to come. Hatred still seethes within me, but I can turn in on and off at will. There is a major breakdown, a radical change about to occur in the social order of our times.

That change will be spearheaded by me. I am the only one strong enough to extract revenge on those deserving it.

The hard part...the hard part will be dealing with the Judas contingency.

Not needing to sleep, I get up and take a peek outside the door to my room. The halls are empty. At this hour, I would expect as much. I notice my door will lock behind me if I leave, and not knowing if I wish to return here or not, I feel I should prepare myself for all eventualities. I search the clothing of the passionless nurse and grab a set of keys from her pocket. Finding one that fits the door, I smile and hold the keys in my hand. There's not much choice actually. I don't have any fucking pockets in the hospital garb I'm wearing. Bare-ass to the breeze, I venture outside my room and head down the hall.

I need a shower, and I need some new clothes.

It takes a while, but I soon discover a room which needs no key. Opening it, I find what I'm looking for. The hot water beating down on me feels great. Watching my tormenters' blood go down the drain makes me feel even better. I fill my mouth with the cleansing liquid and swirl it around, intent on getting rid of the blood still clinging to pockets of attachment. At the rate I'm healing, I shouldn't have to worry about that for too much longer.

Not wanting to go overboard too soon, I gently brush my teeth, and marvel at how much fresher I feel from that alone. Adding some under-arm deodorant increases my feeling of self-esteem. From a stack of nicely folded doctors' pants and shirts, I grab what I need. I'll have to go commando as there is nothing in the way of underwear to be found. Non-slip booties with surgical socks over them are next, and I complete the look with a mask hanging down from my neck, and a nifty operating room cap.

I look more like a doctor than the doctors do. Even my face is shaved and looking good. I suppose it was easier for the medical team to do what they were doing if I didn't have facial hair. So much for the grand beard I sported before being jailed in this hell-hole.

This is a good time to be wandering the halls, searching for what I need. Only a skeleton crew is working.

The nurses' station midway in the hall way is empty, so I slide behind the counter and get on the computer. I don't have to worry about codes or passwords. The sucker is a toy in my hands. It doesn't take long for me to find what I'm looking for.

"Who are you, and what are you doing on my computer?"

I stare at the nurse who should have been here at the counter. "And who are you to challenge me? It appears to me that the nurse responsible for this desk abandoned her station."

Daggers fly from her eyes. "Well, Mr. Smarty Pants, since no one else is around and I had to use the bathroom, I had no other choice."

"Likely story."

She lunges in my direction to get her barrage of foul-mouth words out. I can't afford to have her alert the entire floor, so I have no choice but to shut her up. *For good.* I break her neck with a sharp twist and conceal her body on a lower shelf, wrapping bedding and fresh towels around her.

The room where the blood is stored is easy to find, and everything is well labeled. *Yes, here are blood samples taken from me at every stage of my disease and so called treatment.*

My mind clicks away at its new-found speed, analyzing everything. *Oh, sweet Jesus. The Judas contingent will be brought to their knees.*

I fill syringes with my blood at all the various periods of my diseases and label them. Placing them in a medical transport bag, I calmly walk to the exit door and bid adieu. "I'll return," I say under my breath. "Fear not."

There is no need for me to find a means of transportation this morning. With every step I get stronger, feeling the power of what I have become course through my veins and arteries. No more do I have to deal with the debilitating blood clots in my legs and lungs; no more do I need to take pussy steps for fear of pushing my arthritis to its very limits, knowing I can't have the artificial knee I need but can't get because I would bleed out on the operating table.

That was then, and this is now. No longer am I beset with so many maladies as to make treating any of them contingent on dealing with the totality of the situation.

John J. Jorgenson is first on my list of visitors this fine morning. My trusted lawyer, the one to whom I entrusted the monies in my trust funds for my children. The bastard sold me out and will now pay. With every step I take on the way to his fine mansion, my mind clicks faster, and my determination to see justice done rises.

My old buddy lives alone, his wife having left him many years ago, departing for parts unknown. I never questioned it at the time, but knowing him for the man he is now, I can only surmise that anything could have happened. If she truly left on her own and John didn't have a hand in her departure, I can only say she is a fortunate woman to be rid of the bastard.

John has one of those fancy alarm systems installed at his house, but since I'm now a bionic computer of sorts, I'm able to hack into it and walk in without any trouble. Hungry for the first time since I can remember, I go to the kitchen and find the ingredients for a fine sandwich, cold cuts fit for a king. And a six pack of beer tells me it's nice and cold. Revenge can take a back seat to my hunger and thirst for a few minutes.

I prepare my sandwich, grab a beer, and go to the living room where I can settle back in a grand recliner and enjoy my feast. I'm half way through my sandwich when the light goes on.

"What are you doing here?" John shouts. "You're...you're..."

"Yes, I'm supposed to be in that place they call a hospital, but which in all reality is nothing more than an experimentation center for unwanted humans afflicted with myriad diseases. In other words, a home for guinea pigs. This piggy is cured, hungry, and on a mission."

John looks like he's about to shit on the floor. "Yes, John," I say, "you're part of my mission."

I take a deep swig of my beer and watch John's color turn to an ugly shade of pale. A Vampire would have more color than what he displays at the moment. "But…"

"Too late for that, John. You did me wrong, and I'm not in a forgiving mood. The good folks at Bauckham would love to have you as a test subject. It seems their only success story wandered away from the facility. Can you imagine that? You wouldn't do that, would you? No, I'm sure you wouldn't. You would want to hang around and be the poster child for the super cure."

My hand lifts the bag containing my blood. "See this satchel, John? It's loaded with blood. My blood. All of it was taken before my cure."

John gets closer to dropping that load of shit on the floor. "You're not…"

"You are a clever rascal. Your mind has figured it all out. Your flesh appears to be pale. Anemic. You need some blood. I'm your delivery boy. Best thing? It's free. How great is that?"

Before I can utter another word, John bolts from the room. He tries to, at any rate. I'm up and out of the chair with speed I didn't know I possessed. I grab him by his shoulder, spin him around and hit him with a straight right fist to his temple. He drops like a rock.

Good job, Robert. It feels good to be strong again. In fact, you have never felt this strong.

For whatever pain the bastards at Bauckham inflicted on me, I'm a fucking freak now. Yes, that's it. I could be one of the X-Men; I don't care about the computer chips whizzing about my veins and arteries. Being in the state I'm in, possessing the powers I have, makes up for it.

I open my little black bag, not the least like the one the doctors carried around in the old days. When I was a child, doctors made house calls. You weren't a number *then*. A patient was an individual and was treated with respect. Poor John. I have no intention of showing him any respect.

Which of my blood packets should I share with John? I know. All of them. A cornucopia of contagion will soon course through his veins.

Injection after injection is administered to his veins. I watch in rapt awe as the show before me is played out, act after act. Though John is still not conscious and his words cannot tell me the pain he is experiencing, I can see it through the expression on his face and the contortions his torso is undergoing.

Yes, John. It hurts, doesn't it? The pain will only increase, buddy boy.

It takes a while, but when consciousness returns to my former friend, I say, "If you go to Bauckham to get treated, tell them Robert Heinz sent you. I'm leaving you now. There are others I must visit."

I wash my hands well before I leave. No way do I wish to get any contaminated blood on me. The mini-computers would protect me, but that's still a chance I don't wish to take.

As angry as I am at my daughter for selling me out, I can't extract revenge on her. Her mother and her new man are my targets. They knew what they were doing. My guess? Even now they are chuckling over it.

The merriment is about to end for you two.

He works at the King Soopers in town. The overnight shift. At one time he worked for me at a Buffet in town, but after all the kindness I showed him, sticking up for his sorry ass when the other managers wanted to fire him, he played slap and tickle with my ex. I don't know what the slut saw in him. He had a circulatory problem and couldn't get it up half the time. Maybe I was too much man for her. I don't know. It doesn't matter anymore. I wouldn't touch her with John's cancerous dick at the moment.

When I get to the store, I go around back to the loading dock. Even though he works all over the store, the docks are a favorite place for him. The man is a thief. His car is parked close by, so I'm sure when the opportunity arises he will manage to squirrel some goodies away. How do I know? He did it at the buffet. Why change now?

No one is there, so I go into the shadows, away from the lights, and prepare my syringes.

David walks out after a while, carrying some stolen merchandise. While his hands are still filled, I come up behind him and jam a syringe into his neck. He drops the food and stares at me in terror.

"Good evening, David. You're looking well, but not for long."

As he backs away from me, the pain hobbling his movements, I lunge at him and empty the other syringe into one of the snakes forming on his forehead.

"Wow, David, you should really get those fast expanding arteries checked out. They could be serious. Of course, they are a perfect target for my payload of disease."

His hands rush to his head, trying to ease the pressure in his skull, but it is too late. Blood starts gushing out from everywhere, his mouth becomes a slack piece of pulp, and his head literally explodes.

Shit! I've heard of this happening before, but I have never had it happen to anyone I knew.

I've been cheated! He died in a flash without having to suffer the way I did. Damn him!

Careful not to walk through the pond of blood surrounding his body, I grab my satchel and leave. My ex-wife is next on my list. She deserves the cancer in my bag more than anyone I know. Her moment of darkness is on the horizon.

It is almost time for the sun to rise when I reach her house. I peak in through the windows, looking for the perfect way to get in without the children seeing me. Shit, they're already up! Something is happening. The kids are scurrying around, the older ones getting dressed, and then helping the younger children with their clothes. My oldest, the one who sold me out, runs to the van and starts it up.

I hide in the shadows, wondering what's going on, there not being a clue that I can get from this.

"Hurry!" my ex shouts. "We have to get the baby to the hospital now!"

I shouldn't care about the baby. It's not mine; it's David's. But I *do* care.

The wail of sirens charges through the early morning air, and the EMTs dash out and rush into the house. Within minutes, the baby is in the ambulance and it rushes down the road, the van behind it. With the coast clear, I sneak into the house. There are oxygen bottles everywhere, some empty and some full. It's obvious the baby is still on oxygen.

Now what do I do? As much as I want to kill the bitch, I can't go through with my plan now. Revenge will have to take a back seat to what I just witnessed. The baby needs his mother, and so do my children. Her pain will have to come from knowing she is alone, a single parent having to provide for eight children.

Damn it anyhow! A conscience. I still have a fucking conscience. Yet, I can't allow that to botch up my plans for the rest of what needs to be done. A few innocents will be taken down, I'm certain, but some things need to be stopped, and I'm the only one capable of doing it.

I return to John's house. Money. I need some. Hopefully, he's not home and I can hack into his files and figure how to get some of the long green. My account should be a cinch to access. I know all the particulars on that. Years ago, when I was still well, I had squirreled some money away in trust funds for my kids. At the time, my ex knew nothing about it. Even then I had suspicions about her. Perhaps John has not mentioned anything to her about the funds. My guess? He wanted to use the money for himself.

John's fancy-schmancy car is not parked in his garage when I peer in. Good news for me, and bad news for John. He was certainly in no shape to drive anywhere when I left him. Shit! On the other hand, if he had an accident, that makes two of my wanna-be cancer victims going to their next life without suffering the way I did.

His files are a cinch to hack into, and I was right about him dipping into my trust funds. About half of the money has been doled out to one of his personal accounts. Hmmn. A click here, one there, and the money goes back where it belongs, as well as some extra cash. He's not in any shape to be using any of the money. I might as well not let it go to waste.

With some tweaking of my account, I create a fictitious person and bogus ID so I can send funds to myself. Robert Heinz is now also Charles Gorham. That will keep the NSA boys from figuring out who I am. No in person transactions needed. All online. Sweet.

My internal computers are proving themselves to be invaluable.

So, where might my buddy John be? Would he have been stupid enough to have gone to Bauckham? Maybe. His puny mind might have figured since I was cured, the same thing could happen to him. If he did, this big house of his will be empty. I need a place to stay for a little while. Yet, with the way things are going in this country, I'm not sure I would be safe here. Big Brother could come knocking on the door at any moment.

I walk to my bank and close my account, withdrawing all the funds, and taking it in cash. The bank is leery of doing this, but I need this done before word from Bauckham spreads and people start looking for me. Later, I can put this in my new Charles Gorham account. Allison, my personal banker, suspects something is up, she knows I've been ill for a while, but she pushes this through before the hot shots catch on to what's happening.

"Thanks, Allison," I say. "I'll make this up to you."

She merely winks at me and I leave, waiting for her to come outside and grab a smoke. Once the line is gone inside, she's out and walks over to me. "You're waiting on me, aren't you, Robert?"

"Yes, I need a place to stay, and you have a young child and could use some extra cash. I only need space to set up a computer, a bed, and a shower. Does two grand a month sound fair to you?"

She looks at me as if I'm crazy. "That's far too much. I have an empty room downstairs, but I can't charge you that much."

"Sure you can. I insist. The only stipulation is that no one knows I'm there. Long story. I'll explain later."

"But…"

I count her out the money and say, "Could I have your key please? I'll have one made for me and return it to you."

She reaches into her purse, places the money inside and gets her key out. "Thank you, Robert. I can really use the money. Things have been tight since my husband was laid off."

"We're both helping each other, Allison. Thank you. I'll be back in a jiff with the key."

She goes back inside, and I walk down to the hardware store to get the key made. After it's finished, I go to Allison's house. I know where she lives. She walks to work and I've walked her in a couple times. The hardware man did good. The key works like a charm. I return Allison's key to her and hustle off on my errands. First stop is a rental place where I buy a computer. No questions asked. Cash in their hands, and they're happy as punch.

Allison doesn't have internet hookup, but it doesn't matter. I hook into a neighbor's Wi-Fi, and get busy with what I need. After a couple hours, all my questions are answered and I get offline and wipe out any evidence I was on this stranger's Wi-Fi. Yes, it messes things up for them, but they'll get it repaired soon enough.

Next stop, the supply Sergeant. It's only a block away, and the scent of the old GI clothing and gear smacks me deep inside my large nose the instant I walk in the door. George stares me down and walks over to me, smart enough to not shout out. "Robert, how did you…how did you get out?"

"You wouldn't believe me, George. It hasn't been easy."

"I'm glad you're back. How do you feel?"

"Great. For all the shit and all, I'm cured. Let's go to the back room."

"Sure. Follow me."

The back room is quite the place. Hidden inside huge safes, concealed behind row after row of racks loaded with military goods, are weapons and explosives of every type imaginable. At least that's what was in them when Bauckham came knocking on my fucking door.

"Do the safes still have in them what they did before, George?"

"Yes, they do, Robert."

"I need some plastic explosives, my friend."

"Do I dare ask what for?"

"Not yet. If all works out, I'll be back."

"I'll be waiting on you. The guys will be ready to help out too."

"Great. Is the same team here?"

"Most of them. A few were rounded up by the locals and the Feds."

"For what?"

"The usual trumped up shit. Nothing's changed since you went inside the joint, except . . . except it's gotten worse. Everyone is ratting out their friends and neighbors, their own family even, so they can get some bucks. Times are hard unless you're one of the elite."

"Time to stop that shit, George. It starts here. With me."

"You're only one man, Robert. An army is needed to fight the injustices we live with."

"What's that saying the Army has, George? An Army of One? Not that we can trust our own Army anymore. I will be that Army of One. We'll go from there."

"I can't talk you out of this?"

"You know me better than that. I'll be back for the rest of you."

"That's what I thought you'd say. Help yourself to what you need."

I'm an old explosives guy. In 'Nam, I was the best. I'll be the best again. I take what I need and place it in a duffle bag.

"Holy shit, Robert! That's enough to blow up the biggest building in town, and then some."

"That it is, George. Gotta love it."

"Unless you're on the wrong side."

"The wrong side doesn't need any love. Fuck them!"

"You're well on the way. Good luck!"

"Thanks, buddy. I'll be back. Ready the team."

George nods, and I leave. What I have in mind is a one man show. This will start the dominoes falling.

I carry the duffle bag back to Allison's house and go back down to the empty room which I have taken over. Using my skills from long ago, I set everything up. In no time at all, I'm ready to go.

Swinging the duffle bag over my shoulder, I go to the bus stop and wait for the Northeast bus to arrive. It stops a couple blocks from my destination. "Senior," I say, when it arrives, and I hop on it dressed in medical garb with a non-matching duffle bag. No money needed from this guy.

A half hour later and I arrive at my bus stop and walk the little distance to Bauckham. No one questions me as I walk through the doors and saunter into the doctors' locker room. I grab a lock from the duffle bag and toss it inside for safe keeping. Recon time now.

Room after room I check. All the patients are in the advanced stages of cancer. None of them are even close to where I was before I left. What I was hoping for will not come true. With a heavy heart, I plan my attack.

Going back to the locker room, I get the duffle bag out and do what my soul says I must. Bomb after bomb is placed at every point predicating a weak structural link. I set all of them for the top of the hour, a mere twenty minutes away.

I take too long with the last bomb. The plastic explosive isn't cooperating with me. A fucking security guard catches me and gets on his phone before advancing towards me. Reaching into my duffle bag, I grab an AR15 and blow his ass away. A sound like thunder echoes down the hallway. Shit! I got too cocky.

It's one against at least twenty from what I can tell. Not good odds. I don't worry about it. Maybe they'll think this bomb I'm in front of is the only one and won't go looking for any others. If that's the case, so be it. I'll sacrifice myself for the cause.

The blood courses through me; the high I'm experiencing is unreal. Even knowing I can't win, the joy of seeing this bastion of Hell and its bastard protectors being torn to shreds from my last-ditch efforts pumps me up.

Time is running out. The clock on the wall says there is only a minute to go before this place is toast. I move as far away from the bomb I've been protecting as possible. There is no way I have time to get outside, but a full bomb blast on me is not the way I plan on going either. Not knowing when it is set to go off, the security people move in on it.

Seconds away…mere seconds.

Blood and guts fly everywhere as the bomb detonates. The walls and ceilings all start collapsing in on each other as I watch in amazement.

You haven't lost your touch, Robert. You always were the implosion expert. Another job well done.

Not even a minute goes by, and it is all over. Dust settling is the end of it. Bauckham is no more.

A crowd gathers around the scene of destruction. George is among them. "Damn it, Robert!" he mutters. "I knew you were headed here. I offered to help you, you crazy fucker. Why didn't you let me?"

The authorities move in, not that there's anything they can do. Everyone's dead as far as they can see. They'll keep looking for survivors, but it will be a useless task. "Whoever did this was a pro," they think.

Everyone gathered to watch the rescue efforts leaves as the cops virtually shove them out of the way. There are things inside the building no one is supposed to see. As with everything else, big business owns the entire police force in this town.

Once the crowd is dispersed, the people combing through the rubble stop searching. The higher ups have given the word. No survivors would be a good thing. Anyone found alive will not remain that way for long.

The night becomes as black as the darkest raven. Away from the outside of the pile of rubble, in a place complete covered over by debris, there is movement.

A hand pushes its way through the rubble...

ABOUT THE AUTHOR

Blaze McRob has penned many titles under different names. It is time for him to come out and play as Blaze.

In addition to inclusions in numerous anthologies, he has written many novels, short stories, flash fiction pieces, and even poetry. Most of his offerings are Dark. However dark they might be, there is always an underlying message contained within.

Join him as he explores the Dark side. You know you want to.

15

My Name Is Charles
By TW Brown

To my best friend ever...Steve Hobart. You were too good to leave so soon. And to everybody else who's had friends or family afflicted. May their lives be peaceful and may you share in all their happiness.

The old man grasped the armrests of his wheelchair and braced for the impact of the body walking right for him. What had once been one of his nurses was now something from a nightmare. The white smock had turned black from the long-since-dried blood where the nurse's throat had been torn out.

The smell made the man gag, but he'd been out of food for two days; all that came up was watery bile. A ribbon of dense, sticky drool hung like an opaque cord from his chin for a moment, similar to the dark one hanging from the nurse's.

A scowl deepened the wrinkles on the face of the man in the wheelchair as he struggled to remember. It was futile, he couldn't recall his own name, much less that of the doctors, nurses, and others who wandered the halls. On good days, he couldn't remember the screaming, or things like seeing the pretty, dark-haired nurse who gave the best sponge-baths falling under several bodies; bodies that bit and ripped and tore. On good days, he couldn't remember all the blood.

Today was not a good day.

He recollected being in his wheelchair after having a nice push down to the huge window that looked out over the city of Chicago and Lake Michigan. Then, the screams came. It was unlike anything he'd ever heard, and that included his time in Korea where men had died around him what seemed like every single day of the two years he spent in that godforsaken place.

No, this scream was different. And everybody seemed to realize it. He didn't remember seeing stories on the news earlier that night. Or any of the other stories that had been broadcast the four days previous. He only vaguely remembered that, for some reason, his precious Cubs had not been on the television at all.

Soon, the screams were coming from everywhere. Then, he'd seen the doctor. Only, the young man seemed...*wrong*. One arm was all bloody, and he was sickly looking. And the eyes...they were gooey and bloodshot, but something about that was wrong, too. The blood looked black, which really stood out against the pus-like whiteness that coated the eyes.

The doctor had stepped into the room and stopped for a moment. The head moved in little jerks...like a bird's. Then the doctor had come for him, mouth open, drooling. He remembered the smell that seemed to pour off the doctor much like the drool dripping from his mouth. Then, another person came in behind the doctor and that's when the man really knew there was something terribly wrong.

This second person had been a woman. Not a doctor or nurse, she was wearing what was left of her hospital gown. Only she'd been ripped open at the belly. Strands and bits of her insides were still tumbling out of the horrid gash. Both of them came towards him, arms outstretched, mouths working.

They reached his chair, leaning in, oblivious to the man's weak attempts to bat them away. He remembered hands, cold and sticky with blood, grasping his arms. Both leaned in and he felt mouths brush his skin, then...nothing. They stood and turned, walking out of the room and into the cacophony of screams echoing in the halls.

That scene would replay several more times over the coming days...weeks. The man had seen others fall to these... people? Were they still people? He didn't know. His memory being what it was, he lost track. And sometimes it seemed like it was happening for the first time all over again.

Eventually, the screams stopped. The man, unable to get out of his wheelchair rolled around looking for anybody, familiar or otherwise. He was alone. Scared. Confused. He knew something was terribly wrong. Only, he couldn't get what was left of his mind to clue him in on what it was.

And that is how he remained as the days turned to weeks. Sometimes he forgot everything and spent hours or even days re-experiencing the initial horror of the sights that filled the floor he remained trapped on. He was incapable of using stairs, and there would be no elevator coming. A fire on one of the lower floors which—fortunately or otherwise—burned itself out quickly, left the building without power on that first terrible night.

The man didn't eat much, and for the past several days he'd survived on plastic bottles of Ensure. The last of those containers was now empty and cast aside in a corner. Four of the dead who'd shared the floor with him all these days had wandered into the room, probably drawn by the sound of the can clattering on the dirty linoleum floor.

Every time he left the room, or made a noise, *they* came. *They're more forgetful than I am,* the man mused. The worst part was when they touched him with their cold, dead hands. It used to be the smell, but he'd been stuck in this chair so long that he could no longer smell them over himself. Sometimes, when he shifted positions even a tiny bit, the sores and filth now keeping him welded to the chair would tear and send a wave of stench up to his nostrils that would make him gag or be physically ill.

This small group came, carelessly colliding with him and his wheelchair. But, as always, it was as if they were repulsed by the cancer that was eating at him from within. They leaned in close, and as he'd done hundreds of times before, the man shut his eyes and prepared for death to come in the form of teeth. As always, he was disappointed.

He watched them turn and leave. Angry and frustrated, he followed them, cursing and yelling, although even yelling, his voice was barely above what most people would consider conversational volume. More came, but in turn, each one eventually wandered away, paying little more attention to him than they did each other.

The man rolled to the window at the end of the long hallway. He passed the nurse's station where one of those things was actually sitting at the desk with the receiver from the telephone in its dead hand, its mouth working slowly as if in conversation. As he rolled past, the creature rose, following him, pulling the phone's handset free and falling in his wake as he rolled through the garbage-strewn hall. When he stopped, the thing came in close, its cold mouth brushing the side of his face like a perverse kiss. Then, it wandered away leaving the man alone at the window.

As the setting sun cast beautiful purple and orange streaks across Lake Michigan, the man winced. A pain bloomed in his chest, shooting down his left arm and turning his hand into a claw. The man's heart usurped cancer's hold and claimed his life. Just before his eyes glazed over in death, the man had one, final clear thought.

My name is Charles.

ABOUT THE AUTHOR

Welcome to MY world...Tucked away in the Pacific Northwest with my wife Denise, a Border Collie named Aoife (pronounced EYE-fa), a guitar collection, and an increasing number of aquariums sporting a variety of fish (cichlids are my new favorites), I live for football season when I can cheer on the Oregon Ducks my Super Bowl Champion Seattle Seahawks. I am a fan of Cookie Monster, KISS, and Dr. Who (along with most things British).

His blog can be found at: twbrown.blogspot.com/

You can contact him at: twbrown.maydecpub@gmail.com
You can follow him on twitter @maydecpub and on Facebook under Todd Brown, Author TW Brown, and also under May December Publications.

267

Let's Scare Cancer To Death

16

Survival
By Rhonda Hopkins

For my grandmother, Lavada Moore.
Nanny, thank you for watching all those classic horror movies with me when I was a child and for giving me my love of the genre. Cancer took you away far too soon and I miss you every day.

Sarah's gaze met her twin's fear-filled blue eyes. "I—"

"It's no use. The cuff is too tight. You're going to have to leave me." Dana put her free hand on Sarah's, stilling their frantic motions.

"No. I won't leave you. Maybe I can…" She turned, taking in the empty basement—the cement walls, exposed pipes, and her sister handcuffed to one of the metal cylinders. A small amount of light trickled in through the one lone window, but there was nothing she could use as a weapon. Unless…

She strode over to the dangling pipe from which she'd managed to extricate herself earlier. Grabbing the unattached end, she tried wresting it clear of its fittings, her own wrist dangling handcuffs which clinked against the metal with each pull. Rust and time made it impossible to remove.

"Sarah—"

"No." Tears ran down her face. "I can't leave you, Dana."

"You have to. It's the only way we're both getting out of here. You have to go for help."

Sarah knelt beside her sister who reached out and wiped her thumb across her cheek, brushing the tears aside.

"I'll be okay until you get back. I won't give them any excuse to throw me out to those..." Dana choked back the word they'd both been avoiding. "Creatures."

Realizing there was no way she could take on all three kidnappers without a weapon; Sarah accepted she had to have assistance to save Dana. Hugging her sister, Sarah kissed her cheek. "I love you, Dana. Be strong. I'll be back just as soon as possible."

Heavy footsteps reverberated on the stairs. Dana pushed Sarah away. "Go now. Before it's too late."

Stretching upwards, she tried to raise the window, but it wouldn't budge. She took off her t-shirt, wrapped her hand, and knocked out the glass, ducking as shards rained down on her. Pain shot through her palm all the way to her shoulder, but adrenaline fueled her and minimized the hurt. She unwound the red fabric and smoothed it hurriedly across the sill.

The door crashed inward as one of the men who'd captured them ran into the room. "What's going on here?" He took in the situation and bee-lined for Sarah, grabbed her legs and pulled her down from the window. Still holding one arm, he backhanded her across the face. The edge of his ring ripped across her forehead; the pain almost blinding. Blood gushed from the wound.

She jerked away from him and took on the fighting stance she'd been taught, feet set apart at shoulder width. Sarah grabbed the dangling cuff in her hand and put all her force in the punch to the man's jaw. His head snapped backwards. Before he could react, she stepped back and struck out with her right foot, making contact with his left knee. The crunch of breaking bone and his scream told her she'd done some major damage even before he fell to the floor.

The other two kidnappers pounded down the stairs.

"Sarah! Go!" Dana screamed.

She grabbed the window sill and pulled herself upward and through the opening; glass slivers cutting her where the shirt didn't cover. She yanked her legs through, turned and gave one last look at her sister and saw her mouth, "I love you."

Two men crashed through the open doorway. One ran for the window as the other stopped to check out their injured friend.

Sarah took off running around the abandoned building to the parking lot in front. Her black Expedition was one of three cars parked there. The abductors had taken their keys and cellphones, so she fell to her knees on the pavement beside the left rear tire and reached into the wheel well. Her fingers fumbled for the magnetic box and she issued a silent prayer of thanks when she found it. She got in the car and hit the locks just as the man they called Ron sprinted around the side of the building. The inside light illuminated the car's interior giving away her location.

Her shaking fingers pulled the key from its container. She managed to insert it and start the car in one try. Ron banged on the passenger window with one hand, the other pulling on the handle. He yelled and hurled obscenities as she squealed away from him and onto the street.

***

In the two hours they'd been held captive, things had deteriorated drastically in the city of Fort Worth. A smattering of abandoned cars littered the streets along with the dead. Bodies savagely torn open and covered in blood had fallen along the roadway, across cars and railings. But even worse…Some of them walked. Some of them walked with hideous gashes and missing appendages. Some of them walked with their guts hanging on the outside as they shambled along the dark streets. Some of them walked—while dead.

Sarah maneuvered around the unmoving vehicles, searching for police or anyone who could help. The blue and red flashing lights from police cruisers and ambulances indicated an emergency personnel presence. But they were overwhelmed. Those she saw either fought zombies—no other word for them—or assisted the wounded. Some were injured themselves or had become one of the reanimated dead. She'd find no help there.

Her body shook from shock and cold. Goosebumps peppered her flesh. But she drove on until she came to a dark side road and pulled into a group of trees, cutting the engine and the lights. She listened carefully for a few precious moments but heard nothing.

Blood dripped down her face from the gash at her hairline. Sarah reached for the injury with a trembling hand. Warm wetness coated her fingers and she jerked them back, startled by the amount. The coppery smell filled the car.

"It's okay. It's okay," she whispered to herself. "Even minor head wounds bleed a lot."

Lightning flashed and thunder boomed instantaneously. Startled, Sarah screamed. She clamped a hand over her mouth, cutting off the sound. "Got to get a grip. Dana's counting on me." Her breath caught in her throat as she thought of her twin still in the hands of lunatics. "I can't fall apart now."

Turning on the overhead light, she stretched around to the back seat and pulled her gym bag into her lap. She unzipped it and dug out the towel she'd packed that morning.

How could things have gone to hell in such a short time?

She pressed the towel against the laceration and held it there, while turning off the light with the other hand. She looked out at the darkness. Other than the rain, wind, and other forces of nature, there was nothing moving. But that could change in the space of a breath; she knew only too well.

The area looked familiar. She was just on the outskirts of Fort Worth and knew someone who lived a couple of blocks away. Hopefully she'd be able to get some help. But considering the animosity between them, she was just as likely to be turned away.

"Not gonna freakin' happen."

Her skin prickled with the low temperatures. She hadn't dressed for the cold front which came in while being held inside the building. She'd expected to be home well before it hit. She threw the towel in the backseat, grabbed a t-shirt from the gym bag and pulled it over her head, ignoring the smell of dried sweat from her workout earlier in the day. The handcuff snagged in the armhole, halting its descent. Sarah jerked it loose and pulled her arm through. The black tee was better than nothing, but she still shivered.

She started the engine, jacked up the heat, and slammed the car into gear. She drove with the lights off, hoping to avoid any unwanted attention.

Some areas were completely dark. Electricity seemed to be out in some places, but not all. And some people appeared to have backup generators as there were lone spots of brightness against the darkness.

She found the street she was looking for, although it was difficult to distinguish one house from another. The electricity still functioned here, but many of the street lamps had been broken with only a few to illuminate the affluent community. However, the pretentiousness of the home she sought stood out, even in the dark. She slowed to a stop and checked the surrounding area before turning off the Expedition. Upon exiting the vehicle, she let the door close with a barely audible click.

Within seconds she was soaked; her blonde hair plastered against her scalp. The rain washed the blood down her face as she made a dash for the cover of the front porch.

Noise could create a problem, so she tried the door first, but of course found it locked. Holding her breath, she knocked softly.

Just as she lifted her hand, a sound carried through the rain and she whipped around, ready to flee. An old man shuffled alongside the house across the street, seemingly oblivious to the pounding rain. He'd knocked over a trashcan. Could be just the unsteady gait of a senior citizen. It wasn't discernible at first. But then the wind changed and she picked up the smell of blood and decaying flesh.

Oh, God, no. Please. Not now. Adrenaline surged through her body.

Turning back, she knocked a little louder. Almost immediately she heard something on the other side of the door as if whoever was there had been waiting for her to leave.

"Meredith. It's Sarah. Open the door. Hurry!"

"Sarah. Go away. It's not a good time." The haughty tone of the woman was mixed with fear and something Sarah couldn't identify.

She would have laughed if she hadn't been so afraid. "Of course it's not a good time, Meredith. It's hell out here. Let me in…please." Meredith liked when people groveled. So she'd grovel if she had to.

"No. Get away from the door!"

Sarah half turned to see where the old man had gone and found him at the edge of the street as if listening. She didn't know how the dead could hear, but then again, she didn't know how they walked around either. Fortunately with the rain and wind, it was unlikely he'd heard her. So far. Rage filled her.

"Meredith, if you don't open up this door in the next three seconds, I swear I'm going to break every one of your damn windows. Now let me in!"

So much for groveling.

Sarah wasted no time when she heard the deadbolt disengage. She grabbed the knob and turned, pushing in at the same time.

Meredith gasped and stepped back. "What do you think you're doing?"

"I need your phone. Where is it?" She walked through the foyer into a dark living room.

"You're getting my floors all dirty. Wait here." Meredith started to turn around, but stopped at the low menace in Sarah's voice.

"What the hell is wrong with you? We're in the middle of a zombie apocalypse and you're worried about your floors? That's appalling even for you." Sarah was incredulous.

Meredith sat on the sofa and flipped on the lamp on the end table. "What are you talking about? Have you finally gone completely over the edge to insanity?"

"Oh my God. Are you trying to get us killed?" Sarah jumped for the light, nearly toppling it in her haste. She righted it and turned it off. "Just tell me where the phone is, I need to call the police. A couple of thugs are holding my sister hostage."

"Your sis...I...I've no idea if you're crazy, or what's going on, but the phones are out. I've been asleep all day and tried to call Rudy just before you got here. I guess the storm took them out. I just checked. I forgot to charge my cellphone. You interrupted before I could plug it in." Her voice sounded weary.

Sarah found the small flashlight on her key ring and turned the light on Meredith. She looked frail and gray, her hand pressed against her stomach. She'd obviously been sick. Normally put together impeccably, she now looked unkempt; her pajamas wrinkled and sweat-stained, a scarf covered her head.

"Are you okay, Mere?" She sat down next to Meredith, and appraised her co-worker.

The woman grimaced, holding her hand up in front of her eyes. "Get that out of my face. And you know I hate when you call me that." Meredith's eyes focused on Sarah's wrist and she gasped. "What the hell? Why do you have a handcuff on? What have you done now?"

Sarah sighed. "Look, we've got bigger things to worry about right now. I managed to get away from the guys who grabbed us, but I couldn't get Dana free. I have to help her. And if you haven't noticed, the world is going to hell without even the proverbial hand basket. Where's Rudy?"

"In Chicago. He was supposed to be back last night, but he called and said flights were delayed and it'd be today. I haven't heard from him though and I'm worried." Concern marred her features. She looked more vulnerable than Sarah had ever seen her and older than her forty-two years.

"I'm sure flights have been cancelled until this…this epidemic is under control. But he's got guns, right? I know he does. You've talked about his collection. So where are they?" Sarah got up and brushed the wet hair off her face.

"You're bleeding! Something really has happened, hasn't it?" Meredith struggled to get up and then swayed before finding her balance. Her gaze traveled over the rest of Sarah and the cuts and abrasions on her arms, the dots of blood on her t-shirt.

Conflicting emotions warred within Sarah. She could tell Meredith was really ill, but her sister was in danger. She needed help. And she needed it fast.

"Meredith, please, tell me where the guns are. I really need to get back to my sister before they feed her to those monsters." Her voice broke. Just the thought of what they'd threatened made her gag.

"Feed her to—" Meredith looked at her for a few seconds and then moved off toward a room at the back of the house, reaching out for the wall every few feet. "I hope I don't regret this. Point your flashlight down this way."

They entered a study and Meredith pressed a button hidden under a desk drawer. A panel slid open in one of the walls, a light switched on illuminating the contents. Sarah spun around and checked, but there were black-out curtains on the windows, so they were probably safe enough.

Turning back, she gaped at the weapon stash. *You've got to be freakin' kidding me.* There were all kinds of firearms; from handguns to assault rifles. She moved into the recessed area and picked up a Glock, removed the magazine, and found it loaded. She sent it home again and chambered a round. Different types of holsters took up one shelf. Sarah found one that would work and slid it over her shoulder. She gave thanks that her older cousin had been a gun aficionado and had passed along his knowledge as well as a self-defense education. He'd made certain she and Dana knew how to protect themselves. She hoped he was okay. If anyone could survive a zombie apocalypse, it was Brian.

She turned to face Meredith. "Which of these are you most comfortable with?"

"Me? I don't know anything about guns. That's Rudy's thing —" She wobbled and grabbed her stomach. "Oh, God." Meredith staggered from the room and made her way to the bathroom a couple of doors down, with Sarah following. The door slammed in front of her, causing Sarah to jerk to a stop so she wouldn't crash into it. Retching sounds carried through the wooden barrier. She hesitated a few seconds before entering.

Wash cloths were stocked near the sink as if waiting. Sarah grabbed one and ran cold water over it. She squeezed the excess out and handed it to Meredith who was on her knees, crumpled against the wall. She looked embarrassed, refusing to make eye contact as she wiped her face with the cool cloth.

"I thought you'd been on vacation for the last month. But you've obviously been sick. What's wrong?" Sarah knelt beside her.

Meredith paused, emotions flitting across her face before she came to a decision. She flushed the toilet and reached out her hand. "Help me up."

Sarah rose and grabbed her hand, tugging gently until she was standing. Meredith took a toothbrush from the porcelain holder and put paste on it. "I didn't want anyone to know, but I have cancer. Yesterday was my last chemo treatment. I took leave because I couldn't hide the effects any longer." She brushed slowly, but expending even that little bit of energy seemed to wear her out.

"I'm so sorry." They'd had their problems in the past, but Sarah would never wish such a horrible disease on anyone. "What's your prognosis?"

"The doctor is hopeful. He thinks I've got a really good chance to beat it." Meredith rinsed her mouth and then gripped the counter to steady herself.

Sarah's mouth turned up into a brief smile. "Well, I'm sure you will. I've never met anyone so stubborn in my entire life."

Meredith's mouth moved, not uttering a sound. Finally, she got out one word. "Pot."

Sarah's eyes widened. "Kettle."

They stared each other down and then both burst into laughter.

"Well, that felt good. Here," Sarah placed an arm around the woman and was surprised at how thin she had become, "let me help you into the study where you can sit down for a minute."

Easing into a large leather chair which seemed to swallow her, Meredith asked, "Who has your sister?"

"Three guys taking advantage of the chaos. I had picked Dana up and when we stopped at a corner, two of them jumped into the backseat. One of them held a gun on her, while the other gave me directions. We ended up at an isolated building just a little ways from here where another of their psycho friends waited on them."

Sarah found a black bag in with the weapon stash and began filling it with guns and ammo. A few hunting knives found their way in as well.

"I know you're not comfortable with guns, but do you know how to use any of these?"

"I went to the range with Rudy a few times. I can manage. Just pick out something easy." Meredith pushed herself up and started for the doorway. "I'm going to go change clothes."

While her co-worker was in the bedroom, Sarah looked over the selection. Glocks were her favorite and easy to use. No safety—just point and shoot. But Meredith was so weak, she probably wouldn't have the strength to rack one. She found a .38, loaded it, and found a holster for it. She finished loading the weapons in the bag, placing a 9mm in another holster at her back.

"Sarah?" Meredith called from down the hall. "Can you help me with this?"

Entering the room, Sarah saw a bag on the bed already filled to capacity. Surprisingly, it looked like sensible clothing inside. She rarely saw Meredith without her designer threads. She'd definitely married well. Their investigator salaries from the family court could not have afforded any of the luxuries Meredith had become accustomed.

"What's this?"

Meredith had been busy filling a bag with toiletries and medications. She zipped the small case and put it in the larger one. "It's a go bag. Or at least that's what Rudy calls it. He insisted I have one ready to go in case of an emergency. I guess he was right." A soft cry came from the woman and a tear escaped, rolling down her cheek. "I hope he's okay."

"You just have to believe he is. And I'm sure he'll find his way back here to you as soon as he can."

Sarah held the gun and holster out and Meredith took them, copying the way Sarah had put hers on. "This is real, isn't it?"

"Yeah, it's real. Why don't you rest here and as soon as I can, I'll come back and make sure everything is okay. Then we'll figure out what to do." Sarah turned toward the door, slinging the strap of the gun bag over her head, wearing it cross-body style. She needed her hands free.

"No way. I'm going with you. You'll need help getting your sister." Meredith tried to pick up the bag but didn't have the strength. Frustration at the way the cancer and treatment had zapped her stamina showed in her face. "You'll have to carry this though."

Sarah knew what it cost the woman to have to admit to any weakness. She'd always acted like she could do everything better than anyone else. And there it was—the main problem between them. Meredith continuously tried to make Sarah feel inferior, which had worn thin after four years.

"You're too ill, Mere. You can't help me fight off the psychos. I promise. I'll come back and we'll make some decisions about what to do next."

"I'm coming. I know I'm too weak to help much, but I can stay in the car and I'll know where you and your sister are. If there's a problem, I can go get help. You need—" A loud crash came from down the hall.

"That sounded like a window breaking! Come on, Mere. You obviously can't stay here now."

Sarah grabbed the bag, and ran for the door. She looked back to check on Meredith's progress and saw a glint of steel coming from the study. A machete. Why hadn't she seen it before? She raced into the room, seizing it from where it hung on the recessed wall. She found the button under the desk and closed the panel once again hiding the stash. They may need to come back for the rest later. She made it back to the hall by the time Meredith drew even with her.

They reached the front door and Sarah checked through the peephole. She couldn't see anything from such a limited area, so she opened the door a crack, peeking through. She shut it again just as quietly.

"Okay. There's nothing just in front of the door. But I could see movement to the side, probably where the window was broken. I'm going to go get the car and pull it up here to the door. Be ready to move when I pull up." Sarah gently touched the woman's shoulder.

Meredith opened her mouth as if to object, but closed it again and nodded.

Taking a breath, Sarah gathered her nerve and pulled keys from her pocket. Thank God she'd left the SUV unlocked. She opened the door and stepped out, peering to the left. Bile rose in throat. She gagged silently, but forced it down.

There had to be at least five of the dead gathered around a man half in and half out of the window. Loopy strands of what could only be intestines were pulled from the man's body. Blood and gore covered what remained of him. As long as she lived, she'd never forget the wet, slurpy sounds of the zombies feasting on their prey or the sounds the man made as he died.

Sarah must have made a noise because, as one, the creatures spun in her direction. A couple turned back to continue feeding on the man, digging faces into his stomach cavity. The others started her way. She froze, hearing the strange gurgling type growl coming from the corpses.

"Sarah, run!"

Meredith's words snapped her out of the trance and she ran for the Expedition. The zombies moved faster than she thought they could. But what did she know? She only had books and film to go by. Fiction. She couldn't allow herself to presume anything.

Her chest heaved and she gulped for air, fear making it difficult to breathe. The rain still fell in torrents and she slipped on the sodden ground, but managed to stay upright. After what seemed like forever, she reached the driver's door and jerked it open. She shoved Meredith's go bag into the backseat and was trying to get the other bag's strap over her head, when a hand grabbed her arm, dragging her back.

Sarah cried out, nearly dropping the machete as the seat belt wrapped around it. She finally got it free and turned toward her attacker only to gasp. Half of the woman's face had been chewed off—teeth, gums and tongue showed through the gaping maw. She swung the blade, impaling the woman through the chest. But it didn't stop the already dead cadaver. *How can you kill something that's not alive?*

She yanked out the machete. Before she even realized she'd done it, the blade tore through what was left of the woman's face, piercing the brain. As she pulled it out, blood and bits of the organ coated Sarah's hands and arms. The zombie fell, taking the other two to the ground with her. Sarah wasted no time climbing into the SUV. She slammed the key into the ignition before her legs had even cleared the doorway, surprised she'd been able to hold on to it.

An arm shot up through the doorway, and Sarah watched in horror as one of the dead tried to pull himself up. She turned and kicked out, making enough contact to force the zombie back to the ground. She wrenched the door closed with one hand, while shifting into drive with the other. The two she'd left at the side of house had finished with the man in the window, and were moving toward the front door where Meredith waited.

Or rather…where Meredith should have been waiting. *Where the hell is she?*

***

Sarah drove up onto the lawn and plowed into the two zombies shuffling toward the front door. One fell under her tires with a sickening crunch. The other flew backwards but was already trying to rise. Thankfully his injuries were too severe.

She maneuvered the Expedition so the passenger side was as close to the front door as possible. She opened the door just as a scream came from inside the house.

Sarah bolted out of the SUV and inside the home. She jerked to a stop, taking in the scene before her. Meredith had skewered the old man from next door with a poker from the fireplace. He wiggled and pushed himself toward the woman, arms reaching, jaws opening and closing while Meredith tried to reason with him.

"John? Please, John. Oh, my God. What's happened to you? We're friends. Please don't do this," Meredith cried, but finally released the hold on her weapon and backed up.

"He's not John anymore, Meredith. He's become one of those dead things. A zombie." She pointed to the large gash in his throat and shoulder. The monster which had once been a gentle older man whipped around to search the new noise, another source of fresh food.

Taking two large steps, Sarah used the machete to cut through his skull and into his brain. He dropped to the floor, no longer moving.

"Oh, my God! Oh, my God! Oh, my God!" Meredith gagged, her hand over her mouth, eyes wide with shock. She turned toward Sarah, realization in her eyes. "I thought...even after you found out I was sick...that—"

"That I was messing with you?"

"Well, not about your sister, but I thought surely there was another explanation. There couldn't really be zombies."

Meredith looked as if she was ready to fall over. "Come on—let's get you in the car." She reached for her, but Meredith pulled away.

"Wait. Let's get these. I thought your sister might need them, and who knows what we'll need." She pointed to a pile of blankets, pillows and two coats. She shoved her arms into another jacket she pulled from a chair and grabbed a small bag. "Cellphone and charger," she announced as she held it up.

"Good idea. But we need to go now before more of those things show up." Sarah grabbed the pile stacked on the sofa and led the way to the front door. She heard the door close behind them as she stuffed everything but the machete into the backseat. When she saw Meredith struggling to get inside the huge SUV, Sarah said nothing, but helped to lift the woman into the seat, startled to realize how little she weighed.

Meredith breathed heavily, her chest expanding as she gasped for air, just the little exertion zapping her strength. "Thanks."

"No problem."

Sarah shut the door. The zombie she'd left on the lawn had given up trying to stand and now crawled toward them. Sarah strode over to him using the machete to open his skull. Wiping the blade on the man's clothing, she looked around and saw more shapes shuffling toward them from the dark. She hurried around to her side of the SUV, hitting the locks as soon as the door closed. Even before the truck started to move, Meredith had the charger out and was turning on her phone.

She tried a few times, but finally gave up, resting her head against the window. "911 is busy. It's not even putting me on hold."

"It figures. There's so much going on. Thanks for trying though."

Silence filled the car as they drove toward the building where Dana waited; each woman lost in thought. Meredith finally picked the phone back up again. "Who should I try to call for you?"

Sarah blinked back a look of surprise. She'd thought for sure Meredith would have already tried to reach her husband. Instead she was thinking of her. Not only that, but she'd gone back into the house gathering things for her sister and all of them. She was definitely going to have to give this new Meredith some thought.

"I guess my cousin, Brian. He's about the only family Dana and I have. He was in East Texas this past week, so I don't know if he's back yet." She gave the phone number and waited as the numbers were entered, but Meredith didn't push send right away.

"If he doesn't answer, do you want me to leave a message for him?"

"Yeah. I guess. Hmm…" Where should they go after they rescued Dana? "The only place I can think of that can be made fairly safe right now is the courthouse. With it being Saturday, there shouldn't have been many people there when this thing started. Tell him we're going to check it out, and if the phones go out, we'll leave a message there if we have to go elsewhere."

She listened as the woman beside her placed the call, hope dashing as she heard her leaving a message rather than being able to verify he was still alive.

Sarah placed her hand on Meredith's arm. "Thank you. Why don't you try to reach Rudy?"

"I guess I'm afraid. What if I can't reach him? He's all I've got." She sniffled, but Sarah could tell she refused to let the tears fall.

"Just leave a message like you did for Brian. He'll know where to start looking for you. Just because you can't reach him doesn't mean he's not okay. There's just so much going on and he could have lost his phone." She paused briefly before adding, "Besides, you're not alone. We have each other and we're going to be fine."

Meredith took a deep breath and then dialed. Sarah felt the palpable anxiety in the car lessen as Rudy's deep baritone came through the phone's tiny speaker. She listened while concentrating on edging around the people, the dead, and the cars on the busier roads. Occasionally she bumped into and over things and the walking nightmares. Meredith didn't even acknowledge what was happening around them except with worried glances and fear-filled eyes. She kept her voice even and light trying not to worry her husband. Apparently he was still in Illinois, but had managed to get a car and had already headed toward Fort Worth. He was traveling with a few other men from the area he'd had meetings with while there, so he wasn't alone. Sarah heard Meredith's sigh of relief which probably didn't carry through the airwaves.

The night got even darker as Sarah drove off the main roads onto a long drive toward the building where Dana was being kept. She turned her lights off as she left the asphalt and moved cautiously through trees scattered throughout the property. Coming to a stop on the side of the building where she'd busted the window out earlier, she shoved the gearshift to park and turned off the engine. She'd parked the length of a football field away to keep from being heard and hoped Dana would be in shape to run that far when she finally got her out.

"I love you, too. Be careful." Meredith blinked back tears, and disconnected the call as she faced Sarah.

"I'm glad you reached him and he's okay."

"Me too. Listen…I want to thank—"

"Don't thank me. You've helped me with guns and ammo and—"

"Yeah, but I wouldn't have even known anything was happening before it was too late..." Meredith grabbed Sarah's hand. "So thank you. Now how do we get your sister out of there?"

"I'm going to go inside that window and hope she's still there." She pointed to the frame with the broken glass. "If she's not in the basement, I'll have to search the building, so it might take a while. But I saw their cars when we circled the building. They probably thought I wouldn't make it back."

"Are you sure? We could try to find someone to help you."

"No. I can't wait any longer. I don't know what they may be doing..." She gulped back a cry. She'd been strong so far; she couldn't give in to fear now. She cleared her throat. "Once I leave, you scoot over here. Don't go outside the car for any reason. Just climb over the console and lock the doors behind me. Adjust the seat and be ready to drive." Sarah rummaged in the door's pocket and came up with a plastic bag. "If you feel the need to throw up, use this. It won't be pleasant, but it's better than going outside. Keep a lookout—360. Don't let anyone inside the car except me or Dana. Even if it looks like they need help. Just...don't. Get your gun out and be ready to use it. Any doubts at all, you use it. Okay?"

Meredith waited a few seconds but then nodded. "Okay. But how will I know it's Dana if she comes out by herself? I've never met her."

"She's my twin. We look exactly alike." Sarah laughed softly, remembering a few of the times they'd played the "switch game" with their parents and others.

Meredith gasped. "There are two of you? How did I not know that?" She sounded horrified and Sarah laughed a little louder.

"Yeah. But she's a lot nicer than me." She winked and then became serious again. "Okay. If we're not out in an hour...God I hope it doesn't take that long...then go on to the courthouse and we'll meet you there." She checked her Glock once more; made sure she had an extra magazine in the holster and picked up the machete.

"I'm not leaving you here."

"Only if we're not back in an hour. Look, we could get held up for some reason and I don't want them finding you here. If we have to, we can make it there on our own." Sarah didn't say what they both were thinking: That she and Dana might not make it out. Inside the console she dug around until she found two small flashlights. "I'm putting this one right here on top in case you need it. It's small but it puts out a lot of light, so only use it if you have to. You don't want to give away your position." She tucked the other into the front pocket of her jeans.

She reached over and gave Meredith a one-arm hug, turned off the interior lights, and opened her door. "See ya soon." And she slipped out into the night.

***

Crossing the damp grass at a sprint, Sarah wished rain was still falling to help mask the squishy sounds of her approach. She reached the side of the building and leaned against it catching her breath before sliding toward the window.

She took a couple of deep breaths trying to ease her rapid heart rate. The blood still galloped through her veins, pulse pounding. She looked back at the SUV. Everything seemed fine there.

Holding her breath she peeked around the window's frame. Nothing moved. No sound carried outside. Deftly she pulled the flashlight from her pocket and shined it around the interior. The basement stood empty. Sarah turned off the light and pocketed it again. Her shirt had been removed from the sill, but most of the glass was missing too. It would be easier getting inside than it had been getting out. She sat on the wet ground and shimmied to the window feet first. She grabbed the top pane, arched her back, and eased herself down onto the floor. She cringed as glass crunched beneath her sneakers.

She ran to the stairs and hid under them, waiting to see if anyone had heard and would come to investigate. There was no sound until her sister's scream filled the air. She bolted from her hiding place and up the stairs, managing to stop herself before bursting through the door and losing the advantage of surprise.

Dana's heartrending scream mocked the silence again and Sarah knew she had to act. She opened the door, peering out into the dark hallway. At least there was some ambient light from windows letting her see shadows. After a few seconds, she entered the hallway allowing the door to click softly closed behind her.

Doorways filled the corridor. Some open. Some closed. She found some locked and walked past those. The others she stopped beside to listen briefly before moving on. The building had housed medical offices, but had closed recently. Although abandoned it was still in decent condition. Only a layer of dust, some debris, and a slight musty odor gave away its current disposition.

"Bitch! You bit me!" one of the men roared from ahead. A slap echoed in the hallway.

Sarah hurried to the door. A lump lodged in her throat when she saw the sick bastard on top of Dana. Her sister's hands were pulled above her head and cuffed to the leg of a sofa, the only furniture in the room. Her shirt had been ripped open and her lip bled down her chin.

Sarah didn't even think. Didn't even know she had moved until she found herself beside the man. The machete's blade cut cleanly through his side and he fell to the dirty carpet, trying to cover the gushing wound with both hands. He gurgled, blood flowing from his mouth and then he was silent, his eyes glazed and staring.

A new sound and Sarah jerked around to see the man she'd escaped from earlier struggling to get off the couch with his broken leg. His arm came up and Sarah found herself face to face with the barrel of a gun. She flung herself to the side while sweeping the machete at his arm. He reared back but only enough to spare his limb. The metal of the blade clanged against the firearm and it flew across the room. He fell back moaning against the cushion, sweat pouring down his face, his body racked with fever from the break.

"Stay down." Sarah breathed slowly, trying not to hyperventilate.

"Go to hell." The man spat in her direction.

She wasted no time, jamming the edge of the blade against his throat. She spoke softly, "Listen to me carefully. I've had a really bad day, today. So stay back and you might live."

He held eye contact for a few seconds before dropping his gaze. Something he saw must have made him believe she'd reached her threshold for crazy.

Squatting next to the dead man, she turned out his pockets. Thinking about taking a life, no matter how wicked, caused her gag reflex to engage, but she slammed it down. There'd be time for personal accountability later. The handcuff key tumbled out amongst the coins from his jeans' pocket and she wasted no time before dropping beside her twin.

Her fingers brushed the hair out of Dana's eyes and the tears from her cheeks. "Are you okay?"

Dana gulped in air, staunching the flow of tears. "Yeah. Yeah, just get these off me." She jerked the cuffs.

Sarah unlocked the handcuffs and rubbed her sister's wrists and hands before Dana threw her arms around her. "I knew you'd come back. I'm so glad you're okay." She shivered, chill bumps racing across her skin.

Sarah pulled back and looked from Dana's open shirt to her own gore covered one. "Hey you. Take your shirt off." Sarah motioned to the man on the couch.

An evil grin lit up his face. "You want some of this don't you?"

"Idiot! Just take off your shirt."

"Bitch, you broke my leg. I ain't givin' you shit."

"Have it your way." Sarah moved toward him, but in the end, she didn't even have to threaten him again. He pulled the shirt over his head and threw it at her, grunting at the pain in his leg when he shifted. She straightened it out and handed it to Dana.

"I don't mean to be ungrateful, sis, but I really don't want to wear anything that's touched any of them." She tried to hand it back.

"You're freezing, your shirt won't stay closed, and we have a long walk. It's either this or mine decorated with zombie brain. Your choice." Dana looked from the shirt in her hand to Sarah's.

"Fine. Although, I'm not sure I'm not getting the short end here." She huffed, yanking it over her head covering the ripped shirt.

While Dana dressed, Sarah unlocked her own cuff finally free of the metal chaffing her wrist. She checked the corridor again to make sure they were still alone.

Sarah stood over the man again. "Where's your friend?"

"You just killed him," he said, pointing to the prone figure on the floor.

She picked up the gun she'd relieved him of and checked it. "Not him...the other one. Ron." She handed the weapon to Dana. "It's loaded and ready to shoot. You just have to pull the trigger." Dana nodded and took the gun. Sarah turned back to the couch. "So? Where is he?"

"He left to go get some food."

"Both cars were here when I got back. He has to be here, so you'd better keep talking if you want to keep breathing." She waved the machete in his face.

"I don't know. That's what he said. He was going to get food. If he's back, I don't know where he is." His eyes widened and she thought he might be telling the truth.

She nodded. "I'm real sorry to have to do this, but..."

Sarah raised the knife over his heart and plunged downward.

"Sarah!" Dana grabbed her arm, halting the blade's decent. "What are you doing? You just can't kill him. He's got a broken leg and he's unarmed."

Sarah pulled her sister to the other side of the room and whispered, "Dana. It's hell out there already. We have got to get out of here and get somewhere safe. You know psychos like this. What if he tries to come after us because we got away? Because I broke his leg and killed his friend?"

"But…" She gulped.

A thump made them both jump around. The man was no longer on the sofa, but crawling toward the door, groaning each time he had to move his broken leg. His breathing was labored. His leg probably wouldn't make it without medical intervention.

"It's a new world out there, Dana. New rules. Only those who are willing to do the hard things are going to survive."

Tears formed in her eyes and she brushed them away. She'd spent her whole adult life so far helping people. Trying to make the right choices. Now she'd killed one man. Sure he'd been about to rape her sister, but he was still dead because of her. Could she kill someone unarmed and unable to defend himself?

"Who am I kidding? I don't think I can kill him like he is."

Sarah pulled her shoulders back and faced the man again. "Because of my sister, you're getting a reprieve. I'm not sure you'll make it with a break like that and no help, but if you do— do yourself a favor and stay away from us. If I see you again, I'll assume you're a threat and I *will* kill you."

She grabbed Dana's hand and pulled her to the door. Easing her head around the door, she found the corridor clear. To the left, a glass doorframe led to the outside. Sarah ran ahead and tried the door. It opened. She held it for her sister and motioned her forward.

They both took deep breaths when they emerged into the night air and moved to the side of the building. As Sarah passed the corner, a hand reached out and grabbed her, pulling her against a hard chest, a knife at her throat. He knocked the knife from her shaking hand and took the guns from her holsters.

"Sarah!" Dana pulled the gun and held it out in front of her with both hands. Sarah knew she hadn't practiced shooting in years, so she was a little surprised when her sister fell into a proper stance without hesitation. An engine roared in the distance.

"Drop the gun or I'll open up her pretty little throat." Dana hesitated and the man yelled, "Drop it now!" The sharp blade sliced upward, cutting a line across Sarah's right cheek. She couldn't hold back the scream that tore from her throat. The blood felt warm as it flowed down her face and neck. Even worse, she saw Dana relaxing her arm, about to drop the gun.

"Dana! Don't…think about Brian. You know he'd want you to survive. You know *exactly* what Brian would want you to do."

Her eyes met identical ones across the distance. They stared at each other, communicating without words. Dana straightened up, aimed the gun and pulled the trigger just as Sarah let her legs go limp and dropped as far as she could.

Blood spattered across Sarah. Ron pulled her backward on top of him when he fell to the grass. But it was only a reflex. His eyes were closed and his arm slowly fell to the side. Dana tugged her up and used the bottom of her shirt to wipe the blood from her sister's face. Sarah winced at the contact.

"Ouch! Careful there."

Headlights lit them up as the Expedition barreled toward them. Dana spun around, lifting the gun in front of her where Sarah knocked it down just as quickly.

"No! She's with me."

Meredith opened her door, weakly pulling herself out on the running board to look over the top. "Are y'all okay?"

Nodding, Sarah pushed Dana toward the passenger seat. "Yeah. Thanks for coming for us. Dana, this is Meredith. Meredith, Dana."

While Dana got inside the Expedition, Sarah retrieved her weapons and walked vigilantly over to Ron's still form. A monster on the inside, she marveled at how normal he looked. How they all looked. She knew from years working within the courts that looks could definitely be deceiving. She'd always thought those capable of such atrocities should at least have a warning mark of some kind tattooed across their forehead to give the rest of humanity a fighting chance. They definitely should not be attractive.

The shot had torn a hole through his chest, but he still chugged in breath. She tried to force herself to end him once and for all, but regardless of what she'd told her sister about doing the hard things, she just couldn't do it. She reasoned that he probably wouldn't survive such a severe wound anyway as she walked back toward the other women.

"Do you want to drive?" Back in her seat, Meredith clutched the door handle.

"If you think you feel up to it, then I'll just ride back here." Sarah opened the back door and waited. She was exhausted and just wanted to rest a moment.

Meredith looked her over and nodded. "I'll be fine. We don't have that far to go."

Pulling herself into the backseat, she found the towel she'd used earlier and held it to her cheek to stop the blood flow.

Dana turned around to face her. "I don't think it's too deep, but we need to get it disinfected soon."

"I have a first aid kit in my bag. We can take care of it when we get to the courthouse." Meredith eased the SUV onto the drive and toward Lancaster Avenue.

Exhaustion flooded Sarah as the adrenaline she'd been running on fled her body. With her sister safe and them hopefully on their way to a secure location, she let herself relax against the backseat. Her wet clothing clung to her skin, the heavy thickness of blood on her shirt reminding her of the day's horrors. It felt as if her body had turned to ice. Her teeth chattered and she shook uncontrollably. "H-h-heat." She could barely get the word out.

Dana turned to face her, took in the situation and turned back to adjust the temperature and to make sure the back vents were on. "You're freezing. Here, put one of these blankets around you." She leaned over the console to the back to hand one to Sarah, but Sarah stopped her.

"N-no. I'll be f-fine in a m-m-minute." She hugged herself. "We'll n-need those, and I'm all n-n-nasty with zombie guts."

"We'll find more. Go ahead and use it." Dana tried once again to hand the blanket to Sarah.

"No. I'm really better already. Just needed the h-heat. Th-thanks though."

"Your sister's stubborn." Meredith chimed in; her total focus still on the road in front of her.

Dana laughed. "Don't I know it? Thank goodness though. I wouldn't have made it without her today."

Meredith nodded. "Me neither."

The women sat not speaking. The only sounds came from outside, where the dead attacked the living. Car horns blared and screams filled the night. Try as they might, they couldn't help but stare at the horror surrounding them. People fled cars stalled in traffic, trying to get in others, or into nearby buildings. Some outdistancing the zombies. Some not. A woman's body hit the side of their truck. Blood and gore spattered against Dana's window and the Expedition rocked. Two of the dead had her held there while their teeth chewed their way into her flesh.

"Oh God. We have to do something." Dana moved to open her door but found herself shoved back against the seat.

Sarah held her there. "No…we can't. There's nothing we can do. It's too late."

They watched helplessly as the woman slid to the ground and other zombies came to feed upon her.

"Screw this." Meredith backed up the vehicle, getting just enough room to go up and over a trio of zombies on the ground next to the front tire and across the median to the other side where traffic was less dense. Dodging what she could, she made better progress.

Meredith's reflection in the rearview mirror showed she was fading fast. "Mere, if you'll stop when you can, I'll drive the r—"

A shrill scream eclipsed all the other noise. Sarah's head jerked around to her window.

Dana gasped. "That sounded like a kid."

All three searched the surrounding area. "There! Next to that building." Meredith pointed to her left.

"Stop the car." Sarah moved to the other side of the vehicle, and grabbed the door handle.

Dana looked over her shoulder. "I thought you said—"

"I know what I said. Just stop the car, Mere! It's a kid for Christ's sake." Sarah opened the door before the Expedition came to a full stop and ran toward the girl.

When she saw Sarah coming at her with the machete, she screamed again, but froze in terror.

Sarah dropped the knife next to her as she knelt beside the child. She looked her over and figured her to be about four or five. Blood covered her pink shirt and pants, but she didn't see any injuries. "Are you okay? Where's your mom?" She had to repeat the question twice before the girl pointed. Sarah saw a man crouched over a woman, hugging her to him half a block away.

"Is that your dad?"

The girl nodded as she whispered, "She tried to bite me." Tears flowed down her face and she gulped for air. "She bit daddy and he..." The child sobbed unable to finish.

Sarah rose, picked up her machete, and pulled the girl into her arms. The child's face nestled against her shoulder, her sobs quieter, but they still racked her small body. Sarah motioned for Meredith to follow as she moved cautiously toward the man and obviously dead woman. She kept the girl's face pressed against her chest, so she wouldn't see the bashed in face which used to belong to her mother.

A flap of skin hung from what was left of the woman's mouth, her teeth and face covered in gore. A brick lay near her head stained with her blood and brain matter. The man clutched her to him, whispering over and over how sorry he was. He had a huge chunk of flesh missing from his arm and another from his chest. His head turned and his eyes met Sarah's.

"Maggie? Oh, my God, Maggie. Are you okay?" He reached for her, noted how her head pressed against Sarah, and then looked down at his wife. He laid his wife down and tried to stand, but couldn't. He'd lost too much blood. Instead, he scooted backwards a few feet and held out his hands.

Sarah leaned down to place the girl in his arms just as a blast came beside her. She whipped around to find Dana standing there, gun in hand. A zombie staggered toward them, unafunaffected by the large bullet hole in his stomach.

"Aim for the head!" Sarah turned a full circle. Others had heard the gunshot and were now on their way.

She shook the man's shoulder. "We have to go now. More are coming." She tried to get him to stand, but he looked at her then back at his injuries.

He held his daughter against him, covering her ears as best he could. "I'm not going to make it and I don't want to put her at risk. Please take care of her. Please." His stroked the child's back and begged Sarah with his eyes. Sarah stifled a sob and nodded. "That's Janine." His chin pointed at the woman he'd left to hold his daughter one last time. And I'm Paul. Campisi. Please help her to remember us." Tears fell quietly down his face. Sarah nodded again and he brushed the tears aside.

Dana fired three shots at the approaching dead. Time was running out, but she thought they could give him a few seconds more with his daughter.

"Maggie? Maggie, look at me, honey." He gently moved his child so she could see his face. "Your mommy and I love you very much." Sarah didn't know how he found the strength, but he held back the tears as he looked at his daughter for the last time. "But you have to go with..." He looked up.

"Sarah. That's my sister, Dana."

He turned back to Maggie. "Sarah and Dana are going to take good care of you and make sure you're safe."

"No! I want to stay with you and mommy." The girl wailed and wrapped her arms around her father's neck.

"I know, sweetie, I know. I want you to be with us, too. But..." He caught his breath and held back his own sob. "You need to go with Sarah." Tears fell then as he hugged Maggie one last time.

296

"We have to go! Now!" Dana shouted. She fired another couple of shots, but there were more zombies ambling toward them than they had bullets.

Sarah moved quickly, taking a struggling Maggie from her father's arms. "We'll take care of her, Paul. I promise you." She pressed the curly brown head against her chest and ran for the SUV with Dana on her heels.

Another kid ran past her and she shouted for Dana. Her sister turned just in time to grab him by the shirt. He clawed at her, yelling that a zombie had him. He kicked her shin, and punched her in the stomach, but she held on.

"Kid! Hey, kid! I'm not a zombie. Stop fighting me or we're both gonna get dead." He finally stopped struggling and looked at her. His wide chocolate eyes were filled with fear as he took in the horde nearly surrounding them.

Dana turned him around and pointed. "See that black SUV there at the curb? Run and open the back door and climb inside. We're right behind you." His eyes took in Sarah and Maggie. Sarah had to give him credit. He didn't even hesitate. He just took off running.

The stench from so many decaying bodies made Sarah gag. Her eyes watered. She could barely see to make it to the vehicle as the boy disappeared inside. He tossed the blankets in the back, leaned out, and helped Sarah get Maggie in the backseat, while Dana went around to the front passenger side. Dana fired off two more rounds while Sarah dispatched what once appeared to be a fireman, but now was missing both arms—one ripped from the shoulder and the other at the elbow. Bones, muscle and tissue hung from the stumps.

Sarah jumped in beside Maggie, slamming the door. The locks clicked into place as Meredith drove through the mass of corpses. She tried to block out the sounds of flesh rending and bones crunching. Maggie pressed herself against Sarah. The boy moved closer to them and she put an arm around him as well. Other than everyone's rapid breathing, no one uttered a sound until they were clear of the mob.

A few street lights still burned and Sarah took a minute to assess the boy. His creamy mocha complexion was clear and he breathed easier than he had been. His clothes were splattered with blood, but not enough for her to think he'd been bitten. When he realized he was under scrutiny, and had pressed himself against her, he backed away to the far side of the seat, trying to hide the fear that ate at all of them.

"I'm Sarah. This is Maggie." She rubbed the still sobbing child's hair. Pointing, she said, "That's Dana. My twin."

"Well, duh." He rolled his eyes and she laughed. At least some things could still be counted on to be normal.

"And the lady driving is Meredith." She leaned toward him and whispered loud enough for it to carry to the front seat. "But don't call her Mere. She hates that. Right, Mere." She laughed again as the woman gave a weak glare via the rearview mirror. It felt good to laugh. But she was afraid if she laughed too much she might not stop. Instead she turned to their newest passenger. "What's your name?"

"Dexter." He looked at her with resignation. "Yeah, I know, but my mom named me that before the show. Most people call me Dex."

"Hi, Dex. How old are you? You handled yourself pretty well back there." Dana faced them, peering around her seat.

He snorted. "Yeah. I let a girl beat my a—" He looked over at Maggie. "...butt."

"Yeah, but this girl has training. It's been a while, but I still have a few moves. My sister there, now she's awesome. She's kept up the training and can whip grown men's...butts." She winked. "She's already kicked a few today and saved my behind."

"Yep. And she saved mine right back. We make a pretty good team." Sarah looked down at the girl in her arms. She'd exhausted herself crying and now slept, although she whimpered occasionally. She adjusted Maggie so she sat across her lap and cradled her. Looking back at Dex she asked, "So how old are you?"

"Eleven. I'll be twelve next month." He pulled his shoulders back, making himself appear bigger. "How old is she?"

"Not sure yet. We'll have to wait until she wakes up. I'm guessing about five. What do you think?"

"Yeah. I have a cousin about her age." He leaned against the seat, lost in his thoughts.

"We'll try to get you back to your family soon."

"My mom died when I was a baby. I was living with my grandma, but…" He blinked back tears. "The zombies got her."

"I'm so sorry. We'll see if we can find any of your family as soon as we can. If we can't, you're always welcome with us." Dana reached back to pat his knee.

The vehicle made a turn and slowed. "Look, the doors are boarded up. I guess that means someone's in there." Meredith pulled the car to a stop in front of the red brick building. "So what do you think?"

"I think I'm exhausted. And if someone's in there, it has to be someone who has a keycard since the building wasn't open today except for a few supervised kid visits. If they've got the windows boarded, then hopefully they've cleared the courthouse, so that's one less thing we have to do. Right?"

The running engine was the only sound for a few moments. "Yeah. I think we should try it. What do you think, Dex?"

He looked surprised Dana had asked him. "Let's do it."

"There's the underground garage that's restricted to Judges. Let's see if we can get in that way." Meredith eased the truck around the building and down an enclosed ramp which made it difficult to see if one didn't know it existed. She stopped outside the gate. "I put my bag in the back earlier, along with my purse. Could you find my purse for me, Dex?"

"You have a keycard for the gate?" Sarah looked at Meredith's smirk in the mirror. "Of course you do." She watched Dex hand over the purse.

"Franklin gave it to me not too long ago." She mentioned the name of a judge whom she'd wrapped around her finger long before Sarah started work there. While the other judges loved her, she could never get Franklin Montoya to cut her any slack. No doubt he'd been influenced by Meredith's dislike of her. Sarah shook her head. None of that mattered anymore. Not a lot she'd deemed important previously mattered any longer.

"Thank goodness he did. I hope the code reader is still working," Sarah said.

Meredith lowered her window and inserted the card. Everyone let out the breath they'd been holding when the large gate rumbled upward. It started closing as soon as they were inside.

Before they could park, a door opened up and three men rushed outside brandishing assault rifles, yelling. "Keep your hands where we can see them! Stay in the car! Stay in the car!"

***

A gasp caught in her throat, but she teared up when she recognized the men. "Well, I feel better already." A collective sigh filled the interior of the car. Sarah pressed the button; her window slowly lowered. "Eric? It's Sarah."

A large man with deeply tanned skin, six-feet two-inches and close to two hundred pounds, lowered his weapon and moved toward her. The other two stood guard.

"Sarah?" He leaned in the window, cupping her face in his hands. "Thank God." He opened the door his gaze taking in the other passengers. He motioned to the other men. "It's okay. It's Sarah and Meredith. And someone who looks a *lot* like Sarah." He smiled briefly. "You must be Dana."

"I must be." She smiled back at him. "So you're Eric. The man my sister has been going on and on about for the past six months. Eric this and Eric that—" She rounded the SUV to stand beside her Sarah.

"Dana! What the heck?" After all they'd been through, and now she wanted nothing more than for the floor to swallow her.

Eric's laugh echoed in the garage. "Six months. Really? We've only been on two dates in the last month and I had to work my butt off for those." Amusement shown in his dark brown eyes.

"Well, one thing you can say about our Sarah...she ain't easy."

"I am so gonna get you for that." She bumped Dana's hip and changed the subject. "So it looks like you guys have things under control here."

"Took a while, but it's secure for now. Let's get you inside."

"Good. Cause I really don't feel well." Meredith slumped in her seat.

"Meredith? You okay?" Sarah touched her shoulder.

"Yeah. I will be. I just need to lie down for a while."

"Well let's get you all inside."

The other two men came forward. Eric tried to take Maggie from her, but the girl gripped her tightly even in sleep. "It's okay, I've got her."

He grabbed Meredith's bag and tossed the blankets, pillows and jackets to Robert, one of the other Sheriff's deputies. Theodore helped Meredith from the truck and hopped in, adjusted the driver's seat and backed the SUV into a spot near the door.

Once inside, Eric led them down a stark cream-colored hallway and stopped at a bulky metal door. His keycard opened it quickly and he motioned them inside. Sara stood there looking from the door to the keycard. "If the electricity goes out..."

"We won't be trapped in there," Eric said. "There's a manual override as well as keys for every room and cell."

Once inside, the door clanged shut behind them. It was a large space with twenty cells where prisoners were held when they had court cases pending. A bulky metal door closed it off to the rest of the building. No one would be able to get through it easily. The section also housed the building's security equipment. Outside and inside views showed up on several monitors, some in night vision green.

"We'll figure out something better later. For now, the electricity is still on here and the backup generators are in good order. We can see anything coming at us. And we can heat this area a lot more efficiently than the whole courthouse. There are beds in the cells here, too. I always wondered why they bothered to put in beds when no one stayed overnight, but I'm glad—" Eric dropped the bag he carried and grabbed Meredith as she swayed. Picking her up, he started down the hall to one of the cells.

"I can walk, Eric. Put me down." Her weak voice didn't carry far.

He ignored her protests, carrying her into small cell. He sat her on the bed. "You don't have any blood on you, so I'm assuming you haven't been bitten. Is that right?"

She sighed. "No. I haven't been bitten. Chemo's kicking my ass. I just need to rest."

He nodded and looked her over. "Okay. We'll get you some food soon. Just relax."

"Where can I..." Sarah indicated the child in her arms.

"Over here." He showed her into another cell.

Sarah laid Maggie down. "I really need to clean her up a little bit. I don't suppose you'd have anything I could put on her?" She brushed the hair away from the child's face.

"We raided the sheriff's office a little earlier. We have tees and sweats. Even the women's small will swallow her."

"It'll do for now." She looked around. "I've only been down here once before, but I seem to recall it has a shower area. I can get some water to clean her up."

He pulled her against him, just holding her for a minute. "She can wait a while. She's sleeping and I have a feeling when she wakes up, she's going to need to see a familiar face." He pressed against her, leaned back and looked her up and down. Pulling her back against him, he laughed. "Is that a flashlight in your pocket or are you just happy to see me."

Sarah snorted and pressed her hand against his chest, pushing away from him. "You're a nut. But I am *very* happy to see you." She brushed her hand down his sweatshirt. "I got your shirt all dirty though."

Eric took her by the hand and led her to a supply cabinet where he pulled out sweats for her and Dana as well as a couple of towels. "You two look like you've been through hell. So go get showered and changed. If you're up to it, rinse your clothes while you're in the shower, so you'll have your own stuff tomorrow. Or I'll do it a little later. We've had time to rest some. When you're out, we'll see to your injuries and I'll get Robert to make some sandwiches. "

"Great! I'm starved." Sarah whirled around to see Dex behind her.

"Hey, Dex. This is Lieutenant Alvarez . Why don't you hang with him a minute while we go grab showers, then you can take one and we'll all eat then. Okay?"

"Okay, but hurry. Don't be taking one of those hour-long girl showers." He rolled his eyes.

Laughing, she hurried back to her sister. Her laughter ceased when she found Dana curled on the floor against one of the corners of a cell. She rushed to her, taking her in her arms. "What's wrong? Are you hurt?"

Dana continued to sob, her words barely understandable. "I k-killed him."

Not understanding at first Sarah asked, "Who? Who did you kill?" Then she knew. "You mean Ron? Back at that building?"

Dana nodded.

"Oh, honey, you didn't kill him. I checked. He was still alive when we left. I tried to finish him off, but just couldn't." She pushed her sister back and looked into her eyes. "You *did not* kill him."

Dana gulped back sobs and rubbed her face. "I'm sorry. After everything you've gone through—"

"Hush. We've all been through terrible things today. We've all had to do things we wish we hadn't and this is just the beginning. I'm afraid there's a lot more we're going to face than we ever thought possible." She hugged her and then pulled her up, handing her a towel and sweats. "I've already had a couple of meltdowns today. We're definitely entitled, but a hot shower is going to make us both feel better."

A short time later, clean and in comfy sweats, Sarah did feel better. Sore, but better. She sat on a chair facing Eric as he disinfected the cuts to her forehead and cheek.

"Ouch!" She jerked her head back.

"Don't be a baby." Eric put some antibiotic ointment on the cuts and then covered both with bandages. A few other scrapes and scratches were taken care of before he ran his finger along her cheekbone. "I'm afraid this one's gonna leave a scar, but it won't be bad."

She smiled, turning so her lips brushed his palm. "Thanks for taking care of me."

He drew her into his lap and against his chest. "I'm so glad you thought to come here. We're planning to go look for a few family members as soon as it's light out and you were at the top of my list to find."

She hugged him, grateful to have someone care that much about her and to know her feelings were returned. Only two dates, but they'd known each other a little over a year—ever since he transferred as head ranking personnel from the sheriff's department at the courthouse.

"You have absolutely no idea how glad I am to see you here. I didn't think you were supposed to work today."

"I wasn't. But Malone called in with a family emergency." They both sat in silence as they thought about what the emergency may have been in light of recent events.

"Meredith told us she saw you doing some kind of ninja stuff tonight. Where'd you learn that?"

She snickered. "Not quite ninja. Just some basic stuff and a little martial arts. Mostly just plain dumb luck for the most part. Brian, our cousin, taught self-defense to us both as well as making sure we knew how to handle all kinds of firearms. He encouraged us to keep training over the years."

"Your folks didn't mind him teaching you girls all that?"

Sarah lowered her eyes and her voice softened. "Brian was only 7 years older than us when he took us in. Our parents were killed in a car accident by a drunk driver when we were sixteen. He was our only family and he fought like hell to keep us out of the system. He wanted to make sure we could protect ourselves, plus it was his way of spending time with us—doing what he enjoyed. I really hope he's okay."

"I'm sorry. I didn't know about your parents." His finger lifted her chin and he placed a gentle kiss on her lips.

"It was a long time ago." She stood up. "Thanks for fixing me up. I need to go take some food to Meredith and see if she needs anything. I'll be back in a bit." She kissed his cheek and left him to ponder his thoughts.

Meredith sat up and leaned against the wall next to the bed, making room for Sarah.

"Here." She handed her a wet cloth. "I thought you might want to freshen up a little. And I brought you some soup. There are ham sandwiches, too. I just didn't know what you felt like you could eat." She sat, holding the bowl while Meredith ran the cloth over her face and hands

"Thanks. Soup sounds good." She took the bowl, sipping a little from the spoon. After a few bites, she put the bowl in her lap and leaned her head against the wall. "Actually, I've been waiting to talk to you."

Meredith said nothing for moment. Sarah waited, giving her time to collect her thoughts.

"I want to thank you for helping me out today. I wouldn't have made it without you."

"No thanks necessary. I'm just glad we all got here safely. And we wouldn't have if you hadn't been able to drive us here. *And* get us inside. I'm afraid we would have lost the kids. So thank you for getting us through that horde."

Meredith waved her off. "No. I know you didn't have to bring me along. I wouldn't blame you for not wanting to. I've been a real bitch to you since you started working here." Sarah started to speak, but Meredith continued. "Seriously. I know I have. And I want to apologize. There was never any reason for it. Other than my jealousy."

"Jealous? Of me? Why on earth…"

"I worked hard to get to the point I was everyone's go to person for investigations. Then you came along and with all your passion—well, everyone was so impressed right off the bat. It didn't matter if it was a client, an attorney or even a judge. If you felt something deeply enough, you just didn't quit." Meredith raised her gaze to Sarah's. "I used to have that…that intensity. But I was just burned out. Oh I still did my job and did it well, but the fire wasn't there and everyone knew it. Especially when you showed up."

"I just wanted what was best. I did the custody investigations and tried to make sure that—"

"That the kids came first. I know." Meredith leaned forward and grabbed her hand, squeezing gently. "There really was no excuse for the way I treated you and I am very sorry."

Sarah scooted closer and hugged the woman. "I didn't make it easy either. I certainly could have been less defensive and made more of an effort."

They sat silently for a moment. "Yeah. You could have," Meredith said matter-of-factly, lifting the spoon to her lips. Looking at Sarah's shocked face, she started laughing and before long Sarah joined in.

***

Epilogue
4 Months Later

Sarah moved through the marble lobby with two-story ceilings, her footsteps echoing around the large empty space. Pushing through the double doors, she stopped to take in the scene. It was lunchtime and while eating was on the agenda, so were discussions about the future. They'd made a large square out of the tables so all the adults could see and be heard. The children had their own area today and were engrossed in play as well as eating. Eric waited on Sarah to return from taking a tray of food to Nathan, a young man who'd shown a lot of promise in defense. He took a turn watching the cameras while the rest of them discussed their options.

There were now twenty-six of them making their home at the courthouse. While there was plenty of room and the building had been able to withstand attacks from the dead and the evil-living, they were going to need to be able to grow their own food soon. They'd definitely had close calls and they had lost people, but they were as safe as they could be considering the situation. They'd even been lucky to save a solar expert fighting off a horde by himself during one of their trips outside and they now had solar-powered energy. They just needed to decide whether to move or figure out how to secure their food supply. Foraging trips became longer and more difficult with each run.

Sarah made her way to the table stopping beside Dex and Maggie. Dex made her proud, taking Maggie under his wing and treating her like a little sister. She bent down and kissed them both on the head, even though she knew Dex thought he was too old for such displays. He ducked but grinned at her. There were seven kids living there now. Maggie, at six, was the youngest and Jose, fifteen, the oldest. Some came with a parent. Some were on their own. But no one was really on their own anymore. They all took care of the kids and in making sure everything got done. They'd had their adjustment periods, and there were a couple of people who made things more difficult than they need-ed to be. But still, they'd done well. Much better than some. They'd been fortunate.

"I think I should be at the adult table today." Jose stared directly at Sarah, not blinking.

She thought of all the young man had seen and had to do. How he took charge of the kids when necessary and the decisions he'd had to make over the last few months. She nodded. "You're right, Jose, you should be." She looked at Dex. "You're in charge here until we're done." She watched as his chest pushed out in pride before moving on with Jose by her side, carrying his plate and glass.

She pulled another chair to the table and motioned for him to sit. People looked up, saw Jose and nodded their agreement. Sarah took a seat between Dana and Meredith. She and Meredith had become close friends after their mutual apologies. Looking her over, Sarah was pleased to see the healthy glow to Meredith's skin. Her hair had grown back in and she'd been able to put on weight. Although there had been no way for them to check, it looked like she'd beat the cancer, just like she said she would.

Eric raised his voice and was about to start the meeting when the radio squawked. "Incoming. We have survivors and zombies nearing the gate. Survivors may not make it. It's gonna be close." Everyone dropped their utensils, grabbed their ever-ready guns, knives or whatever weapon they had and headed for downstairs.

Sarah moved toward the kids' table but found Dex already ushering them toward the security area. They'd be safe there locked in with Nathan. She ran back, grabbed half her sandwich and ate on the run.

Survival now came one moment at a time. But Sarah knew they would do everything they could to survive.

The End

ABOUT THE AUTHOR

Award-winning romantic suspense and horror author, Rhonda Hopkins, has learned firsthand that truth is stranger than fiction. Her two decades of experience working closely with judges, attorneys, and within the legal system as an investigator for her state and family courts provide her characters with a depth and realism that gives truth a run for its money. Having come in contact with the best and the worst that society has to offer, Rhonda's imagination is filled with story ideas.

Rhonda is working hard on future episodes in the SURVIVAL series. If you enjoyed this one, sign up for her Newsletter (http://rhondahopkins.com/newsletter) so you'll get first notice of new releases.

You can connect with Rhonda at:
Website (http://rhondahopkins.com)
Facebook (http://facebook.com/RhondaHopkins.Author)
Twitter (http://twitter.com/Rhonda_Hopkins)
Google+ (http://google.com/+RhondaHopkins)
Goodreads (http://www.goodreads.com/RhondaHopkins)

You loved their stories and are hungry for more? Well here are some great choices to start with!

Eli Constant-DEAD TREES--http://www.amazon.com/Dead-Trees-Eli-Constant-ebook/dp/B00APYKD7G/

Heath Stallcup--Return of the Phoenix--
http://www.amazon.com/Return-Phoenix-Heath-Stallcup-
ebook/dp/B00AV8NB48/

Gregory Carrico--Children of the Plague--
http://www.amazon.com/Children-Plague-Gregory-Carrico-
ebook/dp/B00BUZ3EKW/

Claire C. Riley--Odium--http://www.amazon.com/Odium-Dead-Saga-Claire-Riley/dp/1492873535/

Armand Rosamilia--Dying Days--
http://www.amazon.com/Dying-Days-Armand-Rosamilia-
ebook/dp/B004RVZXN2/

Catie Rhodes--Forever Road--http://www.amazon.com/Forever-Road-Peri-Paranormal-Mysteries-ebook/dp/B00C6MYQXW/

J. Thorn--Preta's Realm--http://www.amazon.com/Pretas-Realm-Haunting-Hidden-Trilogy-ebook/dp/B005FI5Z0W/

Chantal Boudreau--Fervor--http://www.amazon.com/Fervor-
Chantal-Boudreau-ebook/dp/B004RZ28FE/

Mark Tufo--Zombie Fallout--http://www.amazon.com/Zombie-Fallout-Mark-Tufo/dp/145151705X/

Michael James McFarland--Fallow Ground--
www.amazon.com/Fallow-Ground-Michael-James-McFarland-
ebook/dp/B00I6J075U/

JULIANNE SNOW

GLIMPSES
OF THE
UNDEAD

Julianne Snow--Glimpses of the Undead--
http://www.amazon.com/Glimpses-Undead-Julianne-Snow-
ebook/dp/B00GHU3IIS/

TW Brown--That Ghoul Ava meets Th Queen of the Zombies--
http://www.amazon.com/That-Ghoul-Ava-Queen-Zombies-
ebook/dp/B00C4NO7ZA

"Not all monsters have scales or claws."

–Cheri Yori

COURTING JUSTICE CASE ONE

PREDATOR

RHONDA HOPKINS

Rhonda Hopkins--The Consuming--
http://rhondahopkins.com/my-books/courtingjusticeseries/

MAY DECEMBER
Publications

The growing voice in horror
and speculative fiction.

Find us at www.maydecemberpublications.com
Or
Email us at contact@maydecemberpublications.com

www.ingramcontent.com/pod-product-compliance
Lightning Source LLC
Chambersburg PA
CBHW032142190626
46814CB00005BA/1801